T0036190

Also by Jennifer Hartmann

Still Beating

Lotus

June First

JUNE FIRST

JENNIFER HARTMANN

Bloom books

Cover design by Cat at TRC Designs
Cover images © biletskly_e/Depositphotos, Subbotina/Depositphotos, Yulia/Adobe Stock

Published by Bloom Books, an imprint of Sourcebooks
P.O. Box 4410, Naperville, Illinois 60567-4410
(630) 961-3900
sourcebooks.com

Originally self-published in 2022 by Jennifer Hartmann.

Cataloging-in-Publication data is on file with the Library of Congress.

Printed and bound in the United States of America.
VP 10 9 8 7 6 5 4 3 2 1

For my husband, Jake. My rainbow after every storm.
All of my books are secretly dedicated to you,
but I think it's time we make it official.

PART I

THE FIRST TRAGEDY

1

FIRST BLOOD

BRANT, AGE 6

"YOU'RE SUCH A FARTKNOCKER, BRANT!"

Wendy and Wyatt speed away on their bicycles, the tires spitting up mud and grass blades as they cut through the neighbor's lawn.

A fartknocker.

What does that mean?

I watch them go from the edge of my driveway, while Theo kicks up one of the loose stones that rim our mailbox. Dad is going to blow a gasket if he sees a rock out of place. He loves weird stuff like mailbox rocks, perfectly edged sidewalks, and grass that looks greener than my babysitter's new hairdo.

I don't really get it.

I don't get fartknocker either.

"Wendy is a dweeb," Theo mutters under his breath.

"Sounds better than a fartknocker."

"It is."

The sun sets behind an extra fluffy cloud, making it look like a giant piece of cotton candy floating in the Midwestern sky. My stomach grumbles. "Want to stay for dinner?"

Theo tries to fix the stone with the toe of his sneaker, but it doesn't look the same. Dad will notice. Theo sighs, popping his chin up and gazing down at the end of the cul-de-sac where the dreadful Nippersink twins disappeared. "Is your mom making that chili?"

"No, it's fish." My mom loves to cook. Aside from giving me cheek kisses and tummy tickles, I think it's her favorite thing to do. I love the food she makes, even brussels sprouts.

Even fish.

"Yuck," Theo says. He glances at his property, the ranch-style house made of bricks, two down from mine, and shrugs. "Besides, I think my mom might have a baby tonight."

"Really?"

"Maybe. She said her belly felt like a hyena was chomping through her loo-der-us."

"That means the baby is coming?" I shove my hands into the pockets of my shorts, frowning at the image that pops into my head. That sounds really bad. It sounds worse than when I got bit by Aunt Kelly's cat because it looked sad and I wanted to feed it one of my apple slices. I caught a fever the next day. "I thought babies were a happy thing. What's a loo-der-us, anyway?"

"I dunno. I think it's the thing in my mom's belly that the baby lives in. Sounds gross to me."

A shudder ripples through me. That does sound pretty gross. I always wanted a brother or a sister to grow up with, but Dad works too much at the office or in the yard, and Mom says it's hard to take care of little babies that poop and cry all the time, so I guess it's just me.

At least I have Theo.

He's my neighbor and best friend, and maybe his new baby brother or sister will feel like mine, too. Maybe we can share.

"What do you think you'll name the baby, Theo?"

My eyes follow Theo as he hops onto the ring of stones around the mailbox, trying to balance himself. He slips and lands on his butt, right in the wet grass, and when he stands up, blotches of brown mud stain the back of his jeans. He rubs at his bottom, making a groaning sound. "How about Mudpie?"

We both laugh, picturing a cute little baby named Mudpie. I skate my gaze around the cul-de-sac, a new name flashing to mind when I fix on a fluttering insect with sunshine wings. "I like Butterfly."

"Yeah, okay. Mudpie if it's a boy, and Butterfly if it's a girl." Theo nods, still massaging his sore butt. He sweeps sandy-blond bangs away from his forehead, revealing eyes glinting with the same dark-blue color as his shirt. "Hey, Brant, maybe you can come over and meet her after she's out of Mom's belly?"

I'd love that!

I'm about to reply when I register what he just said. "Her?"

Theo shrugs again, scrunching up his nose. "I think it's a girl. I can just picture her wearing little pink dresses and giant bows. She'll be real pretty, don't you think?"

"Yeah, I bet she will be."

"I'm going to take good care of her. I'll be the best big brother ever," he says, bobbing his head with a prideful smile. It's the same smile Dad has when he stares at the lawn after a fresh mow. "I'll be like Mario, and you can be Luigi if you want. She'll be Princess Peach, and we'll protect her from all the bad guys in the world."

I picture it. I envision grand adventures and battles, sword fights and bravery. The images shoot a tickle straight to my heart.

I always wanted something worth defending, and Mom won't let me have a puppy.

Theo's new baby will have to do.

"I like that idea, Theo. We'll make a great team."

Our daydreams are interrupted when Theo's mother pokes her head out of their house, her belly so round and large, it holds the screen door open all by itself. There must be something as big as a watermelon inside—there *must*.

Maybe we should name her Watermelon.

"Theodore! We're heading to the hospital!"

Theo's dad rushes out, carrying at least seven bags, two dangling from around his neck. His face is beet red, the same color as the van he tosses the belongings into, and he looks like he might faint. He might even have a heart attack. He's sweating a whole lot.

"Now, Son! We're having a baby!" his father shouts, tripping on a divot in the driveway as he races back to the front of the house.

My friend's eyes pop. "She's coming, Brant! Did you hear that?"

"I heard it," I say eagerly, a little bit jealous of my friend. I want a baby sister. In fact, I'd trade anything in the world for a baby sister.

You hear that, sky? I'll trade anything for a baby sister!

I'm not sure why I tell my secret to the sky, but Mom always looks up at the ceiling when she says her prayers at night. Maybe she's talking to the sky.

Maybe it listens.

The cotton candy cloud doesn't answer back, and neither does the setting sun. The birds don't sing. The treetops sway and shimmy, but they are also silent.

My wish is stolen by the early summer breeze, never to be heard.

Theo mounts his bicycle, waving goodbye at me as he scoots along with his feet. He nearly topples over on the sidewalk, shouting with excitement, "See you later, Luigi!"

I grin at the name. *Luigi.* It means I'm a fighter. A protector.

A hero.

And it's a lot better than *fartknocker*.

"Bye, Mario," I yell back.

Theo almost tips over again when he tries to send me another wave, the bike swerving madly, but he catches his balance and darts home just as his father races his mother to the van. She's holding her plump belly, making awful, painful sounds. She sure doesn't look happy.

I don't get it.

"Brant, honey…it's almost dinner time."

I startle and glance over my shoulder. Mom is waving me inside from the doorway, her dark-honey hair whipping her in the face when a gust of wind rolls through. "Coming," I call to her, stealing a final peek at my friend hopping into the vehicle with his parents. One more excited wave from Theo sends them off as they pull out of the driveway with squeaky tires.

"Come inside, Brant. You can help me butter the garlic bread."

Pivoting, I let out a sigh and jog through the grass to my front stoop. Mom wraps a tender arm around my shoulders, then kisses the top of my head. I look up at her, twisting the hem of my shirt between my fingers. "Theo's mom is having a baby tonight."

She smiles, resting a palm atop her own belly. It's flat and slender—the opposite of Theo's mom's. There are certainly no watermelons hiding inside. "Oh my goodness. I knew it would be any day now." Mom glances up, watching the van disappear around the corner. "I'll have to make them some casseroles when they return. Is Theo excited?"

"He's really excited." I bob my head. "He said I can visit when they come home. Can I, Mom?"

Two brown eyes gaze down at me like warm melted chocolate, and she gives my shoulder a light squeeze. "Of course. The Baileys are like family," she murmurs. "And maybe I'll reconsider that puppy you keep asking me about."

"Really?" My own eyes ping open, wide as saucers I'm sure. "Can we name it Yoshi?"

"I don't see why not."

I hop up and down, anticipation coursing through me. "Thanks, Mom."

Another breeze sweeps by, causing Mom's long hair to take flight like a sparrow. She closes her eyes for a moment, tugging me close to her hip. "You're a good boy, Brant. Your heart is kind and brave. Maybe…" Her words vanish within the breeze, and I'm confused at first…a little worried that something is wrong. Then she finishes with "Maybe we can start over somewhere. Just you and me."

"What about Dad?"

I wait for her answer. My body sags against my mother, her scent a familiar comfort as her fingers trail through my mess of hair. She smells like something sweet. A dessert of some kind—honey and caramel. Maybe even taffy apples.

"Tomorrow, it will be June." Her voice is just a hush, and I hardly even hear her. My mother sweeps her palm down the nape of my neck, then my back, giving me a light pat before she pulls away. "June always feels like a new beginning."

I think about her words well into the evening. I think about them while sitting around the dinner table as Dad talks about how Collins at the office sabotaged his spreadsheets, then yells at Mom for overcooking the salmon fillets. He even throws a fit over the stones around the mailbox, blaming the neighbor dog for getting off its leash and ruining all of his hard work. I keep my mouth shut as I smash my glazed carrots into tiny spheres of mush, not wanting Theo to get into trouble. I knew Dad would notice.

He loves those rocks.

As bedtime rolls around, I still can't stop thinking about Mom's words. I don't know why.

June always feels like a new beginning.

What did it mean? And why did Mom want to go somewhere without Dad?

Mom tucks me into bed that night, singing me a lullaby. She hasn't sung me a lullaby in a while—not since I was in preschool. Her voice is soft and glowing, almost like how I picture the moon. If the moon had a voice, it would sound like her. She singsongs the words, telling me that over the rainbow, bluebirds fly. I think about bluebirds, and I think about rainbows. The words make me feel happy, but she sings it so sad.

She reads me my favorite book about Dumbo the elephant, while my own stuffed toy, a floppy gray elephant named Bubbles, is tucked in my arms. Mom cries as she reads the story, just like she always does.

Then she places a gentle kiss to my hairline, whispering by the light of the stars from my window, "I'll always protect you."

I snuggle under my striped bedcover, a smile hinting on my lips, listening as her footfalls fade from the room.

Dreams try to find me, but my mind is restless.

I'm thinking about Wendy and what a dweeb she is. Wyatt too.

I think about the puppy we're going to get…Yoshi. I wonder if he'll make friends with the neighbor dog.

I wonder if Dad will like him more than the neighbor dog.

I think about my mother's voice made of moonglow, and I wonder why she said those things to me on our front stoop.

And finally, I think about Theo's baby.

Mudpie or Butterfly?

Is Theo's mom's belly still big and full? Did the baby come out of her looder-us yet?

Maybe it'll be two babies, just like Wendy and Wyatt. One for Theo, and one for me.

We can both be Mario.

As the minutes tick by, my thoughts begin to quiet, and I'm whisked away by a magical dream. I'm in the sky, sitting atop the crest of the banana moon.

It's loud up here.

I'm drowning in the chatter of a thousand wishes.

And somehow, somewhere, I think I hear my own…

I'll trade anything for a baby sister.

"Brant."

I'm shaken awake by a familiar presence. At first I'm confused, wondering if I missed the school bus, but then I remember that it's summer break.

My eyelids flutter open as a hand grips my shoulder. It's still so dark in my bedroom. It's still nighttime. I blink, trying to make sense of the shadows. "Dad?"

"Wake up, Brant. Wake up."

His voice doesn't sound right; it sounds frightful, like he's somebody else. A different person. I sit up straight, rubbing at my sleepy eyes and clutching Bubbles the Elephant to my chest. "Am I in trouble?"

Dad's face is glistening in the glow of my night-light. He's sweaty and breathing funny. "I love you, Brant. Forgive me."

I can only stare at him. I don't understand.

"Hide under your bed," he orders, tugging at my arm. "Come on."

My tummy starts to swirl with dread. Tears rush to my eyes. "I'm scared."

"Be a good boy. Please."

I want to be a good boy, so I obey. Squeezing Bubbles in a tight grip, I scoot my butt off the mattress until my feet touch the floor. Dad reaches for me then, taking me by both shoulders and giving me a firm shake. My eyes can now see him better in the dark, and I notice a few scratches etched into his cheeks, mean and red. "Where's Mom?"

A weird look washes over his face, pinching his eyebrows together and causing him to tremble as he holds me. He lowers himself to both knees, until we're face-to-face, and the lump in his throat bobs up and down. Fingernails are digging into my skin, and it kind of hurts, but the fear hurts me more. "Listen carefully, Son," he says in a stranger's voice, low and gruff. Sad. "I want you to crawl under your bed and stay there until the sun lights up your room. Do you understand?" Dad places his navy-blue phone with large number buttons into my hand, forcing my fingers around it. "When the sun comes up, dial 9-1-1. But this part is important… You have to promise me you'll do it, okay?"

Wetness trickles down my cheeks. I nod. I don't know what else to do.

"Don't go downstairs."

Don't go downstairs. Don't go downstairs. Don't go downstairs.

The words echo inside me, over and over. I have to obey. I have to promise.

"Okay, Dad."

He relaxes just a little. "I love you. We both love you. You know that, right?"

"Yes, I know," I tell him through my tears. I'm not even sure why I'm crying, but it feels like I should.

With a short nod, he begins guiding me beneath the bed, so I get down on my hands and knees and crawl, flattening myself to my belly and slithering the rest of the way under. It's extra dark, littered with stray toys and playing cards. The dust tickles my nose. Curling my body into a ball, I pull Bubbles to my cheek and let him collect my falling tears as my other hand fists the phone. Dad crouches lower, mouth parted like he's about to speak, but his lips only tremble with words unsaid. He swipes a meaty paw down the center of his face, then ruffles his hair.

I think he's about to leave me here, so I blurt out, "Mom said she'll always protect me."

Danger prickles my skin. I don't feel safe.

And Mom isn't here.

More sadness creeps into my father's face, but he still doesn't speak. He doesn't comfort me like Mom would.

Right before he stands, he reaches for me, stealing away the hand that clasps my toy elephant. "One more thing, Brant," Dad says, peering at me sprawled underneath the bed with his wild, tear-filled eyes. He chokes a little, making a sound I might never forget. It sounds like every nightmare I've ever had. Giving my fingers a final squeeze, my father makes that choking noise again, something like a cough, or a cry, or an awful goodbye. He pulls back and whispers through the wall of darkness, "Cover your ears."

He jumps up, turns, and walks out of my bedroom.

I watch as his sock-covered feet move farther and farther away, and then my door closes shut.

Click.

Silence enters the room.

My heart thunders loud, my breaths coming so quick they match the beats. Bubbles comforts me the only way he can, pillowing my cheek as I lie there with my knees to my chest.

I try to remember everything my father told me. There was so much.

"When the sun comes up, dial 9-1-1."

My fingers curl around the phone.

"Don't go downstairs."

Why can't I go downstairs? I want my mom. I need her to protect me from these things I don't understand.

I think there was one more thing…one last thing I'm supposed to do, but I can't remember.

What was it? What was it?

Tears pour out of me, and my throat stings, my mind racing.

"One more thing, Brant…"

I can't remember. *Oh no, I can't remember!*

My bedroom floor is cold and dark, so lonely. I'm scared.

I've never been more scared.

As I call out for my mom, crying and shouting, my father's final plea flashes to mind.

Oh, yeah!

Cover my—

Boom.

A loud crack causes me to jump, my whole body shivering as my eyes flare wide open. I think maybe it's just fireworks. I still hear them sometimes, right outside my window, leftover celebrations from Memorial Day. They paint the sky in pretty lights and colors, and they make me feel happy inside. They make me smile.

But I don't feel happy right now. I'm not smiling.

I don't think it was fireworks.

I cover my ears anyway, even though it might be too late. The heels of my hands dig into either side of my head, closing in sound, while I bury my face into the gray softness of my stuffy.

That's where I stay for a long time.

Hours, maybe. I'm not very good at telling time, but it could be hours.

And I know I'm supposed to wait until the sun peeks over the clouds and brightens my bedroom, but my muscles are hurting. My body is stiff and achy, my neck sore. It's getting hard to breathe under here.

Making a decision, I press the numbers on the phone that Dad told me to dial. Nine-one-one. A lady answers, but I don't say anything. Dad didn't tell me to say anything. He just told me to press the numbers.

I slide my way out on my tummy, my palms pulling me forward. I snatch up Bubbles before I stand, then I pace out of the room on my tiptoes, trying to be as quiet as possible. I promised Dad I wouldn't go downstairs, so I don't want him to hear me.

He can't know I broke my promise.

My insides feel fuzzy and sort of itchy as I make my way through the darkened hallway, the only sounds being the creaky wooden floor and the *whoosh* of a ceiling fan. I take careful steps down the staircase. It almost feels like I'm sneaking a peek of the tree on Christmas morning, checking to see if Santa came and brought me presents wrapped in colorful paper and glittering bows.

It's not Christmas morning, though.

And what I find when I reach the bottom of the stairs is not an abundance of gifts with my name on them. There is no joy. There is no wonder.

There is only a terrible nightmare.

Blood.

Fear.

A scream.

My scream.

I squeeze my eyes shut, blotting it all out. Then I reopen them.

It's real, it's real... Oh no, it's real!

Bubbles slips from my hand, landing in a pool of red that seeps from a hole in my father's head. There's a gun resting beside him—the same kind I've seen in movies and TV shows.

My mother is lying beside him, too. She has something wrapped around her neck, causing her mouth to hang open and her eyes to bug out. I think it's my father's work tie.

It's purple.

I hate purple. It's the worst color I've ever seen.

Mom doesn't look at me, even though her eyes are open. She's quiet and still, just like Dad. "Mommy?" My voice hardly sounds real. It's so high and squeaky, stuck in my throat like Laffy Taffy. I step around my father and his river of blood, then throw myself at my mother. She doesn't move. She doesn't hold me.

She doesn't protect me like she promised.

I sob against her chest, begging for her to wake up, crying for her to read me stories and sing me lullabies. Needing her to tell me this is all a bad dream.

That's where strange men find me a short while later, dressed in uniforms, their faces filled with horror, just like how my dad's face looked when he left me in my bedroom all alone. They rip me away from my mom, and I kick and scream and cry harder, my arms extended, reaching, pleading, as they pull me out the front door.

Away from her.

Away from Dad.

Away from Bubbles.

Someone wraps me up in a blanket even though I'm not cold. They tell me nice words in a nice voice, but I can't make sense of anything they're saying. Ambulances pull up with red and blue lights, sirens blaring, joining the police cars lining our cul-de-sac. Neighbors step out of their houses, cupping their mouths, shaking their heads, and staring at me with curious eyes.

Not Theo, though.

He's not home. He's at the hospital with his mom and dad and new baby.

Voices whisper around me, and I try to make out some of the words:

Dee-oh-ay.

Murder.

Suicide.

He killed her.

Poor kid.

Tragedy.

I bend over from my perch in the driveway, reaching for one of the ruddy stones that has fallen astray near the mailbox. Holding it in my hand, I stare at it, grazing my thumb over its smooth edges.

I think Dad loved this rock more than he loved Mom.

I think he loved it more than he loved me.

I clutch it in a tight fist, looking up at the midnight sky that twinkles with stars and unclaimed wishes. I realize then that maybe this was my fault. Maybe I killed my parents. Maybe I traded them in for a silly wish.

Only…I don't have a baby sister.

I don't have anybody.

My bottom lip quivers, and the tears fall hard.

I squeeze the rock.

Then I set it back in place.

2

FIRST IMPRESSION

BRANT, AGE 6

Aunt Kelly sweeps her fingers through my hair, her rings cold and clunky against my head. She looks like Mom a little when she smiles, and her eyes are the same dark brown, but she doesn't smell as sweet. She smells like her cat. The one that bit me.

"This will be good for you, Brant. I know you're scared right now, but you'll see. This is right... This makes sense." She glances over her shoulder, and when she twists back to me, her eyes are shimmering. "This is what Caroline wanted."

I look around her, knowing exactly what made her eyes fill with tears.

The house. My house.

We're standing on Theo's front stoop, just two properties away from my yard. The grass is overgrown, littered with dead dandelions. Dad wouldn't like that.

I'm silent as Aunt Kelly makes a gasping sound, covering her mouth with her hand. It trembles a bit. Her whole body does.

My head dips down, chin to chest, and I stare at the little cracks in the porch step. I'm not sure what I'm supposed to say. I'm not sure what I want to say.

"Oh, sweetie, come here."

I'm pulled into Aunt Kelly's arms as she hugs me tight, my nose pressed into her belly. She smells different when I'm this close, and I can almost pretend she's Mom. Maybe they used the same laundry soap.

"I'll come visit you, okay? I promise," she whispers, ruffling my hair again. "I know how confusing this must be for you, but the Baileys will raise you right. You'll have siblings to play with. You'll have a good family to grow up with—more than I could ever give you." Her tummy heaves against my face, like she's trying to catch her breath. "This is what your mother wished for, so you just have to trust that. Do you understand, Brant?"

I swallow, then nod. I don't really understand, but I think it's the answer she expects of me. It works, because when she finally pulls away, there's a smile breaking through her tears. It reminds me of when the clouds dance around in the sky, playing hide-and-seek with the sun, and the sun wins. Triumphant.

"Good," she tells me, bobbing her head up and down and clasping my face between both palms. Her rings burrow into my cheekbones. "That's good."

Aunt Kelly rings the doorbell. It chimes throughout the whole house, spilling out through the screen door. It's followed by hurried footsteps down the hall. Familiar footsteps.

Theo greets me in the entryway, halting in place when he sees me standing on his stoop with bags and suitcases waiting by my feet. He hesitates. I've rung his doorbell so many times, and he never hesitates when he sees me.

I guess he knows. I guess he knows that my parents got killed, so that makes him hesitate.

"Brant," a voice calls out. It's Theo's mom, all dressed up in a polka-dotted skirt and white blouse, wearing lipstick, and curls in her hair. She looks like how my mom would look whenever we had guests come over—only, Theo's mom has yellow hair like the dandelions in our yard before they shriveled up and died. Her eyes are different, too. They're blue.

And her belly doesn't look like a watermelon anymore.

I reach down to the porch stoop and pick up the new elephant stuffed animal Aunt Kelly bought for me. I haven't named him yet. He looks a little bit like Bubbles, but he's not Bubbles.

I miss Bubbles.

"Come in, please," Theo's mom says. She pushes open the screen door and waves us inside. "I made cookies and lemonade."

Aunt Kelly places her hand on my back, pushing me forward as she gathers all the bags. When I'm standing inside the foyer, I look over at Theo. He looks at me.

We just kind of stare at each other while he scuffs his foot back and forth on the carpeting.

"Thank you again, Samantha," Aunt Kelly says to Theo's mom. "I know this was…sudden. And with the new baby and everything—"

"It's okay. Really," she replies. Her voice is low and soft, almost like she doesn't want me to hear. "Caroline was my dearest friend. Taking in Brant is more than a privilege. It's a gift."

A gift.

That's a weird thing to say; I don't feel like a gift. Gifts are fun and exciting, and they make people smile. Nobody is smiling right now.

Everyone looks sad.

"Please keep in touch," Aunt Kelly mutters through more tears. "I'd love to visit as much as I can. I travel for work all the time, so it's hard with my schedule, but I want to be a part of his life."

"Of course. You're more than welcome any time."

Theo takes a small step closer to me, his eyes drifting to the Super Mario backpack resting beside my ankles. He shoves his hands into the pockets of his gym shorts and nods at the bag. "I got the new Paper Mario game. It just came out."

I blink, then clear my throat. "Yeah?"

"Yeah."

My mind wanders, filled with past memories of holing up in Theo's bedroom with his Nintendo 64 games, while his mom popped in with pizza rolls and Hi-C Ecto Cooler juice boxes. It wasn't even that long ago. I'm not sure how long it's been since The Bad Night, but it's still summertime. We're supposed to go back to school soon—first grade for me, and second grade for Theo.

The women give each other a hug before Aunt Kelly tugs me toward her again, kissing my cheeks and dampening them with her tears. "You're very loved, Brant. Don't forget that."

I nibble at my lip, watching her pull away. She tousles my hair a final time and says goodbye, sharing a look with Theo's mom, then spinning around. When she steps outside and shuts the door behind her, it sounds so loud that I can't help but jolt in place.

It's quiet in here now.

Theo and his mom are staring at me, like they don't know what to do with me. Almost like I'm a stray puppy who ran away from home and got lost.

I squeeze the stuffed animal to my chest, pretending it's Bubbles.

And that's when something fractures the silence.

A small cry.

My eyes go wide, curiosity poking at me. A hopeful little feeling.

Theo perks up, straightening in front of me, and his mom bends over, hands to her knees, then smiles brightly. "Would you like to meet Theo's new sister, Brant?"

A sister!

Theo was right. She *is* a girl.

Somehow, through all the confusion and sadness, amid the tears and uncertainty, a tendril of joy slithers its way into my heart. I'm not sure what it means, but it causes my feet to move, and I start marching toward the direction of the tiny wail.

There, in the center of the living room, is a swing. It's white and soft, singing lullabies and rocking back and forth, side to side. I almost don't see her at first, swaddled inside a blush-pink blanket, but then a foot peeks out, kicking the air aimlessly.

My breath sticks in my throat.

Theo's mother comes up behind me, her hand falling to my shoulder with a squeeze. "She's eleven weeks old."

There's a lump in my neck that feels tight, so I try to swallow it down. I've never seen a foot so little before. She must be fragile, just like a snowflake when it lands on your skin. I'm too scared I'll break her, so I just stare at her for a few seconds before a question pops into my mind. "Did you name her Butterfly?"

A burst of laughter greets me. Theo's mother shakes her head as her fingers glide down my arm—a gentle touch, like Mom used to do. "Her name is June."

June.

June always feels like a new beginning.

My own mother's words sink into me, words I've buried deep. Words I've tried so hard not to think about. I slam my eyes shut when her face flickers in my mind, her warm eyes and silky hair. The shape of her face. The way her upper lip was thinner than the bottom one, but it didn't make her smile any less perfect.

The truth is, my mother wasn't wrong when she told me that June was a new beginning. It just wasn't the beginning anybody wanted. It was the beginning of a horror movie, or a scary book. A nightmare. It was nothing like the magical fairy tales she'd read to me every night at bedtime.

I take a step back, away from the swaying cradle.

Maybe I don't like Baby June.

Is she my wish? Is she what I traded my parents for?

Theo slides up beside me, fiddling with his overalls. "Do you like her, Brant?"

"I don't know."

All I know is that *she's* here, and Mom and Dad aren't.

"Come on," Theo's mom says, her tone a little lower, a little sadder. "Let's get you set up in your new room, then we can have some cookies."

It turns out that my new room is also Theo's room. I guess I'll be sleeping over for a while, and they ran out of rooms for me. June has her own room—the nursery, Theo called it—painted pink and gray, decorated with elephants, from her little wooden crib to the spinning mobile to the patterned border along her walls. I poked my head in, clutching my own elephant toy to my chest. I didn't like her nursery because it made me think of Bubbles.

"How long do you think I'll be here, Theo?" I ask my friend while pulling shirts and underwear and pajama sets out of my suitcase. Theo and I each have our own dresser, along with our own bed. There's a television sitting atop a desk in between the two dressers, complemented by a Super Nintendo system, as well as a Nintendo 64. A few posters line the walls. I wonder if I'll be able to bring over my favorite posters from my old bedroom.

Theo bounces on his bed with his butt, watching me unpack. "How long? Forever, I guess."

"Forever?"

"That's what my mom said."

A strange feeling pinches my chest. *Forever.*

Aunt Kelly didn't tell me much. She said the details didn't matter, and the only thing that mattered was that I was safe. That I would be okay.

But forever is a really long time, and I wonder why she didn't think that mattered.

Everything has been confusing since The Bad Night. So many strange people, so many questions I didn't know how to answer. Aunt Kelly told me they were called social workers and thera-pits, and they were good people. They would help keep me safe.

I stayed at Aunt Kelly's for a while. She said we had to wait for something called the Court to tell us what to do next. I didn't know what that meant, but maybe it was the place where Theo and I play with our basketballs sometimes.

Aunt Kelly's house was okay. She lives right over the Illinois border, in a little townhome in Wisconsin. Her cat had to stay locked up in the laundry room so I wouldn't get bit again, but every time I walked by the gate, it would hiss at me. I couldn't really sleep well, either, and most of her food tasted too spicy, but she was nice and treated me well. She gave me a handful of Skittles every night before bed and picked out all the purple ones. I don't like purple. Aunt Kelly said the dentist might get mad at her, but at least I was going to sleep with something sweet.

I sit back down on my bed after my clothes are placed into drawers. Some things came from my old closet, and some things are new from Aunt Kelly. I put the old things on top of the new things so I can wear them first.

I'm twisting a loose string on the bedspread around my finger when Theo tosses me something. It's a stuffed butterfly toy. "What's this?" I wonder, squeezing it between my hands. It's soft and bright, but it looks like a girl's toy.

"My grams let me pick it out for the new baby." Theo shrugs. "I told my parents I was naming her Butterfly since she was a girl, but they didn't like that name."

"Why not?"

"I dunno. They said we don't name new babies after bugs, but then they named her after a month. That doesn't sound like a people name either."

Pondering this, I stare down at the pink and yellow butterfly toy. "Do you like her, Theo?"

He flops down onto his back, head to pillow, and situates his arms behind his neck. He lets out a long sigh and says, "Yeah, I really like her. I love her, even."

"More than your video games?"

"Probably the same amount."

Our conversation in my driveway stirs in my thoughts, bringing back images of colorful adventures and battles. Swords and weapons. Mazes and monsters.

At the center of it all is a little princess.

I wonder if Theo still wants to pretend we're heroes, just like Mario and Luigi. I'm about to ask him; I'm about to see if he wants to create our own grand adventure together, with June as the princess, but it's almost like he read my mind.

"We'll protect her, you and me," Theo says, gazing up at the glow-in-the-dark galaxy stickers pressed to his ceiling. "I'm Mario, and you're Luigi. And June is Princess Peach."

"Okay," I tell him.

"You still want to, right? You didn't forget?"

I quickly shake my head. "I didn't forget. We'll keep her safe from all the bad things in the world."

As I say it, I realize I don't know how to do this yet.

And then I think—

Neither did my mom.

A loud cry startles me awake.

I shoot up in bed, sweat dotting my brow, my chest already tight with fear.

"Forgive me. Don't go downstairs. Cover your ears."

My heart pounds against my ribs, and when that cry rings out again, I *do* cover my ears.

At first I don't know where I am. Memories bury me like an avalanche, and

I think I'm walking down my staircase with Bubbles held close for protection. My mom said she'd protect me, but she's not here. I don't know where she is.

It's so quiet. I'm breathing really fast. Something is wrong, but I don't know what.

I'm scared.

I want my mom.

I guess I say it out loud because Theo answers back.

"It's okay, Brant. That's just June." He sits up from the other side of the room, slightly illuminated by the neon-green dinosaur lamp on our shared bedstand. "She does this every night. Don't be scared."

My heartbeats start to slow as the fear dissipates. I lower my hands from my ears, staring at my friend through the darkness. "She sounds so sad."

"Yeah. Mom says babies cry a lot because they need something."

I wonder what she needs. When I was scared or sad, I would always reach for Bubbles. He made me feel better.

An idea nudges me, so I whip off the bedcovers and climb down from the mattress. "I'll be right back."

"Where are you going?"

"I want to help June."

I'm still not sure if I like her yet, but I want to help her. I don't want her to be sad like me. Looking around the glowing green room, I locate the stuffed butterfly sticking out from underneath the bed, then I tiptoe my way into the hall. Baby June's nursery is right around the corner, and her tiny cries lead me through the dark. When I poke my head inside, I'm greeted with kicking legs and a scrunchy face.

I squeeze the butterfly. "Hi, June. I'm Brant."

My voice is low, just a whisper, and I don't think she hears me. June keeps kicking her legs, her arms joining in with little balled-up fists. Her eyes are closed tight, her mouth wide open with no sound coming out, as her head twists side to side.

Taking a few steps closer, I stop at the side of her crib. Then I toss the butterfly toy over the railing. It lands beside her on the mattress, startling her enough for her eyes to ping open.

"I brought you something, June. I hope you like it."

My efforts are shattered when June instantly starts to cry.

Oh, no.

She doesn't like the toy.

She hates it.

She hates it so much, she turns redder than Mario's hat. June's whole face scrunches up again, silent at first, like she's building herself up to a giant crescendo, and when her shrieking wail finally breaks free, I jump back from the crib, mortified.

It's not long before Theo's mother rushes into the nursery, tying her robe at her hip. Her hair is a mess, her eyes tired-looking, and she blinks a few times when she spots me in the middle of the room, standing frozen to the elephant-shaped rug.

"Brant?"

Thinking I might be in trouble, I start to stutter. "I–I'm sorry, Mrs. Bailey. I was trying to make her less sad, so I brought her a toy. I–I didn't mean to make her madder."

I'm rambling loud over the ear-piercing cries. My own cheeks feel just as red as June's.

Theo's mom offers me a little smile, then rushes to the crib to scoop up the squawking baby, bouncing her up and down. Up and down. She pats at her back, strokes her tiny head sprouting with dark tufts of hair, and makes hushing sounds that make *both* of us feel better.

A peacefulness enters the room. A mother's love.

She takes the baby with her to the rocking chair and plops down, while whispering cooing sounds into June's ear. When the baby quiets, Theo's mom's eyes lift to me. They don't look like angry eyes. They don't look like Dad's eyes when Mom didn't cook something right or forgot to make the bed. Her smile returns and she says, "That was very kind of you, Brant. Thank you."

I bite my lip. "You're not mad?"

"Of course not," she tells me, and I believe her. She ushers me forward with the flick of her wrist. "Here, come closer."

Fidgeting for a moment, I inch my way toward the rocking chair, my gaze fixed on the squirmy little thing draped over its mother's shoulder. I swallow. "I guess she just needed her mom."

Theo's mother doesn't reply, but her eyes look wet in the gleam of moonlight spilling into the room. She holds her hand out to me, and I take it, and then she whispers, "I'll love you like my very own, Brant. I'll love you like Caroline loved you. You have my word."

She doesn't say any more, but she holds my hand for a long while, even as she rocks back and forth with June on her chest. She hums a lullaby. It's not the same one Mom sang to me, but it makes me both happy and sad at the same time. Happy because I feel loved.

Sad because the person I love most isn't the one holding my hand and singing me lullabies.

When I traipse back to my bedroom after June is carefully returned to her crib fast asleep, I see that Theo is also asleep. He's facing the opposite wall, one leg sticking out of the blanket and hanging off the bed. He snores a little, and it makes me laugh.

I dip inside my own comforter, prepared for sleep to steal me away.

But I don't make it very far.

June starts crying again.

My eyes pop back open, and I stare up at the ceiling, wondering what she needs this time. Does she miss her mom already? The butterfly toy didn't work very well, but—

Wait!

A new idea sweeps through me, pulling me back out of bed and guiding me toward the nursery with a toy dangling from my grip.

June's cries are squeaky and small when I enter the room as quietly as possible. I don't want to scare her. I edge closer to the crib and peek through the grates, watching her writhe atop a sheet made of white and gray stripes. She's a curious little thing, all bright-red cheeks and wriggling limbs. Her shrieks turn loud and screechy, like one of Mr. Canary's speckled roosters I got to meet on our last school field trip. She makes my head pound and my ears ring.

I toss the new toy over the crib rail, and my elephant stuffed animal drops beside her on the mattress. Baby June flails her hands around until a tiny fist locates the toy and clamps the long elephant's nose, squeezing tight.

And then…she goes quiet.

Her cries cease. Her movements become less jerky and mad. The shrieks have turned to coos, and I stare in wonder through the crib slats as June turns her head to look at me.

Our eyes lock, making my insides feel fuzzy. I lower myself to my knees, my own hand curling around one of the rails, while the other reaches in between the slats to touch her. I rub her tummy like I would a puppy, then trace a finger down her twitchy arm. She's warm and soft. She smells like bubble baths.

"I don't have a name for him yet," I murmur, pressing my forehead against the rails. "You can name him if you want."

The elephant thrashes lightly in her grip.

Her eyes are still pinned on me, wide and inquisitive and dark blue, looking almost black in the shadowy room. June coos, then makes a noise that sounds like "aggie." It's cute. It makes me giggle as my hand makes its way to hers.

"Okay, then. We'll call him Aggie."

Tiny fingers clamp around my pinkie, stealing my next breath. She clings so tightly—as if she needs me for something, as if I'm important, and that causes my belly to flutter. My chest tickles, too. I like the feeling: being needed, wanted.

Claimed.

I feel claimed.

And after losing everything I love, it feels really good to belong to someone.

Ah, yes. The moment it all began.

The moment six-year-old me peered into June's crib as she held my finger in her tiny fist, while clutching a toy elephant in the other. I still remember the feeling that came over me, clear as day.

It felt like I would never be lost again.

Of course, I was only a kid at the time, so I didn't fully understand the magnitude of such a feeling—how could I? Our story was impossible to predict.

But…I knew something.

I knew that Baby June had claimed me in that moment, and she never stopped.

She claimed me like the sunrise claims the morning sky with lightness and blush, promise and wonder.

She claimed me like a cyclone funneling through a quiet town, taking no prisoners.

She claimed my good and my bad, my light and my dark. She took my broken, ugly bits and molded them into something worthy of display. She turned my agony into art.

June claimed me in a way that could ultimately be defined by a single word:

Inevitable.

3

FIRST BREAK

BRANT, AGE 6

"You're still a fartknocker, Brant Elliott."

Wendy sticks her tongue out at me while we wait at the bus stop as her brother, Wyatt, snickers under his breath. The Nippersink twins are dreadful.

I ignore them both as we all stand together at the end of the cul-de-sac with Theo's parents and Baby June. Theo is playing with his Game Boy, sitting beneath a vibrant maple tree, while red and orange leaves float and flutter down around him.

June wiggles her arms around inside the stroller, messing up the fuzzy blanket I had carefully wrapped her in. "Aggie."

My smile blooms to life, prompting me to pat the head of the stuffed elephant resting beside her. "Aggie's right here, June. He'll play with you while I'm at school today."

Wendy sneers in my direction. "Babies can't talk, Brant. Don't be stupid."

Theo's mom is bickering with Theo's dad about who was supposed to bring the garbage to the curb. I'm supposed to call them Samantha and Andrew, but my mom always told me that we don't call grown-ups by their first names—it's rude.

I kick at a loose stone on the sidewalk, raising my eyes to Wendy. "I'm not stupid."

"You're pretty stupid. You're talking to a baby who can only drool and cry."

"You're wrong. She does lots of things."

June learned how to roll over last week, from her tummy to her back. It was incredible, and I saw it with my own eyes, but she only did it that one time. She does other things, too. She smiles at me a lot, she flaps her arms like a baby bird, and she says two words: *Aggie* and *Ga*. I think she's the smartest baby in the whole world.

"Whatever." Wendy shrugs, tugging at her ponytail. Her hair is brown like mine, but underneath the autumn sun, I see glimmers of red. Red like the devil, probably.

I feel a hand on my shoulder, so I glance up to see Mrs. Bailey smiling down at me with warm blue eyes. She's pretty, just like June. I wonder if June's eyes will turn light blue like her mom's, or morph into copper like her dad's. Right now they look dark navy, mirroring the gloomy October sky.

"Are you excited for your classes today, Brant?"

I've been back in school for a little while now, and summer has faded into fall. We're learning about pumpkin farms. "I guess."

"Something tells me you'll have a great year, kiddo," Mr. Bailey adds, bumping me on the shoulder with his fist. I quirk a smile in return. "I need to get going, hon. Another day, another dollar." He bends down to plant a kiss against Mrs. Bailey's yellow hair, his eyes dancing with love. They look so much different from my dad's eyes. Even when Theo's parents argue with each other, it never feels bad like it did when my parents fought. It doesn't make my heart gallop like a wild stampede, or make my belly swish with panic.

Mr. Bailey is really nice. He walks us to the bus stop every morning before going to work at the computer office with his mug of coffee. It's never in a paper cup with a lid like some of the other parents' when they wait with us, and I often wonder how he never seems to spill a drop. It's brimful, piping hot. Steam rolls off the top like little plumes of smoke. Mr. Bailey loves coffee almost as much as he loves Mrs. Bailey.

Lifting his hand with a wave, he retreats back down the cul-de-sac, calling out, "Have a remarkable day."

He always says that. He never tells us to have a good day, or even a great day… It's always *remarkable*.

I wonder if he had told my own dad to have a remarkable day on the day of The Bad Night, would everything have been different? It's hard to do bad things when someone wants you to be remarkable.

The bus roars to life around the corner, causing Wendy to hop up and down, her ponytail bouncing with her. She loves school, a lot more than I do. It's probably because she has so many friends. I used to have more friends, but when school started up this year, all the kids looked at me funny. Same with the teachers. I guess everyone had heard about what happened to my parents. Maybe they think that if they get too close to me, it will happen to them, too.

Theo jumps up from his perch beneath the glowing maple, handing off his Game Boy to his mother. She stuffs it into the diaper bag draped over her shoulder, then leans down to give him a hug.

I flash back to standing on my old front porch with Mom. That was the last time we ever hugged beneath a golden sky. Memories burn me, scents and feelings. Mom smelled like taffy apples at the summer carnival, and her love for me was just as sweet. I miss it.

I miss her.

The bus rolls up, tearing me away from the memory. June squeaks out baby noises that sound like gibberish, flailing her arms around beneath the awning of the stroller. It almost looks like she's waving goodbye to me.

I can't help but smile.

"Bye, June," I say, dashing toward the school bus, my backpack slapping against me as I run. I turn around at the last second, calling out, "Have a remarkable day."

I'm sitting at the dinner table that evening, feeling dejected. I didn't have a remarkable day, even though I tried. In fact, it was a really bad day.

Wyatt gathered all his friends up, and together they teased me on the playground.

They called me an orphan.

A stray.

A loser.

I spent so long in the bathroom crying in one of the empty stalls that Principal Seymour came in searching for me and brought me to his office. He gave me a little paper cup of water and a lollipop, then told me to sit down in his oversized rolling chair until I felt better.

The lollipop was purple.

I dropped it into the garbage can when he wasn't looking.

Principal Seymour called Theo's mom, telling her all about what happened. She picked me up from school early, and we rode the whole way back to the house in silence as June squeezed my finger beside me in her car seat. It was the only thing that made my heart hurt a little bit less.

It's still quiet at the table as I mush my cottage cheese with a fork, only pretending to eat it. I wonder if it's so quiet because Mr. and Mrs. Bailey are mad at me for going to the principal's office.

Theo's voice bursts to life beside me as he shovels bites of chicken into his mouth. He talks through his chews, announcing, "I'm the student of the week. I have to make a poster board all about my life." He kicks his legs back and forth underneath the table. "That's pretty cool, huh?"

Mrs. Bailey dabs at her mouth with a napkin. Her hair is pulled up into a giant bun with a pen sticking out of it. There's always a pen in her hair, sometimes two or three. She says it's because she's always misplacing them, and you never know when you might need a pen. "How exciting, sweetheart. I'll pick up the supplies tomorrow and take the disposable camera in to print out some photos for your board."

"Can you take a picture of me and Brant? Since he's my new brother?"

I frown as my utensil clangs against the plate. "I'm not your brother."

"Yes, you are. Mom said so."

"No, I'm not. I'm your friend, and I'm just sleeping over for a while until I can go live at my house again."

Silence settles in.

Theo makes a weird face, then shrugs, taking in another mouthful of chicken. I glance up at his parents, and they're both staring at their plates, looking like they want to say something but don't know what.

Mr. Bailey finally clears his throat. "Brant…you won't be going back to your old house. Nobody lives there anymore. Your new home is here, with us." He says it gently, but the words sound so sharp and callous. So final. "Do you understand, son?"

Son.

No, that's not right.

"I'm not your son, Mr. Bailey. My parents are Caroline and Lucas Elliott."

Theo's mom chews her bottom lip with her teeth, then pulls the pen out of her mound of hair, twirling it between her fingertips. She doesn't write anything with it. She just spins it in circles, back and forth, like it's helping her think. "Brant, honey, I know this is difficult. I can't even imagine how hard this must be for you—"

"Can I be excused?" The question spills out of me, and I push my uneaten plate away.

They glance at each other before Mr. Bailey gives me a small nod.

I leap from my chair and race down the long hallway to the room I share with Theo. June is taking a nap in her rocker, so I slow my steps when I pass her nursery, sparing her a quick peek. She looks so peaceful, so innocent, and I wonder what she's dreaming about. Maybe her dreams are filled with visions of bluebirds flying high over the rainbow, just like I used to dream about whenever Mom would sing me that lullaby song.

I wonder if she's dreaming about her parents who love her—who are still alive to tell her that they love her—and I wonder if maybe *she's* the one flying high over the rainbow, as free as a beautiful bird, without any worries or fears.

And then I wonder…

Why, oh why, can't I?

A nightmare found me.

A terrible, ugly nightmare found me in the middle of the night, one that scared me so much I climbed out of my bed, soaked with sweat, and did a bad thing.

I took June.

Mrs. Bailey lets her sleep in her rocker or swing some nights. She says it's because June will wake up if she's placed inside her crib, and then she'll never go back to sleep…and Mrs. Bailey really likes sleep.

Luckily for me, tonight was one of those nights.

I made sure my footsteps were small and quiet as I ventured my way down the hall and into June's nursery. She was already awake, but she wasn't fussing. She was just lying in her rocker, kicking her feet, and making sweet little sounds I couldn't decipher. Her eyes were big and round, and I swore they lit up just for me when I hovered over her. "Don't be afraid, Baby June. I'll protect you."

It took me a few moments to unclasp the buckle, but when she was finally free, I gathered her to my chest and picked her right up. She sure was heavy for being such a tiny thing. Carrying her down the hallway to the front door caused me to sweat even harder. It made my breath come fast and quick, too. My heart pounded inside my chest.

I remembered to bring her pacifier with us—Theo calls it her nom-nom—as well as her favorite pink blanket to keep her warm. My arms were too full of June to grab Aggie, so I'll need to go back for the toy later.

June was a real good baby. She hardly made a peep when I set her down on the welcome mat to slip on my sneakers and a light jacket and open the front door. She only cooed and gurgled when I clutched her to my swiftly beating chest, then hauled her down the short sidewalk as a mild breeze followed alongside us.

And she only smiles with her gums when we finally land in front of my old house.

"This is where I live, June," I tell her, bouncing her softly up and down like her mother does.

June chirps back, "Ga!"

Theo's dad said that nobody lives here anymore, but that's not true. This is *my* house. I live here.

There's a sign stuck to the front lawn with big letters and a picture of a strange man's face. He's happy and smiling, and I wonder if he's trying to steal this house from me.

I lay June on the grass on her back, and she squirms among the long blades, watching me as I skip away to the front porch. It's dark outside, and the porch light isn't on, but I notice a box attached to the doorknob that looks like some sort of lock.

The door won't budge.

How will I get inside?

This isn't right. This is my house, and I should be able to open the door and walk right into my own house.

Sadness crawls all over my skin, so I scratch at my arms, my mind racing with possible solutions. June still looks content, tickled by the early fall breeze as she clasps her fingers around a tall weed. She doesn't appear to be cold, but I pace over to her and tighten the blanket around her wiggly body just in case.

As I straighten, my eyes skate over the yard, falling upon the mailbox.

Dad's beloved rocks stare back at me, and an idea blossoms.

My heart skips.

And before I can second-guess myself, I jog the rest of the way over to the mailbox and grip a ruddy rock inside my palm.

You shouldn't do this, Brant.

This feels wrong.

Oh, but I must...

My thoughts battle it out as I traipse back to the front of the house and come to a complete stop, facing the main window.

I swallow my fear and glance over my shoulder at June, muttering the three words that have haunted me ever since The Bad Night: "Cover your ears."

Then I twist back around and throw the rock right through the window with all my might.

Glass shatters. I jolt at the noise. June starts to cry.

"It's okay, June. I'll be right back for you."

Darting up to the porch, I start to climb through the broken window, instantly slicing my hand on a jagged piece of glass when I pull one leg over the ledge. Blood oozes from the wound. My head feels light and dizzy.

Keep going. Keep going.

Ignoring the stab of pain, my body rolls the rest of the way inside until I hit the floor, landing on my back. It takes a moment for me to catch my breath, but then I'm on my feet, heading toward the front door and successfully swinging it open. I race out into the yard to collect a shrieking June and hobble my way back inside, shutting the door behind me.

"Shh…don't cry, Baby June. You're okay. I got you," I hush her, rocking her in my arms. Blood stains her favorite pink blanket, and my eyes pop in horror. "Oh, no…"

There's so much blood.

The gash on my palm looks deep and angry, and I can't stop the rush of red from seeping out. June must sense my unease because she wails even louder, her arms extended and tremoring.

I have to be brave. June needs me. My house needs me.

Placing June on the fresh new layer of carpeting lining the floors, I unwrap the blanket coiled around her and use it as a bandage for my hand. Dad used to watch shows with lots of blood, and the people did this sometimes. They would wrap their wounds in towels or cloth.

Satisfied with this remedy, I bend over June and stroke her silky curls with my uninjured hand. "I'll keep you safe. I promise."

She calms a bit, her lips quivering as her cries quiet to soft whimpers. I wonder if she's scared… *I sure hope not.* I promised I'd always protect her, but how could I protect her if I'm here and she's in a different house?

I had to take her. I just *had* to.

When I'm confident June is happy again, entranced by the carpet fibers tickling her fingers, I trudge up the staircase to my old bedroom in search of Bubbles. I'd take June with me, but I don't think I can carry her all the way up the stairs. My arms are too tired. Instead, I'll just have to bring down some blankets and pillows for us, as well as Bubbles and my favorite night-light to keep the shadows away.

I make my way up the steps and around the hall, my heartbeats slamming loud and hard against my ribs. A giddiness possesses me, carrying my legs the rest of the way, eager to see my old room for the first time since The Bad Night.

Only…the excitement is snuffed out the moment I reach the threshold.

My breath catches.

Tears coat my eyes.

It's gone.

My room is gone. It's nothing but an empty shell.

The walls are stark white. The bright-blue color that reminded me of a summer sky has been painted over. My furniture is missing. The posters have been torn down, leaving behind no evidence that they were ever there at all. Even my bed is gone.

Bubbles has vanished without a trace.

Bubbles, where are you?

I collapse to my knees, sucker punched with grief. Everything is gone. Wyatt and his friends were right. I'm just an orphan, a loser. I've lost everything.

June's little cries cut through my tears, and I remember that she needs me.

I haven't lost everything… *I still have June.*

Making my way back down the stairs, sniffling, I run the back of my wrist across my face, erasing the rest of my sadness. "I'm sorry, June," I whisper raggedly, lowering myself beside her on the carpet. My hand throbs with pain, but I force it away. "I didn't mean to leave you so long."

She makes a *ga-ga* sound when I tuck my arm around her middle and pull her close. We lie there together on the floor of the living room, in the exact same spot I found my parents. Another tear sneaks its way down my cheek, and I glance up at the ceiling, just like Mom did whenever she said her prayers at night. "I'm here now," I say out loud. "I'm home."

I wonder if Mom and Dad are flying high over the rainbow, waiting for me. Maybe they couldn't find me because I wasn't here. They didn't know where to look.

I'm here now, my mind echoes, over and over again.

Maybe they will finally come back for me.

Maybe they'll fly home.

My parents never found me, of course, but somebody's parents did.

Gary Keebler's parents, to be exact.

They lived next door and were awoken by a suspicious sound that night. It had been me, chucking a rock through the window like a miniature Butch Cassidy in the making.

The Keeblers brought us home, much to Samantha and Andrew's horror.

Samantha was hysterical. Absolutely hysterical. In all the years I've known her, I've only seen Samantha Bailey cry three times, and that was one of them.

The second and third times came much later.

I needed stitches in my left hand, but miraculously, Baby June came home without a scratch on her. I promised I would keep her safe, and I kept that promise. I kept it for a long time.

I kept it for as long as I possibly could.

But…I should have known no one can keep a promise like that forever.

Not even Mom.

But I'll get to that. First, you should know that night triggered a new chapter for me and the Baileys. Not only was it the last time I ever set foot into my childhood house, but it wasn't long before I left the Baileys' house, too.

Less than two months later, we moved.

4

FIRST STEP

BRANT, AGE 8

"It's a good day to save someone," Theo hollers. "Hurry up, Peach!"

He's yelling over his shoulder at us, while I hang back with June, who is already running out of steam. She's only two, and her legs are so little.

She makes a scowl that looks more adorable than mean. "Me June!" she calls back.

Theo calls her Peach, just like in Mario, but June doesn't like it.

We're running through the acres of our backyard, home to a plethora of fruit trees, vegetable gardens, and a custom-built tree house made by Mr. Bailey. We've lived here for almost two years now, and it might be my favorite place in the whole world—for a few reasons.

One, it doesn't remind me of The Bad Night. I don't have to look out the front window and see my old driveway, and I don't have to stare at the familiar bricks and stones while I wait at my bus stop. I don't have to ride my bike past the sad, overgrown lawn, or look at the porch and think of the very last time my mother called me a good boy.

Two, I have my own bedroom. The Baileys made sure to buy a house with an extra bedroom just for me, and even though I spend a lot of time in Theo's room playing games and making forts—and even more time in June's room with puzzles and building blocks—I have a private space to draw and do my homework. I have a quiet bed where I can dream alone. Mrs. Bailey tucks me in each night and reads me a story, reminding me that Mom is watching over me.

I dream a little easier, imagining my mother floating over the rainbow, smiling wide, smelling like caramel and taffy apples.

And three...June took her first steps in this backyard, on her first birthday.

It turns out she was born in the early morning hours of June first. That's why Mr. and Mrs. Bailey gave her that name. She was born right around the same time my parents died, and I'm not sure what to think of that yet. All I know is that I was sad on June's first birthday, really sad. Everyone walked around the house all quiet and mopey, not knowing what to say to me. I wouldn't even have known it was the anniversary of The Bad Night, but Theo spilled the beans during a video game marathon, telling me he overheard his parents talking about it. Aunt Kelly stopped by to visit, filling my palm with multicolored Skittles, minus the purple ones of course, and giving me wet cheek kisses. She told me she was visiting my momma's gravestone. I didn't want to go, so she said she'd try again next year.

But here we are...*next year*. A whole year went by, and I still didn't want to go.

I wanted to stay here and celebrate June's second birthday—because when June turned one year old, the most amazing thing happened.

She walked.

And not only did she walk...she walked straight *to me*. She hobbled right into my arms.

Nobody could believe it.

June had the biggest smile on her face, and she said my name the best she could, which sounded a little bit like "Bat!" She says it better now, but she still can't really say her R sounds.

"No wun," June tells me, tottering to a stop, winded and overly dramatic. We haven't even run that far. "I sit."

She plops down in the lush grass, her stuffed elephant dropping beside her. "Aggie tired."

Theo halts his pace, groaning from a few feet ahead. "We haven't even made it to the haunted castle yet."

The haunted castle is the tree house. It's also an enchanted castle, an underground cave, a lava pit, an evil fortress, and a mystical tower. June is too small to climb up the ladder, so we created a fort underneath it just for her. She's the princess, and we're the heroes.

It's our favorite game.

Well…it's mine and Theo's favorite game, anyway. June would rather play in her ball pit and watch *Blue's Clues* all day, munching on Goldfish crackers.

"Be right there!" I call to him. "June wants to rest."

"Just put her on your back and carry her, Brant. Time is running out."

June perks up at this, leaping into my arms. "Pig-back!"

"Okay, okay, hop on."

I gather June onto my back as her wrists clasp my neck, her legs wrapping around my middle. She's still so heavy for being just an itty-bitty rag doll. Hunching forward so she doesn't slip, I make sure to grab Aggie, and we slowly march our way over to the tree-house fort, where Theo is already waiting inside, pretending to fight an evil ghost with a tree branch.

"Don't worry, Peach. I'll save you!" he shouts.

June makes a sassy little huff, then slides down my back to the ground. "You siwwy."

She can't really say her L sounds either.

I take a seat in one of the inflatable chairs Mr. Bailey blew up for us, and June follows suit, jumping into my lap. Her butterscotch curls tickle my nose, smelling like a mix of baby powder and the lilac bushes that fence our front porch. Her hair is a magical thing. It's darker during wintertime, almost brown, then fades to golden in the summer months.

June spins in my lap, her chubby hands planting on either side of my face. "Bant. Stowy."

Her eyes glow blue in the afternoon haze. They are light, light blue—even lighter than Mrs. Bailey's eyes. Sometimes I think I can see right through them. "You want me to tell you a story?"

She nods emphatically.

"Okay, June. I'll tell you a story…" Then I tackle her to the blankets that line the floor of her fort, my fingers dancing across her torso in a frenzy. "After I tickle you!"

Her laughter warms me, her limbs flailing as she tries to dodge my attack. "No mo! No mo!"

I lift up her T-shirt, patterned with ice cream cones, and blow raspberries onto her round belly.

She laughs harder. She laughs so hard her face turns red like a ripe strawberry.

"I'll save you, June!"

Theo leaps into action, waving his invisible sword at me until I fall back, pretending to be defeated. I play dead.

"Super Mario to the rescue," he crows, and I pop an eyeball open to watch as he pulls June to her unsteady feet, then lifts her arm in the air in victory.

I sit up straight. "I'm Luigi, remember? You're not supposed to kill Luigi."

"You were a bad guy in this scene."

"Bant no bad," June pipes up in my defense. She dashes over to me, falling down beside me on the blankets and cradling her knees to her chest. "He good."

"Fine, I guess he's good," Theo relents. His sandy hair falls over his eyes, so he brushes it back with his arm. Freckles dot his nose and cheekbones, and I idly wonder if June will have freckles, too. Right now, her skin is porcelain white, just like one of Grams's china dolls. Theo traipses over to us and sits cross-legged in front of me, tracing his finger through a patch of dirt that pokes through the mound of blankets. "What do you want to be when you grow up, Brant?"

I consider the question. It's not something I've really thought about before. I'm in third grade, and we're learning about so many interesting things—firefighters, doctors, teachers, and pilots. My mind races with potential, with things I can become, and I blurt out, "I want to cook for people."

Mom loved to cook, and I loved to eat her food. Dad yelled about it all the time, but I never understood why. It was so yummy.

I want to make yummy food like my mom.

Theo doesn't look up, entranced by a ladybug that crawls along his finger. "You mean like a chef?"

"I think so. Sure."

"That's cool." He nods. "I want to be a saver."

My brows knit together in confusion. "A saver?"

"Yeah, I want to save people one day. You know, like when we play superheroes and we defeat all the monsters and bad guys. We always win," he explains, still staring at the ladybug, watching transfixed as it wriggles over his knuckles. "I want to be a saver. That's what I want to do."

I love that idea. Theo would make a great saver one day. He's always taking care of June and watching over me, making sure the other kids aren't mean to me.

Even though we moved into a different house, we stayed at the same school. I still have to deal with the dreadful Nippersink twins, Wendy and Wyatt, along with their gaggle of bullies.

One day, on the school playground, Wyatt threw a rock at me. He said he'd heard about what I did that night, when I threw a rock through my old house's window, so he threw a rock at me. It didn't really hurt, but Theo saw him do it.

Theo marched over to us from the swing set and punched Wyatt Nippersink right in the belly, saying, "If you ever hurt Brant again, I swear on my sister's life I'll break your kneecaps then hide your wheelchair so you have to crawl around like a little baby and we can all laugh at you."

He got sus-tended from school, which meant he got to stay home for a few days.

So cool.

Wyatt didn't talk to me much after that, and all the other kids left me alone. Even Wendy stopped sticking her tongue out at me.

That's how I know he'll make a great saver.

"Lay-bug!"

June drops to her knees, her curtain of shiny curls falling over her face. She bends over to stare at the tiny speckled creature skittering along the back of Theo's hand, then gasps with awe.

"That's right," I confirm, moving in closer. "That is a ladybug."

A smile brightens her face, showcasing her dimples and the glints of starlight in her eyes. It always looks like she has stars in her eyes, even in the daytime. June pops her head up, looking right at me, then points to herself. "June...bug!"

I'm confused at first, and then she flaps her arms like a bird...*or a bug*?

"June...bug," she repeats, motioning like she's flying through the air. "Pwetty bug."

"Oh, a butterfly?" I ponder.

She bobs her head in agreement.

A few months ago, I told June that Theo and I wanted to name her Butterfly. Then I found some picture books in her bedroom detailing a variety of fascinating insects, and I zeroed in on the butterfly with apricot wings. She was amazed.

"June, bug," she repeats, pleased with her association.

I smile. And then the words settle in, poking and tickling me like some kind of revelation brimming to life. "Junebug."

"Junebug," she parrots happily.

Theo pokes his head up, inquiring, "What's that?"

"That's what I'm going to call June," I say.

I bet it's a beautiful bug. I bet it's as beautiful as a butterfly.

June smacks her hands together, clapping with delight, then scoots her way back to my lap and climbs up. She nuzzles into me, her little sigh warming my chest. "June wuv Bant."

I wrap my arms around her, my heart feeling fuzzy and full. We all stay in the fort for a while, until the sun starts to hide behind the horizon, dimming our light. Theo rests on his belly, his legs kicking back and forth through the air as he reads comic book after comic book. We tell stories to each other and create elaborate schemes to reenact after school the next day. We laugh and tease and joke, our imaginations as bright as the sun-kissed sky. And by the time Mr. Bailey comes home from work and ushers us inside for supper, June has fallen asleep in my lap, her fine wisps of hair tickling my chin and a dollop of drool dampening my T-shirt.

I place a kiss to her temple before waking her up then heading inside. "I love you, too, Junebug."

The following day, I have my weekly appointment with Dr. Shelby.

She's a kind woman, with a voice that sounds like a pillowy cloud. Dr. Shelby isn't like a regular doctor. She doesn't poke me with metal sticks, or shine lights into my eyeballs, or press on my belly with cold fingers.

She just talks to me. She plays with me. Sometimes she draws with me.

I glance up at her from my perch on the bright-orange area rug, aimlessly dallying with one of those colorful bead mazes. Dr. Shelby is watching me with one leg crossed over the other and a pad of paper on her lap. A pencil taps against the notepad, a friendly smile drawn onto her lips.

"You like that bead maze," she notes, bobbing her chin at the toy in front of me. "It's always the first thing you play with."

Sliding an assortment of colored beads along the thin metal bar, I nod. "It's June's favorite toy. It reminds me of her."

We talk about June a lot. My first meeting with Dr. Shelby was shortly after the incident at my old house—the night I took June and cut my hand so badly I needed stitches. I still have a scar etched into my palm.

Dr. Shelby asked me questions about that night, about why I did the things I did. She wanted to know my thoughts. But mostly she asked me why I took June. She asked me that question a whole lot of times, and I wonder if she thought I'd give her a different answer one day.

I never did.

"Because I told her I'd always protect her," I replied.

According to Dr. Shelby, I had actually put June in more danger that night.

I feel sorry for that. I never meant to hurt her or make her scared.

Dr. Shelby situates herself on the couch across from me, jotting down some notes. "How is June? Did she learn anything new this week?"

"Yes!" My excitement flares; I love talking about June and all the fun things she learns. "She learned how to pedal on her trike. It took a long time to get her feet going in the right directions, but she was so happy when she figured it out. She's the smartest girl I know."

"She's very lucky to have two big brothers she can look up to as she grows older."

I stop fiddling with the beads and glance up again. "I'm not her brother. I'm an only child," I explain. "Mom didn't bring home any more babies."

Dr. Shelby is quiet for a moment, then she writes something in the notepad. "The Baileys adopted you, so that would make you the adopted sibling of Theo and June."

"No, I don't have any siblings. I'm an only child."

More silence. More notes.

"Okay, Brant, let's talk about some things that make you happy. How does that sound?"

"That sounds okay," I tell her, shrugging, then leaning back on my palms. "Like June?"

"Sure. What else?"

I chew on my lip. "Video games with Theo. Sweet things like muffins and cake. Bubbles, even though he's gone. But mostly June."

"That's great," she says through a smile. "Maybe you can think of some more things and tell me about them at the next meeting."

When I left to go home that day, I was still thinking about those things. I thought about happy things all through dinner, and when I took a bath, and when Mr. Bailey helped me with my math homework, and when I tucked June into her new toddler bed, and when my own head hit the pillow.

Mrs. Bailey sits beside me on the mattress, and it squeaks beneath her weight. "Did you have a good day today, Brant?"

She always asks me that. I stare at the pens stuck inside her blond bun, noting that one of them is Theo's Mario pen. It makes me smile.

It makes me happy.

"I guess so," I tell her, picking at the bedcovers. "Dr. Shelby wants me to think about things that make me happy."

"I love that. I bet you can think of a lot of things."

Snuggling under my comforter, I nod. "Yeah." I'm about to turn over and settle in for the night when a thought strikes me. It's something that used to make me very, very happy. I blink, then gaze up at Mrs. Bailey with curious eyes. "Can you…sing me a lullaby?"

Her grin stretches wide, lighting up her face, just like when June smiles. "Of course. Is there anything you want to hear?"

I swallow. "My mom used to sing one to me. I can't remember the words… but there were bluebirds and rainbows. The words made me happy, but the song sounded sad."

"I think I know that one." Mrs. Bailey scoots closer to me, pressing her fingertips to my forehead and brushing aside my scruffy bangs. She clears her throat. "Tell me if this is right…"

The moment she starts humming the tune, I'm drenched in familiarity. Tears rush to my eyes in an instant. "That's it," I croak out, my throat stinging and itchy. "That's the lullaby."

She stops humming and tells me, "It's called 'Over the Rainbow.' It's one of my favorites."

"Mom didn't sing it for a long time because she said it made her cry sometimes. But she sang it to me on the night…" My voice trails off, a tear breaking free and sliding down my cheek. "She sang it to me that night."

Mrs. Bailey's eyes gleam with her own tears, and she licks her lips with a quivering sigh. "Okay, Brant," she whispers, her thumb grazing my hairline with a lingering touch. "I'll sing it to you from now on. I'll sing it every night until you grow too old for lullabies."

And she did.

Every single night, until I grew too old for lullabies, Samantha Bailey would tuck me into bed, comb my hair with gentle fingers, and sing me that song. I looked forward to it. It kept me close to Mom, so she never strayed.

And then one night, I started singing it to June.

Only, I changed the words a bit.

Somewhere, over the rainbow, Junebugs fly…

5

FIRST DANCE

BRANT, AGE 10

"Have a remarkable day."

Mr. Bailey sips his hot mug of coffee at the edge of our long, wooded driveway. He's in a robe today, and platypus slippers, which are garnering stares from the bus driver. I didn't even know what a platypus looked like until I saw his slippers.

"Bye, Mr. Bailey. See you after school."

Theo runs ahead of me, climbing up the bus steps and waving over his shoulder. I hesitate briefly, my eyes stuck to the front door of the house, waiting to see if a familiar little face will wave me off. June sleeps in too late some mornings, so I don't always see her before I leave for school.

Those are the days that are a little less remarkable.

With a sad sigh, I hang my head and pivot toward the school bus.

"Bwant! Wait!"

My heart leaps with relief.

I hear the screen door clap shut, then turn to discover June running as fast as her tiny legs will carry her up the driveway with bare feet. Aggie dangles from one hand, while the bottom of her nightdress skims the pavement. She's a vision of whipping hair and erratic limbs.

"Brant, time to go," the bus driver declares.

"One minute, Miss Debbie!"

Mr. Bailey shakes his head, like he's a little embarrassed for the delay, maybe a little sorry, but he doesn't tell me to hurry up or move along.

June catapults herself into my arms, nearly knocking me backward. "Have a marker day, Bwant!" she tells me, squeezing me so hard that I wheeze. *Marker* means *remarkable*. She'll only be four years old next month, so she still struggles with her vocabulary. Then she waves madly to the school bus, to where Theo's hand is poking through a crack in the window. "Bye, Theo!"

"Bye, Peach!" Theo yells back.

"Brant…" the bus driver says again. "Last call."

"Okay, sorry!" I let go of June, smiling my goodbye as I pace back toward the bus. "See you after school, Junebug. I can't wait for your recital tomorrow."

She twirls the hem of her *Little Mermaid* nightgown, her copper-colored hair swinging with her. June has her very first dance recital this weekend. She's been practicing since last fall, and I can't wait to see her perform, all dolled up in a lollipop dress.

"I dance!" she says, hopping up and down. "Bye!"

I finally make my way to the school bus, where Miss Debbie is tsking her tongue. She sighs, then closes the mechanical door behind me. "If you two weren't so darn cute, I would've left without ya."

Sheepishly, I make my way down the aisle of the bus, looking for a vacant seat. To my surprise, Wendy Nippersink pats the space beside her.

"You can sit with me, Brant," she says, glancing my way with an unreadable expression.

I falter for a second, but don't want to hold the bus up any longer, so I slip into the seat. Craning my neck around Wendy and her devil hair, I wave to June and Mr. Bailey as the bus begins to roll away. June is held up high in her dad's strong arm, while his other hand grips his coffee mug. They are both smiling behind us as we disappear down the quiet street, and I swear his platypus slippers are smiling, too.

"Why'd your dad have big brown ducks on his feet?"

Wendy's equally big brown eyes are staring right at me, her lashes so long they almost reach her eyebrows. "He's not my dad."

"Yes, he is."

"No, he's not. He's Theo's dad."

She twists around, pulling herself up to her knees and finding Theo, one seat behind us. "Your dad is Brant's dad, too, right?"

I remain facing forward, a little groan of irritation tickling my throat.

Theo replies, "Nope, he's only my dad. And June's. Brant just lives with us."

"That makes no kinda sense." Wendy huffs her disagreement, falling back down to her butt with a swishy sound. I can see her watching me out of the corner of my eye, but I don't dare look at her. "So, why'd he have ducks on his feet, anyway?"

"He didn't. They were platypuses."

"No such thing."

"Fine, Wendy. No such thing." I'm really annoyed with her, so I cross my arms, lean my head back, and close my eyes.

She pokes me in the ribs with her finger.

"What?" I bark.

"Wanna play after school today?"

Wendy never asks me to play, so she must be up to no good. "No, thanks."

"Why not?"

"Because you've always been rotten to me. I don't like you very much."

"Maybe I like you."

My eyes snap open. She's staring at me, all wide-eyed and innocent looking, but I know better. "You're a liar. You called me a fartknocker."

"That was before I liked you," she says, her composure cool and calm, like we're talking about classwork or something minor. She gives her high ponytail a sharp tug, tilting her head to one side. Two eyes like cinnamon are glittering in my direction, and with a satisfied smile, Wendy mutters, "I do like you, Brant Elliott. You'll see."

June is the sweetest little lollipop I've ever seen.

She barrels toward me from the restroom, twirling the rainbow tulle of her spring recital dress. Bright-pink lipstick, the color of Mrs. Bailey's potted orchids, is smudged along her lips, and her skin shimmers with glitter as she dances through the lobby. The scent of hairspray follows her, necessary for her perfectly coiffed bun to remain stiff like a statue when she bounces up and down. "Look at me! Mama made me look pwetty, just like her."

Mrs. Bailey chuckles as she trails behind June, wearing matching lipstick, her own bun carefully secured into place. Not a single pen sticks out of it today.

June's recital is being held at the performing arts center of a local community college. We're all waiting in the lobby while the dancers are ushered to their respective classes, where they will stand by to perform on the big stage in the auditorium.

Theo is huddled up in a nearby chair, trying to hide himself in a baggy hoodie because, apparently, he spotted Monica Porter in a sequined peacock dress. I guess he has a crush on Monica Porter, but that doesn't really explain why he's hiding. He pokes his head out of the gray fabric to glance at June. "Look at you, Peach. You look like a real-life dancer."

"I am, silly! Watch this." June plants her hands upon her hips, then bends her knees. "Plié…" She pops back up. "And straight!"

We all clap.

Mr. Bailey looks like he might cry as he kneels down in front of June, fluffing the hem of her skirt. "My baby girl at her first recital…"

"I not a baby, Daddy. I almost *four*." She holds up five fingers.

"That's right. How could I forget?"

June grins from ear to ear, sashaying in her dress as the multicolored sequins gleam like prisms. Her cheeks are painted with rose blush to match her lips, and there's a colorful accessory clipped to her bun that resembles a pinwheel. Light-brown hair glints like gold beneath the ceiling lights. She turns to me, her smile still as bright as her dress. "Will you dance with me, Bwant?"

"Dance with you? I can't dance, Junebug. I'm no good at it."

"You can do it. Mama says to believe in yourself."

A smile quirks on my lips. Mrs. Bailey does say that a lot. She told me once, after I had a string of nightmares about The Bad Night, that our minds are the most powerful tool we own. Whatever we believe about ourselves is sure to come true. It reminded me of my favorite rainbow song. Reaching for June, I nod, accepting the offer. "Okay, I'll dance with you."

She squeals, bobbing up and down on her ballet slippers, and springs forward until she's in my arms. I parade her around in clumsy circles, spinning her until she almost topples over, giggling so hard my belly aches.

"Let me get a picture," Mrs. Bailey chimes in, scrambling through her giant purse. "Hold still, you two."

June wraps two tiny arms around my middle, smashing her cheek to my hip. "Cheese!"

The flash goes off.

"Theodore, come here. And remove that awful sweatshirt. You're covering the nice sweater vest that Grams made for you."

Theo drags himself over to us, his eyes darting around, scouting the crowd for a familiar blond peacock. "Yeah, yeah. I'm coming."

We take an assortment of photographs before two dance instructors file over to us to collect June. One of the teachers bends down and holds out her hand. "June Bailey, look how beautiful you are. It's time to go," she says softly. "Are you excited to dance for all the moms and dads tonight?"

I'm surprised when June's smile slips, and her eyes go wide. She shakes her head.

"No? Are you nervous?"

She nods.

A sad little feeling sweeps through me. I don't want June to be nervous; she's been so excited to dance on the big stage. I kneel down beside her, clasping her hand until she turns to face me. Pale-blue eyes glint with tears. "Junebug, what's wrong? Why are you nervous?"

Mrs. Bailey appears flustered, setting her purse down and tugging at June's wrist. "Let's go, June. Your teachers are waiting."

"No!"

"Sweetheart, you're fine. This is what you've practiced for all year." Embarrassment dots Mrs. Bailey's face, the flush creeping down her neck. She gives June another tug. "You're going to do great. I promise."

June manages to pull free, dashing back to where I'm still kneeling and flinging her arms around my neck. Her bottom lip quivers. "Will you dance with me, Bwant?"

"I can't do that. I'm not a ballerina like you. I haven't even practiced."

"I show you my dance moves, okay? Watch…"

She steps back and starts to do a twirl, but I stop her. "I'm sorry, but I can't. You have to be brave and do it all by yourself."

"I no like being brave." She pouts, dipping her chin to her chest.

The teachers fidget restlessly beside us, one looking at her wristwatch.

I clear my throat, tilting June's head up to look at me. A tear slips down her rouged cheek, so I brush it away. "It's hard to be brave. Scary too," I explain. "But the best part about being brave is the feeling that comes after."

She sniffs. "What's that?"

"It's pride, I think. You feel proud of yourself for doing that hard thing. Everyone else is proud of you, too, and that feels really good." I glance up at Mrs. Dailey, who is staring down at us, her expression mixed with softness and alarm. Maybe even pride. I keep going, returning my attention to June. "Junebug… remember when I was really scared to go down that sledding hill last winter?"

"Yes," she mutters.

"Then when I was finally brave enough to go down, everybody cheered for me? I felt really good inside. I felt happy. And it was so much fun… I did it a hundred more times."

"I 'member."

"Well, it's sort of like that. You just need to be brave that first time, then all the other times come easy. And maybe you'll love it so much, *you'll* want to do it a hundred more times."

A teacher cuts in, stretching a smile. "We have to go now, June. There are coloring books and crafts waiting for you with the rest of the class. How does that sound?"

June looks at me with her wide, watery eyes, as if she's waiting for my approval. My reassurance. She squeaks out, "I be brave like you."

My heart swells. I nod eagerly. Proudly.

"I dance now." June pummels me with another tight hug, planting a kiss on my cheek before she releases me.

Standing up, I watch as she takes her teacher's hand and prances away, her head held high. I wave. "I'm proud of you, Junebug."

June calls back over her shoulder one more time, "I be brave!" Then she rounds the corner, her rainbow lollipop dress disappearing out of sight.

A strong hand squeezes my shoulder, so I look up, finding Mr. Bailey gazing down at me with gentle brown eyes. They remind me of hot cocoa. "You're a remarkable young man, Brant."

Remarkable.

There's that word again. I don't feel very remarkable. All I felt was sad because June was sad, and I wanted to fix that. I wanted her to be happy.

I'm still digesting his words when a flash of cerulean and emerald catches the corner of my eye. My head twists to the left, just as Theo jumps behind me, hiding from the two peacocks waving at us from across the hall.

It's Monica Porter and Wendy Nippersink. They're all made-up in their recital costumes, looking pretty.

Pretty?

I just called Wendy Nippersink pretty. Gross.

Theo mumbles into my back, "Are they gone?"

"No."

"Let's get out of here, Brant. This is humiliating."

"Why?" I wave back at my schoolmates a little awkwardly, then shove both hands into my pockets.

"Because I'm wearing that hideous vest Grams made for me, of course," Theo says.

"So? It's not that bad."

"There are little baby sheep playing harmonicas all over it."

I shrug. "I guess it would be cooler if they were playing drums."

"Hi, Brant. Hi, Theo."

The girls traipse over to us, and I nudge Theo with my elbow until he pops up beside me, swiping at his hair and trying to cover his vest with his arms. I teeter on the balls of my feet and give them a nod. "Hey. You guys are dancing tonight?"

Of course they're dancing tonight. Why else would they be dressed like peacocks?

My embarrassment flares, but not as much as Theo's. His pale skin breaks out into blotches of red, almost like hives.

"Yeah, we're dancing," Monica responds. Her eyes light up when she glances at Theo. "I like your vest."

I think Theo might faint. His own eyes bug out, his words stuttering in his throat. "Um, I... Yeah, it's not mine. It's Brant's."

My head whips toward him.

"He likes sheep. And harmonicas. And I just put it on by mistake, thinking it was a different vest. A much, much cooler vest." He coughs into his fist. "Because I'm cool."

I just stare at him, confused. We all do.

"Oh, well, that's...cool." Monica forces a smile.

Luckily, Mrs. Bailey intercedes, sending a "hello" to the girls, then telling us it's time to go find our seats in the auditorium. I'm grateful for this. I'm also really mad at Theo for being a liar.

"Bye, Brant," Wendy says, while Mr. and Mrs. Bailey collect their things and Theo runs ahead of them like a chicken. "I'll wave to you when I'm onstage."

I'm shocked silly when she lifts up on her tiptoes and gives me a little kiss right on the jaw. My cheeks grow hot, and I splutter, "O-Okay. See you in there."

Wendy blinks her long lashes in my direction, her reddish-brown hair piled high on her head, not a lock out of place. Must be that magical hairspray. Then she takes Monica by the arm, and they skip off to join the rest of their group, leaving me bewildered and stumbling to catch up to the Baileys.

When we're settled into our seats a few minutes later, I shoot Theo a glare. He's hunched low in his seat, his knees drawn up. "Why'd you lie, Theo? You made me look like a dummy."

"I dunno. I'm real sorry, Brant."

"You didn't have to lie, you know. I would've said it was my vest if you asked me to."

His head pops up, his eyes big and curious. "Really?"

"Yeah, really."

A silence settles between us. I pick at the buttons on my dress shirt, waiting for what Theo will say next.

He finally sighs, sitting up straighter in his seat. "Maybe you should be Mario. You're a lot braver than me," Theo tells me, glancing in my direction. "I can be Luigi."

"No." I shake my head. "You're the saver. I'm the sidekick."

"But—"

"Mario doesn't just stop being Mario because he gets scared. He keeps fighting. He keeps going and going until he defeats all the scary things," I say, my voice hushed in the quiet auditorium. "Think about it. He gets a whole lot of chances before he gets it right."

Theo bites at his lip, nodding his head as he faces forward. He's silent for a beat before he whispers, "Yeah. You're right."

A shot of happiness ripples through me.

Pride.

And that's when the lights dim to dark and the curtains open. That's when the announcer welcomes us, and the show begins. That's when the dancers walk out onto the stage, the youngest group going first—*June*.

They are mere silhouettes on the shadowy stage, but when the lights ping back on, neon and pastels, June stands in a line with five other ballerinas with one hand on her hip and the other clinging to a vibrant lollipop accessory.

I leap from my seat. I can't help it.

I whoop and holler so loud, the whole crowd of parents laugh. Theo laughs, too. Mrs. Bailey hides her face behind her palm, while Mr. Bailey tugs me back down to my chair, and I continue to wave like a lunatic to the tiny performers onstage.

June spots me, her face beaming.

She only breaks character that one time, right at the beginning, waving back at me and accidentally dropping her lollipop. But the moment the music starts, she dances like a dream, like she was always meant to dance.

She is flawless.

She is magical.

My heart flutters with joy as I watch June skip around the stage, twirling and proud, confident and strong. She takes a bow, and the crowd erupts with applause.

She is brave.

June never stopped dancing after that.

She loved it so much, she did it a hundred more times, then a hundred more. She told me once, a long time ago, that that recital might have been her very first memory—only, she doesn't remember the recital itself.

She remembers me.

She has a vivid recollection of me rising to my feet in a sea of people, shouting like a maniac, calling her name and cheering her on. She also remembers what I told her when she got scared. The thing about being brave. She said she's kept those words with her all her life, clinging to them tightly whenever she has felt afraid.

I wish I could admit to doing the same... but fear is an ugly, unpredictable beast, and the greater the fear, the more strength it takes for us to face it.

I've had a lot of fears over the years, but only one has truly torn me up, shredded me from the inside out, and nearly killed me.

The fear of losing June.

Two years later, I came face-to-face with that fear.

6

FIRST FALL

JUNE, AGE 6

THE LEAVES ARE CRISP AND crinkly beneath my rain boots as I stomp through the backyard, following behind Brant and Theo.

I can't help but startle when thunder rolls in the distance. It's Halloween night, and everything feels a lot spookier on Halloween night. The dancing tree branches, the roar of the wind, and even thunder. *Definitely thunder.*

We're still in our costumes after a long night of trick-or-treating in a nearby subdivision, since we don't have many neighbors on our quiet street. Theo is Mario, Brant is Luigi, and I'm Princess Peach. Mama took lots of pictures, and everyone told us we had the best costumes they ever saw. I collected so much candy in my bucket that Dad said he had to take some of it for himself or else the bucket would break. He took all of the Snickers bars because they were the heaviest.

Brant spins around to glance back at me, carrying a flashlight in his fist. He points it under his chin, waggling his eyebrows as shadows and yellow light dapple his face. "Where's Aggie? Don't you want him to keep you safe from the ghost stories?"

I shiver when a dank draft sweeps through. "He's still handing out candy with Mama. You and Theo will keep me safe," I say, my small legs trying to catch up.

"Did he dress up in a costume, too?"

"No. He's already an elephant."

Brant's face brightens with a smile, reminding me of a lightning bug at dusk. I stare at him for a moment, and the prickle of fear fades away. His face is handsome and brave, with eyes like the earth: a little green, a little brown. He has dents that pop up on both cheeks when he smiles wide, and Mama says they're called dimples. I love Brant's dimples. I pretend they were made just for me.

"Are you sure you wanna come, Peach?" Theo takes long strides toward the tree house, adjusting his Mario hat with one hand and carrying a big bowl of popcorn with the other. I can hardly see him through the darkness. "We're going to tell really scary stories."

Another chill rushes down my spine. "How scary?"

"You'll probably have nightmares for the rest of your life."

Ghouls, goblins, and wicked witches cackle in my mind, causing me to pick up my pace until I'm right beside Brant. "Will you protect me, Brant?"

He switches off the flashlight and stuffs it into his pocket. "You know I will. I'll always protect you."

"What if I die, and you can't save me?" I reach for his arm and cling hard, nearly stumbling through the grass. "What if *you* die?"

"Whoa, hey..." He stops suddenly, facing me, both of his hands gripping my shoulders. He's taller than me—a lot taller. He's tall and strong, and he makes me feel safe. "Why are you asking these things, Junebug?"

"Because it's Halloween, and scary stuff happens on Halloween."

"Yeah, but not *that* sort of scary stuff. You should be thinking about ghosts and jack-o'-lanterns, not—" His words clip short, and his eyes seem to fog over. Brant stares off just beyond me with shadows swirling in his faraway gaze, but before I can question where he's gone, he's back. He returns to me, and he's normal Brant again. "Don't think about those things. Promise me, June."

He must be mad. He called me June instead of Junebug, just like when Mama hollers at me and says my full name: *June Adeline Bailey*. I gulp, nodding my head. "I promise. I swear it."

"Good."

Theo calls over to us from the tree-house steps, balancing the bowl of popcorn in one hand. "C'mon, you slowpokes. We need to summon warlocks and raise zombies from the dead! Mwahahaha."

I giggle to hide the fact that I'm spooked. Brant hauls me onto his back, carrying me the rest of the way to the tree house, then climbs up behind me in case I slip on the ladder. Dad finally allowed me to climb the tree house all by myself last year, but only if Brant or Theo are with me. A light drizzle sticks to my hair as I make my way up, and I tell the boys that I'm shivering because I'm cold—even though that's not the truth. I'm scared of the ghost stories.

Brant takes off his jacket once we're huddled inside, draping it over my shoulders. "That should warm you up. Your mom said she'll bring us hot cocoa, too."

I crawl across the blankets laid out over the wooden planks, settling into Brant's lap and pulling the jacket tighter. Theo sits across from us, tossing popcorn kernels into his mouth. Lanterns are placed in every corner, illuminating the small house, while raindrops whisper atop the roof.

We talk about our night by the glow of the lanterns and Brant's flashlight, laughing about Mr. Sandman's silly horse costume, comparing candy hauls, and teasing Theo about how Monica Porter unclipped his suspenders and his pants fell down right in front of the entire neighborhood.

I'm having the best time. We aren't even telling scary stories, which makes it better.

And then Mama calls up to us from the bottom of the tree house, her hands full of hot cocoa cups. But that's not what has my insides whirling with a queasy feeling.

It's Monica Porter and Wendy Nippersink standing beside her, still dolled up in their costumes. Monica is a mermaid, and Wendy is a devil.

She really is a devil.

"Your friends are here, kids," Mama says, climbing up the ladder halfway and popping the cocoa into the tree house. "Can I send them up?"

She has a funny look on her face when she glances at Brant and Theo. She even winks.

"Yeah, okay," Brant replies. He twists in place, then removes his Luigi hat to comb his fingers through his hair before situating it back on his head.

I stay firmly rooted to his lap.

"Hi." Wendy pokes her head in first, pulling herself up all the way. "What are you guys up to?"

"Nothing. Just about to tell some ghost stories." Brant shines the flashlight under his chin again, and Wendy giggles.

Monica appears next, immediately snuggling up next to Theo, her mermaid fin twinkling turquoise in the lantern light.

"Look at you," Wendy says to me, coming up beside us. "You look adorable, June."

I finger the princess crown still attached to my hair with bobby pins, scowling as I press my back to Brant's chest. "I'm Princess Peach. Brant and Theo protect me from the bad things."

"Like spooky ghosts and monsters?" She wiggles her fingers at me, making a ghostly sound.

"No, that's silly. Monsters aren't real."

Monica chimes in. "You mean the *really* bad things? Like what happened to Brant?"

Everyone is quiet. I feel Brant's muscles go stiff, so I swivel my body to glance up at him. His expression is as white as the ghosts we just spoke of. "What's that mean, Brant?"

I'm not sure what Monica is talking about, but something in the air changes. Something in *Brant* changes. He doesn't smile or laugh. He just stays quiet, wrapping an arm around my waist, almost like he's trying to protect me from whatever bad stuff Monica is talking about.

Theo throws a piece of popcorn at Monica. "We don't talk about that."

"Why not?" She laughs, swatting at his shoulder. "You said you were telling scary stories. Maybe Brant can tell us about what happened to his parents."

"Will you tell us, Brant?" Wendy adds. She scoots closer to us on the blankets, her eyes glinting with devilish curiosity.

Brant is squeezing me too hard. I don't think he means to, so I pluck at his hand, entwining my tiny fingers with his until he relaxes and lets out a hard breath into my hair.

"Not with June here," Brant finally replies, his voice sounding shakier than normal. "Maybe someday I will."

"She's just a little kid," Monica insists. "She won't even—"

"Not with June here."

My skin itches with confusion and unease. I'm not sure what anyone is talking about, but Brant sounds angry, and I hardly ever hear him sound angry. When I turn around in his lap again, his face looks pale. He looks afraid.

That makes *me* feel afraid.

I scamper from his crisscrossed legs, landing on my knees in front of him until we're facing each other. His earthy eyes seem darker than usual, but maybe it's because it's nighttime.

Monica grabs the discarded flashlight and starts talking into it like a microphone, ignoring Brant's order. "My big brother told me the story of the haunted Elliott house," she begins, her tone low and frightening. "Once upon a time, on a dark and dreary night, little Brant was woken up by a terrible thing… Gunshots. Death. Blood. So much blood…"

I wince. My eyes flare, terror sinking into my tummy.

"Monica! You're being a biatch," Wendy exclaims.

Theo also voices his aggravation from behind me. "Quit it, Monica. Not cool."

But their words blend together into a blur of nothingness because all I can focus on is Brant, and all I hear is the thundering of my heartbeats. There's a terrible, awful look in his eyes; I think he might throw up. Even his hands start to shake as he sits there, our gazes locked, my insides curling up like the dying leaves outside. "What does that—" I start to say, but I'm cut short.

"Junebug," Brant whispers, and he's still the only thing I hear. Monica prattles on, spewing gibberish behind me, but Brant's words are what slices through the fog. "Cover your ears."

He almost chokes on those words.

His voice breaks.

And I'm too young to understand what that means, but I think…

I think it hurts.

I think Brant is in pain.

I'm frozen to the checkered blankets, not sure what to do, when Brant quickly jerks forward and plants both of his hands over my ears. There's a deep frown between his eyes, wrinkling his forehead. His skin glistens with sweat. His chest moves up and down with giant breaths.

My own hands lift, covering his, and then I close my eyes.

I can't hear anything.

I feel safe.

I feel protected and loved as Brant holds his hands over my ears, shielding me from the awful story. I'm not sure what Monica Porter was talking about, but it was scary enough to scare Brant, so it must be *really* bad—especially because Brant is one of the bravest people I know.

I'm safe. I'm safe.

And just like that, noise returns. Brant whips his hands away from my ears and stands to his feet, hurrying away. Giggles from Monica follow him out of the tree house, and I turn to watch as he disappears down the ladder.

"Brant, come on," Monica calls out to him. "We were just having some fun. You don't have to get all weird about it."

Wendy crawls over to the opening, shooting a glare toward her friend. "You wench…that was so evil. What's the matter with you?"

"Whatever."

Both girls climb out of the tree house, then Theo scurries to follow behind them. "Hey, wait for me…"

They all leave.

They all leave me up here.

Raindrops are my only friend as I look around at the shadows and lantern light. The wind howls, the tree branches scrape the roof. My mind spins with frightening things, like boogeymen and black bats. Tingles race up and down my spine, and tears wet my eyes.

I'm afraid. I'm all alone.

I want Theo.

I want Brant.

Crawling on my hands and knees, I make my way over to the tree-house door and peer down over the edge. It's so high up—I've never climbed down all by myself before.

Maybe I should call for help. Maybe I should wait for someone to fetch me. My dad says I should never use the ladder without a grown-up.

My fingers curl around the blankets, my heart thumping hard against my chest.

I think I'm going to wait up here. They'll come back.

They must.

But then the wind howls again, hissing like a snake, and I panic. I'm stolen by blind fear; all I want to do is run inside and bury myself in my Winnie the Pooh bedcovers, clutching Aggie in my arms. Pivoting around, I slide backward on my belly until my feet poke over the ledge.

I lower myself out in an attempt to climb down the ladder.

Only, a terrible thing happens.

I miss.

I miss the first step.

And then I'm falling, my scream the only thing howling louder than the wind.

7

CAST THE FIRST STONE

BRANT, AGE 12

"COVER YOUR EARS."

My father's last words echo in my mind, and I lean back against the brick siding, pressing a palm to each ear, as if I'm still trying to keep them out.

Boom!

A gun.

Blood, fear, deafening silence.

A hideous purple tie coiled around my mother's throat.

And then…

A scream.

At first, I think it's *my* scream. My mind is playing cruel tricks on me, replaying that awful night. The images are too close to the surface, trying to pull me under. I think about the tools Dr. Shelby has given me over the years to keep the maddening thoughts at bay, and I try to channel my "strong self" over my "hurt self." I squeeze my eyes shut.

Be brave, Brant. Be strong.

But then my blood swims with ice.

No, that wasn't my imagination. That was something else. That was…

June's scream…?

Horror spirals through me when reality fractures my gruesome, miserable thoughts. I had only run around to the side of the house to catch my breath, to collect some air—to get away from Monica Porter and her disgusting words—and I just needed a few minutes. I was coming back.

I was going to come right back.

My feet kick into action, and I round the corner through the backyard, running as fast as I can. Mr. and Mrs. Bailey are already racing through the sliding back door, while Theo and the girls jog from the other direction, blocking my view.

"Oh my God. June!" Mr. Bailey's voice is booming, frantic.

No, no, no.

My heart is in my throat, my lungs burning with fear. "Junebug!" I push blindly between Wendy and Monica, shoving my way past Theo, until I'm standing over June's crumpled body in the wet leaves. *No!* I'm sobbing instantly, falling to my knees beside her. "June…Junebug, wake up!"

"Don't touch her, Brant," Mr. Bailey orders, then turns to Mrs. Bailey and says in a frazzled breath, "Samantha, call an ambulance."

She makes a strangled gasp and darts back into the house.

Tears are sliding down my face faster than the rain that pelts us. I rock back and forth in the grass beside June, watching as Mr. Bailey presses two fingers to the side of her neck.

Is she breathing? Is she dead like my parents?

She can't be. I won't survive it.

"She's breathing," he says, a rush of relief spilling out of him. He looks around at us all, his dark, wet hair matted to his forehead. His cheeks are bright red, his eyes wide and filled with grief and alarm. "Everyone, stay back."

I want to reach for her. I want to cradle her in my arms and whisper in her ear that I'm sorry—I'm sorry I failed. I failed to protect her like I promised I always would.

How could I be so careless?

Sniffling, I drink in her sweet face dotted with a light spattering of freckles. Her princess crown is cracked, lying beside her in the soggy grass, and her hair is camouflaged by the golden-brown leaves. June's eyes remain closed; she lies perfectly still. Motionless.

Just like Mom and Dad.

A rage I've never felt before infiltrates me, and I jump to my feet, spinning around to face Theo. He's wide-eyed and mortified, completely silent as he links his hands behind his neck and shakes his head. Mr. Bailey continues to tend to June while sirens blare in the distance, and that's when I crack.

I let my anger loose.

Theo's misty eyes shift toward me, and both Wendy and Monica back up when they see the look on my face. I must look wild, crazed.

Swallowing back a stormy growl, I descend on Theo, shoving at his shoulders until he tumbles backward, his butt slamming against the ground. "Where were you? How could you leave her up there all alone?"

"I–I didn't…I wasn't—"

"It's *your* fault if she dies! I'll never forgive you." My teeth are bared, and I'm nearly snarling like an animal. I *feel* like an animal.

"Enough, both of you!" Mr. Bailey bellows before turning back to June. "That damn tree house is a death trap. I should have known."

We all startle, then freeze.

Theo sits up straight and buries his face in his hands. He shakes and quivers as regret pours out of him, while guilt pokes at me. I feel the anger morph into something else—something even worse.

Maybe I'm wrong. Maybe it's *my* fault.

I'll never forgive myself.

Choking back another sob, I drop to the grass beside Theo and pull him into my arms. I hug him tight, apologizing over and over. "I'm sorry, Theo. It's my fault. I left first," I chant, our tears falling together, our respective guilt breaking us in half. He hugs me back. "It's my fault."

Red and blue lights illuminate the backyard, and when I look up, Mr. Bailey is talking to a medic, while Mrs. Bailey crouches down beside her daughter, stroking her soft, sandy hair. Monica and Wendy have moved to the patio, sitting together beneath the table umbrella and hugging themselves against the deep chill that has seeped into the Baileys' backyard.

Wendy catches my stare and mouths to me with sorrowful eyes, *"I'm sorry."*

I look away.

I sit in the grass beside Theo with my broken heart and broken promise, watching and waiting for good news as June is moved onto a stretcher and carried away.

All I can do is wait.

Theo sits quietly beside me in a hospital chair. We're both slouched over in our sodden Mario and Luigi costumes, waiting for the doctors to give us permission to visit June.

Whatever a concussion is, that's what June has. She has a broken arm, too.

She must be so scared.

Silence stretches between me and my best friend, the guilt eating us both alive. I feel bad for leaving June up in that tree house, and I feel bad for blaming Theo for it. None of us should've left that tree house—we're all to blame. And I know we're both going to be in big trouble when we get home. I can see it in Mr. Bailey's eyes. He's hardly said a word to us since we got to the hospital, and the quieter he is when he's mad, the worse the punishment. His eyes are rimmed red, swollen and puffy, and his left eyebrow keeps twitching as he taps his feet in perfect time. Mrs. Bailey sits next to him, her head resting against his shoulder as she stares at the floor.

"Do you hate me, Brant?"

Theo finally ruptures the uncomfortable silence, and I jerk my attention toward him. Gnawing at my bottom lip, I shake my head. "No. I don't hate you."

"But you did," he says. "I saw it in your eyes when you pushed me down."

I slink lower into my seat, as if I can hide from what I'd done. The anger, the rage. It was a terrible thing to feel, almost like poison sailing through my veins, and I wonder if it's the same feeling my father felt when he killed my mom.

The thought steals my breath. My stomach curdles.

What if I turn out like him?

No!

I'll never get that mad again. I'll never react with violence.

I make a silent vow to myself as I fight back tears. "I hated myself, and I took it out on you. It'll never happen again, Theo."

He swallows, staring straight ahead. "You were right, you know. It *was* my fault. I was the last one to leave the tree house, and I wasn't even thinking about June." Emotion rushes to his voice, and he sniffs, swatting at his eyes. "I was thinking about Monica Porter. A dumb girl—a dumb girl who was cruel to you, and I didn't do anything to stop it. I let you down, and I let June down."

I'm not sure what to say, so I don't say anything at all.

"I'm going to be better, Brant. Promise. A better brother, a better friend." He looks my way, his deep-blue eyes glimmering with resolution in the artificial light. "I won't let you guys down ever again."

A smile pulls to the surface, and I nod. Then I hold out my hand to him. "Okay, Mario."

Theo relaxes with relief and shakes my hand. He tips his red hat with the other. "Thanks, Luigi."

The tension drains from the air, and that's when a doctor approaches the Baileys, seated across from us on stiff, ugly chairs. He says five words that cause my heart to gallop with joy. "She's going to be okay."

She's going to be okay.

They are the most wonderful words I've ever heard.

I love them so much, I store them away in my galloping heart, knowing they will never leave.

It feels like ages go by before I'm able to visit June, but when we're finally summoned to her recovery room, I snatch Aggie from the empty table beside me and make my way down the corridor.

"Brant!"

When I step into the room, my eyes widen. She's hooked up to cords and monitors, and the image makes my chest pinch tight. June is far too little to look so broken. A clunky white cast adorns her right arm, but it doesn't take away from her beaming smile. I return it instantly. "Junebug."

Racing to her bedside, I watch her baby blues glisten with a glaze of tears. She doesn't even notice her parents filing into the room, followed by Theo. I have her full attention. "I didn't mean to fall. I'm sorry."

"Don't you ever apologize, June. It was an accident." I pull Aggie out from behind my back, watching her eyes grow even wetter. When I discovered June was going to have a cast, I rushed to the bathroom and wrapped his little elephant arm in a spool of toilet paper to match. "Aggie wanted to have a cast just like you."

"Oh, wow!" she exclaims, reaching for her favorite toy with her good arm. "Thank you!"

The Baileys rush toward her, besieging her with tender hugs and kisses. Theo cries quietly into her pillow as he lies down beside her, apologizing for leaving her all alone. There are so many tears, so many whispered words, so many thankful thoughts. I watch from my perch in the corner, grateful I was made a part of this family.

Where would I be without them?

When emotions have settled, June reaches for me again, so I curl up beside her on the small bed, breathing in the scent of her lilac hair. "Thank you for bringing me Aggie," she murmurs, snuggling into me. "I was scared without him."

I smile sadly. "I know you were, Junebug. I had a stuffed elephant when I was your age, and he always made me feel better when I got scared."

"Really?"

"Yeah, really."

She ponders this, blinking up at the ceiling. "What happened to him?"

I knew the question was coming, but it's not the time to give her the gory truth. It's not the time to explain Bubbles's fate—that he was part of a massacre, stained with my father's blood and tossed away like garbage.

Maybe it'll never be the time to tell her that.

"I lost him one day," I opt for, my voice hitching slightly.

"You lost him forever? Not just for a little while?"

I swallow. "I lost him forever."

Closing my eyes, I try not think about my old childhood comfort. Instead, I drink in the comfort of June and her warm breaths and her swiftly beating heart.

"I'll find him for you someday, Brant," she says, squeezing my hand in hers. "I promise."

I realize it's a promise she can't keep, but I smile anyway.

"Can you sing me the rainbow song now?"

Mrs. Bailey pulls her chair closer, right next to June's beside, and runs her hand along my arm. "How about we both sing it?"

June nods with enthusiasm. "Yes, please. It's my favorite."

It's my favorite, too, Junebug.

It used to be my favorite because it reminded me of Mom.

Now, it reminds me of June.

While Mrs. Bailey twines her fingers with mine and sweeps a loose tendril of hair from June's forehead with her other hand, she sucks in a deep breath. My eyelids flutter closed.

We sing.

We all made promises that night.

I promised I would never react with violence again, and, well...I did a pretty damn good job of keeping that promise. I only went off course one time, years later, and I like to think I had a good reason for doing that. (Wyatt Nippersink might not agree.)

But that was it.

The fear of snapping, of doing irrevocable damage like Lucas Elliott had done to my mother in a moment of what the detectives called "blind rage," was a highly effective motivator over the years.

And then there was Theo's promise.

Theo hardly left June's side after the tree-house incident. He was overly protective, fiercely loyal, and, unlike me, unafraid to lash out at any person who put June in harm's way.

Even if that person was his best friend.

Even if that person was me.

Lastly, there was Andrew Bailey.

Andrew made his own promise that night. He swore it was the last time we would ever set foot in that godforsaken tree house.

Come sunrise, it was nothing but a pile of firewood.

8

FIRST NOEL

BRANT, AGE 12

Mom always preferred the colorful twinkle lights over the white ones.

I stare at the beautifully assembled Christmas tree, shimmering with all the colors of the rainbow, and it makes me think of her. My mom. She loved Christmas, and she loved rainbows.

June races into the front room, spinning the skirt of her holiday dress. Her light-chestnut hair is coiled into corkscrews that bob over both shoulders as she practices the moves she's been learning in ballet class. She spent a good portion of her classes in an arm cast over the last two months, only participating in the less complex routines, but that didn't seem to lessen her drive. My little ballerina is more dedicated than ever—and as of a few weeks ago, she's finally cast-free.

She even asked for shiny tap shoes for Christmas, so I spent all of my allowance money on the perfect pair. Mrs. Bailey offered to buy them for me, but it felt less special somehow. I wanted to buy them with my own money, so I worked extra hard in the yard with Mr. Bailey, raking leaves and collecting wood from the old, splintered tree house.

June is going to love her shiny shoes.

"What's a june bug look like?"

I glance over at her still dancing in circles around the coffee table. The lights from the tree reflect off the sparkles in her emerald dress, and I smile wistfully. "It looks like a rainbow butterfly with glittery fairy wings."

"Wow!"

I feel guilty for lying, but I realized too late that I'd named her after a hideous creature with long, creepy legs and a poop-colored shell. It might be the ugliest thing I've ever seen.

June plops down onto the couch beside me, nuzzling against my shoulder. "Do you think Santa will come? Have I been good this year?" Her feet kick back and forth as she stares at the illuminated tree in front of us. "He might be mad about the tree house."

"Don't be silly, Junebug. You've definitely been good this year. Brave too."

She sighs. "I'm not brave."

Before I can respond, Mr. Bailey trudges in through the front door, covered head to toe in white snow. His skin is stained from the cold, his nose so pink it's actually red. He doesn't look happy as he stomps his boots against the reindeer welcome mat. "It's really coming down out there. We've gotten four or five inches in the last hour."

Mrs. Bailey appears from the hallway, clasping a dangly earring into place. Her hair is down tonight, curled like June's. "That bad, huh?"

"Yep. I knew we should have upgraded to four-wheel drive before winter set in."

"Money's just been tight, Andrew. With the higher mortgage from the move..." She glances my way, clearing her throat. "You know how it's been."

"Yeah..." He runs a gloved hand up and down his face, then pulls off his snow-kissed hat. "I don't think it's safe to drive tonight. Maybe we should stay in."

A gasp leaves me. "But it's Christmas Eve," I proclaim. "What about dinner?"

We were supposed to have dinner at Aunt Kelly's tonight. I haven't seen her since June's sixth birthday, and she got a new cat. She told me so in a letter she wrote to me. This one is just a baby kitten, and it's much nicer than her other cat.

Theo skips down the hallway, joining us in the living room upon hearing the news. "He's right, Brant. I looked out my window and the car is already covered again, and Dad just cleaned it," he says. He pulls off his snowman sweater, revealing a plain white tee underneath, and I'm certain he's just trying to get out of wearing the new sweater his Grams made for him. "It's not safe."

"I want to see the kitten," June adds, her lip jutting out in a perfect pout.

"We can't, Peach," Theo tells her. "What if we crash and you get hurt again?"

There's a seriousness laced into his tone, causing the room to fall silent. Images of June lying crumpled in the grass slice through my mind, and I grind my teeth together. Theo's been extra protective of June since it happened—we both have.

June isn't at all charmed by his concern. She folds her arms over her chest with a frown. "What about my pretty dress? What about Mama's earrings and Theo's nice sweater from Grams?"

Theo grumbles.

"We must go!" she insists, rising from the couch and running toward her father. Mr. Bailey sighs wearily, plucking the gloves off his hands one by one. "Please, Daddy? We're all dressed up, and Aunt Kelly was going to make my favorite ham."

He shakes his head, patting her on the shoulder. "I know you were excited, June, but safety comes first. Our car won't make it in this blizzard. Maybe we can order in?"

"No. I hate that idea."

Mrs. Bailey unclips her earrings. "We could order pizza."

"Yeah!" Theo agrees.

"We can't have pizza on Christmas Eve!" June stomps her feet, acting petulant. She might even cry. "Pizza is for when Daddy watches sports all day. We need to have a feast on Christmas Eve."

An idea swims through my mind, so I clear my throat, standing to face the Baileys. "Maybe I can help." I shrug, tucking my hands into my khaki pockets. "I can cook Christmas Eve dinner."

I'm not a cooking expert, and I'm still pretty young, but I watch a lot of cooking shows. I even help Mrs. Bailey in the kitchen sometimes, jotting down notes and recipes onto index cards. Last week for breakfast, I made a hollandaise sauce for our eggs, which impressed Mrs. Bailey. She said *she* wasn't even able to make a good hollandaise sauce.

I want to learn more.

I want to cook Christmas Eve dinner so June will get her feast.

Hesitation ripples around me, even as June bounces up and down, pleased with the suggestion. Theo slides down to his knees by the Christmas tree, fingering the array of multicolored presents glinting beneath the lights. He chimes in with his own approval. "I like that idea. Brant is a really good cook."

"Well…all right," Mrs. Bailey consents. She relaxes, gifting me with a warm smile from across the living room. "I'm not sure if we have much of a selection, but I'm sure we can whip up a few things. I'll help you get organized, Brant."

Excitement whizzes through me. The last time I helped cook Christmas Eve dinner was the year before my parents' deaths. I was only five years old, so I couldn't do much, but I have a vibrant memory of standing in front of the stove on a little wooden stool, helping my mother stir a pot of mashed potatoes. I recall her being on edge that evening, worried about how the potatoes were going to turn out. They were my father's favorite. He liked them with extra butter, not too much garlic, and with no pieces of the skin left behind. I spent a long time picking out tiny peels of potato skin, and when she wasn't looking, I added an extra heap of butter, plus a sprinkling of pepper and seasoned salt.

My father loved them.

Mom was over the moon happy.

Smiling, I race around the sofa into the kitchen with eager steps, ready to scour through the pantry and refrigerator for dinner items.

If there's a chance I can save the day, I have to do it.

I want to see June as happy as my mother was that last Christmas.

Homemade lasagna, potato salad, cranberry sauce, beer bread, macaroni and cheese, and gooey cinnamon buns—that was the dinner I'd created with all of the ingredients we had on hand. I know it wasn't perfect, but it was certainly a feast, and the Baileys were stunned by my creations. Mrs. Bailey helped me swap dishes from the oven and assisted in a few various tasks, but overall, the meal was entirely made by me.

June was so happy.

I don't know if I've ever seen her so happy.

She tried a bit of everything with a huge smile on her face, then told me I was the best chef in the whole world. Truthfully, seeing her joy was the best Christmas present I could ever ask for.

Christmas Eve wasn't ruined. I'd saved the day.

Now we're all huddled around the tree in our holiday pajamas with cocoa and cookies. Our bellies are full, but not too full for the treats we're inhaling faster than the snow falling down outside. Mr. Bailey has disappeared down to the basement a few times for unknown reasons, but we're finally all together, drinking in the moment.

June is in my lap, her back pressed to my chest as she gazes at the tree with a look of wonder in her eyes. It's magic, really, and it makes my heart skip a few beats as I watch the joy flicker across her face.

Mrs. Bailey pipes up from the reclining chair, her hair now in a messy bun with a holiday-themed pen stuck in it. Her Rudolph slippers nearly rival Mr. Bailey's platypuses. "Brant, I have an early Christmas present for you…if that's okay."

Of course that's okay!

I'm instantly giddy. Nodding, I straighten, while June lets out a gasp of excitement from my lap. Her hair tickles my chin when she resituates, clapping her hands together.

"I know what it is!" she chirps, bouncing up and down. "Can I give it to him, Mama?"

"Hey, it was my idea," Theo counters.

Mrs. Bailey stands, setting down her mug of "grown-up" cocoa we're not allowed to taste. She bends over near the tree, plucking a small present from the pile, and for a moment I'm transported back in time to that last Christmas at my old house. I picture my mother in her red flannel nightdress with curlers in her hair. She looked so sad, even though she was always smiling. She reminded me of the rainbow song—a sad melody disguised with happy words.

She'd read me a story about dancing sugarplums and rosy clatters. It was a magical story with strange words, but what I remember most about that night was the way my mother grazed her fingers up and down my spine, her voice a lullaby in itself. Everything felt so perfect in that moment. Dad had locked himself away in the bedroom, so there was no fighting, no tears. It was only me and my mom, drowning in Christmas magic, reading stories by the fireplace with colorful twinkle lights glimmering off the tree.

The memory fills me with warmth.

It fills me with regret.

It fills me with a touch of madness because it's not supposed to be like this. She should be here right now, sharing a grown-up cocoa with the Baileys and singing us to sleep with our favorite song.

I'm brought back to the present when Theo snatches the gift from Mrs. Bailey's hand and rushes it over to me. He's smiling so big, I can't help but let the bitterness fall away. For as much as I hate that my mother is gone, I can't be angry for what I have now. I could never regret this family, or this home…I could never regret spending Christmas with my best friend and little Junebug.

"It was my idea, but June wrapped it," Theo explains, plopping down beside me on the area rug. "Go on, open it."

June scurries off my lap and faces me on her knees, far too eager to see what she already knows is inside.

Mr. and Mrs. Bailey have their arms around each other as they settle on the couch beside us, and I swear there are tears in Mrs. Bailey's eyes. The lights are reflecting off of them.

What could it be?

Swallowing, I peel back the candy-cane wrapping paper. It's a tiny present, just the size of my fist, but my heart starts to thump nevertheless.

And when I unfold the gift that sits inside, that same heart nearly detonates.

I discard the paper, staring down at the treasure in my hand, my chest achy. My throat tight. My fingers tremoring.

June is quick to point at the discovery, her voice high and chipper. "Look,

Brant, it's your mama! She's so pretty. And that's you when you were as small as me."

"Do you like it, Brant?" Theo wonders, his eyes wide and curious.

I glance around the room with my own wide eyes before slipping my gaze back to the gift. It's an ornament. It's an ornament shaped like a gingerbread house, with a photo inside.

My mother and me.

I've never seen this photo before. She's crouching down beside me, her hands squeezing both of my arms. I'm looking at the camera with a cheesy grin, and she's looking at me. Her smile is so happy, so proud. So alive.

She's looking at me like she never wants to let me go.

I have something smeared across my face, maybe chocolate, and my long-lost friend dangles from my grip.

Bubbles.

June announces with pride, "I couldn't find your elephant friend, but Mama found this picture in the attic, so I did my best. He's not lost anymore. He'll live in this picture with you forever."

I look up at her, silent and stunned. I'm not sure what I was expecting to find, but it wasn't this. I open my mouth to speak, to thank the Baileys for such a kind gift, but nothing comes out. My words are stuck in my throat like caramel.

So I just trail my eyes around the room again. I suck in a breath.

And then…

I cry.

I can't help it.

Emotion seizes me, and I clutch the ornament in one hand, while my other hides my face from the worried onlookers. I cry so hard, I don't even know where the tears come from. It's been so long since I've cried like this.

A loving arm wraps around my shoulders, followed by a voice. A soothing voice. A voice that reminds me of my mom, which only makes me cry harder. "Oh, Brant…I'm sorry, sweetheart. We didn't mean to make you cry…"

I know they didn't mean it. They meant to give me a precious thing, and I'm making them feel bad. Sniffling, I swipe at my eyes and lift my head, my bottom lip still quivering. "Th-thank you. I'm sorry I got sad. I just…I miss her a lot."

Theo pats my back, his own eyes looking watery. "Want to hang it on the tree?"

I nod.

Rising to my feet, I wipe away a few more stray tears and approach the artificial pine. Mr. Bailey speaks up from the couch, and when I glance at him, I think maybe he was crying, too.

"Why don't we hang it at the top?" he suggests, joining me, reaching for the ornament. "Right beneath the glowing star."

"Okay," I say, sniffling.

He holds me up high, allowing me to place the ornament on the tree, and we both take a step back. A smile replaces my sadness. It almost feels like she's looking down on me.

June tugs at my pajama shirt, so I dip my head to give her my attention. She's holding Aggie in her arms. "You can sleep with Aggie tonight," she tells me in a sweet voice. "He always helps me feel better when I'm sad or scared."

The sentiment almost makes me cry all over again. I hold in the tears, forcing a smile. "That's kind of you, Junebug, but he's your friend. I'll be okay."

"Will you tuck me in?"

Mrs. Bailey nods her approval as Theo races to the couch and hops onto his father's lap. They both laugh, and the image tickles my heart. I sigh. "Sure, I will. Let's go."

We traipse down the hallway to her bedroom. I watch as June leaps into her bedcovers, bouncing atop the mattress with a big smile. She snuggles beneath the blankets, curling up into a ball. "I'm sorry you got sad, Brant. Did something bad happen to your mama? Is that what Monica Porter was talking about in the tree house?"

I chew on the inside of my cheek as I settle down beside her. "Yeah, it is. But I don't want to talk about that right now," I say softly. "I really love the gift. It made me cry in a good way."

"A good way?"

"Yes. It was so thoughtful, and I felt a lot of love in that moment. Sometimes a lot of love can make you cry."

Her brow furrow. "I don't cry about love."

"Maybe you will someday."

"That doesn't sound so good. I don't think I want a lot of love."

"It's a good thing to have," I tell her. "The downside is, the more love you have, the harder it is to lose it."

Her little pink lips pucker as she contemplates my words. I don't think she understands, but I don't expect her to. June is still so young, immune to the hard consequences of love. The parts that hurt. Right now she's only experienced the beauty of it.

"Good night, Junebug," I whisper, leaning down to press a kiss to her forehead. "Dream of june bugs flying high over the rainbow, lemon drops, and chimney tops."

"Like the ones Santa goes down." She giggles.

"That's right."

I'm about to stand to leave when she calls to me once more. "Hey, Brant?"

"Yeah?"

"I don't think I want tap shoes anymore," she says, pulling the comforter up to her chin. "I want Santa to bring me something else."

My heart stops. "What do you mean? You were so excited about tap shoes."

"I know, but that's not what I really want."

Oh, no. What am I going to do?

I gulp hard, biting at my lip. "Okay. What is it you want, then?"

"I want a sword."

"A sword?"

"Yes, a sword for fighting. A sword to make me brave, like you."

"You don't need a sword to be brave, June. Bravery comes from here." I press my hand to her chest, right over her heart. "I don't have a sword."

Her big blue eyes twinkle in the glow of her night-light. "That's just what I want, Brant. Do you think Santa will get it for me?"

"I..." My mind races with anxiety. It's way too late to change my gift now, and I doubt she'll be getting a sword from anyone else. June will be so disappointed on Christmas morning. Heaving in a deep breath, I stretch a smile. "We'll have to see, but for now, it's time to get some sleep. Merry Christmas, Junebug."

"Merry Christmas, Brant."

She sends me a final smile, then closes her eyes and buries herself under the covers.

I step out of the room, my heart squeezing tight.

I'm not sure what to do. June seemed so excited about shiny new tap shoes, and now she's going to hate them. Now she wants a sword.

The image of my little ballerina with a mighty sword causes me to laugh out loud through my worry. What a sight that would be.

When I step out of her bedroom, I lean back against the wall and try to come up with a plan. It's after 9:00 p.m. on Christmas Eve in the middle of a blizzard. There's no way to even get to a department store right now, even if one were open. And I know *I* don't have any toy swords, and neither does Theo, and...

Wait!

A thought springs to life. My skin tingles with a possible idea.

Marching down the hallway, I half jog into the living room, calling out for Mr. Bailey. He glances up from his mug of cocoa. "Everything okay, Brant?"

"I think so. I hope so," I spit out, checking the time on the giant wall clock. "I need your help with something."

"Anything."

Anything. No questions, no hesitation.

I smile.

"I need a sword."

Christmas morning is a blur of chaos.

Wrapping paper, bows, garbage bags, toys, boxes.

Laughter, squeals, music.

Mr. and Mrs. Bailey are still in their robes, clutching mugs of coffee and munching on leftover cinnamon buns. Snow still flutters from the sky outside the window, creating the perfect backdrop for such a magical morning.

June is tearing through her final haul, her hair in complete disarray. Her curls from the night before are half undone, the toffee-toned strands dancing with static, and her feet are no longer adorned with slippers but with shiny tap shoes.

She rips open the last gift and peels the cardboard back, revealing a Barbie Dreamhouse. I don't miss the way her smile slips, just slightly. "Wow, cool," she says, digging out the toy. "Thanks, Santa."

I lean back on my palms, watching from my perch on the rug. It's been a wonderful Christmas. Theo and I got the newest Nintendo system called the Wii, along with an assortment of new games. We got clothes, posters for our bedrooms, and the Baileys even gave me cookbooks with my very own apron that says CHEF IN TRAINING.

I have everything I could ever want.

Except one thing.

June is quietly playing with a puzzle when she crawls over to the couch and hops up, sighing dramatically. Her little shoulders deflate as she blows a piece of loose hair out of her face.

"What's wrong, Junebug? Do you like your gifts?"

"Yes, I love them." She swings her legs back and forth. "I love my tap shoes the best. And the bath-time dolly."

"Then why do you look sad?"

She shrugs, glancing away. "I didn't get a sword. I guess Santa didn't think I was brave enough."

Sharing a look with the Baileys, I climb up beside her on the couch and pat her knee. "Remember what I told you last night? You don't need a sword to be brave. Bravery comes from the inside."

"I guess."

"I'm serious, June. Being brave is a choice, and choice is the greatest weapon of all. I promise, you don't need a sword."

June worries her lip, gazing up at me with a wide-eyed stare. Her eyes glimmer like the tinsel on the tree. "You mean it?"

"Of course I mean it."

"Okay, then," she nods, a smile lifting. "I'm brave. I'm the bravest girl in the whole wide land."

My grin is bright. "Say it again, Junebug. Louder."

"I'm the bravest girl in the whole wide land, and I don't need a sword!"

We all laugh when her squeaky voice cracks, and I pull her in for a tight hug. Pressing a kiss to the top of her head, I whisper gently into her ear, "Go look behind the tree."

Her eyes pop. "Why?"

"Something just appeared like magic."

She only falters for a second before she leaps from the couch cushion and darts around to the back of the tree. A little voice calls out with astonishment, "Another present!"

Theo waggles his eyebrows in my direction, and Mr. Bailey gives me a wink. June drags the long, narrow gift from the back wall to the center of the room and begins to shred the paper.

When the gift is revealed, she gasps.

A wooden sword, painted pink and silver, stands tall in her two eager hands.

"Whoa!" she squeals with delight.

Mr. Bailey and I stayed up nearly all night carving June a homemade sword from the wooden pieces of our old tree house. He loved the idea, and he loved that something that caused so much pain could be reused for something joyful. My painting job isn't so great, but June doesn't seem to notice. She's so happy, near tears, holding the sword high in the air with all her might.

"Look at that, June," I say, standing to my feet. "I guess you don't need a sword to be brave, but it sure is nice to have."

"I love it! Santa is the best!"

I chuckle, reveling in the enchantment glowing in her eyes. Someday she'll know who really made her that sword, but for now, there's nothing more special than Christmas magic.

Mr. Bailey clears his throat, slapping a palm against his wife's knee and rising from the love seat. "Well, since we're on the subject of surprises, I think Santa might have one more trick up his sleeve. I found something this morning with a tag that said 'For June, Theodore, and Brant.'"

My heart stutters, and I share a surprised look with Theo and June.

We've already received so much for Christmas… *What else could there be?*

"I'll be right back," Mr. Bailey declares, disappearing down into the basement. He returns after a few moments of curious silence, while Mrs. Bailey sips her coffee through a smile. His arms are full of a giant box wrapped in glittering Santa paper that he sets down between us on the rug. "Go on. Open it up."

We all glance at each other again.

Theo dives in first.

June and I lean over the box while paper flies and cardboard tears, desperate to get a peek of what hides inside.

When the final flaps are pulled apart, Theo jumps back.

June screams.

The Baileys laugh.

And I…

Well, I jump up from the rug, hop up and down, and shout to the heavens with my arms stretched high. "*A puppy!*"

It was a puppy, all right.

A tiny black-and-tan dachshund, hardly bigger than my hand, and something I'd been wanting since the neighbor dog licked my fingers through the fence of my old backyard.

It took six years, but I finally got the puppy I'd always dreamed of.

I'll never forget standing on my front porch beneath cotton-candy clouds, telling my mother I was going to name him Yoshi…so, that's exactly what we named him.

Yoshi was a constant companion over the years. For a little while, we pretended he was actually *Yoshi and continued to act out our heroic video game scenarios with June as the princess in peril. We didn't have the tree house anymore, but we still had fruit trees and gardens and many wild acres to explore in our backyard.*

But Theo and I were getting older.

And as the years pressed on, our imaginations faded, replaced by something far more intriguing…

Girls.

9

FIRST KISS

BRANT, AGE 15

TODAY IS JUNE'S NINTH BIRTHDAY, and Aunt Kelly is here because it's also the nine-year anniversary of my parents' deaths.

It's a celebration and a mourning all in one, and it's a combination I'll probably never get used to.

The adults are gathered on the patio, chatting beneath the freshly bloomed trees with tea, cappuccinos, and a basket of cookies and muffins I baked, while June and her schoolmates run through sprinklers in the backyard. Yoshi is hiding from the sun beneath the patio furniture, and Theo and his new girlfriend—who happens to be Monica Porter—are cozied up on the swinging bench, lazily kicking their feet as their laughter floats over to me through the screen door.

"You should go this year, Brant," Mrs. Bailey says, coming up behind me with a tray of vegetables and dips. "Kelly really wants you to."

I pull my bottom lip between my teeth. "It's June's birthday. I don't want to be sad and depressed on her birthday."

"It'll always be her birthday on this day. You have to go sooner or later, right?"

A heavy sigh leaves me, and I tug back the lace drapes. Aunt Kelly comes by every year on June first, hoping I'll finally tag along and visit my mother's grave.

It's not that I don't want to—

Well...maybe it *is* that I just don't want to.

I'd rather be here, with June, celebrating another year of her life instead of wallowing in the life I lost.

I pivot, leaning against one of the table chairs bejeweled in pink and white tissue-paper pom-poms and glittered streamers. Tasteful ballerina-themed decor is featured throughout the entire main level, and it looks like a little girl's dream party.

Mrs. Bailey sets the food tray beside me on the table, deflating with her own sigh. She eyes me in a way I've come to expect when she's about to spew out sage advice that I probably won't appreciate. "I know you're scared to go, sweetheart. I know it's hard. But I'll never forget what you told June all those years ago at her very first dance recital..." Her flaxen hair glints with specks of silver beneath the recessed lighting, reminding me that she's getting older.

I'm getting older.

I turned fifteen this past April, and I'm finishing up my last week as a high school freshman. Stubble has sprouted along my jawline. My voice has progressed from young and squeaky to almost manly. A deep baritone settled in over the past year, and while it was an embarrassing transition, it was one of multiple newfound changes.

Scratching at the stubble that always feels itchy, I lift my gaze to Mrs. Bailey, waiting for her to proceed.

She smiles. "You just need to be brave that first time, then all the other times come easy."

I guess I was the one with the sage advice; she's just using it against me.

Too bad I'm too much of a coward to take it.

I push up from the chair and shake my head. "Maybe next year," I murmur, clearing my throat and glancing out through the cracked drapes again. "Do you think they're ready for cake?"

Changing the subject to pastries sounds more appealing, so I shuffle toward the birthday cake I whipped up, smeared with raspberry frosting and chocolate drizzle.

I love cooking. I love baking.

And according to everyone who eats my food, I'm pretty darn good at it, too.

I think I've taken after my mother in that sense, and I wonder if she'd be proud of me.

My sleeveless shirt hangs off my gangly frame as I move. I shot up to nearly six feet tall, but I've hardly filled out in the muscle department yet. Theo lifts weights every day, so he's bulking up more than me, hoping to try out for the football team next year. I may join him if I can pack on some more weight.

Before I reach the refrigerator, the sliding door squeaks open, and I turn to see a soaking-wet June barreling over the threshold. She's in a swimsuit and pink tutu, her chestnut hair drenched and limp. "Is it cake time?" she chirps. She does a pirouette in the kitchen, gracefully spinning on the ceramic tile with her wet bare feet, then throws me a smile. Her hair is long now, so long that the ends tickle her hips. "I'm starving."

"Coming right up, Junebug." I grin.

"June, you're dripping everywhere," Mrs. Bailey scolds, shooing her back outside. "And you're bringing in grass blades… Out with you."

"Cake!" she shouts at me through her giggles, then disappears into the sea of squealing children. Mrs. Bailey pinches the bridge of her nose, laughing lightly, and before she can take the tray outside, the door slides open again. June pokes her head inside, looking frantic. "Brant, I need you! You have to hurry."

My eyebrows lift. "Why?"

"There's no time for questions. It's an emergency!"

Points for drama *and* suspense.

Chuckling under my breath, I sweep past Mrs. Bailey, swapping an amused grin with her, and follow June outside into the unknown "emergency."

Two minutes later, June is on my back, piggy-back style, her bathing suit soaking through my T-shirt. Long, wet hair smacks the side of my face every time I take a giant stride through the yard, while a mass of sugar-infused nine-year-olds and a tiny dachshund chase us. Her hands are like prunes from hours in the water, and her high-pitched shrieks batter my eardrums as the children gain on us.

"Faster, Brant, faster!"

"I can't go any faster. The grass is too wet."

"You must!"

I fill my cheeks with air and plow forward as June's grip tightens around my neck, nearly strangling me.

Apparently, there was no emergency. June just wanted to prove that I gave the best piggyback rides in the world, and now eleven other third-graders are on my heels, wanting to experience it for themselves.

The things I do for this kid.

"Yeah, Brant…faster!" A different voice calls out to me this time—a familiar voice. When I twist my head to the left, Wendy Nippersink is waving at me from the sidelines in a dangerously short sundress and with a deadly sparkle in her eyes.

The distraction causes me to slip, and we go down.

Crap.

I reach around my back on instinct, holding June as well as I can as I plummet face-first into the sprinkler-soaked grass. Her scream transforms into a fit of giggles when she pinwheels off me, and I just lie there trying to decide if my chin is more bruised than my pride.

It's not.

Rolling onto my back, I catch my breath as a curtain of ruby-red hair inches into my line of sight, hovering above me. Wendy asks worriedly, "Are you all right, Brant?"

Yoshi licks my face, like he's trying to bring me back to life.

Theo is next to appear, frazzled, racing straight to June. "Holy hell, Peach… you good? Did you break anything?"

"I'm good!" She's still laughing.

I'm still trying to find a way to erase the last fifteen seconds of my life.

I pull up on my elbows, glancing at June just to make sure she *is* good. She appears unscathed, so my heartbeats manage to settle with relief. A swarm of children surrounds us, followed by Monica and a few of the adults, and I clear my throat, reaching my hand out to June to help her up. "Sorry, Junebug. I guess I deserve to have my title stripped as world's best piggyback giver, huh?"

Her nose crinkles, her freckles scattering. "That was really fun! Can we do it again?"

"I wanna do it!"

"My turn!"

June's friends descend on me, but I'm saved in the nick of time when someone snatches my wrist, dragging me away from the inevitable siege. I glance back over my shoulder at June, catching the way her blue eyes dim as I retreat, despite the hazy sunshine causing the water droplets to glimmer on her skin. My heart falls a little when she slowly sulks away, but the scent of coconut perfume pulls my attention back to the girl who still has her fingers coiled around my wrist.

My skin heats when our eyes meet.

"You sure you're okay, Sonic?"

I falter, fumbling for words. "Sonic?"

"The hedgehog, dummy." Her flash of teeth softens the insult. "You're fast."

"And clumsy, apparently."

"Maybe you were just distracted," she winks, tugging me toward the swinging bench. "Come sit with me."

Wendy smooths out her mint-green sundress that seems to complement the rosy undertones of her hair, then takes a seat. I sit beside her, leaving a few inches between us. Coughing a bit, I ask, "What are you doing here?"

"Monica texted me. Said there would be cake," she tells me, studying her crimson-tipped fingernails. "I can't resist cake."

The way she looks up at me then has me feeling like *I'm* the cake.

I gulp. "Cool. I made it myself… It's raspberry-flavored."

"My favorite."

Her cinnamon-dusted eyes look lighter in direct sunlight, almost like copper coins. I feel like I need to break our stare, so I dip my gaze, landing on the cleavage poking out from the top of her dress. It's honestly not a better thing to focus on, but I can't seem to look away this time. She's filled out over the past year, growing bustier, looking more like a woman every day.

Making me feel more like a man.

Biting my lip, I force myself to glance back up at her, fidgeting when I notice the little smile creeping onto her lips. She caught me gawking at her chest like an idiot.

"Hey, do you want to meet me at the park later? After the party?" she inquires.

"The park?" Swiping my suddenly sweaty palms along my grass-stained thighs, I wonder if there's something else laced into her invitation. The only time I've been to a playground in the past few years has been to take June. "Why do you want to go there?"

She shrugs. "I guess you'll have to find out."

I'm pretty sure she's flirting with me. I gulp again.

"Cake time!" Mrs. Bailey calls out from the patio, enticing a dozen children to race over to the party table.

June drags behind her friends, looking sluggish and melancholy. Even her tutu looks sad as it hangs off her petite frame. I frown and tell Wendy I'll be right back, then shoot from the swing and jog over to June. She perks up a little when she spots me coming toward her. "Junebug. Are you having fun?"

"Sure, I guess. Are you having fun?" Her gaze slips around me to where Wendy is languidly swinging on the bench, now joined by Monica.

"I am if you are."

June's cheeks stretch into a genuine smile. She takes my hand in hers and guides me to the table where her friends are seated, eagerly awaiting birthday cake. "I'm going to make my birthday wish. Can you sit next to me?"

"Of course I can."

Aunt Kelly gives my bicep a gentle squeeze when I sweep past her. "Your mama would be proud," she says to my retreating back.

I wince slightly, then turn around to give her a small nod.

"Okay, everyone," Mr. Bailey announces, plucking a lighter from his pocket. He runs a hand through his dark, receding hairline, dotted with a line of sweat. "We want June to have a remarkable day, so we're going to sing 'Happy Birthday' as loud as we can. Ready?"

"Ready!" the guests shout.

I pull out a chair beside June, watching her face light up with magic. She has dirt stains on her skin and tangles in her hair, but I've never seen her look so radiant.

She's still holding onto my hand as the off-key singing voices ring out around us, and I give it a little squeeze, causing her smile to burst tenfold.

And when the final note is sung, she closes her eyes, gathers in a giant breath, then bends over the table to blow out the candles, my hand still tucked inside hers.

Everyone claps. She bobs up and down, doing an elegant twirl.

"Happy birthday, Junebug," I say, matching the joy I see on her face.

June smiles even wider as she leans in to me, then whispers against my ear, "I wished for your mom to come back."

My heart stalls. A rush of air leaves me.

Before I can put together a string of words, June spins away and starts chanting, 'Cake!' over and over, while Mr. Bailey passes out plates to outstretched hands.

I stay rooted to my chair as her wish rockets through me. The next twenty minutes spin by like a blur, my mind preoccupied with a different life, my heart thundering with remorse.

I'm slumped back in the chair, staring blankly, when Aunt Kelly announces her departure. She taps my shoulder. "Are you sure you don't want to come along, Brant? No pressure, of course, but…it would be a blessing if you did."

Blinking myself back to reality, I glance up at her, then rise from the folding chair. I scratch at the nape of my neck, thinking of the nicest way to get out of this. "I, uh…think I'm going to stick around for June. I'd hate to leave her party."

She smiles sadly, knowingly. "I understand. If you ever change your mind, I'm only a phone call away."

"Thanks, Aunt Kelly."

She moves in, giving me a strong hug. She always holds on to me a little longer than anyone else who hugs me, and I can't help but wonder if she's trying to soak up the remaining remnants of my mother.

Aunt Kelly says the rest of her goodbyes, and the party guests trickle out one by one, until the sun starts to set behind the clouds. Wendy sends me a coy wave as she leaves, Monica trailing behind her, texting furiously, and Theo smacks his girlfriend on the butt before he darts inside the house.

It's just me and June now. She digs her finger into what's left of the raspberry frosting on her birthday cake, then licks her lips. "This is so good, Brant. You're the best cook ever."

I still feel rattled, but I force a smile. "Only the best for you."

"You don't love Wendy more than me, right?"

"What?" Her question takes me off guard, so I turn my body until I'm fully facing her. "Why would you ask me that?"

She shrugs, her hair starting to dry beneath the setting sun. "You looked at her funny. You always look at her funny when she comes over."

"I don't..." My mind races with a proper response. "I don't love Wendy at all. I could never love anyone more than I love you."

"You mean it?" Her eyes widen to sky-like orbs, looking even bluer outside in the natural light.

"Of course I mean it."

"You went to sit with her today instead of playing with me."

A tinge of guilt ripples through me. "I'm sorry, June... I didn't mean to upset you. The older we get, the more friends we're going to have, so my time will be divided. But you have to know that you'll always be the most important thing in my life. Theo's too."

She throws her arms around my neck, burying her face against me. I hug her back as she mutters into my shirt collar, "I have the best brothers in the whole world."

I tense in her embrace, loathing that word.

Truthfully, I don't know why I loathe it. She's my adopted sibling, after all. There's a legal document to prove it. But I've never felt anything familial for the Baileys, and I don't mean that in a negative way. I have always just felt like I've grown up in a home with my very best friends and nothing more. Not for lack of love or connection—not at all. I can't really explain it. Maybe it doesn't feel that way for other adopted kids, and that's wonderful; it's a beautiful thing to feel like you're being raised by blood, but for me, it's simply felt...*different*.

June pulls back, planting a kiss to my cheekbone. "I'm going to change into my pajamas. Can you watch the new Hannah Montana movie with me?"

"Sure, I—" I cut myself off, remembering my mysterious park date with Wendy. I swallow, backtracking. "Well, not tonight. I'm sorry."

"But it's my birthday."

"I promised another friend I would see them tonight, but I should be home in time to tuck you in and sing you the rainbow song. Would that be okay?"

She scowls. "Are you going to see Wendy?"

I frown, pursing my lips together. I'm not sure why she's acting so defensive about Wendy. "Yes."

Tears rush to her eyes, causing a dagger to pierce my heart. June leaps from her chair, nearly tipping it backward, then stomps her bare feet into the house.

She doesn't say another word to me.

Even after I freshen up and traipse downstairs with Theo in an attempt to say goodbye, June just watches the television screen in silence, burrowing beneath her fuzzy blanket on the couch, ignoring me. I sigh. I realize she's only nine, so it shouldn't hurt me…

But it does.

"You made it!"

Wendy glides back and forth on a swing, her reddish hair separated into two low-hanging pigtails. Monica swings beside her as Theo and I approach from the edge of the playground. Wood chips crunch beneath our sneakers, and I ruffle my hair, clearing the tickle from my throat. "Hey."

"Lookin' good, ladies." Theo spins his baseball cap front to back. He always knows the right things to say. He's only a year older than me, but it feels like decades.

Monica hops off the swing and darts toward her boyfriend, leaping into his arms and wrapping her long legs around his middle. Her ashy-blond hair glitters beneath the lamppost. "I missed you," she squeals, leaning in to him.

They kiss.

They kiss for a long time, tongues tangling and groaning noises sounding from both of them.

I'm only standing a foot away, so it's awkward. I glance at Wendy, causing her to dip her chin as she bites at her lip, a smile hinting. Not knowing what else to do while Theo and Monica suck face, I stuff my hands into my denim pockets and saunter over to her on the swing. "So..."

She looks up, like she's waiting for more.

I've got nothing.

A giggle slips out, and she nods her head to the swing beside her. "Sit."

"Okay."

I do what I'm told, collapsing onto the swing seat and pushing myself back and forth with my feet. I look over at Wendy, and she looks at me. We laugh, then glance away.

"Have you ever kissed a girl before?"

Her question has me choking on absolutely nothing. Swallowing back a coughing fit, I heave in a deep breath and shake my head. My cheeks feel hot as mortification sets in. "No...have you?"

She smiles, mischief lighting up her eyes. "Nope. I haven't kissed a girl before."

I realize my poorly executed question and duck my head, that stupid Katy Perry song springing to mind. "You know what I mean."

"Yeah, I know," she says, making a hissing sound as she sucks her bottom lip between her teeth. "I kissed a boy once. Last summer at the carnival. He won me one of those stuffed-animal prizes, so I felt like I owed him, you know?"

"Sure, I guess."

"He's not the one I wanted to kiss, though."

My lips suddenly feel dry, so I lick them. "No?"

Wendy shakes her head back and forth, digging the toe of her sandal into the wood chips. When she looks up at me, blush stains her cheeks. "I wanted to kiss *you*, Brant Elliott."

"Me? Why?"

"Because I like you."

I suppose that's a sensible enough reason. "Is that why you asked me to come here tonight? To kiss me?"

"Maybe."

My belly flutters with unfamiliar feelings. I'm not sure what I'm supposed to do with this information.

Maybe I'm supposed to kiss her.

Monica laughs loudly when Theo picks her up, propping her over his shoulder so she's dangling upside down. "Put me down, Theo! You better, or I swear you're not getting any tonight."

Getting any.

I know that means sex.

Theo and I are close, so we've talked about sex—specifically, the fact that he's having it and I'm not. His first time was with Monica Porter earlier this year. He'd snuck out of the house through his bedroom window, just like in the movies. I guess they both had sex together for the first time in the back of Monica's parents' Land Rover, which sounded uncomfortable to me, but Theo said it was one of the greatest moments of his whole life.

He told me I should try it, too.

I swallow, returning my attention to Wendy. Her eyes darken. Summoning my courage, I ask her, "Ever had sex before?" My skin flushes as the words spew out of me, and I'm really hoping she doesn't notice.

Wendy's eyebrows lift, like she wasn't anticipating the question. "Oh, um... no. Just that one kiss."

"Yeah, same here." I backtrack, clearing my throat again. "I mean the sex part. But I'm sure that's obvious, considering I haven't kissed anybody."

I think I'm rambling. I feel kind of sweaty, too.

Wendy pops up from the swing and holds a hand out to me. "Come on."

"Where are we going?"

"Just for a little walk."

Theo and Monica are lost in their own world, so I fight back my nerves and accept Wendy's offer, clutching her hand in mine and standing from the swing. We stroll through the park, hand in hand, as a light early-summer breeze skims our faces. "So..."

"So," she repeats through a laugh. "Are you going to kiss me or what?"

"What?"

We stop walking, and Wendy swivels toward me, a timid smile still in place. "The 'what' wasn't an actual option, you know."

She bites her lip again, and I drop my gaze to the gesture. Gritting my teeth together, I inhale sharply. "Right. I know."

"Well? Are you?"

No. Maybe. Probably. Yes.

My heart thumps wildly. "I'm thinking about it." Cursing myself for being a chickenshit, I scrub a palm down my face and tell my jackknifing heart to shut up. Then I raise both hands and cup her cheeks, maybe a little too roughly. She gasps in surprise, so I loosen my grip. "Sorry…"

Wendy's tongue pokes out to moisten her lips as she glances at mine. "I'm not."

"This is okay?"

"Yes. It's more than okay. It's what I've been thinking about for years."

"Years, huh?" Gnawing at the inside of my cheek, I flick my thumbs across her jaw. "That's a long time to be thinking about kissing someone."

"I'm certain it'll be worth the wait."

We exchange a glance before I lean in, my breaths coming quickly and unsteadily. Nerves sweep through me, and I beg my body not to tremor so I seem like an inexperienced fool. I part my lips, and so does she. Dipping closer, I inhale a final breath before closing the gap between us, my mouth fusing with hers. I kiss her lightly at first, just a tickle or caress. We just kind of hover, her hands lifting to my hips and resting along my belt.

Wendy makes a little squeaky sound, something like a gasp. I take it as an invitation to kiss her deeper, flicking my tongue against her upper lip. She makes the sound again, louder this time.

And then her tongue plunges into my mouth, making me teeter and causing my skin to flush hot. It almost feels like an out-of-body experience as I cup her face between my palms, the tips of my fingers twining through her hair while we kiss.

She holds me tighter, our lower bodies pressed together. I wonder if she feels what my body is doing. I wonder if it scares her.

"Brant," she whispers in a scratchy voice, pulling away slightly. "You're a really good kisser."

My eyes flutter closed. "Am I?"

I feel her nod in my grip. "I'd like to keep kissing you. All night if you'll let me."

"Yeah, I'd like…" I'm about to concede. My body is begging me to concede.

But something stops me, and I pull back farther, opening my eyes. I told June I'd be home early enough to read her a birthday bedtime story. "Actually, I should probably go. I promised June I'd read her a book before bed since it's her birthday, and it's getting pretty late."

Wendy's forehead furrows as she slicks her tongue along her lips. "You want to stop kissing just to read your little sister a story?"

I'm not sure I like the implication woven into her tone. "Yes." Then I add, "And she's not my sister."

"Okay, then." She pulls away from me, smoothing out her hair. "Have fun."

"You sound angry."

"I'm not angry. Just disappointed, I guess."

"It's not like we can never kiss again. I just have something else I need to do tonight."

"Something more important, you mean."

I take a step back until we're at least a foot apart. "Well, yeah. It is, actually."

Wendy folds her arms over her chest, pursing her lips as she looks away. Her cheeks are tinted pink, and I'm not sure if it's because of our kiss or because she's mad that the kiss is over.

She looks upset with me, and that doesn't feel fair.

Inhaling a quivering breath, Wendy still refuses to make eye contact. "Maybe my brother was right. Wyatt said I was wasting my time pining over you. Said you weren't worth it."

"That's nice," I mutter bitterly. Just the sound of Wyatt's name has my blood boiling with painful memories. He was awful to me during the most vulnerable time of my life.

They both were.

And now all I can think about is the fact that I left June alone on her birthday to kiss a girl who used to torment me.

I keep pacing backward. "I'm going to go. Have a nice night, Wendy."

She seems flustered at my departure, softening her stance. "Brant, wait," she says. "I didn't mean it like that, you know. I'm just feeling a little rejected here."

"It wasn't a rejection," I tell her. "It was a 'to be continued.' But I'm not sure I want to continue it now."

Wendy's eyes go wide.

"See you at school on Monday." I spin around fully, marching back through the park and heading home. I pass Theo and Monica cozied up in one of the play structures making out, so I holler a goodbye before I disappear.

"You're leaving?" Theo asks, poking his head out above the slide.

"Yeah, I'll see you at home."

"Okay…see you there, Luigi."

"Later, Mario."

And then I break into a run, racing down the quiet sidewalk until I reach our secluded neighborhood of towering trees and a single gravel road. The rocks crunch beneath my soles, my lungs burning with adrenaline. I run all the way to my front door, then push inside, glancing around the front room for June.

But it's only Mr. and Mrs. Bailey snuggled up on the terracotta-toned sofa, whipping their heads in my direction as I plow into the house like a hurricane. "Brant? Everything okay?"

Instinctively, I swipe at my mouth, as if they can tell by just looking at me that I'd been locking lips with Wendy Nippersink. "I'm fine. Where's June?"

"She went to bed about fifteen minutes ago," I'm told.

My heart stutters. She went to bed without my lullabies and storybooks—without my promise that I'd be here to read to her and say goodnight. She was probably devastated.

I fly up the stairs.

"Don't wake her, Brant," Mrs. Bailey calls up to me. "She's probably already asleep."

"I won't."

I'm a liar, but I'd rather be a liar than a promise breaker.

Carefully poking my head through the crack in her door, I glance inside the shadowy room that's brightened only by her ballerina night-light. There's a lump beneath the bedcovers with a little brown head of hair peeking out. A gray elephant rests under her chin.

Ignoring Mrs. Bailey's warning, I step into the room.

"Brant?" June sits up straight, her hair a mess of static.

Thank goodness.

I race to her bedside, falling to my knees and taking her hand in mine. "Junebug…I'm sorry I was late."

She studies me in the dark, her eyes sad. "I waited up for you."

"I'm really glad you did. Do you forgive me?"

"I guess." She shrugs. June pulls Aggie closer to her chest, wrapping both arms around him. "Did my birthday wish come true?"

My insides clench. Her innocent nine-year-old wish thunders through me, wreaking more havoc than it should.

It warms me, too.

It warms me because little girls should be wishing for roller skates, or a new bike, or dolls that talk and cry. They shouldn't be wishing for things like my mother coming back.

But she wished it for *me*, and that's everything.

Sweeping my hand over her forehead, I smile softly. "That wish can't come true, June. When people die, they don't come back. It was really nice of you to ask it, though."

"What's the point of wishes, then?" She frowns.

"Well…I'm not really sure. They give a lot of people hope, I guess."

"I'd rather that they just come true."

"Yeah." I chuckle lightly. "Me too."

June looks up at the ceiling, her racing thoughts twinkling in her eyes. "Brant? If that wish won't come true, can I wish for something else?"

"Sure."

"Okay…I wish that we can be together forever."

"Forever, huh?"

She nods, picking at one of Aggie's worn ears. "Forever and ever. That one will come true, right?"

I hope so, Junebug.

And sometimes, hope is all we have.

"I bet it will," I say, kissing her on the temple and rising to my feet. I turn to leave the room, pausing in the doorway to whisper two final words into the dark. "Happy birthday."

I bet you're wondering if June's wish came true.

I'd love to tell you that, but it would spoil the ending of the story.

And to understand the end, you need to know the middle.

I'll warn you, though—it's not a pretty middle. It's messy and complicated and at times soul-crushing beyond comprehension.

I'm going to fast-forward three more years, to a snowy afternoon in December. I still think about that day, even after all this time. It still haunts me. It still keeps me up at night.

It was the day I feared June's birthday wish was lost forever…

10

FIRST SNOW

BRANT, AGE 18

"June's gone."

Theo and I both jolt from our places in front of the television, our Final Fantasy marathon forgotten. Yoshi scrambles off the bed, nails clicking against the hardwood floor while he darts from the bedroom as if he's equally daunted.

"What?" I blurt out.

I heard her the first time. Maybe I just didn't want to hear her.

Samantha Bailey pulls a blue ink pen out of her hair and begins clicking the end of it over and over, as if that might tell her where June went. "She wanted to go to the mall to meet up with her friends, but I told her no because of the snowstorm, and—"

"I'll head to the mall." I'm already pulling a wool sweater over my head and beelining toward the doorway. It's the first snow of the season and it's coming down fast and hard—but I'll drive all over this town until I find her, shitty tires be damned.

Theo is right on my heels. "Who was she meeting there?" he calls over his shoulder to his mother. "I'll see if she left her phone behind."

"She's a preteen," I remind him. "She didn't leave her phone behind."

Samantha trails behind us with panicked breaths. "Lord help me… I'll call Celeste's mother again. I already tried twice and it went to voicemail."

I pop my snow boots on one by one, nearly tipping over in the foyer. Theo tosses me my car keys, and I catch them easily as I say to him, "She could have walked down to Celeste's. It's not far. And if she's not there, we can split up. Cover more ground."

"Aye-aye, Luigi."

"I'll stay here in case she comes home. If she's not back within the hour, I'm calling the police," Samantha says worriedly as we zip up our puffy coats. She places a hand over her heart, gripping the fabric of her cardigan with glossy eyes. "Please, be careful."

Nodding, I signal at Theo and we both make our way out into the December blizzard. Big fat flurries tumble down from a pearl-gray sky almost as fast as my heart is jackhammering inside my chest. I stomp through the several inches of freshly fallen snow, and we both hop into my Corolla, hoping the squealing belt I need to replace doesn't snap and get us killed.

Where the hell are you, Junebug?

She's growing up fast.

God…she's growing up *too* fast. She'll be a teenager in six months, and we've already been getting a taste of what's to come—the hormones, the sass, the emotions.

The boys.

Jesus—the boys are going to kill me. She has a crush on a kid named Marty, and I don't even know Marty but I already want to sit Marty down and interrogate the crap out of him in regard to his intentions with June.

I realize he's twelve.

Of course, he will only have twelve-year-old intentions, like going to the junior high dance, or eating pretzel bites and ice cream cones at the mall food court. Possibly ice-skating down at the rink.

But hell, you never know, and sociopaths can be identified early these days.

What if he's a miniature Ted Bundy in the making?

What if he's a *Dexter* enthusiast?

What if he's…

What if he's just like my father?

"You're thinking about her, huh?"

I flip on my wiper blades and ruffle the snowflakes out of my hair, trying to reverse out of the unshoveled driveway. The car reeks of Wendy's Newport cigarettes. "Aren't you?" I counter, craning my neck to look out the rear window.

"Of course I am. Peach is taking the whole princess-in-peril thing to a very realistic level." He throws a slushy boot up on my dashboard, shaking his head of sandy-brown hair before slinging it back against the headrest. "She's too smart for her own good, you know."

"Yeah, I know." The tires resist when I step on the gas, tossing up sheets of white. I make three more attempts, then smack the wheel when we don't budge. "Damn it."

"Hell, I'll shovel under the—"

"No time. We're walking."

Theo falters. There's a fleeting pause, but it's not hesitation I see when our eyes connect, my hazel locked on his dark blue. It's a common thread. It's a bond we've shared since I was six years old, when we stood at the edge of my driveway and made a promise to protect a little girl.

"Let's go," he says, swiftly moving from the vehicle and throwing up the hood of his oyster-toned coat. "Save Peach, then celebrate by kicking your ass at Mario Kart for old times' sake."

Shoving the car keys into my pocket, I shuffle up beside him and adjust my hat over my ears. Theo's nose, slightly turned-up and dotted with a light spattering of freckles, is already turning pink in the upper-twenties temperature, while little plumes of smoky breath dance through the air as he walks. We trudge down the secluded street toward the more populated neighborhood where Celeste lives, nearly shoulder to shoulder.

"You know, I've been thinking," Theo muses, sifting through his pockets for the cigarettes he quit smoking two months ago. As if suddenly remembering, he tenses up, his jaw clenching. "I think it's time I finally figure my shit out. Take those first steps. Get out of my parents' house."

My own breath transforms into icy tendrils as it hits the air. "I'll help with whatever you need."

"I know you will." We share a quick glance before he ducks his head. "Shit,

I've been a mess since Monica went off to college. Wallowing, you know? I really thought she wanted to stay local and make it work, so I put my own dreams on hold. Then I was too devastated to care about my dreams…but it's time, man." Theo lifts his chin, exhaling deeply into the winter draft that rolls through, glancing up at the clouds. "I want to be a cop."

I'm instantly transported back in time, camped out beneath the wooden tree house in our backyard with Theo and June. She was transfixed by a whimsical ladybug dancing across her brother's finger as I blew raspberries onto her chubby belly, and it was the very first day I called her Junebug.

It was also the day Theo announced his dream.

"I want to be a saver."

Emotion rockets through me. A full-circle feeling. "That's incredible, Theo," I say, turning to look at him through the angry fall of snow. "I mean it. That's really incredible."

"Gotta maintain my Mario credibility, eh?" A smirk curls along his lightly stubbled jaw. "My trusty sidekick can hold down the fort here with June. For a little while, anyway."

I nod tersely, and we quicken our gait.

The truth is I don't have much going for myself either. I graduated from high school this past spring with a dead-end job at a convenience store and an on-again, off-again girlfriend I only like half of the time. Maybe I should start thinking about college.

Culinary school.

Hell, even a line-cook position at a local diner would be a start.

Something has been holding me back, though…

Fear.

Fear that something will happen to June if I'm away at college or working long hours. Fear that she'll start dating the wrong guy in a few years and I won't be around to keep an eye on her. Fear that she'll get into an accident, or meet some predator on the internet, or start doing drugs.

Fear that I won't be able to protect her.

It's a senseless fear that has me spinning my wheels and chasing my tail… but, damn it, it's real. It's pervasive. It's all-consuming.

Wendy keeps telling me to move out, to move in with her, but I'm not ready for that yet, and she doesn't understand *why*.

And I don't have an answer that holds any weight.

It's hard to explain something that feels intangible.

As we're about to cross the busy road into the suburban subdivision on the opposite side, a familiar car slows down at the mouth of our street, and we hop backward to avoid getting showered with wintery sludge.

It's Andrew Bailey.

He inches his window down, his head and elbow poking out. "Your mother called me, so I left work right away. I already checked Celeste's house and she's not there."

"Shit." I kick at the snow, my anxiety spiking. "Where could she have gone? I know she's been moodier lately, but it's not like her to run away..."

Theo moves around the hood of the car to the passenger's side, his feet sliding over the wet snow. "Wherever you're going, I'm going with. We can head to the mall. Maybe a friend's mom picked her up."

"You coming?" Andrew asks. He glances at me, the worried look in his eyes surely reflecting my own.

I consider it.

But I shake my head, knowing we'll be more productive if we split up. "I'll search on foot. She could've wandered off to the park or the sledding hill."

A nod. "You have your phone? Keep me posted."

"Yeah, I will." I give the top of the vehicle a pat, then step back while Andrew does a three-point turn and drives off toward the mall.

Cold wind whips me, shooting a chill down my spine. I tug my hat down further, rub my gloved palms together, then start walking.

McKinley Park is only a few blocks away, and June would ride her bike there frequently when the weather was milder. I'd go with her on occasion. Even when my high school friends were out partying and socializing, I'd be at the playground with June, shooting hoops, roller blading, or tossing a football back and forth.

That's always how it's been, though.

When she calls me, I'm there. If she needs me, I'm hers.

I was the one who missed the school's homecoming dance because it fell on the same night as June's dance competition.

I was the one cheering the loudest in the stands when her team scored first place in the regional division.

I was the one who took her out for ice cream to celebrate that night, then walked with her to the park where we sat on the swings and sang "Over the Rainbow" together beneath a sky of stars and moonglow.

And I'm *still* the one singing her lullabies.

I will be until she outgrows them.

My heart skips as I pick up speed, dodging mud and slush as tires whiz past me.

Where the hell are you, Junebug?

She knows better than to just take off in the middle of a blizzard.

But she's twelve, and I suppose twelve-year-olds don't always consider the consequences.

Not all adults do either.

My boots march through the accumulating snow until I veer off to the left and find the entrance of the park. When I round the corner, past the giant mound of snow that doubles as a sledding hill, past the clusters of squealing children and bundled-up parents…

I see her.

I see her. I found her. She's okay.

Junebug.

Her cheeks are windburned, her long, light chestnut hair fluttering beneath her earmuffs. She brushes snow from her blue snow pants as she watches a group of kids skip stones across the surface of the frozen pond. Her Grams had bought her those same snow pants in purple for her birthday…but June knows I hate purple.

So she begged her mother to take her to the department store to exchange them for a different color.

Just the image of her wearing them for the first time causes my heart to stutter.

I take a moment to catch my breath, bending over, hands to my knees. The relief of finding her alive and well is overwhelming and nearly cripples me.

But that relief is quickly replaced by niggling alarm when I notice who the other kids are—or rather, the fact that they're not really kids at all. She's surrounded by a bunch of seventeen and eighteen-year-olds, most of them unsavory.

One of them the worst of the worst.

Wyatt Nippersink. Wendy's treacherous twin brother.

What the hell?

I straighten, my muscles locking. Then I move in closer, until the sound of her sweet voice captures my ears.

"I should go home, now," she tells the crowd of notorious troublemakers. A few other children, various teens and preteens, float around the edge of the pond, dipping the toes of their boots onto the ice, then jumping back with laughter. June's expression looks apprehensive as she glances around. "I only wanted to make snow angels. My brothers don't like you."

Wyatt sucks on a cigarette, his ears red and irritated from the cold. "Go on, Juney. It's your turn. You can't chicken out on us."

My hackles rise. I have no idea what Wyatt is up to, but the asshole has had it out for me ever since I broke up with Wendy that first time in the middle of junior year. He's always been a bully, but he took it to a highly personal level that night, almost breaking down our door, yelling about Wendy and her broken heart.

I suppose I couldn't entirely blame him for looking out for his twin sister. June and I aren't even related and I'd do the exact same thing for her.

But this is different. This is crossing a line.

I advance on the group, a good ten yards away.

"I don't want to," June argues, stepping up to the iced-over water and peering down. "It's too slippery."

"Don't be lame. I'll go right after you, promise."

My pace quickens and I call out to her. "June!"

She snaps her chin up so fast, her earmuffs fall back on her head. Crystalline eyes that parallel the frosty pond widen when she spots me running toward her. "Bra—"

Wyatt snatches her by her puffy coat sleeve, then slings her onto the ice, laughing. She slides on her knees to the center of the pond, scrambling to stand.

My stomach drops.

"Go on, little ballerina," Wyatt taunts. He flicks his cigarette butt by his shoe, blowing ribbons of smoke out his nostrils. "Show big brother your pretty twirls."

One of his friends mimics a ballerina, tiptoeing in a dainty circle in the snow, and everyone erupts with laughter.

June can't keep her balance on the ice, her feet sliding everywhere. "You jerk!" she shouts, cheeks reddening with outrage. "Why did you do that?"

I barrel down the final hill that separates me from the group. "June, don't move! I'm coming."

"Brant to the rescue," Wyatt sneers. He spits near my boots when I slide to an erratic stop. "Just having some fun."

Ignoring him, I look around for an object to hold out to her. A large stick. Something.

I don't trust the ice—it's not stable. It hasn't been consistently cold enough yet.

June's legs splay when she tries to steady herself, her arms flailing, and then she plummets backward, her bottom slamming down hard on the icy surface.

My blood freezes.

Everyone laughs.

June looks like she wants to cry.

"June, hold still—" I start to tell her, but as a tear slips down her cheek, she tries to pull herself up anyway.

And that's when I hear it.

Crack.

We all hear it.

It's a mere fissure at first, but it's enough to cause everyone to go deadly silent. June's eyes flare. She stares at me from a few feet away, completely still, and I feel like time stops in that moment. It's the pause button on a movie reel. An eerie intermission. The wind howls with a timbre of terror, and the snowflakes sting my skin, and everything feels heavy. Or weightless. Or both.

The ice continues to split—ugly veins branching out, contaminating piece after piece.

"Brant..."

June murmurs my name from the middle of the pond, and it's the frailest whimper, a fearful plea.

It's the last thing she says before the ice collapses underneath her.

"June!"

Her scream tears through the park, then she plunges into the icy water.

I don't think.

I just move.

Wyatt rambles beside me, "I didn't know, dude, I just thought—"

I don't listen.

I. Just. Move.

I race onto the ice, hoping it holds me long enough to reach her, but it crumbles quickly, disintegrating into slush.

"Brant!" Her head pops up long enough to choke out my name again, her arms thrashing wildly, and then she disappears underwater.

I follow. I crash through the arctic surface, nearly suffocating on the cold. My bones chatter. My skin goes numb. My blood swims with ice.

But I keep moving.

It's not deep, but June is already sinking from shock. Sailing toward her, I wrap my arms around her middle and drag her up to the surface. Her skin looks discolored. Blueish...almost...

Purple.

I feel sick.

Dizziness tries to yank me back under, but I plod forward to the snowy edge, where Wyatt and his friends have already vanished, replaced by worried onlookers. Cold water and ice chunks lap at my torso, and I feel like I can't breathe. My lungs have shriveled into glaciers.

I'm shivering. Close to blacking out. Everything is fading.

June, June, June.

It's a miracle I reach land, somehow finding the strength to pull her up onto the snow. A man runs over and assists, bringing her out safely before helping me from the water.

I collapse.

I collapse beside her, shaking uncontrollably, rolling until I'm nearly blanketing her small frame. "Junebug…" I croak out. I tap her cheek, my fingers twining through her icicled hair. "Junebug, please. Please, please."

She twitches.

She splutters.

She starts coughing up water, her body convulsing, then instinctively reaches for me as she gasps for breath. June tremors with cold, her deathlike fingers curling around my wet coat.

It's all I need.

It's all I need to know before I buckle on top of her with frigid exhaustion and slip away.

11

AT FIRST BLUSH

JUNE, AGE 12

A FEVER CLAIMS ME.

I wake up on Christmas Eve, curled into my bedcovers, trembling with chills. It feels like I'm in the water again, fighting for air, desperate for warmth. Shaking, flailing, sinking…

Petrified.

A phlegmy cough rattles my lungs as I roll onto my side, pulling my knees to my chest and burrowing deeper into my quilted blanket. Sunlight pours into the room, alerting me it's daytime, but it hardly feels like I've slept.

What time is it? Is everyone opening presents without me?

My eyes feel heavy. They narrow against the daylight, too weak to absorb the happy sunshine. I try to call out for my mom but my voice is too small. Only a little squeak breaks through, and I start coughing again.

I'm cold. So cold.

The mattress shifts beside my shivering body, and I feel him looming over me before he speaks. He's warm. He's perfect.

He's my everything.

A hand reaches out, gathering my sweat-soaked hair and letting it drop against the pillow. His breath flutters into my ear, followed by my favorite word in the whole world: "Junebug."

I inhale a shuddering breath, holding back another cough. "I'm sick, Brant. I'm really sick."

"I know."

"I need medicine."

Brant's fingers interlace with mine, and he tugs me until I roll over onto my back. Two earthy orbs stare down at me. He has eyes like soil and grasslands, and they make me want to run and play in open fields.

But not today… I'm too sick.

"I want to show you something," Brant says, his dark-brown waves of hair falling over his eyes. He sweeps it back with a smile. "Are you ready?"

"I–I don't think so." My mouth feels dry, like I'm choking on a mouthful of cotton balls. I blink through my fevered fog and stare at the little dark freckle that dots the underside of his bottom lip. It stretches as his smile grows. "I might need a doctor. My teeth are all chattery."

"I know what will help. Let's go."

"Where are we going?" Curiosity pulls my heap of weakened, sweaty limbs from the comfort of my bed. Brant wraps an arm around me, hoisting me to unstable feet. "Is it far?"

"Not too far. Just over the rainbow."

I squeeze his bicep for leverage. "Huh?"

"Come on."

There's a dull pulsing in my temple, pounding in time with my heartbeat. I hold on to Brant's arm with both hands as a coughing fit has me doubling over. "I think I have the flu, Brant. Or mono."

"It's pneumonia. You'll be okay."

"Pneumonia? My gramps died from pneumonia," I tell him, panic causing my head to throb harder.

Brant keeps me upright, smelling like Ivory soap and spearmint chewing gum. Sometimes those scents mingle with fresh herbs, as he's always cooking in the kitchen. Basil, thyme, sage. Comfort smells. He glances down at me, his dimples so striking against his strong jawline. "But you won't," he says. "Now, open your eyes."

"My eyes are already…" My words trail off when a giant castle appears before me, tall and proud, made of pink bricks and lemon drops. It stands amid dancing clouds and rainbow stars. I gasp. "Where are we?"

"I told you, Junebug," Brant replies, letting me go and strolling ahead. "Over the rainbow."

"That's not real. That's just a song."

He's in a tuxedo now. It's a brilliant blue, like the robin's eggs that hatched on our front door last spring. Their nest was built on the Easter wreath Mom made from straw and twigs.

Just when the thought crosses my mind, three baby robins fly across my vision, and I swear they wave at me with their flittering wings.

This fever is making me batty.

I rub at my eyes, confusion causing my vision to blur. "Brant, wait… D-don't leave me here."

"I'd never leave you. I love you."

"How much?" I'm not sure why I ask it, but I do.

"To the moon and back." Brant pauses, his brow furrowing. "No, that's not enough. How about…over the rainbow and back again," he settles on. Then he winks. "Hurry up, Junebug. You can't be late for the wedding."

The wedding?

I'm not prepared. I have no speech, no gift, no pretty dress. I'm wearing my gym shorts from school and an old dance T-shirt stained with fever sweat.

Forcing my legs into action, I race forward on the pastel bricks, trying to catch up to Brant. He disappears through the grand foyer glimmering with golden pixie dust.

A familiar voice greets me when I step inside. "June!"

I spin to my left, finding a shock of dark red hair bouncing over two slender shoulders as she dashes toward me.

Wendy Nippersink.

This isn't a dream. This is a nightmare.

My lips pucker. "What are you doing here?"

"I brought you something," she coos, adjusting a glittering tiara on her thick head of hair, then leaning in to pinch my cheek. "A beautiful gift for a beautiful girl."

I crinkle my nose at the cheek pinch.

Wendy has always been nice to me, so sometimes I feel bad for not liking her. But she's not always nice to Brant, and that's what matters most to me.

I wish he'd break up with her for good.

She trails her hand to my brown hair, letting it flutter between her fingers. "I named him Rupert."

"Him…?"

And then there's a unicorn.

I scream.

Wendy presses a finger to my lips, hushing me. "Shh. You'll startle him. Rupert doesn't like loud noises, enclosed spaces, or double negatives."

"What is happening?"

She stares at me like *she's* the one confused, petting his prism-colored fur. "You don't like him?"

Rupert neighs.

"Where am I? How is this possible? Why is there a unicorn?"

"He's here for the wedding, of course."

Wooziness causes twinkle lights to dance behind my eyes. I press the heel of my palm to my forehead, inhaling a deep breath. When I start coughing uncontrollably, there's a gentle pat along my spine. I massage my throat, then glance behind me.

My eyes pop with disbelief.

It's Brant's mother.

She looks exactly the way she looked in the Christmas ornament photograph, with cocoa-butter hair and marmalade eyes. Pure warmth and sweetness. "I–I–I don't understand…"

"Oh, June. I couldn't be happier."

"But you're—"

"Dead?" She smirks, ducking her head. "I suppose I am. But magic can happen over the rainbow…if you dare to dream."

Brant's mom appears to float down a long corridor, so I follow, my fever creeping its way back and heating my ears and neck. She leads me into a Victorian-style room—or a room I'd expect to find back in the olden days, with jewel hues and vintage furniture, busy wallpaper and heavy drapery.

Brant's mother—*I think her name was Caroline*—taps the top of a tufted armchair with a curling iron in her grip. "Come, now, June. Let's get you all dolled up."

"I'm sorry, but I'm too sick." I begin to sway, my fever spiking. "I can't make it to the wedding."

"Oh, but you must. You're the bride."

What?

"Yeah, Peach, you can't bail on us. I spent hours writing this speech."

I whirl around, spotting Theo collapsed on a floral settee. He clears his throat, a slip of paper clutched in his fist. He's also dressed in a fancy tuxedo. "Theo?"

"'Once upon a time, my mom was going to have a baby, and I just *knew* it would be a girl,'" he reads, his opposite hand waving animatedly. "'I was going to name her Butterfly, but someone else came along and gave her a different name—*Junebug*. Not at all a glamorous bug, but the name sounded cute nonetheless. Just like my baby sister. And they both have wings, which was fitting... because this little girl was destined to fly.'"

There's a tickle on my back, so I arch my neck and discover two giant wings stuck to my shoulder blades. They flap all by themselves.

Flip, flap. Flutter, flutter.

This is madness. This can't possibly be real. I race over to Theo, shaking his shoulders as I demand, "Please, take me back home. I'm going to miss Christmas. None of this makes sense!"

He only smiles.

"Please," I repeat, my grip on him slackening. "I'm not supposed to be here, Theo."

A sigh leaves him, a hand lifting to curl around my wrist. "Of course you are, Peach. Everything in your life has brought you to this day."

"Impossible. I'm only twelve! I'm too young to get married."

"None of that matters here, little sis."

"Oh, Theo, please take me home..."

I collapse beside him on the settee, and he pulls me close. "You are home, silly. Besides, I haven't even finished reading you my speech."

"Can't you tell it to me on the day I *actually* get married? In real life?"

Theo pauses, dipping his head for a minute before meeting my gaze. His eyes twinkle with a galaxy of stars as a soft smile touches his lips. "I think I'd rather tell you now."

My head radiates with pain. My lungs feel heavy and full, desperate for reprieve. I rest my temple on his shoulder, while chills pulsate through me. "Fine," I relent.

"Excellent." He claps his hands together. "Okay, Peach, listen closely because this next part is important. Got it?"

"I got it."

"Good. Now, don't forget…" Theo inhales a big breath, then opens his mouth to speak.

Nothing comes out.

His mouth is moving, but there's no sound.

Frowning, I lift up from his shoulder. "I–I can't hear you, Theo…"

"And there you have it. You won't forget, right?"

No! This is maddening! "Say it again," I beg. "Please, Theo! I couldn't hear you."

"It's time!" Caroline announces, ushering us out the doorway as she floats over the threshold. "You look absolutely lovely, June. Just wait until he sees you."

Theo jumps up and follows. "Speech time!" he says, then prances ahead of me.

He truly frolics.

"Wait, I'm coming!" I'm suddenly wearing a leotard with an extravagant skirt made of tulle, silk, and shimmering gems. A rainbow train follows behind me as I make my way to the ballroom I'm compelled to be at and somehow know the way to.

I'm stopped at the entrance by Wendy, who looks to be crying. Mascara tracks down her cheeks as she pulls the tiara from her own head and gifts it to me. A watery smile greets me as she secures it into place, my hair magically curled and dusted with glitter. I touch it with tentative fingers. "Thanks," I murmur.

"It looks better on you, anyway." She shrugs. "Congratulations, June."

The doors open all by themselves, revealing my friends and family waiting in diamond-crusted pews. All eyes are on me as I step into the ballroom. My heart sputters with nerves, my fever heightening. I'm afraid I might pass out.

My mother dabs her tearstained cheeks with a handkerchief, smiling brightly as I walk down the colorful aisle. Dad gives me a thumbs-up, hollering over at me, "You look remarkable, honey!"

I nibble my lip, looking on both sides of me. Theo looks to be practicing his speech, Grams is knitting an ugly sweater, my school friends are blowing noisemakers, Aunt Kelly has an armful of cats, and even Yoshi is perched on a pew with a biscuit in his mouth, tail wagging.

And Brant…

Wait. Where's Brant?

I spin forward in a panic, only to be stopped short by a unicorn.

Rupert neighs. I lurch back.

And when I trail my eyes upward, I finally find Brant. He's perched atop the unicorn with two stuffed elephants in his lap. One is Aggie, and the other looks to be his old stuffed toy…*Bubbles*. I wonder where he found Bubbles. Smiling fondly, dreamily, he holds his hand out to me. "Ready, Junebug?"

"What?" I croak out.

He's still dressed in his vibrant blue tux, and there's a streamer floating from Rupert's tail that reads JUST MARRIED.

Mortification rockets through me when I realize…

Brant is my groom!

"Y-You're the one I'm marrying?" I stutter as the room starts to spin.

"Of course." He frowns with a sprinkle of confusion. "Who else would it be?"

Anyone! Anyone else!

"You're my brother," I say, disoriented. Dizzy with confusion. "Take me home, Brant! Please!"

"Calm down, Junebug. I'm not really your brother."

"You are! I can't marry you!" I plead. "Please, I'm sick. I need medicine. I need…" I start to sway again, consumed by furious fever.

My legs wobble, too weak to hold me upright any longer. Stars dance behind my eyes as everything around me blurs. Voices turn unintelligible. Colors meld into light. Noise transforms into…beeping…

Beep. Beep. Beep.

I blink.

Artificial light spills into my vision.

I draw in a sharp breath, hardly achieving a lungful when I start coughing. It's a wet, ugly cough—it hurts. *I hurt everywhere.*

A hand touches my forehead, gently pushing back my damp hair, and my eyelids flutter with familiarity. The scent of Ivory soap tickles my nose. "Brant…"

"Shh. Don't try to talk, Junebug. I'm here."

My head swivels to the right, and I see him. He's sitting beside me in a chair, while I lie on a bed made of white. Starchy sheets are pulled up to my chest, and the light in the room is harsh and blinding. I squint my eyes, trying to see Brant better. "Are you real?"

The dream spirals back to me, causing me to blush profusely. I'm hopeful the heat from my fever is disguising my humiliation.

I dreamed I was marrying Brant!

Strange images flicker through my mind—from unicorns to vintage settees to Brant's mother floating from room to room.

Madness. Delirium.

I've never had a dream so realistic before. So…*bizarre.*

"I'm real. That fever really took a toll on you," he says softly.

There's worry gleaming in his earthy eyes, spun with green and brown. Moss and clay. His hair is a mess of darkish waves—not quite curly, but not straight. Thick locks coil behind his ears, making him look young and boyish.

He's not a boy, though…he's eighteen. He's officially a man.

And he's my brother—sort of.

I dreamed I was marrying him!

I can't seem to meet his eyes as my embarrassment continues to climb. My cheeks heat and my ears burn. "How did I get here?" I mutter to the ceiling tiles.

The last thing I recall is dragging myself up the staircase, weak and warm, while Brant prepped Christmas Eve dinner. Mom said she'd check on me in a bit.

And then there was Rupert.

Brant takes my hand in his, squeezing lightly. "Your fever spiked really high… It was over one-oh-five. You were hallucinating. Scared us all half to death."

When I brave a glance in his direction, his face looks pained. Truly pained. I swallow back the sting in my throat.

"I thought I lost you in that pond," he continues, looking just beyond me. He's quiet for a beat. Reflective. "Tonight I thought I was losing you all over again."

Tears rush to my eyes. "I'm here, Brant," I whisper, my voice ragged and strained. "I'm here."

Well…I *think* I'm here. Truthfully, I have no idea what's real anymore. For all I know, the room could dissolve into outer space at any given moment and I'll be floating on a shooting star, dressed in a snorkeling suit and top hat.

Brant lets go of my hand, leaning over the side of his chair. His hair falls over his eyes in thick waves, so he brushes it back as he straightens. "I brought you something."

"It's not a unicorn, is it?"

He falters, then laughs. "No…it's not a unicorn. It's something else—two things, actually." Brant lifts both arms, revealing his gifts. In one hand, there is Aggie. In the other, there is the custom-built sword I received for Christmas six years ago. "Something for comfort, and something for courage."

My eyes continue to prickle with tears as my heart swells to twice its size. "Thank you. You always know how to make me feel better."

I think about my dream, and how Brant had both Aggie and Bubbles resting in his lap as he sat on top of Rupert. Our two beloved elephants had finally met.

How I wish that were true.

"That's because I love you, Junebug," he whispers. Brant bends over, pressing a light kiss to my hairline. "So much."

"How much?" I ask.

My voice cracks. My throat tickles.

He inches away, peering down at me with all the love in the world. His handsome face is all I see. His warmth is all I feel.

I gulp.

"To the moon and back," Brant says.

"That's not enough," I murmur, inhaling a frayed breath. Then I smile, with Aggie tucked beside me on the hospital cot, a hand gripping my sword while the other holds on to Brant. *All the things that make me brave.* "How about... over the rainbow and back again?"

PART II

THE SECOND TRAGEDY

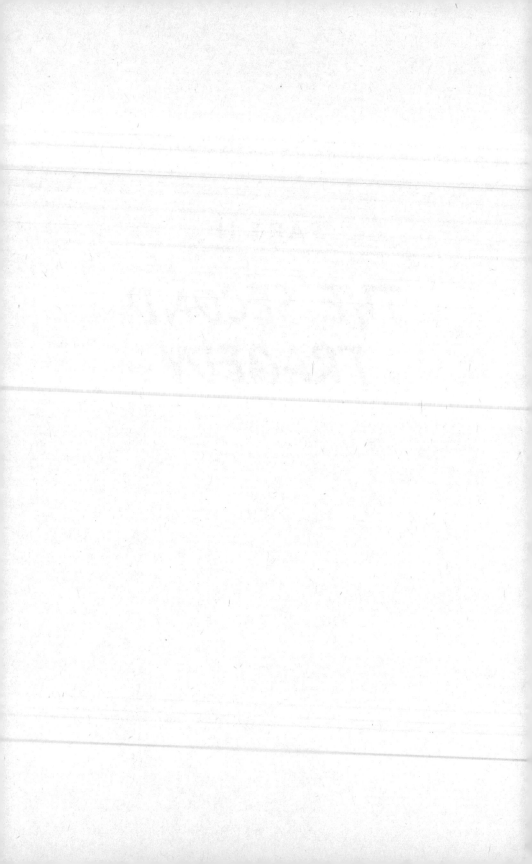

12

FIRST BASE

JUNE, AGE 14

CELESTE GASPS THROUGH A MOUTHFUL of strawberry-glazed doughnut. "Hayden is coming?"

"He said he was. Marty too."

Marty. Sigh.

A warm July breeze causes the tree branches to shimmy as I sit on the patio with my best friend, twirling a can of Dr Pepper between my fingers. My sunglasses block the glare from the afternoon sun blazing down on us, and my long hair is woven into a single braid over my shoulder. One of my favorite songs, "Dangerous" by Big Data, is playing, the perfect soundtrack to this summer Saturday as my friend and I chat about the upcoming soiree.

I stretch my legs, hoping for a semblance of golden glow. I'm pale like Mom, my porcelain skin practically allergic to sunlight.

Annoying.

Leaning back in the lawn chair I'm happily content, when I'm startled by something hitting me in the face.

"Put some clothes on, Peach. Jesus Christ." Theo tosses a beach towel at me as he strolls out through the patio door.

I scoff, lifting my sunglasses. "I'm wearing clothes. Jeez."

"Those aren't clothes. That looks like the shit you used to dress your baby dolls in, for Christ's sake."

Glancing down at my teeny denim shorts and tight halter, I purse my lips. "You're being a hypocrite. You're not even wearing a shirt."

He scratches at his bare chest—bronzed, because he was blessed with skin that does that.

So not fair.

"I'm not a fourteen-year-old girl who looks twice her age," he barks back. "Brant's got a friend over who said, and I quote, 'Little sis has got legs for days and a nice rack to boot.' No." Theo whips his hand though the air like he's trying to slice oxygen in half. "Fuck. No. I'm not having you eye-raped on my watch, absolutely not."

Celeste and I share a look before she turns away, hiding behind her half-eaten doughnut.

"You're really embarrassing, Theo," I mutter, throwing the towel onto the patio pavers. "It's not my fault if some guy wants to be a creep."

"No, but you can sure as hell give him less to creep on." He storms over to me, picks up the towel, then drapes it over my bare legs. "Until I have the authority to arrest any asshole that has the balls to put his eyes on my kid sister, cover yourself. I mean it, Peach."

I stick my tongue out at him, then lower my sunglasses, indicating the end of the discussion. Theo hovers over us for another beat, folding his arms and silently glowering like a big brute. His hair has recently been trimmed short, longer on top and buzzed around the sides, making him look more dominating than I know he is. Theo is a softie on the inside, regardless of his muscles, surly attitude, and new macho haircut.

He has more freckles than I do, but they're lighter, like a smattering of sand. Like the honeyed color of his hair. Theo looks more like our father with his sharp angles and square jaw, but his eyes are blue like Mom's—dark, dark blue, reminding me of steel.

Steel armor, steel blades, steel gallantry.

Steely overprotectiveness that often drives me mad.

The moment he marches away, I toss the towel.

"Yikes, your brother is obscenely protective."

Filling my cheeks with air, I blow out a breath, sipping on my soda. "Lucky me."

Theo is finishing up his last year at the police academy, so he thinks that gives him some kind of free pass to act like the law around me. He's already scared away two boys who made the mistake of stopping by the house to study. As much as I love him to death, I really can't wait for him to move out once he gets a position on the force. He's totally embarrassing in front of my friends.

Thankfully, Theo is going to his girlfriend's apartment tonight, which means he won't be around when I have my little get-together. We all graduated from eighth grade last month, so Mom said I could throw a summer party as long as everyone clears out by 9:00 p.m.

Celeste mock-shudders beside me. "Super lame. I'd die if I had two older brothers breathing down my neck."

"Yeah, it's rough." Setting my soda can beside me on the side table, I tinker with the fringe on my shorts. "Anyway, do you think we should set up some games for tonight?"

"Ooh. Truth or dare?"

My chin pops up, and I bite my lip as a wave of thrill rolls through me. "Definitely. And maybe…spin the bottle?"

"Oh my God. With Hayden?" She clasps her chest with her hand, throwing her head back. "Stick a fork in me. I'm done."

We both giggle.

"Have you kissed anyone yet?" Celeste asks midchew, swiping crumbs off her leggings. Her dirty-blond hair is piled high on her head, shimmering in the sunny haze. "I kissed Jordan last month at the beach bonfire. I think I told you."

I clear my throat. "You did."

The beach bonfire.

The beach bonfire I was banned from going to because Brant and Theo found out about it and told Mom and Dad there would be drugs and debauchery.

There wasn't, of course. It was held at Adam Plankton's beach house with his parents and grandmama who likes to wave her cane around, threatening to smack anyone with alcohol on their breath. Sure, maybe a few kids made out, but honestly—we're only fourteen.

I think everyone was just excited to stay out past curfew.

Chewing on my thumbnail, I shake my head. "Nope, not yet. I haven't had much of an opportunity. My brothers seem to think that I'll get pregnant in the mere presence of the opposite sex."

Celeste snickers. "Welp, maybe tonight's the night." She singsongs, "'June and Marty sittin' in a tree…'"

"Don't be immature." I smile deviously, plucking the towel from the pavement and chucking it at her.

She laughs. "Bitch!"

When our giggles ebb, I fall back onto my lounge chair, drawing up one knee. My thoughts float to Marty. Specifically, kissing Marty.

My skin hums with nerves.

I've been curious about boys for a little while now. My body has been evolving, growing, becoming more mature. My breasts began to bud shortly before my thirteenth birthday, growing fuller and more pronounced with each passing month. I went from wearing a sports bra to needing a B-cup within a twelve-month span.

The boys at school teased me at first…

And then they stopped teasing me, suddenly wanting to be my friend instead.

The patio door slides open, and Yoshi comes barreling out. He's eight years old already but still acts like a puppy, with his short, stubby legs, high-pitched yelp, and overly excited tail. Running in circles around the patio table, he pauses to lick a crack in the pavers where something must have spilled, then darts out into the backyard, disappearing around a mulberry tree to chase a squirrel.

My smile is still in place when I glance up, watching Brant saunter out onto the patio in a baseball cap, white T-shirt, and athletic shorts. "Where's your friend?" I inquire, recalling Theo's comment.

Brant closes the door behind him, then flicks his gaze back and forth between me and Celeste. He doesn't say anything at first. He just approaches us on bare feet and with an unreadable expression, bending down to scoop up the beach towel then plopping it onto my legs. "He's out front working on my car. The brake pads are shot."

I take the hint, grumbling internally and adjusting the towel so I'm more covered. "You know I'll be dating soon, right?"

"I'm only protecting you from the wrath of your brother. He's going to blow a fuse if he sees that you lost your towel again."

"Yeah, well, Theo wishes he could keep me in a glass jar on his bookshelf. He's gonna have to realize he can't protect me forever."

Brant seems to flinch at that. Something crosses his face, pinching his eyebrows together for a split second before he shakes it off. "Try telling him that."

"I have. He just says, *'Nice try, Peach. You're hilarious, Peach. A real comedian, you are, Peach.'*"

Brant's lips twitch. "Sounds about right."

Celeste perks up from her chair, taking a swig from her water bottle and twisting the cap back on. "I should get going so I can freshen up before the party," she chirps, glancing at her cell phone, typing out a quick text message, then rising to her feet. "I'll be back at six."

I stand as well, taking the towel and throwing it over Brant's head. He shrugs it off with a smile he can't help, and that makes me grin right back. Celeste gives my cheek an air-kiss, tugs at her messy bun, and strolls around the side of the house to her bicycle, calling out a final farewell.

I stretch my arms over my head, feigning a yawn. "Are you going to Wendy's tonight?"

"No. She and Wyatt have some family barbecue to go to." Brant pulls off his baseball cap, scratches at his unruly mess of brown waves, then returns the hat to his head in the opposite direction. "I'm on chaperone duty."

He says it with a mischievous gleam in his eyes, and I freeze. "You are not."

"Am too. Your dad appointed me, and I plan to take my responsibility very seriously."

"Brant, I swear to God—"

"I have a list of rules. Handwritten, very official."

"Brant…"

He clears his throat, all formal-like. "At least a six-foot distance will be maintained between June Bailey and any person of the male gender while lounging on a piece of furniture, including but not limited to sofas, love seats, and benches. Beds, of course, are strictly prohibited." He's trying to hold back his amused grin, but it's not working. "No music that references sexual acts or genitalia will be permitted. No snacks or foods with any sort of phallic representation will be—"

"Stop. Please, stop." I'm shaking my head, but a burst of laughter betrays me.

"There will be an imposed study break around 7:00 p.m. because education is important." He lifts a finger in the air. "And last but certainly not least, I insist on a mandatory retelling of an embarrassing story from June's childhood every hour on the hour, just to keep things light. I volunteer—"

I pounce on him.

Leaping onto his back, I wrap my legs around his middle, my arms encompassing his neck and squeezing. "You're not funny."

"Humor is subjective," he grits out.

He carries me through the backyard, attempting to shake himself free of me, but I maintain my grip. I don't weigh a ton, but I'm toned and fit from years of dance training. "Okay, but *nobody* thinks you're funny."

"I do."

"Argh, you're infuriating," I say, holding on tighter and pinching his arm for good measure. "Take it back."

"Ouch. If you want to play dirty, I'm prepared." He tugs at my braid.

"Hey! Low blow. You're twenty, and I'm still a kid."

Sort of. I only pull the kid card when it benefits me, and God forbid someone calls me a child when I'm trying to earn privileges or appear older than I am.

"Perfect. Kids love being tickled." Brant reaches around and starts tickling me, his fingers dancing over my ribs until I shriek, then surrender.

Damn it—every time.

He continues to tickle me, even as I slide off his back and try to escape, my giggles escalating as I writhe and squirm amid the onslaught. "Stop!" I squeal, my lungs gasping for air.

And then my lungs feel like they're *actually* gasping for air.

"Wait, wait…st-stop," I pant, trying to catch my breath.

Brant must notice the shift in mood because he instantly releases me. "Whoa, you okay, Junebug? Did I hurt you?"

"No, I..." My hand lifts to massage my chest, and I'm drenched in confusion and mild embarrassment. It feels like my lungs aren't filling with air fast enough. While I noticed a similar feeling at dance practice the prior week, I brushed it off. I'd been getting over a little cold, so I figured that was why. When my heart rate starts to decelerate, I finally inhale a satisfying lungful, my nerves subsiding. "Sorry, I just got a little winded there."

Brant props a finger under my chin, tilting my head up until we're eye to eye. There's worry etched into every crease, every shadow, every pore. His gaze tracks over my face, trying to read me, trying to put the pieces together until he's confident the threat has passed. A breath leaves him as he lowers his finger. "I don't like that."

His irises glow with affection and a trace of unease, the sunlight causing the green flecks to glint brighter than the brown. I'm lost in the sepia swirl for a moment before I duck my head, crossing my arms over my chest. "It was nothing. I'm fine." Forcing a smile, I slug him gently on the shoulder. "Nothing to worry about. You may have won this battle, but you'll never win the war."

My teasing falls on deaf ears, though; the tension is too high, the concern still heavy in his stare.

I bite my lip, trying to think of something else to say. "You know—"

"Hey. Brant."

Brant looks over my shoulder, then moves past me. "All finished?"

Swiveling around, I trail behind Brant as he makes his way to the patio, where the friend working on his car hovers in the doorway. The guy is a grease bucket, with stringy black hair, oil on his skin, and a lecherous look in his ruddy eyes when he notices me approaching.

I fiddle with the hem of my halter top, only to realize the gesture pulls the man's attention to my exposed midriff.

I'm not sure if it's intentional or subconscious, but Brant moves in front of me as if to block the guy's view. "What do I owe you?"

Skeevy dude coughs into his fist, then swipes his dirty hands along his jeans. "Two-fifty."

"Great. I'll meet you out front with cash."

I hang back, playing with the split ends of my braid, half watching as the man nods and disappears into the house. "He seems like—"

"He's not my friend," Brant declares, his back still facing me, his focus on the patio door. "He's just some auto mechanic I know through Phil."

"Oh..." I blink, not understanding the point. "So?"

"So," he says, finally pivoting toward me and pinning his eyes on mine. He swallows, his irises darkening like storm clouds in the desert. "I wouldn't be friends with someone who looks at you like that."

My heart flutters with a peculiar feeling as I chew on my cheek. Clearing the tickle from my throat, I murmur, "Okay."

He holds my gaze for a single heartbeat, then turns around to head inside.

"Be right back!" I exclaim, setting down my red Solo cup filled with iced tea. The sky is gray and dusky, laden with clouds and disappearing daylight. Tiki torches and string lights illuminate the patio as my group of friends mingle and dance to the pop music radiating from Dad's fancy speakers. He let me borrow them so I didn't have to waste my cell phone battery.

It's halfway through the party, so I skip upstairs for a bathroom break. Brant is in the living room with Mom and Dad, binge-watching *Breaking Bad*, but I know he's only half paying attention. The other half is tuned in to the party and, more specifically, my particular involvement in said party. I'm almost positive he installed secret cameras outside and is checking the footage on his phone to make sure I'm not being drugged or date-raped or participating in beer bongs or body shots.

Or the Nae Nae dance.

He'd find that equally unacceptable.

His eyebrow arches in my direction as I whip up the staircase with a beaming smile, sending a quick wave to my parents.

All is well. I'm totally not going upstairs to obsessively brush my teeth in anticipation of a game that involves kissing.

I shut the bathroom door behind me, then check the mirror. My hair is a little frizzy from the July humidity, but my loose curls have held up pretty well. I fluff them with my fingers, then pop on some more deodorant and Victoria's Secret perfume. The indigo sundress I'm wearing complements my eyes, and the glue-on eyelashes help, too. Finishing up with a dab of shimmery lip gloss, I adjust my bra so my cleavage is more pronounced, and head back down the stairs.

Dazzling my family with another flash of white teeth, I wind through the kitchen and disappear outside.

"There you are!" Celeste announces, yanking our mutual friend, Genevieve, in my direction. Both girls wander up to me, and Celeste mutters under her breath, "Behind the big mulberry tree in five."

My mouth dries up, and I instinctively smooth out my dress, as if that will prepare me for my first kiss. "Who all is playing?"

"Everyone," Gen says. "We're going to play in two separate groups, so everyone doesn't disappear at once and send up red flags to your parents. But don't worry… Marty will be in our group." She winks at me.

I lift my wide, terrified eyes, searching for Marty. He's laughing with two other boys, Hayden and Josh, leaning back against a food table. His short brown hair is smoothed over with hair gel, causing it to gleam beneath the lantern lights. "Okay."

"You look like you might vomit, June," Celeste whispers to me. "You sure you're good?"

"Of course. I'm perfectly great."

The two girls share a glance, then shrug. "Let's head over now. The boys will join us in a few."

I gather my wits and traipse across the lawn, meeting up with a few other girlfriends along the way. Gen pulls an empty Pepsi bottle out of her hobo bag, her thick black eyebrows dancing with trouble as she collapses, crossed-legged, in the grass.

My heart pounds furiously.

I take a seat between two friends, playing with my hair while I try to ignore the butterflies swimming in my belly.

Marty appears from around the tree a few moments later, accompanied by four other boys. "Hey, ladies. Got room for us?"

He's grinning wide, devilishly.

He's grinning right at me.

I gulp, forcing a smile that probably looks unhinged. "Of course. Come on over." My voice cracks a little, confirming my derangement.

"Excellent."

The boys situate themselves, forming a circle, Marty sitting directly across from me. One of my friends sets a piece of cardboard from our firepit stash in the middle as a flat surface for the bottle to spin.

"June, you go first," Marty speaks up, his chocolate eyes starry. "It's your party."

The flirtatious smile hasn't left his face, and my cheeks burn with horrible anxiety. I wring my palms together, nodding my consent. "Sure, okay."

I'm damn near trembling as I reach for the glass bottle.

Humiliating!

Screaming at my arm to act normal, I laugh lightly while whispered chatter mingles around me. I suck in a quick breath, then flick my wrist. The bottle spins wildly on the cardboard, and I watch it twirl, over and over, slowing… slowing…

Marty reaches out, stopping it, the neck pointed directly at him.

My friend Arya giggles beside me. "That's cheating," she chides.

"Whoops." He shrugs, clearly not caring. "Look at that."

Fresh nerves sweep through me. My skin flushes hot, tingling with uncertainty and a trace of fear.

This shouldn't be scary. This shouldn't be scary.

I laugh, awkwardly this time, which I suppose is better than psychotic. My lips feel dry and chapped, so I slick them with my tongue.

Marty zones in on the fleeting gesture, then pulls himself to his feet. He holds out a hand to me. "My lady," he says with formal whimsy.

I beg my knees not to tremble as I rise to a stand. They obey, mostly, but I do nearly trip on some wood chips as I step forward. "I've, um…" I swallow hard, glancing around the circle before meeting his gaze. "I've never kissed anyone before."

"I know."

"You know?"

Marty nods. "I'm honored to be your first."

I lick my lips again, then nibble the bottom. Marty is cute and sweet—*and young*. He looks so young, just a boy, a kid…and that's because he is.

I'm not sure why the thought filters through my mind.

I'm young, too. We're the same age.

Tucking my long, heavy ribbons of hair behind my ears, my cheeks pinken even further when Marty reaches out to graze a finger along my jaw. "Ready?" he asks.

I'm grateful that he asks, that he doesn't just take. I nod.

"Okay." He smiles, biting at his own lip before leaning in.

A breath catches in my throat, and then his lips meet mine. Warm, wet lips. They just sort of hover at first, testing the waters, sampling a taste. Then he presses into me more, his breath hot against my mouth. I'm not sure what to do, but I part my lips on instinct and wait, wait for him to do more, to make another move.

He does.

Marty pushes his tongue into my mouth as his arm lifts, wrapping around my lower back, while his opposite hand cups my cheek. I hear him groan when our tongues collide. I feel something hard pressing into my lower abdomen when our bodies meld. My back arches, and he kisses me harder, swirling his tongue inside my mouth, tangling it with mine as my hands clutch the front of his shirt for steadiness.

My own tongue moves, trying to find rhythm. Trying to meet his sloppy thrusts.

And then it ends abruptly.

A hand curls around my upper arm, lurching me backward, yanking me away from Marty. My feet stumble, and I nearly collapse into the hard frame flush behind me. I crane my neck up, my eyes widening when they meet with Brant's.

Crap.

He stares down at me, his jaw clenching with quiet anger, his fingers still wrapped around my arm. "Party's over."

The shock dissipates, quickly replaced by outrage and embarrassment. I tug my arm free. "What the hell, Brant?" My lips feel bee-stung, my cheeks flaming hot. Glancing around at my friends, everyone is rising to their feet, collecting their things, refusing to make eye contact, while Marty smiles sheepishly and trudges away through the grass, leaving me alone with my brother. I cross my arms, my defenses flaring. "I can't believe you did that."

"Are you kidding? You were sucking face with some kid I've never even met before. You're just a child, June."

"I am *not* a child. I'm a teenager. I'm about to start high school!"

He swipes a hand through his untamed hair. It's shaggy, spilling over his ears and forehead. "I'm just trying to protect you. I don't even know him."

"You don't have to know him," I spit back. My temper escalates as I take a step closer. "You embarrassed me. You embarrassed me in front of all my friends, including my crush."

His eyes close briefly, as if he's reining in his own emotions. "Let's go inside."

Brant reaches for me, but I pull back sharply. "Don't touch me," I seethe. "I hate you, Brant. I truly hate you."

He flinches, his hazel eyes flaring with subtle turmoil.

Guilt coils around me instantly.

Brant looks away, massaging the nape of his neck as he whispers softly, "Don't say that." He shakes his head a little, then repeats it. "Don't say that, Junebug."

My chin drops to my chest, tears stinging my eyes—a mix of regret and low-simmering anger. But my pride is too mighty for me to apologize, so I simply say nothing at all.

I walk away.

I stalk across the lawn, up to the patio, meeting up with my friends who are lingering in the doorway. Pausing briefly, only once, I brave a glance behind me, looking across the dusky yard and landing on the mulberry tree.

Brant still stands there, right where I left him, with that same awful look on his face.

13

FIRST OFFENSE

BRANT, AGE 22

"That motherfucker is dead. Stone-cold *dead*."

Theo's hands ball at his sides as we march through the sand together, the smell of a summer bonfire mingling with marijuana and citronella.

Volatile waves radiate off the man beside me, and I know there's nothing I can do to talk him down, but I still try. "You worked hard to get your badge, Theo. Don't lose it over a scumbag like Wyatt."

Wyatt Nippersink—I *really* hate that name.

Theo scoffs at me, as expected. "I appreciate the effort, but I plan on losing my badge tonight. I'm going to shove it down his fucking throat until he chokes."

Well, shit.

I'll be honest, my own blood is boiling, but I've spent years practicing how to temper the heat to ensure that I don't burn anybody.

Theo is the opposite. He's all venom and vitriol.

And when it comes to June?

Watch. Out.

Wendy spilled the beans to me that Wyatt was going to a party on the beach at Celeste's family's property, and that she overheard June's name come up while he was talking with a friend.

Illegal substances, underage drinking, and sixteen-year-old girls—sounded like the perfect party for a cop to drop into.

Flames flicker a few yards away, and laughter floats over to us on a muggy mid-August draft.

Her laughter.

Junebug.

"Don't worry, Peach… I'll save you," Theo hollers, cupping his hands around his mouth.

June is a silhouette of peachy sundress and long brown hair tumbling over both shoulders as she jumps up from a hand-carved bench. She shoves a beer bottle behind her back to Celeste, who rises beside her in an attempt to be inconspicuous.

Even though Theo bristles to my left, emanating hot-blooded fury, June's eyes are fixed on me as we approach the fire. Her full lips part, as if wanting to explain herself, yet realizing there's nothing she can say that we don't already know.

Wyatt stands lazily, flicking cigarette ashes into the flames. The orangey undertones in his hair are more striking when reflected off the blaze of the fire, and the smirk on his face is instant and organic. I wonder if it ever goes away. I'm almost positive it's permanent. "Nice of you to join us, fellas," he croons. He then turns to June and says, loud enough for us to hear, "Why don't you be a doll and grab our guests a beer?"

"You're a dead man, Wyatt," Theo spits through his teeth, kicking up sand and grit when we reach the firepit. He wastes no time in grabbing Wyatt by the shirt collar and fisting hard, dragging him forward until they're nose to nose. "Why are you here with my goddamn sister?"

Wyatt shoves himself free with a caustic laugh, then runs a hand through his coarse mop of shoulder-length hair. "Violent threats, police brutality…" He sticks a finger in the air. "Hold up, I should write this shit down."

"You won't have a hand to write with in about two fucking seconds. Then you can lick your wounds in a jail cell tonight."

"What's the offense?" Wyatt sniffs, looking pointedly at Celeste. "Not my booze. Not my bud. Not my property."

Celeste cowers guiltily.

I hold my arm out in front of Theo to keep him from jumping the asshole, while my eyes trail back over to June. Her arms are crossed over her chest, covering the low-cut neckline of her dress. My anger bubbles, knowing she wore a skimpy dress for the son of a bitch I'm trying to prevent Theo from bludgeoning to death. I grit my teeth. "Consider this a warning, Wyatt," I bite out, returning my attention to the man still smirking, his arrogance thick and heady.

Theo pushes through my arm barrier. "What the fuck, Brant? No. Absolutely fucking not. He's not getting off that easy."

Wyatt's grin stretches as he steals a glance at June. "Not anymore, thanks to the party crashers."

I let Theo go, and he flies.

"Theo!" June finally speaks, dashing over to the brawl. "Stop, damn you!"

I grab her by the arm, pulling her back before a flying fist accidentally clips her. "Get in the car," I tell her, watching as the ambient orange flames light up her doe-eyed expression. "Now, June."

She blinks, hesitating briefly, then tugs her arm free of my hold. Her features morph from contrition to contempt as she paces backward through the sand.

One of Wyatt's friends separates the two men before I can jump in, severing the escalating altercation. Wyatt swipes a smattering of blood from his lip, laughing through his weighty breaths. "I think you broke the law, Officer," he sneers.

"And here I was, trying to break your face."

Wyatt releases an unamused chuckle, then rolls his neck, pinning his attention on me. His grin curls. "Little Juney's all grown up now, huh?" Sweeping his gaze over my shoulder to where June retreats, he taunts, pitching his voice so she hears him, "She's got some real porn-star titties on her."

My blood pressure instantly spikes, my muscles locking. I feel fury swimming through my veins, and I know Theo can sense my unraveling because he quickly throws his own arm up to block me from pouncing. I swallow. "What did you just say?"

"I said your sister has nice tits."

Everything inside me screams at me to react.

Defend June.

Keep June safe.

Protect June at all costs.

My eyes lock with Wyatt's, and he just stares at me, waiting, begging for me to make the first move. He wants me to. I'm his target, and he knows my weakness.

I step forward, endorphins rippling with the prospect of a fight.

But Theo blocks me again. "Don't, Brother… This fuckhead isn't worth it." Wyatt whistles under his breath, while Theo shoves me backward, slapping one hand on my chest, the other gripping my bicep. He knows I don't let my anger loose; he knows my history, my childhood promise. He's protecting me in the same innate way that I'm protecting June. "Get Peach out of here. I'll handle him."

My gaze flicks to Theo, my jaw tense, my throat tight. I nod slightly and move away. "She's not my sister," I mutter to Wyatt, pivoting around until I'm stalking toward June, who stands idly in the sand a few feet away.

Wyatt laughs with icy disdain, calling out, "Yeah, you *wish* she wasn't your sister."

I freeze, eyes meeting June's as the cords in my neck pulse and thrum. Her chest heaves with every swift breath, her cheeks flushed pink.

What the fuck is that supposed to mean?

Choosing to ignore the barb, I press forward, shifting my attention to my car parked at the edge of the beach. I don't look at June as I move past her, repeating, "Get in the car."

She follows, reluctantly dragging behind.

I yank open the door to my beat-up Corolla which has somehow managed to survive five brutal Midwest winters. I've been saving up for a more reliable vehicle, something with four-wheel drive. Maybe a Highlander. It's one of the reasons I haven't moved out of the Baileys' residence yet. While I scored a decent job in the kitchen at a popular restaurant outside of town last year, and I could probably afford to get my own place, I haven't quite committed yet.

Because of finances.

Yeah, that's part of it, sure. It's hard to make it in this state with the high cost of living and outrageous property taxes. I should make sure I'm 100 percent prepared to be fully independent. It's the smart move.

But when June opens the passenger's side door and plops down on the seat, using an unnecessary amount of force to pull her seat belt into place, I know that's not the only reason.

It's not even the primary reason.

A prolonged sigh leaves me, and I falter as I go to stick the key into the ignition. Silence hums around us, as dense as the humidity dampening our skin.

I look over at her. She's still breathing heavily, her cheeks now rosy red, arms crossed in a defensive stance. The scent of lilacs and lemon drops wafts around me, and *hell*...it's ridiculous how gorgeous she is.

When I was sixteen I was awkward and gangly, but she's a vision of beauty and grace, smelling like spring and citrus and looking like a radiant woman instead of the little girl with a crooked grin and golden ringlets I can recall so fondly.

I knew I would lose it when men started noticing her, but I had no idea it would be *this* difficult.

June sweeps a hand through her hair, letting it fall over to one side. The dark tresses are tinged with autumn and honey lights, bringing a gentle warmth to the blue ice glittering in her eyes when she finally snaps her head in my direction. "What did he mean by that?"

My brow furrows, not expecting the question. It trips me up for a second. "Nothing. I don't know." Feeling unsettled, I avert my eyes to the wheel and pop in the key. The car roars to life, sounding as rattled as I am. "He's a damn creep."

I feel her staring at me as I shift into reverse. June fidgets in her seat, adjusting the spaghetti strap of her dress as the tires begin to roll. "You always talk like that. I don't understand it."

"Talk like what?"

"You refer to Theo as *my* brother. Mom and Dad are *my* parents," she explains, her voice a little strained, a little breathy. "You say I'm not your sister."

My jaw twitches. "Technically, you're not."

"Why do you feel that way? Have I not made a big enough impact on your life?" she inquires. There is no anger there, no bitterness. Only a stark vulnerability. "Do you not care enough?"

I slam the brakes, stalling in the middle of the semi-vacant lot as I shift back into park. Ripping off my baseball cap, I run my fingers through my hair and lean back into the seat. "That's not it at all," I tell her. When I return my attention to June, she's watching me with wide, glossy eyes, sliding a hand up and down her arm as if she's chilled. "You know how much I care, Junebug."

"Then why—"

"You wouldn't understand. It has nothing to do with you."

I realize we've never broached the details of my past before—not really. She knows the basics, of course. She knows that my father strangled my mother to death with his work tie after he lost his temper and snapped, then shot himself in the head. She knows I was in therapy throughout most of my childhood, and she knows I don't like talking about it, especially with her.

I never wanted to be that black cloud in her rainbow sky.

June learned most of what happened that night through schoolyard gossip and internet news reports. Possibly from her parents, too. I'm not sure how much they shared with her as she got older.

But she doesn't know the psychological toll it took on me.

She doesn't know that it altered inherent parts of me.

She doesn't know that I made a wish that day, standing in my front lawn, begging the cotton-candy clouds for a baby sister.

And then I got one.

I got June in exchange for my parents, and in the mind of a small, damaged child, it felt like I had caused their deaths. My wish had come true at a terrible price.

It was all my fault.

So I refused to ever see her as my sister. I refused to see the Baileys as my true family because that would make me guilty. That would have given me the darkest, heaviest burden imaginable, and it likely would have snapped me in two.

As I got older, I came to realize that it was simply a tragedy, and there is no logic in tragedy—tragedies just happen—and how we get through them, what we do after, is our only true power over them. But that was how I chose to cope at the time, and even though I understand it now, those feelings have been hardwired into me. There's no going back.

Curling my fingers around the steering wheel, I veer the subject away from my haunted past and focus on the whole damn reason we're sitting in my junky car at 11:00 p.m. on a Friday night. "What the hell were you doing there, June? Why… *Wyatt*?" I shake my head, the disappointment in my voice so tangible, it almost feels like a third passenger listening eagerly from the back seat. "He's bad news, and you know that. He's a delinquent. A deadbeat."

Two blue eyes glance over at me, brimming with something like regret. Maybe an apology. "I don't know, I just… I thought it would be fun. Celeste's older brother was going to come, too, but he had to work, so—"

"Do you have any fucking idea how much I worry about you?"

She flinches.

Our gazes lock tight, as a virile need to defend her simmers in my bloodstream. Just imagining her getting involved with Wyatt, the lowest of the low, has my heart hammering, my hands curling into fists. She's still just a kid, despite her curves and air of maturity. She's only sixteen. A question gnaws at me, and I blurt it before I think about it. "Did you sleep with him?"

She gasps, her eyes going wide.

"Did he put his mouth on you? Touch you?"

"Brant, please…"

"I know I can't keep you from men, or sex, or getting your heart broken, but I swear to God, if Wyatt Nippersink is your first—"

"No!" she says in a burst of appalled breath, her face stained with blush. "God, Brant, please don't ask me things like that. It's humiliating."

She sinks back into her seat, swiveling away from me, her arms folding over her chest once again. I sigh, defeated, and put the car back into drive. "Yeah," I murmur, tires squealing as I turn out of the parking lot. "Sorry."

My anger drains as we make the drive home in silence, and I hate that I allowed Wyatt to get under my skin. I feel like a traitor in my own body.

How did my father feel when he made the decision to murder my mother?

What drove him to wrapping that silk purple tie around her neck?

Was it something she said? Did? Threatened?

Or had he just gone mad?

The unknowns of that night have followed me around my whole life like parasitic hitchhikers. Uninvited, unwanted, but clinging tight, determined to come along for the ride.

And I know the "whys" don't matter because "whys" would give way to excuses, and there are no excuses for what he did.

But that doesn't stop me from wondering why.

We pull into the driveway, and the engine hasn't even been killed when June pushes the door open with her sandals and hops out, leaving only the scent of her flowery shampoo behind.

It lingers. *She* lingers.

I pull the key out of the ignition, exhaling a deep breath, and just sit there, watching her disappear into the house.

The last two years have been a complicated whirlwind of change, muddled dynamics, and ever-shifting tides. Hormones are a vicious, unpredictable beast, and ever since the night I reamed June out for kissing a boy behind our mulberry tree, I caught the unfortunate brunt of them. There were days she hated me—literally *despised* me. Those were the days that twisted me up inside, like brittle rope and barbed wire. All I've ever tried to do was protect her, but it seemed like the more I pushed, the more she pulled back.

The more she slipped away from me.

Samantha told me it was common, that she herself was a menace at that age, and she had taken those destructive, confusing feelings out on the people she'd loved most.

It was natural. Normal.

That didn't make it any easier, though. Explanations and rationales didn't change the fact that the little girl who adored me with her whole heart, who lived for lullabies and piggyback rides, was quickly morphing into a moody, complex young woman with fire in her blood and venom on her tongue.

"I hate you, Brant! When will you move out, already? You're ruining my life!"

Then there were days she loved me like she used to.

She'd sneak into my bedroom and sit cross-legged on the bed, hungry for advice or comfort, eager to share details about her day at school. She'd choose to spend a Sunday afternoon with me, playing video games, going for bike rides, walking down to the beach for swimming and sunshine. She'd choose *me* instead of window-shopping with her girlfriends at the mall, or going to the movies with some boy I secretly wanted to pummel.

"Forgive me, Brant. I didn't mean it. You know I love you, right?"

Those were the days I lived for.

Those are the days I *still* live for—and luckily, they've been more frequent lately. While fifteen was the age of the devil, sixteen has already been so much sweeter, bringing about a mellower dynamic between us.

More tenderness, less toxicity.

More hugs, less hatred.

Until tonight, apparently, when I spoiled her plans of doing God-knows-what with the vile Wyatt Nippersink.

Squeezing my car keys in my fist, I finally exit the vehicle and make my way inside, grateful that the Baileys are already in bed. The house is dimmed, the lights all turned down aside from a few of those scented plug-ins, Yoshi's glowing eyes as he watches me with a wagging tail from his dog bed, and moonlight through the cracked drapes. June must've gone straight to her room, desperate to get away from me and any potential further interrogation.

I trudge up the staircase, turning left into my bedroom, not bothering to flip on the light switch. I'm exhausted, prepared to fall face-first onto my mattress and pass the hell out. Reaching behind my back, I pull my T-shirt over my head, then move toward my dresser to discard my wallet and car keys.

"I never mean to worry you, you know."

Her soft voice stops me in my tracks. I spin around and discover June sitting on the edge of my full-sized bed, her shadowy silhouette barely visible in the darkened room. "June?" I approach slowly, blinking through the hazy wall between us. "What are you doing in here?"

She doesn't respond right away, and I can't see what she's doing or what she's focused on. "I just wanted to apologize," she mutters quietly.

I take another step forward, watching as she takes shape before me, still clad in her peach sundress. "You don't need to. I understand you're sixteen, and you're going to get into trouble and rebel, and—"

"I wanted to apologize for more than tonight," she cuts in. "I wanted to apologize for every time I've made you angry, made you sad, or scared, made you question how much I love you, and how much I always have."

I stare at her, and I notice her gaze drop to my bare chest, mildly illuminated by the soft window light. She fiddles with a loose string on my comforter, averting her eyes to the floor.

"You don't have to do that either." My voice sounds so raw, so naked in this quiet room. Taking a few more paces toward the bed, I sit down beside her, the mattress squeaking beneath the added weight. I clasp my knees with my palms, then glance at her in the dark. My eyes have adjusted, and I can see the mascara streaks smudged beneath her eyes. She's been crying. "Junebug. It's okay."

She sniffs a little. "Sometimes I think about how fragile life is, you know? I go mad, wondering the last thing I said to you before you drove off to work, or before I left for school. Was it cruel? Were we arguing? What if it was something wicked and it was the last thing I ever said to you?"

I'm not sure where this is coming from. A frown furls between my eyes as I sit there, shoulder to shoulder with her, lost for words.

"What was the last thing your parents ever said to you?" she asks suddenly.

My next breath lodges in my throat. The room seems to dim darker, my skin prickling with razor-edged memories. "June, don't…"

"Please, Brant. I want to know about your past, about why you've never seen me as a sister. I feel like it's all related somehow, and I want to understand. I want to understand *you.*" June reaches out, taking my hand in hers and grazing her thumb along my knuckles. I tense a little, startled by the gesture. Unsteadied by the way my heart skips at the contact. "I miss how close we used to be, and I hate that I've caused distance. It truly kills me."

"You're growing up, Junebug," I tell her. "It's natural. Lullabies and bedtime stories don't last forever."

She smiles softly, almost sadly. "Growing up isn't the same as outgrowing. I'll never be too old for the rainbow song."

My heart continues to skip its strange, unfamiliar beats, and I swallow through my nod.

"Can I lie down with you?"

"What?" I shake my head, pulling my hand away. "You're too old for that."

Vivid recollections spill into my mind as I remember the innocent days of little June crawling into bed with me after a nightmare, or falling asleep in my arms after reading her favorite book.

But those years have slipped away, traded for social propriety and seemliness.

"How so?" she ponders, and it's almost as if her innocence was never lost. "You're still Brant, and I'm still June, right?"

I glance at her, gnawing on my cheek. "You're right."

"So what's age got to do with it?"

"It's just not appropriate anymore. I'm a man now, and you're still a girl."

"But we're still the same people."

Blowing out a breath, I look away, tenting my hands. I'm having trouble countering her logic, considering there's nothing unsavory about her proposal. Lying back on the bed, I scoot over to the far wall, making room for her. "Okay, then."

I see her smile brighten, even in the dark. June takes her place beside me, leaving a small gap between us, and we both lie on our backs, gazing up at the popcorn ceiling. We stay like that for a while, drinking in the silence, savoring the connection.

Shifting onto my side, I prop my head up with my palm, studying her profile as she rests with her eyes open, fingers interlaced over her belly. "I want to answer your question."

Her head cocks to the side, finding me through the darkness, her abundance of brown hair spilled across my pillowcase like wild waves. She doesn't reply. She just waits.

I close my eyes, fighting against the urge to pull back. To run from the hard questions and painful memories. It's been sixteen years, but it still feels fresh.

My mother's face forms in my mind, from the short sweep of her nose to the bronzy highlights in her hair. She smells of sugar and caramel crème. I see her hovering over me like an angel, tucking me into bed, sitting beside my legs as I snuggle Bubbles to my chest.

I feel her lips against my hairline. Her hand sweeping along my forehead.

I hear the sound of her voice.

"I'll always protect you," I say, my eyes still closed. "She said… 'I'll always protect you.'"

I'm drenched in a shot of resentment, knowing my mother's words were nothing but kindling in the wind. Knowing she never should have made a promise she couldn't keep.

June moves toward me on the mattress, closing the gap between us. Her breath tickles my bare skin as she whispers, "And your father?"

I don't think about him. I don't imagine the sound of his voice, or his hickory smell, or the gray flecks in his eyes. "'Cover your ears.'" My tone is jagged, my voice rusty. "That was the last thing he said to me."

"One more thing, Brant… Cover your ears."

Perspiration dots my skin, my airways tightening.

Panic inches its way inside me.

I feel lost. I feel scared. I feel abandoned.

I told June I'd always protect her, but how could I promise such a thing, knowing how easily those words can come back to haunt? To terrorize?

She curls into me then, the top of her head tucked right beneath my chin, the wetness of her tears tickling my chest. She hums the tune of "Over the Rainbow," soothing my nerves. Her hands slide around my middle, stroking up and down my shoulder blades, calming the tremors that have settled in. June comforts me until my breathing steadies and my mind clears.

She's my rainbow after the storm.

My arms wrap around her on instinct, and as we lie together, more entangled than I should allow, I can't help but wonder…

Who's protecting who?

When I awoke the next morning, June had already slipped from the covers and disappeared into her own bedroom, leaving her scent on my pillow and her tearstains on my skin. We didn't talk about that night again, but our dynamic changed once again. We grew closer.

In a lot of ways, too close.

And I'm not sure why.

I'll never know why.

But I got out of bed that Sunday, threw on a clean T-shirt, drank my morning coffee, and hopped into my car.

I drove to Wendy's apartment, and I broke up with her.

For the very last time.

14

FIRST BITE

BRANT, AGE 22

"You worried about the new boss?"

Alfie expedites orders for me, making conversation as I carefully slice my signature beef Wellington, quirking a smile at the brilliant ruby color of the meat.

Nailed it.

We're the only restaurant in a fifty-mile radius that serves beef Wellington, and that's because it's a bitch to make. It took me two solid years to perfect, but it's our top seller and the reason I was promoted to head chef last month after only three years of kitchen experience as an assistant cook. Cooks generally need five years and a degree for such an esteemed title, but our old manager, Davis, promoted me anyway.

Swiping the sheen of sweat from my forehead with a dish towel, I glance up at Alfie, then start cleaning the plate. "Not really. Can't be worse than Davis and his cringey jokes that teetered on the brink of sexual harassment."

"Yeah, well, at least Davis was fuckin' funny. Heard this guy is a real jackhole." Alfie snatches two tickets, then reads them off to me. "Another Wellington, medium rare, and a mushroom risotto."

I nod my head at Santiago, who's on the fish station, and pull him over to start the risotto since Lawson is behind. *Again.*

The restaurant I work at was recently bought out by Pauly Marino, a bigwig in the culinary industry owning multiple Michelin-star restaurants in Chicago, Vegas, Seattle, and New York City. It was renamed Bistro Marino, and buzz surrounding the new ownership has circulated throughout our North Shore suburbs, exciting many but terrifying some—mainly the staff.

Alfie reads me another ticket, then sighs. "Last time some executive prick took over a kitchen, I got the ax." He slides two fingers across his neck. "I got too many high-limit credit cards I'm hiding from the wife to get cut from the payroll, man. My side piece appreciates the finer things, you know?"

I ignore him, drizzling hollandaise sauce over asparagus, then sending over the two plates for table twenty. Washing my hands, I gear up for a new round of orders while simultaneously checking on my line cooks and various stations.

The kitchen doors slap open, pulling my attention to the blue-blood-looking man strolling in, smartly dressed in a pristine heather-gray suit, slicked-back inky hair, and a shadowing of dark stubble framing his jaw. Bronzed skin showcases his Italian descent, and while his belly is round and swollen behind the suit jacket, his eyes are razor-sharp.

Pauly Marino.

My new boss.

Smoky tobacco and bergamot overpower the aroma of sautéing garlic when he sidles up beside me, hands linked behind his back. "Name," he deadpans.

I flip the egg that I'm frying for a burger, offering him a tight smile. "Brant Elliott, chef."

His coal-like eyes narrow as he looks me up and down. Intimidation emanates from him, and I'm pretty sure I should be pissing myself like Lawson to my right, but I stay focused, sliding the perfectly fried egg onto the beef patty.

Pauly makes a sighing sound that reeks of condescendence, leaning over to inspect my handiwork. "Those your beef Wellington dishes my customers were eating?"

He poses the question in a way that makes me want to deny all responsibility, but I nod as I garnish the burger. "Yes, Chef."

"That is interesting." Lips pursing with thought, he arches an eyebrow and saunters behind me, presumably off to unnerve another victim. "That is very interesting."

Interesting sounds almost identical to "you're fired," but since Pauly doesn't actually say those words, I keep working.

I work my ass off all night, delivering what I believe to be fifty-seven damn good beef Wellington dishes while overseeing the rest of our menu offerings and trying to decipher Pauly's assortment of long drawn-out sighs that Alfie has dubbed "the sighs of death." I've always been pretty good at reading the room, but hell, I can't figure this guy out.

When the kitchen finally closes and cleaning commences, I pull off my white jacket and join the rest of my staff and coworkers in the main dining area for an impromptu meeting with Pauly before we all clock out for the evening.

"Line up," he orders, sitting in a half-circle booth and sipping an amber liquid over ice. His top three shirt buttons are undone, revealing a sprinkling of dark chest hair. Pauly skims his fingers over his jaw, eyeing us as we dutifully obey his command like toy soldiers. "I would like to formally introduce myself to all of you. My name is Pauly Marino, and I am your former boss."

My heart stutters.

Uhh…former?

"While I appreciate your dedicated service to previous owner Mark Davis, I am a very particular bastard who prefers to handpick and train each member of my team. I wish you all the best of luck in your future endeavors and hope you will come visit me and my restaurant again soon." Pauly gives us a curt nod, then flicks his wrist as if shooing us away. "Discard your aprons by the hostess desk, please. I will have your final paychecks mailed to you."

I exhale a hard breath while my coworkers begin to disperse, mumbling their profanities and disbelief. Alfie slides two fingers across his neck again, mouthing *"Told you."*

Shit. I guess this means I'm unemployed.

June is going to be crushed. She was beyond excited for my promotion and even ordered me a custom-made "head chef" T-shirt with the money she's been earning from working part-time as an assistant dance coach for the little local girls. The odds of me scoring another position like this one, with the awesome salary to boot, are slim to none.

As I rub at the nape of my neck, still processing the news, I pivot to exit the dining area. That's when I'm stopped.

"Except for you, Mr. Elliott."

I freeze, then spin back around. "Come again?"

"You will stay."

"I will?"

Pauly sips delicately on his liquor, rising from the booth with a heavy sigh. "Yes. You will." He sweeps past me, leaving me considerably slack-jawed in the cloud of his bergamot cologne, only to pause before he reaches the kitchen doors. He looks over his shoulder, his charcoal eyes scoping me from head to toe. "In my entire career, I have yet to see so many consistently flawless plates of beef Wellington served to a busy dinner crowd. You carry the skill and finesse of a seasoned executive chef, yet you hardly look old enough to have earned the title of head chef."

I swallow, staring at him in stunned silence.

A tight smile crosses his lips as he finishes. "I look forward to seeing if this was simply a lucky night for you, Mr. Elliott, or if I have stumbled upon someone with the talent and tenacity to become a culinary legend."

My hands feel like they're shaking, so I wring them together in front of me, palms sweaty. I'm tongue-tied, my mouth dryer than the rack of lamb Lawson tried to serve to table number eight. "Um, thank you, Chef. I appreciate—"

"Good night. You will return on Monday at 3:00 p.m. sharp."

He disappears into the kitchen, the doors swinging closed behind him.

And I just stand there.

I stand there until my heartbeats return to normal and his words fully register.

I stand there until a smile stretches across my face.

I stand there, confounded and giddy, gazing up at the ceiling and whispering softly, "I'll do you proud, Mom."

When I pull into the driveway the following day, after spending two grueling hours at the gym, an all-too-familiar red Ford Focus is parked in front of the house.

Great. This is exactly what I wanted to do on the first day off I've had in over a week—deal with my ex.

Wendy jumps out of her vehicle at the same time I do. It's been three weeks since I broke up with her, and needless to say she hasn't taken the news very well.

"Not today, Wendy," I mutter, refusing to spare her a glance as I stuff my keys into my back pocket. "I'm tired."

"Can we just talk about this?"

I hear her sandals stomping through the grass, the scent of her blackberry body mist floating into my personal space as she comes up behind me. Slowing my steps, I feel my shoulders sag with submission. My chin dips to my chest as I say, "It's over. There's nothing to talk about."

"We're just in a rut. You know what they say about the "seven-year itch." It makes sense, Brant. This is just a blip. We'll get through it." Wendy moves into my view, her cinnamon swirl irises shimmering with desperation. She has dark circles under her eyes, and her hair hardly looks washed, let alone combed. "I love you."

The forsaken look on her face softens me just a little. I can't pretend I'm a stone-cold monster or anything. It doesn't bring me any sort of joy to see Wendy so dejected and worn down, begging me for another chance in my front yard, looking like she hasn't slept a wink since I spontaneously showed up at her apartment and said we were done. We were together for almost eight years. I cared about her deeply. I still do.

But we're not right for each other, and even in the beginning I never felt that raw, passionate flame that burns and flickers when two people come together who *are* right for each other.

And, well…I also won't pretend I know what *that* feels like. The truth is, I've only ever been with Wendy; she was my first and only kiss, my first and only sexual partner. She was my first and only experience with romance and relationships entirely.

So, no, I don't exactly know what "right" feels like, but I'm pretty damn sure I know what "wrong" feels like.

I drag my hand down my face, forehead to chin. "Wendy, I'm sorry. I hate to see you like this, but I can't keep doing this with you."

She chews on her nail. "It's because of Wyatt, isn't it?"

"No. I don't like the guy, but he has nothing to do with us."

"So..." She licks her lips, a hopeful gesture, and reaches for my hand. "There's an...*us*?"

Pulling back, I pinch the bridge of my nose, feeling out of my element. It doesn't feel good to break someone's heart once, and doing it over and over again is damn near torture. "That's not what I meant at all. Listen—"

The screen door claps shut behind me, but before I can spin around, two hands wrap around my face, stealing my vision. "Guess who," says a sweet feminine voice.

It's a voice that has the power to turn my anxiety into tranquility in the blink of an eye. My skin hums with comfort and familiarity. With purpose.

Junebug.

Apparently, I say her name out loud, because she whips her hands away and jumps onto my back, whispering against my ear, "Good guess."

I make a huffing sound when June hops on, her arms curling around my neck, legs winding around my torso. Lilac hair and citrus skin infiltrate the blackberry smog that is Wendy.

Wendy's reddish eyebrows lift with curious regard as she skates her gaze to June. Clearing her throat, she acknowledges, "Hi, June."

"Hey, Wendy."

June gives my upper arm a pinch, and I can't hold back a laugh. I clasp her ankles, crossed in front of me, tickling up her calf until she giggles and starts kicking my abdomen with her heel. "Ow."

We're lost in our own little world when Wendy makes a pronounced coughing sound, reminding us of her presence. She tucks a loose strand of auburn hair behind her ear, and her eyes roll back to mine, flickering with something I can't quite pinpoint. She's silent for a beat, studying us. "All right, then. I suppose I'll go. Maybe we can..."

Resituating June by popping her up my back, I give Wendy a nod. "Yeah. I'll see you around." Then I spin toward the front porch, not allowing her to finish her final plea, and not bothering to watch her retreat. June's chin is propped up on my shoulder, bouncing as I pace forward. "You're getting heavy, Junebug," I mutter, trying to keep my grip on her. "I can hardly carry you."

She pinches me again. "Rude, Brant. You can't say stuff like that to a girl. It'll give her a complex." June finally slides down my back when we reach the door, and she skips up beside me, smoothing out her sky-blue dress that matches her eyes. It bewitches me for a moment, the striking color parallel, until June jabs me in the chest with her finger. "Besides, you were just at the gym. You should be more than strong enough to carry little ol' me."

I shake my head, reaching for the doorknob. "How do you know I was at the gym?"

"Because you smell like sweaty gym shoes."

"Awesome. Thanks."

"No problem. You might want to hop in the shower before you head out back to the barbecue."

Oh, yeah. The barbecue.

The Baileys always host an end-of-summer shindig on Labor Day weekend. I was so distracted by Wendy's car that I hadn't even noticed the slew of other vehicles lined up along the quiet street.

Traipsing in through the foyer, I see that the patio door across the way is cracked open, a warm breeze causing the curtains to dance. Chatter and music float in from the patio, while the smell of Andrew's renowned barbecued chicken wafts around me, causing my stomach to sing.

"Dad's on grill duty. Mom was hoping you'd make your epic potato salad, but I said you were too busy working on these guns of yours." June reaches out to squeeze my bicep, bare to her touch from my sleeveless tank. Her gaze floats up to me for a moment before she drops her hand. "You're single, now. Gotta impress the ladies, huh?"

She smiles a little, then looks away. I chuckle under my breath. "I think I'm good being single for a while. I'm in no hurry to jump back into anything."

"Really?"

"Yeah, I—"

"Yo, Luigi! Make me some potato salad." Theo pokes his head through the back door, waggling his eyebrows in my direction. "But first, come meet my lady friend. And my partner, Kip."

It's refreshing to see Theo.

He moved out a few months after getting a position at the Gurnee police department, finally able to afford his own place. He works crazy hours, so the occasional family get-together, lunch date, or "Operation Save June" are the only times I really see him.

June trails my heels as I make my way to the back of the house and step out onto the patio. It's swarming with guests, most of them friends of the Baileys, but June has two classmates hanging out on the trampoline: Celeste, and a raven-haired girl I'm not familiar with.

Theo has his legs propped up on a wicker ottoman with Yoshi in his lap, his sunglasses hiding his slate-blue eyes. There are unfamiliar faces on either side of him—on his left is a man with light-brown hair, a little darker than Theo's but cut in a similar short-cropped military style. He lifts his beer to me in greeting, his cheeks slightly concave, his jaw square.

"Hey, I'm Kip. Nice to meet you."

"Brant." I shake the hand he extends.

Theo pops his thumb to his right, where a tall, long-legged blond sits in a folding chair. Her hair is bleached, shoulder-length with crimpy curls, her skin is tanned, and her eyes shine emerald and amiable. "The good-looking one is Veronica. We got a place together last week."

"Wow, that's awesome." I shake Veronica's hand. Theo really seems to have his shit together, and I couldn't be happier for him. A new career as a dedicated police officer, new coworkers, and a new girlfriend, who already appears to be ten times more stable than Monica. Pulling my attention back to Theo, I excuse myself for a quick shower, then promise to make a batch of potato salad when I'm done. "Be back in a few. Nice to meet you guys."

They send me off with smiles, and when I turn to head back inside, I realize June has vanished, along with Celeste and the mystery friend. They must be partaking in girlie gossip inside.

After saying my hellos to Samantha and Andrew, I stroll back into the house and make my way to the upstairs bathroom to freshen up.

"You *cannot* keep this from us, June. You simply cannot. It goes against every best friend code in the rule book."

June's bedroom door is cracked open as I reach the top of the staircase, and Celeste's voice carries over to me, piquing my curiosity.

Don't eavesdrop, Brant. Keep walking. Leave it be.

I'm going to obey my noble inner voice, but then June replies. "It's so awkward to talk about…" She sighs, then giggles nervously. "Gah, fine, okay… It was…good."

I falter.

"Good? Like, how good?"

"Really good, I think."

"Yeah? Did you…you know...?"

The dark-haired girl speaks up. "We need details, June. Juicy, scandalous details."

"I don't think I…you know," June says with ominous inflection. "But he did."

"Did your mom put you on the pill?"

"Yes."

Holy shit.

No.

God, no.

My stomach pitches, my heart withering with a sickly feeling I've never felt before. I feel winded even though I'm not moving. I feel strangled even though I'm breathing fast and furious.

I feel like I'm dying even though my heartbeats threaten to detonate inside my chest.

"Did it hurt?" Celeste asks.

Go, Brant. Stop listening. Get the fuck out of here.

June squeaks out a tiny, "Not really."

"Girl, it hurt so bad my first time, I even cried. Totally embarrassing."

I hurt.

This hurts *me.*

And I don't know why.

Decay slithers through my veins, polluting my blood with rot.

Why does this hurt so much? Why the hell does this hurt?

June laughs lightly, her voice shaky as she finishes. "It was good for my first time. I'm lucky, I guess."

"I bet you can't wait to do it again, yeah?"

"Definitely."

I force my pathetic, useless feet to move. Swallowing down a mouthful of bile, I stumble toward the bathroom and shove my way inside, taking a moment to catch my breath before turning on the shower until the water is heated to scorching.

I need to burn away this feeling. Singe it off my skin, then peel away every sullied layer.

Stripping down to bare bones, I step into the tub, planting both hands against the tile wall and letting the jets pelt me until my skin turns crimson. I think of June. I think of June, so innocent and good, twisted and tangled with some dumb kid who never cared about her heart, only cared about her body—only cared about bragging rights and a new notch on his belt.

She's too young. Too sweet, too perfect.

It's too soon.

Goddammit.

I shouldn't care this much.

This was inevitable. I can't protect her from sex. I can't protect her from curious hormones or horny boys. I can't hold her back from experiencing the bad and ugly parts of life, like crying her eyes out when she wakes up next to some guy one day, only to realize that he had no intention of giving her the whole world.

And I think…

I think that's exactly why it hurts.

I never confronted June about what I heard that day.

Instead, I let it eat me up inside like battery acid, eroding my skin and gnawing at my bones. It felt like a disease. A cancer, rotting me from the inside out.

But I never let her know.

I couldn't let her see.

I never scolded her, or demanded to know his name, or asked to a see a picture just so I could envision the son of a bitch who took something so precious from the girl I cared for so spectacularly.

She never, ever knew.

And I know now the real reason it hurt so goddamn bad—the painful, deep-seated reason that changed the course of my entire life.

Yeah…I know now.

But I didn't know it then, and I'm glad I didn't.

It was for the best.

Because the moment it hit me, one year later, I wished I had never figured it out…

15

FIRST-DEGREE BURN

BRANT, AGE 23

I BURNED MYSELF TODAY.

I was rushing out a table order, picking up the slack from a fellow coworker, and I grabbed the handle of a cast-iron skillet after it'd just come out of the oven.

Amateur move.

An angry, blistered burn mark has since decorated the underside of my palm, right above the heel where a jagged scar still lingers from when I took baby June on a late-night adventure to my old house of horrors.

After wrapping my hand in a few layers of gauze, I worked hard despite the pain for the next couple of hours, hissing through my teeth the whole time, right up until my lunch break.

Pauly nearly crashes into me as I push through the kitchen doors, pulling off my chef hat. He snatches my injured hand by the wrist, holding it up for inspection. "What do we have here, Mr. Elliott? Workers' compensation?"

I wince, the pain still fresh. "I'm good. Burned myself on a skillet like an idiot, but it's only a first-degree burn. I'll be fine."

"Sometimes you do too much. You are too eager to please. That will be your downfall if you are not careful."

He drops my hand, and I lift the opposite to scratch the back of my neck. I smile thinly. "Thanks. I'll work on that."

"I have no doubt you will, Mr. Elliott." Pauly gives my shoulder a pat as he moves past me into the kitchen, repeating effectively, "Eager to please."

In my year of working under the watchful eye of Pauly Marino, I've learned a lot. I've learned that he never abbreviates anything he says, only speaking in full, articulate sentences, and that he has never once called me by my first name. It's always "Mr. Elliott."

I've learned that when someone is on his good side, he's a wealth of knowledge and inspiration.

And when someone is on his bad side, they don't get a second chance at ever experiencing being on his good side.

I've also learned that Pauly Marino has more talent in his pinkie finger than every chef I've ever worked with combined, including myself, and watching him hone his craft has only made me hungrier to be better. Pauly struck me as the corporate type at first, nothing but a suit who drank overpriced scotch in a stuffy office while his employees sweated buckets in the kitchen.

But that couldn't have been further from the truth.

Pauly busts his ass just like the rest of us, working long hours, staying late to clean and prep for the following day, and masterfully overseeing his kitchen with a strange mix of brash authority and imagination.

As I stare at my hand and splay my fingers, the flesh beneath the bandage still tingles, and I glare at the bumbling mistake. I'm about to step out of the kitchen when Pauly calls out to me once more.

"Mr. Elliott, I almost forgot. Your lovely sister is waiting for you up front."

June is here?

She's supposed to be teaching arabesques to nine-year-olds right now.

I smile my thanks and hurry out the doors, beelining toward the front of the building. As I weave through tables and waiters, Wendy comes into view first, perched at the hostess station, her thick mound of hair pinned back in a clip, recently colored from its natural auburn tone to a vibrant burgundy.

That's right—Wendy works here now.

She needed a job after getting laid off from her customer service position at a call center, so she texted me, asking if we were hiring. We were, and I felt like I kind of owed it to her—not that I had intentionally hurt her or anything, but I did break her heart, and I'm not an asshole; I was sympathetic. Pauly seemed to like her well enough, so she was officially hired on three months ago, and so far things have been smooth sailing. We've kept our relationship cordial and professional.

Sweeping past her, Wendy lights up a little when I tap my knuckles on the wooden station and shoot her a friendly smile. But my attention is quickly pulled to June, who sits in one of the waiting chairs near the doors, her knees bouncing in opposite time, still dressed in her leotard with a pair of leggings and an oversized gray cardigan dangling off one shoulder. She also brightens when she spots me, her chin popping up, eyes glinting with splashes of sapphire and silver.

Both girls react in a similar, wide-eyed way when they see me.

My heart only reacts to one.

"Junebug," I say, my smile blooming as she stands. "I thought you were working this afternoon."

"I was, but I got off a little early and thought I might catch you on your break." June holds up a brown paper bag, crumpled tight at the top. Her high ponytail swings side to side as she steps toward me, tresses billowing like the spiraled ribbon of a kite. Free and effortless, akin to the smile she gifts right back to me. "I brought you something."

My attention lands on the bag. "Please say it's loaded with carbs, great with tea, and rhymes with clones—hint, please tell me there are two."

"Eerily perceptive." She winks, chuckling under her breath. "Two blueberry scones, made with love by yours truly."

"Wait, you made them?" I take the bag from her outstretched hand, then peek inside. "You hate baking, Junebug."

She shrugs. "Mom jumped in before I accidentally added bleaching powder instead of baking powder, but otherwise I pretty much put Gordon Ramsay to shame."

We stare at each other for a beat with identical grins, overly charmed, almost like we're drunk on something, then I break the spell, moving toward the chair to set the bag down. When I spin back around, June's eyes fall to my hand taped with gauze.

"Brant, your hand…" Her gasp spills out in a breath of tender turmoil, and she reaches for my clumsily wrapped palm, clasping it between both of her hands. Her touch is as delicate as her worry-filled features as she grazes an index finger over the bandaging. June doesn't physically pull me closer, but I find myself moving in toward her anyway, and the longer she caresses my hand, the more the gap between us lessens. "What did you do?"

Her eyes are trained on my injury, while my eyes are trained on the way her brow furrows tight. The way she lightly nicks her bottom lip with her teeth. "Touched something I shouldn't have and got burned."

There's a strange huskiness to my voice that has her gaze drifting upward. "You should be more careful," she replies softly, slicking her tongue over her lips. "I hate to see you hurt. What if it gets infected?"

"You worry too much, Junebug." Instinct has my own index finger lifting, skimming the curve of her cheekbone, a token of affection. I almost want to linger, to connect the dotting of dark freckles scattered across her skin, curious as to what kind of art I could create. But I shake the bizarre thought away, dropping my hand as June's cheeks appear to flush a little pinker. "I promise I'll survive."

She laughs lightly, tucking an invisible piece of hair behind her ear. "I suppose it's only a little burn. Sorry. I'm too softhearted."

"You say it like it's a bad thing when it's the thing I love most about you."

There's a subtle shift in her expression, something I can't quite translate, but it makes me wonder if I said something I shouldn't have. I'm about to backtrack when someone bumps into me and I jolt, pivoting in place to see that a line of customers has formed, and here we are, obstructing the entrance, totally oblivious.

"I, uh…should probably eat something and get back on the clock," I say, ruffling my hair, then pointing to the little bag of scones abandoned on the chair. "I really appreciate you stopping by. I'll see you when I get home?"

June bobs her head, stretching a smile. She adjusts the sleeve of her cardigan, pulling it up over her shoulder. "Of course," she murmurs, clearing her throat. "See you there."

She turns to leave, sweeping past me like a sea-born breeze infused with lilacs and sunshine. I stare after her through the glass door as she traipses through the parking lot, ponytail bouncing side to side, arms crossed over her chest. Then I force my attention away and snatch up the paper bag, moving to head toward the kitchen.

Wendy catches my gaze the moment I'm facing her. She bores holes into me, tapping her pen along her notepad as she multitasks with a customer. There's something dark brimming just beneath the happy copper color of her eyes, like a storm brewing while the sun still shines.

It unnerves me.

I scratch at my cheek, duck my head, then make my way to the break room to eat my scones.

"Brant, hold up."

Wendy's voice floats over to me across the parking lot as I stride toward my new Highlander. I purchased it just a few months ago. Used, of course, but in great condition. I'm eager to see how it handles the ugly winters ahead.

I slow to a stop, turning in place to find her jogging over to me in high heels. They click along the concrete, her legs hindered by the black pencil skirt that falls at her knees. "Yeah?"

I'm not sure what she could possibly want. She hasn't broached any relationship discussion since she started working here, and I wouldn't exactly call us friends.

A piece of hair falls loose from her clip. She pushes it aside when she reaches me, her eyes darting every which way until she finally pins them on me. Wendy sighs as she says, "That was weird earlier. With June."

"What?" I'm immediately lost, a little defensive, my arms folding across my chest. "What was weird?"

Another sigh, and then, "The way you look at each other. The way you touch each other. It's almost like..."

What the hell?

"Like what?"

She swallows. "It's almost like you're…involved. Intimately."

My eyebrows lift to my hairline. My stomach swirls with nausea. "Whoa." I stare at her, incredulous, my arms falling to my sides. Words are elusive as her bomb thunders through me, blasting me with buckshot and bewilderment. Throat tight, heart clenched, I mutter through gritted teeth, "Not only are you wrong, but you're completely out of line."

"Am I?"

"I'm telling you that you are."

"And I'm telling you what I saw."

I search her face, looking for an angle. Desperate to uncover some kind of manipulation tactic or wicked intent, but all I see is…*concern*. A sense of alarm.

And I think that shakes me up even more.

"Wendy, listen to me," I say, my voice low. Hoarse, cracking. "I understand you're hurting. I know this hasn't been easy for you, what happened between us, and I'm sorry for that. I truly never meant to cause you harm."

"That's not what this is—"

"But to imply there's something inappropriate going on between me and my teenaged sister is going too far. You're crossing a line."

Wendy pulls her lip between her teeth, worrying it, thinking about her next words. Her head shakes back and forth, just slightly, another piece of hair falling loose. "I promise that's not what this is about, Brant," she says, and there's earnestness laced into her tone. Blunt honesty that cuts me deep. "I'm telling you this because I'm worried. If I noticed it, then someone else will, too." I'm about to counter her claim again, but she cuts me off. "Your sister, huh?"

My lips part, but nothing comes out. I just frown, waiting for what she'll say next.

"That's interesting," she continues, glancing down at the pavement, twisting the toe of her stiletto into a crack. "You never call her your sister. You've always hated that word. Until right now."

Traffic rumbles from the highway behind us, and a sharp breeze blows through, kissing my skin. It feels colder than it really is on this muggy August night. "It's not like that."

"She's gorgeous, Brant. She's stunning and loyal, and she absolutely adores you."

"Stop it."

"This isn't coming from a place of resentment," Wendy tells me, reaching for my hand and giving it a squeeze. I glance down at the contact, but don't pull back. I'm numb. "This is coming from a place of love. I love you, Brant, and I always will. And I'd hate to see you crash and burn."

My eyes trail up to hers, slow and lazy, my defensiveness dwindling to defeat. "June and I are close. Closer than most. We always have been," I explain, hating that I have to explain it at all. *This is madness.* "Nothing is going on between us."

Wendy squeezes my hand one more time, the smallest of smiles hinting on her face, then lets me go. "Good," she whispers. She steps away, another prickly draft carrying her final words over to me. "I hope for both of your sakes you keep it that way."

I'm not sure why she comes to me.

Tonight, of all goddamn nights, when I'm lying here, restless and tormented, replaying Wendy's words over and over again inside my mind.

She comes to me.

"Brant?"

I lift up on my elbows, squinting my eyes through the dark, dragging my gaze over her outline. She's standing right at the edge of my bed, dressed in what looks to be a tank top and shorts. "June," I murmur, already suffocating on her scent. Already twisted up inside because Wendy put dirty, untrue claims into my head and now I can't shake them. "What are you doing in here?"

"I had a nightmare." She fidgets beside me, waiting for an invitation she won't receive. "Can I lie with you?" she asks softly.

"No. You should go back to sleep." I shut her down quickly, probably more harshly than she deserves, and flop back down to the bed, rolling away from her.

The mattress shifts.

A subdued sigh leaves me, and I close my eyes for a moment before twisting back around to find June sitting next to me, her eyes glistening in the dark. "You're still here."

"Why do I feel like you're angry with me?"

"I'm not, I just..." Grumbling with a tinge of frustration, I pull myself up until my back is flush with the headboard. "I'm not angry with you. I'm just tired, and you shouldn't be in here."

"Why not?"

"Because it's late, you're seventeen years old, and you're hardly dressed."

Moonlight leaks in through the window, partially illuminating her white tank, her cleavage spilling out the top.

She bites at her lip. "I'm wearing what I always wear to bed."

"You can wear whatever you want," I say, my tone clipped. "In your own bed."

Silence settles in.

June glances away, her dark hair curtaining her profile as her chin dips to her chest. "What did I do?"

Guilt blankets me, and I sit up straighter. I gaze at her for a moment, reeling in my strange emotions, sorting through my addled thoughts. Rubbing both hands up and down my face, I finally lean forward and reach for her, curling my fingers around her wrist. "Hey. I'm sorry," I say, watching as her head slowly lifts, her eyes finding me through the dark. For a blinding, beautiful second, I see her as she is—my beautiful Junebug, the girl who makes me homemade scones, who lies with me and dreams with me, who protects my heart at all costs. Nothing has changed.

Nothing has changed.

I trace the underside of her wrist with my thumb, inching closer. "You didn't do anything. I just...I had a bad day. I didn't mean to take it out on you."

June nods, twisting herself in my grip until our hands are clasped, fingers interlocked. It's my injured hand. Scratchy gauze still winds around my palm in layers. "Do you think you'll have two scars, now? One from that piece of glass, and the other from the burn?"

"No," I whisper. "The burn isn't serious."

I never told June the whole truth about the scar on my hand. All I told her was that I cut myself on a broken window when I was six; she doesn't know I was breaking into my old house where my parents were killed, hoping to find my lost stuffed elephant and officially move back in.

She doesn't know she was there with me.

I tug her a little closer to me, our hands still intertwined. It's instinct, I think. I don't even mean to. June scoots over on the bed until she's resting beside my hip, close enough that I can make out her chaste features. Pale white skin. Crystalline eyes. A handful of freckles aimlessly sprinkled along her button nose and high cheekbones, like someone tripped with a paintbrush.

A pouty, heart-shaped mouth.

I glance at it.

No. Stop it. This is insanity.

My jaw clenches, Wendy's words fighting their way back inside my psyche. Infiltrating me. Poisoning everything good and pure between us.

I let go of June's hand, dropping my chin to my chest. "I took you that night," I confess.

She's silent for a moment, but I don't look up.

I just wait.

"What do you mean?"

Eyes closing tight, heart humming with wayward memories, I tell her. "The night I cut my hand. You were there. I took you with me."

She moves in closer, somehow. "I'm confused, Brant. Where did you take me?"

"To my house. My *real* house—the house I lived in until I was six years old, until my father decided to slip off his work tie and instead of going upstairs and placing it into his dresser drawer with all of his other work ties, he wrapped it around my mother's neck, strangling the life out of her until she stopped breathing. Until she choked. Until she died on our living room floor with a purple tie around her throat, and a little boy upstairs in bed, dreaming about fucking rainbows."

The words tumble from my mouth, angry memories and bitter breaths, as

June presses into me, her forehead to mine. My eyes are still closed, and it's for the best because I can't look at her right now. I can't see whatever tortured look is shining out through her eyes, or the tear tracks staining her porcelain skin.

I keep going.

I have to keep going.

"You fell asleep in your little bouncer seat that night. I unstrapped you. I picked you up with all my strength and I carried you down the hallway. I put my shoes on, then I stepped outside and walked next door, two houses over." Her forehead is still smooshed against mine, and I hear her sniffle. I hear her breaths catching and hitching in the back of her throat. "I set you down in the grass, and you were so good, June. It was cold that night, October I think, but you were so, so good. I realized I couldn't get inside, so I took one of the rocks that lined our mailbox and I threw it at the window until it smashed into a million fractured bits. And then I climbed through, slicing my hand on the glass." I swallow down the lump in my throat, my molars grinding together. "But I still came back out for you. My hand was bleeding all over your blanket, and I was so worried you'd be scared, but you just lay there with me on my living room floor. You lay there with me when I needed you the most, just like you're doing right now."

She sniffs again, her hands cradling my neck, thumbs dusting over my bristled jawline. "You brought me with you," she rasps out, an air of incredulity in her tone. "I've always been with you, Brant."

I finally open my eyes, lashes fluttering, my heart jackhammering in my chest. June is so close. *She's so close.* "Always."

I inch myself down the headboard, we both move into a sleeping position, and I tug the blanket up over our bodies until we're cocooned in the downy quilt.

We shouldn't be this close. I know it's not right, but I don't fucking care right now, and I don't care about what Wendy might think or what she thinks she saw—all I care about is June.

June, June, June.

My eyelids feel heavy as we lie there, chest to chest, noses gently grazing. Her warm breath kisses my lips with every fervent heartbeat.

I'm content. I'm at peace. She's here, in my arms.

She's always been here.

I'm not sure how much time passes, but I'm roused awake by the feel of more than just her breath upon my lips. There's something else. A tickle at first. Just an erotic tickle.

"Brant..."

She breathes my name against my mouth.

Her mouth is on mine.

June's mouth is on mine.

And I don't push her away. I should, but I don't, I can't, I just can't...

"Junebug, what—"

"Shh. You want this," she whispers, the tip of her tongue brushing along my upper lip. Her pelvis is flush against mine, arousal pulsing through my blood. "You want me, don't you?"

"Yes."

I don't hesitate.

Why don't I hesitate?

"Take me, Brant. Touch me." June pulls her cotton tank top up over her head, her tresses fused with static splaying out over my pillow, her bare breasts highlighted with moonglow as she tugs at my hair, yanking my face down until I'm level with her chest.

No, no, no.

This is wrong. This is so wrong.

A groan spills out of me when I flick her nipple with my tongue, then do it again, and again, until my mouth is wrapped around her breast, my hand palming the other, and she's writhing against me, gasping for more.

I'm hard.

I'm so goddamn hard.

I want her. I need her.

You can't have her. She's seventeen. She's your fucking adopted sister, you fucking freak.

My mind is shrieking with madness, but my mouth is still moving. Still tasting. Still sucking her tits as she digs her nails into my scalp, my name spilling from her lips.

"Brant…yes, please…" she begs. "Please, wake up."

Her voice sounds far away as I drag my tongue up her body to the curve of her neck. "What?" I grit out.

"I said *wake up*."

I inhale a sharp breath.

My eyes ping open.

It's silent in the room, save for my ragged breaths muffled by lilac-scented threads of chestnut hair. My face is buried in her tresses, her back to me on the bed, while she's sound asleep.

The room is dark.

It's still nighttime.

I was dreaming.

Holy shit, it was just a dream.

Only, the horror doesn't wane when I realize that I'm spooning her, my hand cupping her breast, my groin pressed into her bottom, jabbing her with a rock-hard erection.

I fly backward, letting her go as if she morphed into brushfire.

Fuck.

Fuck, fuck, *fuck*.

Sliding to the foot of the bed as quietly as possible, I manage not to wake June as I pull myself to shaky legs, then throw on a T-shirt. She lies there, perfectly still, her breathing languid and steady, the epitome of angelic.

And I dreamed of defiling her.

Sullying her sweetness.

*God…*what the hell is wrong with me?

What did Wendy do to me?

I have to get out of here. I feel like I'm choking on a cloud of filth, desperate for clean air. Racing from the bedroom, I snatch up my cell phone and keys, then pop my shoes on and stalk outside into the humid, late summer night.

I get into my car.

I drive.

And fifteen minutes later, I'm rapping my knuckles against Wendy's front door.

She peeks through the curtain after a minute passes, inspecting who the hell would be knocking on her door at one in the morning. I'm not sure if she's more stunned or relieved to see that it's me.

The door cracks open. She's clad in a white robe, her hair in disarray. "Brant?"

"You're wrong," I tell her, pushing my way through the threshold. Wendy paces back, her eyes wide. I sound menacing. Ready to pounce. "I'll show you how wrong you are."

Closing the gap between us, I tug her robe apart until she's bare before me, clad only in her underwear. Wendy gasps, and we're both breathing heavy, both confused, both rattled to the bone.

I kiss her.

I kiss her hard, crushing her mouth to mine, and erasing June for good.

I burned myself today.

And while I know my hand will heal, some burns are destined to leave a permanent scar.

16

FIRST CLUE

JUNE, AGE 17

My lungs tighten, my chest achy and sore. Nearly bruised.

I take a quick break from the routine, turning to face the wall, then lean over, hands to my knees as I catch my breath. I've been feeling winded more often, especially today after learning the rigorous choreography for a contemporary ballet performance I'm participating in this fall.

Sweat dots my brow, my lungs wheezing.

"Everything okay, June?"

Regrouping, I straighten my spine, stretch, and take a giant swig of water once the boulder on my chest releases. Pivoting with a smile, I nod at my instructor, Camilla. "Perfect," I chirp as I tug at my ponytail. Camilla blinks, studying me for a moment before continuing with the routine.

When the class is over, I sweep back the rogue hairs that slipped loose from my hair tie, damp with sweat, and close my eyes to center my breathing.

"You really nailed it today, June. I'm impressed." Camilla comes up behind me, a light hand sweeping down my back. "You sure you're okay, though?"

"Absolutely," I say without hesitation, despite the way my lungs still squeeze. "I'm excited about this choreography. It's so modern, yet elegant."

"It's grueling. Took me months to fine-tune, but I think we're really going to stand out."

The water bottle crinkles in my grip as I twist the cap back on, ignoring the hum of warning that prickles my skin. I've been losing my breath more often, to the point that it's getting harder to disguise. Episodes have come and gone over the last few years, ramping up in frequency and urgency since summer training began.

I've brushed it off, thinking I've simply been overdoing it, and too afraid to see a doctor due to the off chance that it could be something serious—something that could hinder my dance career.

I want to perform on Broadway.

New York City.

I want the bright lights, the costumes, the treasure trove of opportunity.

And I'm so close. I've been practicing for years, mastering my craft to the point that there's no other option for me.

Only dance.

Having just entered my final year of high school, I've found the future on my mind a lot lately. Mom says I need to narrow down my college selections. I've already been accepted into three—Columbia being my top contender—but…the truth is I'm not sure I want to go to college. Celeste managed to secure a one-way ticket to New York after graduation and will be staying with her aunt while she gets a jump start on her career with a company who hires background dancers.

I want that, too.

I'm just not sure how I'm going to do it yet.

My arms lift into a stretch as I respond, sweat still sheening my skin. "I can't wait. I'm going to spend every waking moment practicing," I tell her.

Camilla's mocha eyes twinkle, her dark brows lifting as her smile grows. She has the whitest teeth I've ever seen. "No doubt in my mind you'll be the star," she says. "You truly have a gift, June."

A shot of conviction floods me.

I want this so bad.

"Thank you. That means a lot to me."

"I only speak the truth. Just don't overdo it, you hear?" Camilla sends me a smile that teeters on the line between worry and warmth. "See you next week."

I watch her go as my fellow teammates chat idly, sifting through their duffel bags for outfit changes. Celeste makes a beeline toward me after Camilla disappears, her golden hair swept up into a big knot. She's grown so much taller than me, by nearly a foot, and while her body is all athletic trim and defined muscle, I'm more soft curves and petite bone structure, needing to work extra hard to maintain my lithe physique.

My ample breasts, especially, are a huge deterrent in the world of dance, acting as more of an inconvenience than an asset—despite what all my girlfriends say.

"Starbucks?" Celeste suggests, throwing her bag over her shoulder. A cropped jersey hangs low off her fit frame, showcasing a black sports bra underneath. "I need my Saturday frappé fix. And maybe a lemon loaf. God, I haven't had carbs all week."

I toss the towel draped around my neck into the hamper, then pull a pair of leggings up over my leotard. "Can't. My brother is picking me up for some bonding time."

"Ooh." Her eyebrows waggle suggestively. "I'd kill for some bonding time with that man."

"What? Gross." I laugh a little awkwardly while reaching for my own duffel. "Theo has a girlfriend, but I'll pass along the compliment."

"No, girl, I was talking about Brant." She chuckles, linking her arm with mine and leading me toward the front exit. "I mean, Theo is cute, but he's more all-American cute. Brant is...*oof.* The other kind of cute, you know? The dirty-thoughts kind."

Flush creeps into my ears. When someone comments about "my brother," my brain automatically assumes they're talking about Theo. I suppose I have two brothers, technically, even though one of them likes to reject the idea.

My thoughts scatter as we dally in the front lobby, waiting for our rides. Brant has been on my mind a lot lately, ever since the emotional night we shared together almost a month ago—the night I startled awake from a nightmare, and instinct pulled me to his bedroom for solace. I know I'm not a little girl anymore, but grown girls still have nightmares. Grown girls still crave childhood comforts, such as precious stuffed elephants, rainbow lullabies, and strong arms attached to white knights.

He told me once, in a hospital bed as I struggled through deadly pneumonia, that he'd brought me Aggie for comfort and my custom pink sword for courage.

Little did he know I already had both.

I had him.

And up until that night last month, I thought I still had him—but something happened, something shifted, and it's something I haven't been able to unravel just yet. Brant has been distant and moody, far from the easygoing man who suffocated me with bear hugs and didn't shy away from piggyback rides, even though I'm far too old.

He doesn't touch me anymore.

He looks at me differently, almost as if I'm a stranger.

He bans me from his bedroom if I dare step foot inside.

Our tender, thoughtful conversations have transformed into superficial chitchat about nothing at all, and the moment I try to delve deeper, he pulls away. He claims to be tired, or too busy, or he simply says, *"Not now, June."*

June.

That right there has been the biggest red flag.

He hasn't called me Junebug.

He hasn't called me Junebug in twenty-six days.

I feel all alone without his smiles and jokes. Mom and Dad are home often, both only working part-time now. My friends are abundant, and Yoshi is a sweet old companion, but everything seems to pale in comparison to time spent with Brant.

I've replayed that night over and over in my mind.

A nightmare had spooked me. I'd dreamed of floating down a river of red, approaching a cave of horrors. It was a black night with cackling winds and crowing trees, a sense of foreboding hanging heavy in the air. Brant had been on the raft with me, and we'd been traveling along a rainbow stream, happily content. I'm not sure what happened, but I think it was lightning. A sinister strike had brightened the sky, and Brant had looked at me in that moment, right as everything flashed, something strange glittering in his earthy eyes. He'd reached for me. He'd reached for my hand across the buoyant raft as if he needed to, as if our very lives depended on it, and the moment we touched, everything changed.

He was gone. I was alone.

Only a dark cave loomed ahead, and as vultures swooped above me, laughing at my loneliness, I'd awoken in a cold sweat, desperately searching for Brant.

I found him in his bed, uneager to see me. My dream swirled through me like a toxin, blackening my relief, soiling my comfort that all was well, that it was just a terrible nightmare.

He hated me.

But then he reached for me with that same look in his eyes. The dream look, filled with hopeless desperation. He reached across the mattress and clasped my wrist, tracing gentle designs onto my skin and apologizing for being cold. And then he confessed a grisly secret.

A grisly, beautiful secret.

"I took you that night."

I listened through my tears, trying to be his anchor through whatever storm he was fighting. Trying to be the rainbow on the other side.

Our foreheads melded together with affection as I held his neck between my palms, clinging tight to every word. Clinging tight to him.

My best friend.

And then I fell asleep in his arms, my dreams molding into images far less frightening.

Only, when I woke up, a new nightmare began.

I was all alone in his bed when the sun came up, his car vacant from its usual spot in the driveway when I'd glanced out the window. Confusion blanketed me. Worry sank its teeth into me. A tickle of trepidation swept through me.

Brant was gone.

And the worst part?

He never really came back.

"Yo." I nearly jolt to the ceiling when two fingers snap in front of my face. "Earth to Peach."

My hand shoots to my heart, my head popping up to discover Theo standing over me in his police uniform. I inhale a jittery breath, then let it out slowly. "Sorry. You scared me."

"I have that effect on people when I'm dressed like this." He shrugs with a smirk. "Thought it would have the opposite effect, but turns out everyone's got something to hide these days." Theo frowns when I just kind of stare at him, my eyes glazed over. "You should be immune, though. Did I interrupt some intense daydreaming or something?"

I shake away the thoughts, laughing through my idiocy. "Sort of. I guess." Reaching for my duffel, I sling it over my shoulder and rise to my feet. "Practice was challenging today. I'll be recovering all week."

"Gotcha. Good thing we're jump-starting the recovery process with ice cream cones down by the riverwalk. You can eat those, right?" He jabs my belly with his index finger. "I know the word 'sugar' is occasionally considered a mild offense among teenaged girls."

Swatting his hand away, I push forward toward the exit. "Yes, Theo, I can have those. I'll have two now, just to be a brat."

"Attagirl."

We make our way outside and into the September sun, hopping into Theo's cruiser and driving the short distance to the downtown riverwalk lined with pizza joints, cutesy boutiques, and ice cream shops. I let my hair down, and it dances through the open window as we parallel park along the bustling street. Jumping out of the car, I prop my sunglasses on my nose. "I thought you were off today," I muse, strolling over to the sidewalk. "Did you get called in?"

Theo adjusts his holster, joining me in front of our favorite ice cream parlor. He sighs, whipping off his own sunglasses and securing them on his head. "Sure did. There always seems to be bad guys to defeat, people to save." A grin curls in my direction as he gives me a gentle slug on the shoulder. "I'm making it sound a lot cooler than it is. It's mostly traffic violations and petty citations."

I return the smile. "Well, I'm glad you were still able to squeeze me in."

"Anything for you, Peach. And anything for cookie dough."

The little bell chimes overhead as we saunter into the shop, the scent of raspberry cream and warm vanilla sugar swirling around us. I purchase a few chunks of fudge for Mom and Dad, as well as a sack of saltwater taffy for Brant.

He's always had a sweet tooth. He told me once that desserts remind him of his late mother.

As the employee scoops the taffies into a bag, I tell her, "No purple ones, please."

She glances at me. "Pardon?"

"No purple. All the others are fine."

Apparently it's a strange request because I get a long, baffled look before she painstakingly removes the purple candies, returning them to the case.

I take the treats with a big smile. "Thank you so much."

Theo and I order our respective ice cream cones, and Theo ends up paying for the whole purchase. I thank him repeatedly because I'm only making ten dollars an hour at the dance studio, assisting the instructors with the miniature ballerinas. Money is tight, going mostly to my cell phone bill and chipping in with gas when Mom lets me drive the minivan.

While we wait for the cones, the young girl scooping out ice cream keeps looking up at me, her dark eyes glinting with curiosity. When she hands me my cone, she nibbles her lip and finally says, "I've seen you at Bistro Marino."

"Oh! Yes, I've stopped by a few times," I tell her, bobbing my head, then licking the melty ice cream dribbling over the side of the cone. "Good memory."

"Your boyfriend is awesome. He's so talented."

I pause, nearly choking on the bite I just took. Blinking up at her, my eyebrows lift. "What?"

"I work part-time as a hostess there. Tuesdays and Thursdays. I've seen you stop in from time to time with his lunch or something. Anyway, I wasn't trying to be nosy, but I wanted you to know that you're lucky. My boyfriend can't even microwave a Lean Cuisine without messing it up." She laughs, bending to make Theo's cone. "You two are adorable together."

I'm speechless for a moment, braving a glance at Theo, who has a single eyebrow raised in confusion. "I–I'm sorry, you must be thinking of someone else…"

She pops her head back up, her ponytail swishing behind her. "Brant. The head chef."

"Brant is my brother. He's not my boyfriend."

A moment of silence passes. A terribly awkward moment. "Oh my gosh, I'm so sorry." The girl hands Theo his order, swiping her hands along her apron. "The way you two interacted with each other, I just thought… Wow, okay. I'm sorry."

She blushes, mortified.

I do the same because I'm equally mortified.

The clerk clears her throat, scratching at her neck as she addresses Theo. "You must be her boyfriend. I apologize for the misunderstanding."

"Also her brother."

Her eyes pop. "Wow. Great, that's…great." She gives us a little wave and moves to make a hasty retreat. "I'll go die now."

Stepping away from the counter, Theo follows behind me and we exit through the glass door, the little bell signaling our departure and sounding far less cheerful on the way out. When I take a bite of my ice cream cone, it tastes like shame.

"That was mildly cringey." Theo falls into stride beside me as we turn onto the riverwalk, where ducks float along the water, hopeful for starchy snacks from passersby. "Your face is as pink as your leotard, Peach."

"Shush."

I feel him watching me as we walk, and my legs inadvertently pick up the pace as if I'm trying to lose his stare. "What was that all about?"

"How would I know?" I wince when my inner sass lashes out. That's not like me anymore. I've evolved from a bratty teenager into a polite and eloquent lady, for the most part, thanks to that one time my mom recorded me in the midst of a hormonal hurricane when I was fifteen. She replayed it back for me once I'd calmed down, and I was so humiliated by my behavior that I turned my attitude around fast. It's heightened my awareness of how other people perceive me, so I make a great effort to always put my best foot forward. Quickly correcting myself, I shoot Theo a small smile. "Sorry."

My brother doesn't seem to take offense, but that's no surprise. Over the years, I've discovered that only two things in this world truly offend him—one of them being people who get offended.

The other: people who have the potential to put me in harm's way.

This includes primarily any person of the male variety who looks at me, talks to me, God forbid *touches* me, and occasionally breathes the same air as me. Apparently, that last one depends on their face. If it looks like the face of someone who might participate in the previous list of offenses, they're toast.

Theo doesn't reply for a few beats, licking his ice cream cone until it molds into a perfect point. Then he murmurs, "I wonder why she thought that."

Heat blooms on my cheeks again, and not even the cold ice cream can counteract it. "Weird, huh?"

"Definitely weird. She said something about the way you two *interacted* with each other… What the hell does that mean?"

"I have no idea. She obviously needs a lesson in social cues."

"I'd say so." He's quiet again, so I assume this humiliating conversation is finally over. "How do you interact? Like, hugging or some shit? Or do you—"

"Theo, this is awkward. He's my brother, and we act how we always act. Can we please talk about something else?"

I feel Theo's eyes on me again. Gallant blue eyes. A sigh falls out of him as we travel beside the river's edge, and when I peek up at him, he's already popping the last bite of cone into his mouth, his attention on the water. "It's a good day to save someone," he says.

I laugh. He always said that when he still lived at home, right before he'd leave for his shift. "It's always a good day to save someone."

"I save a lot less people than I thought I would going into this gig. Where are the damsels in distress? The princesses trapped inside the haunted castles?" Theo's sandy-colored hair parts when the wind blows through it, and as his smile grows, his spattering of freckles seems to multiply. "I rescued a litter of kittens from a sewer last week."

Another laugh spills out of me. "That absolutely counts," I say, licking up the melted ice cream that drips down my hand. "But seriously, I know you'll get your big save one of these days. You were born to do this, Theo."

He throws an arm around me, pulling me close as we stroll down the riverwalk. Giving me a little squeeze, he says, "As long as you believe in me, Peach."

Theo dropped me off at Celeste's house after our ice cream date, and we spent a few hours practicing our dance routine, gossiping, and making plans for the following weekend. Celeste's brother is going to a party, and she wanted us both to tag along.

I'm not much of a partyer, mostly because I have a deep-rooted fear that my brothers will materialize from the walls if I even glance in the direction of an alcoholic beverage, then carry me out upside down after securing me with a chastity belt and pulverizing every boy who had the audacity to be under the same roof as me.

Also beer tastes like wet cardboard after a dog peed on it.

I agreed, though, because I've spent every waking weekend hour devoted to dancing and I could use the social break. I'm not planning to stay long. It's not easy staying out late with Brant still living at home. I swear he refuses to sleep until I'm home safe, always checking to make sure I'm unscathed the moment I walk through the door.

Well, he used to, anyway.

The sun is just beginning to dip behind the horizon as I walk the short trek home from Celeste's and traipse into the house.

Dad is just finishing up dinner, while Mom clears the table. My father swivels in his chair, sending me a hello from across the way as I set my duffel in the foyer. "June Balloon, my darling daughter," he bellows, but it's a charming bellow. He never sounds angry despite the rough baritone of his voice. "Hurry and gobble up some of this gumbo before your mother eats it all."

"Very funny, Andrew," Mom murmurs from around the kitchen corner. "You're like a rabid animal with gumbo, foaming at the mouth when I try to take a single serving."

"I wasn't foaming, dear. It was a subtle froth." He shoots me a pronounced eye roll, then mouths *"Dramatic."*

My dad is a goof. He wears platypus slippers, makes up funny words, and is always rhyming my name with something random. June the Goon when I'm acting silly. June the Typhoon when I'm a grouch. June Balloon, June Lagoon,

June Harpoon—the rhymes are endless. Infuriating at times when I want him to take me seriously, but mostly I've come to treasure them.

Pulling the treats I accrued from the ice cream shop out of my bag, I stroll through the living room and into the kitchen, where exotic spices and cumin sweep under my nose. I hand my father the packaged fudge. "For you and Mom."

His eyes light up as he coughs into his fist, slurring, "Favorite child alert."

"Technically, Theo bought it."

He coughs again. "Second favorite child alert."

Smacking him on the shoulder, I share a smile with my mother, who's placing dirty bowls into the dishwasher. The sack of taffies is clutched in my opposite hand, and I assume Brant is in his room since his Highlander was in the driveway when I got home. "Is Brant upstairs? I got him something, too."

"He is," Mom says. "It's his weekend off. He went up right before you walked in."

My father adds, "He's in a mood. It's good you'll come bearing gifts."

"A mood?"

He shrugs. "Not sure, really. He didn't say much at dinner. But hey, while you're up there, go give your brother a big hug." Dad winks, the precursor to a joke. "A June cocoon."

Good Lord.

I groan, then saunter away from the kitchen to the flight of stairs.

When I move into the open doorway of Brant's bedroom, he's standing by the window, looking out at the dusky sky. Swallowing, I take a few soft steps forward. "Hey."

He hears me because he responds right away. "Hey." He doesn't turn around, though. Brant just stands there with his back to me, arms at his sides, his reflection subtle in the windowpane.

I lick my lips and continue to pace toward him until I'm flush with his back, his body heat sinking into me. The scent of Ivory soap invades me, mingled with a slight trace of spearmint from his favorite chewing gum.

Then I wrap my arms around his middle, pressing my cheek to his spine.

He stiffens.

It's a devastating reaction.

Brant always welcomes my arms, my hugs, my tender touches. He always reacts with equal affection, often upping the ante and picking me up, or tickling me, or squeezing me until I nearly pop. He never tenses up. He never hesitates.

He never stiffens.

"Brant, please," I murmur into the warm cotton of his shirt. "Hug me back, will you?"

It takes a moment—a long, worrisome moment—but he eventually lifts his palm and places it atop my hands that have linked around his torso. It's not much, but it's something.

Brant's head dips when his fingers graze the little plastic bag tied with a piece of twine that I'm still holding onto. "What's this?"

"Saltwater taffy. I picked it up for you today."

"Why?"

Why? What a ridiculous question. Unraveling my arms, I wait for him to turn around and face me. He does—he does right away, his features firm and taut. The radiant rain forest in his eyes, lush greens and rich soil, looks more like a dying swamp. "Because I love you, that's why."

His frown pulls tighter.

"I even had them remove the purple pieces." Taking his hand in mine, I set the little bag inside his palm, closing his fingers around it. "I thought maybe you needed something sweet."

Brant's eyes close for a moment, his fist clenching the gift. His dark silence penetrates me, a blunt dagger right through the heart.

Something's wrong but I don't know what. Something happened but he won't tell me.

I can't help him if he won't tell me.

I have to help him.

I open my mouth to speak, but before I can get a word out Brant snatches my face between his hands and looks me right in the eyes. They flash with something. I'm reeled back into my nightmare, and we're floating on that raft, the sky going dark, the river turning red.

Flash.

Brant moves forward like lightning and plants a hard kiss to my forehead, his thumbs bruising my jaw as he grips me tight. So tight it almost hurts. Then he says in a ragged, broken voice, "I'll always protect you, June."

He lets go, and I nearly stumble back from the loss of him.

My breaths come quick and unsteady, my legs growing shaky as I listen to him storm down the staircase to the lower level. The front door slams shut, and I still stand in the center of his room, my hand to my heart, and my forehead still tingling from the weight of his kiss.

June.

Not Junebug.

He said he'd always protect me…but he has no clue that *he's* the one striking me down.

17

FIRST DIBS

JUNE, AGE 17

I'D ASSUMED WE WERE GOING to a schoolmate's party—maybe Marty, the party king, or even Hayden who will occasionally host something at his parents' sprawling farmhouse.

Imagine my surprise when we pull into Wyatt Nippersink's driveway. His tiny little shack of a house is bursting with so many people, I can hardly move inside, gripping my red Solo cup as if it's my only lifeline.

Celeste pops up behind me, startling me because I didn't hear her approach over the cacophony of beer-pong celebrations, rap music, and belching. "June, there you are!"

"Here I am." My smile probably looks painted on. "How long did you want to stay?"

"Whenever Tony wants to leave, since he's our ride. I don't have to be at my babysitting gig until eleven tomorrow." She chugs down her cup of mysterious red punch that matches mine. "Are you cool with that? I'm sure he'll take you home early if you need to go."

I worry my lip between my teeth. Truthfully, I only came out tonight to mingle with friends and let off some steam. But I hardly know anybody here aside from Celeste and her older brother, Tony...and Wyatt, of course, but he's far from what I'd consider a friend.

Celeste looks so glamorous tonight, dressed in a tight-fitting black minidress, her dirty-blond hair curled over both shoulders. Her lipstick is bright red, enhancing the smile she's wearing.

Twirling the cup between my fingers, I shake my head. "Nah, I'm fine. Whenever you want to leave works for me."

We chitchat for a bit, our voices shrill over the resounding racket of party noise. That's where Wyatt finds us, huddled in a corner, giggling and sipping our punch, a few minutes later. "Juney," he drawls, a wicked gleam in his eye. It always seems to be there when he looks at me. "Big brother let you out of his sight long enough to come play with me, eh?"

I pivot to face him, one hand instinctually tugging down the hem of my denim skirt. He doesn't notice, though, because his gaze is locked on the swell of my breasts poking out from my halter top. "I'm here with Celeste and Tony. It's good to see you, though."

"The feeling is very mutual." Wyatt snatches a pitcher of punch that's been discarded on a coffee table and moves toward me, pouring it into my partially full cup. Liquid splashes up at me, misting my hand. He glances over at Celeste. "Need a refill, honey?"

She holds out her cup. "Fill 'er up."

I take a delicate sip of the punch, wincing when it coats my tongue. This batch tastes a lot stronger than the last.

Better than beer, at least.

"Tell you what, Juney. Have a few more glasses of my magic juice, then come find me, yeah?" Wyatt sends a wink my way, shoving back his mop of auburn hair.

While Wyatt isn't terrible looking—he has a decent build, perfectly straight teeth, and pretty eyes when they aren't leering at me—there's something off-putting about him. Something slimy.

It's almost as if I've always had his attention, even as a young girl. I recall the day at the frozen pond when he'd pushed me onto the ice. I know he was only being dumb and immature at the time and that he hadn't intentionally tried to hurt me or anything, but he was certainly old enough to know better.

And he was old enough to not look at me the way that he had.

I was only twelve years old at the time, yet I'd still felt the prickle of unease when he pinned his eyes on me. A threat lurked inside his golden gaze.

Bristling under his perusal, I simply nod then take a few more gulps of the cocktail. "Sure, okay."

"Good girl."

He saunters away, and Celeste nudges me with her shoulder. "He wants to sleep with you."

"What?" I nearly choke on my last sip. "You think?"

"C'mon, June, you can't be that naive. 'Come find me later'—? That's definitely code for sex."

I suppose she's right. It's not like he'd be interested in going head-to-head in a riveting game of Scrabble. "Wyatt's not really my type. I guess I'll have to break his heart," I tease.

"No? I thought you were into older guys."

A flush seeps into my skin. It's true, in a way. Boys my age have never really held my attention for long. My early high school crushes faded quickly, and I found myself more intrigued by my brothers' friends whenever they would come over. They were so much more mature, engaging. Fidgeting with my cup, I shrug. "Not him."

Wyatt stares at me from across the small living room, and I avert my eyes, my cheeks hot, and gulp down the rest of my punch.

The room spins a little, like I'm dancing on a pinwheel.

After three glasses of "magic juice" I think the magic is finally starting to happen. I'm bounced between dancing bodies, music pulsing through my veins as I sway and twirl.

I think I'm kind of drunk.

I've never been drunk before. Hangovers have never really held any appeal for me, especially with my rigorous dance schedule and the goals I'm determined to reach. Parties and booze will only slow me down, hold me back. Alcohol doesn't fit into my life.

But it doesn't feel half-bad right now as my inhibitions float away like deflating balloons. I'm sweaty and laughing, swinging my arms to the beat of the song. Celeste dances beside me, squealing as she grinds up on some guy, and we both grin wide, young and carefree.

"Told you to come find me." Wyatt's voice is gritty and suggestive as his mouth finds my ear, his body pressed up behind me.

I shiver just a bit. "I was dancing."

"I see that." Two hands roam over me, from my hips to my waist to the underside of my breasts. "Let's go talk someplace private, yeah?"

He doesn't give me a chance to respond before tugging me away from the crowd and leading me down a short, wood-paneled hallway. Wyatt kicks open one of the solid oak doors and pulls me inside with him. When the door slams shut, the click of a lock follows.

It's fairly dark inside the cluttered bedroom. A small lamp provides faint illumination in the corner, and the blinds are pulled up, allowing moonlight to spill in. It's bright enough that I can make out every detail on Wyatt's face as he stalks toward me, a predator hungry for a taste of fresh meat.

I blink the haze from my eyes, my body still buzzing with liquor and music. "You want to talk?"

"Something like that," he says, cocking his head to the side as he advances on me. "Don't really need words to get my point across, though."

Swallowing, I catch a whiff of cigarettes and bourbon mingling with the smell of mothballs in the room. My eyes are fixed on his as he reaches for me. "I'm intoxicated." I feel the need to say it, to inform him.

To remind myself.

An eyebrow arches. "You know where you are?"

"Yes."

"Who you're with?"

"Yes."

Wyatt's smirk curls as he takes his index finger and runs it through my long, flowing curtain of hair, then brings a tendril to his nose. He sniffs it. "You smell like a pretty little flower garden," he says, a low growl rumbling in his throat. "Makes my dick hard."

My breath catches, my gaze dipping to the side.

I'm not sure what I'm feeling right now.

There's a trace of adrenaline swimming through me. No one has ever talked to me like this before. Curiosity floods me.

But I also feel a low hum of warning vibrating in the pit of my stomach, telling me to run.

Wyatt takes my silence as further invitation, dropping my hair to palm my breasts through my halter top. I arch into him with a startled gasp, and he moans in reply. A raw and dirty sound. "You know how many times I've jerked off imagining blowing my load all over these big milky-white titties?" He squeezes my breasts like they're sponges, and I shake my head, eyes slamming shut. "Too many times to count, honey."

Oh God.

The alcohol is making my brain feel fuzzy, my body teetering until I stumble back against a dresser. My heart is thumping frantically in my chest but I can't decipher its beats.

And then he's kissing me.

Hard, wet, demanding. Wyatt shoves my jaw open, stabbing me with his tongue until I almost gag. "Mmm," he groans, slipping one hand between my legs, sliding it upward until he's palming my inner thigh. "You know what this body was made for?"

Words feel unattainable. Only a squeak breaks free.

He replies anyway. "Me."

Wyatt grabs me by the hair and shoves me to my knees, his opposite hand deftly loosening his belt buckle and unzipping his jeans. The denim falls to his ankles while he jerks himself free of his boxers, stroking hard through a groan, still fisting my hair as I remain rooted to the musty carpet, completely frozen.

I'm not sure why, of all moments, Brant's face spirals to mind.

My lashes flutter, my breath hitching.

I picture the look of disappointment in his eyes when he finds out about this. The betrayal. He *hates* Wyatt. Of all people this could happen with, this almost feels like I'm twisting a knife into Brant's perfect heart. Shame floods me, and I flinch as Wyatt thrusts his hips at me.

"Swallow my cock, Juney," he says with a moan. "I want first dibs on this pretty little mouth."

No! Nausea curdles in my gut when the head of his penis nudges between my lips, and I lurch back. "I–I can't… I'm sorry. I just…" Flustered, I fall back on my bottom, pulling my skirt down as far as it will go, then scamper to my feet. "I changed my mind."

I can't do this. I don't want to do this.

Wyatt sniffs. "Yeah, I figured you might."

Pacing backward on shaky legs, I readjust my bra then fold my arms over my chest like a protective hug.

"That's the thing about good girls," he drones, stuffing himself back into his boxers, still fully erect. He tugs his jeans up his hips and finishes, "It's a bitch to close the deal. But *fuck*…it's so damn sweet when you do."

My jaw aches from grinding my molars together. Tears threaten to spill, so I spin around and stalk toward the bedroom door.

He stops me.

He stops me dead in my tracks.

"Think he calls you Junebug when he fantasizes about pumping his cock into that sweet hole of yours?"

I freeze.

My blood freezes, everything freezes.

Color drains from my face, and my stomach pitches. I turn to him slowly, my eyes wide and volatile. "What?"

He shrugs.

He just *shrugs*.

"Are you insane?" My voice trembles with slow simmering outrage. "He's my brother."

"He ain't your brother, Juney." Wyatt zips his jeans back up, then fastens the belt buckle. "Trust me—he's all too aware of that fact."

"You're sick."

"Not so sure I'm the sick one here."

Realization dawns on me, thick and heavy, settling deep. I lose a breath. "This isn't about me," I murmur, my words cracking. "This was never about me. This was always about getting to Brant."

"Can't think of a more enjoyable way to get there." He licks his lips knowingly, then sifts through his pocket, pulling out a pack of cigarettes. Flicking one out of the carton, he holds it out to me. "Smoke?"

I stare at him with shock in my eyes before whirling around tugging at the door until I untwist the lock with shaking fingers, and race from the room.

Tricks. He's playing tricks on me, twisting a beautiful thing into something wicked and perverse. Wyatt Nippersink is a devil, just like his sister.

How could I go that far with him?

Reality slithers through me as a geyser of hot tears pours out of my eyes. I feel gross and dirty. I'm a vile, nasty thing.

I stumble into the living room, my eyes searching desperately for Celeste and her brother, Tony. I need to get out of here. I need to get home, run into Brant's arms. I need him to comfort me and wash away my sins. But most of the crowd has already cleared out, some guests still spilling out the front door as a police officer stands in the middle of the room, filing them through the entryway.

His back is to me, but I recognize him.

Kip!

It's Theo's partner, Kip. He's been by the house plenty of times for summer barbecues. He must have gotten a noise complaint, then came by to break up the underage drinking.

"Kip," I say in a desperate breath, rushing over to him, nearly tripping on my heels.

He spins around, doing a double take. "June?"

My tears are still falling hard. Mascara is surely smeared all over my face, making me look crazed. My hair is tangled from Wyatt's fist, and my clothes are rumpled and crooked.

"Did someone hurt you?" Kip's hands are on his hips, his angled features hard and angry as he approaches me. I don't answer right away, so he repeats the question. "June. Did someone hurt you?"

Pulling my lips between my teeth, a new wave of tears begin to fall. "Yes," I croak out, my eyes dropping to the floor with shame. "I did."

He frowns, stalling right in front of me.

"Please, take me home."

18

FIRST STRIKE

BRANT, AGE 23

MY CELL PHONE PINGS BESIDE me on my nightstand, jolting me into an upright position.

I wasn't sleeping. I can't remember the last time I got a full night's sleep.

I also purposely put my ringer on full volume because I knew June was going out tonight and I worry like crazy about her.

Reaching over to where my phone is charging, I swipe open the text notification.

Kip: I'm bringing your sister home. She was at a party and I think something happened. She's okay, just a little worked up. See you in a few.

I reread his text message a dozen times.

I think something happened.

I think something happened.

I.

Think.

Something.

Happened.

A thousand gruesome scenarios swarm my mind, and my chest literally aches.

I call him instantly.

Kip answers on the second ring. "Hey, we're leaving in a sec. Had to finish protocol here."

"What the hell happened?" Throwing off my bedsheet, I start aimlessly looking around the room for socks, only to realize I'm already wearing them. "Give me an address. I'm on my way."

"No, stay put. We'll be there in ten minutes."

"Address," I demand, and I hear Kip sigh into the receiver. There's buzz and chatter in the background, and I strain my ear to listen for June—*Is she hurt? Crying? Sick?*—but all I make out is muffled static. "Let me talk to June."

"Brant, I promise you she's okay. Whatever happened wasn't serious—"

"Put her on the phone. Now."

A purring of madness whispers in my ear, and I start pacing the bedroom. Hesitation lingers on the other end of the line, a fleeting pause, and then he says, "I'm sorry, but we need to head out. I'm on the clock. We'll be there in ten, okay?"

"Just tell me what the hell happ—"

"Ten minutes."

He hangs up.

Damn it.

I toss my cell phone onto the mattress, pull a shirt over my head, and march downstairs to wait outside on the front porch.

That's where they find me ten minutes later.

Kip's police car rolls to a stop in front of the house, the tires making prints in the mud from the afternoon rain shower. Both doors push open, and I rise to my feet, meeting them on the cobblestone walkway. June looks wrecked—hair knotted, makeup running down her cheeks in inky streams. Two swollen eyes land on me across the lawn, glimmering like sad blue moons. Kip trails behind her, scratching at his clean-shaven jaw.

"Thanks for bringing her home," I mutter, my tone impressively calm. I shove my hands into my pockets to keep them from grabbing June like a madman and demanding answers, or from punching the wooden pillar beside me in the likely chance that I won't like what those answers are.

June ducks her chin to her chest, then moves past me to the front porch, scuffing the toe of her shoe against the cement. She doesn't say a word.

I walk with Kip back to his cruiser in hopes I can get his version of events. "Did someone hurt her? Touch her?"

Kip lifts his hand to rub the nape of his neck, tilting his head skyward. "You know, I don't have any answers for you, Brant. I wish I did. She wouldn't tell me what happened, but I don't think it was serious."

"How do you know?"

"No visible injuries. She said she wasn't assaulted and I believe her, and she refused medical treatment. She said she made a mistake, and that's all she'd give me."

I swipe a hand down my face, glancing over my shoulder to where June is waiting idly on the porch, her head down.

"Listen," Kip continues, "my guess is she had too much to drink, maybe fooled around with some boy, and now she regrets it."

My fists clench. There's a veil of red over my vision.

"Go easy on her… She's finding her way. My own sister did some pretty heavy shit when she was June's age. Happens to the best of us." He gifts me a small smile that does nothing to quiet my demons. "She's a good kid, I can tell."

The twitter of crickets blends with the early autumn breeze, and I close my eyes, forcing myself to relax. Calm down. Get a damn hold of myself because I don't like what I'm becoming.

Nodding at Kip, I slap him on the shoulder and mutter, "Thanks." I *am* thankful. I'm thankful June is in one piece, home safe.

Kip is a little older than Theo and me, pushing thirty, and while I've only known him for about a year, he's fit right into our lives as if he was always meant to. Kip lost his parents in a tragic boating accident five years ago, so I think the frequent Bailey barbecues have tethered him to Samantha and Andrew in a familial sort of way. He also has a sister, so he understands that connection.

He understands us.

Skipping his gaze across the yard to June, he glances back to me, then extends his palm for a handshake. I accept it. "Keep me posted. If you find out any details I'd want to know about, call me, you hear?"

"Yeah, will do."

With a final smile, he retreats back into his cruiser and makes his way down to the main road.

I turn to June.

She's staring at me now, her arms dropped at her sides, brown hair flittering across her face, sticking between parted lips.

Go easy on her.

My fingers stretch and splay as I advance on her. My heartbeats vibrate through me like a power drill. My insides tense with dread, with anger, with a fierce sense of possessiveness over this woman.

No…this *girl.*

She's just a girl.

A teenager, bound to make mistakes. Destined for missteps.

And I know, *I know*…those missteps shouldn't stomp all over me with steel-toed boots, leaving me shattered and ruined.

"Brant." Her soft voice surrounds me, ripping through the rancor. June closes her eyes, long lashes wet and fluttering, kissing the curve of her cheeks. "Brant, I…"

The tips of my shoes land at the porch step, until we're eye level with each other. I ball my hands to keep them from touching her. "Tell me what happened."

"I…" A carousel of emotion dances across her face, and the wind whips through, stealing her breath, as if even nightfall is loath to hear her sins. June swallows, the delicate bob of her throat capturing my attention for a split second before our eyes lock again. She rushes out the words. "I messed around with Wyatt."

I go still.

Eerily still.

June continues, tripping on her words, desperately reaching for me as she begins to ramble. "I–I don't know why I did it, but I hate myself for it. He said cruel things, vulgar things. Things that make me feel dirty and awful, and I'm so afraid you'll look at me different now and I won't survive that. I just won't." She grips my rigid shoulders, lightly shaking me. "I already feel like I'm losing you, and I can't bear to see you slip away from me for good. You mean everything to me, Brant, everything. You and Theo, Mom and Dad. You're my whole world, and I can't lose a piece of my world or it wouldn't be whole anymore."

"Go inside, June."

She blinks. Her mouth is partially open, her next words eclipsed by my command. June's fingers curl around the fabric of my shirt as her head shakes side to side. "What happened to you, Brant? Why did you wake up one morning and decide you didn't love me anymore?"

My heart decimates into kindling, but I don't reply.

I say nothing, and she takes that as a confirmation.

Something in her eyes dwindles, fades like hopelessness. She is nothing but tattered sails in a big sea.

But she doesn't know the real reason for my silence. She doesn't understand that my sea is being transformed by a deadly typhoon, and I refuse to let her drown in the weight of my waves. "Go inside. Now."

"Brant, please—"

Spinning away from her, I stalk toward my car and I don't look back. I can't watch her standing on that porch, a picture of devastation and confusion, as I speed away down our street.

I just drive.

I simmer.

I nearly boil over.

Ten minutes later, my tires are squealing into Wyatt Nippersink's driveway, my car parked diagonally, my door still hanging open as I fly through his front lawn and start banging on his door.

Wyatt cracks the door a few seconds later, his smirk immediate. He pulls it wider slowly, knowingly, resting his arm against the frame without a care in the world. "Howdy-ho," he greets me through the screen. "Look what the cat dragged in. Or should I say…the kitten."

He purrs.

My claws come out, and I yank the screen door open and shove my way inside, grabbing him by the shirt collar and throwing him up against the far wall.

Wyatt laughs, only losing his breath for a moment. "Testy. Didn't mean to touch a nerve. What brings you by, eh?" He sneers, enjoying this far more than he should. When I don't respond, he adds, "Kitten got your tongue?"

My grip tightens, my forearm perched along his throat.

"No, wait," he drawls. "That was my tongue she had."

"Fuck you. *Fuck you.*" I'm breaking. I'm snapping right in two, and Wyatt Nippersink is going to be the first person to feel the aftermath of my detonation. "What did you do to her?"

"Nothin' she didn't ask for, and certainly nothin' she didn't want."

"She's just a child. She's barely legal, you sick fuck."

"Legal is legal." He sniffs, trying to shove me away, but my grip is iron. He laughs instead. "I see how you look at her, Elliott. I know exactly what you're thinking when you stare at those pouty pink lips." Wyatt chokes a little when I press harder, but that doesn't stop him from spewing out more filth. "Bet you're wishin' it was *your* dick she got wet with that hot, willing mouth of hers. Mmm."

My heart stops. My blood swims with black ice.

"She said it was her first time suckin' cock, but I wouldn't have had a clue. I shot my load in a quick minute. Right down her pretty little throat."

I'm going to be sick.

I think I'm actually going to puke all over his ratty Adidas sneakers.

Stumbling back, I let him go. I let him go because I'm too afraid of what I'll do if I don't. My hands sweep through my hair, balling into fists. My head shakes back and forth. I'm queasy and wrecked, and I shouldn't be any of those things, and that's exactly why I *am*. "Why her?" I swallow, watching him readjust his wrinkled shirt. "Why June? She's sweet, and good, and pure—"

"Because she's yours."

He says it so simply, so matter-of-factly.

Because she's mine.

My jaw clenches. My eyes glaze over. My heart hammers with the final thwacks of bitter truth. They pound into me until my bones feel like they're crumbling into splinters and ash. It takes everything I have to ask him in a frail, pathetic voice, "Why do you hate me so much?"

Wyatt straightens, pushing back his golden-red hair. He looks at me as if the answer is clear as day. "You fucked my sister over, so I'm going to fuck yours."

Wendy. This is about Wendy.

I grind my teeth until they nearly chip. "We broke up. It happens. I wasn't *trying* to hurt her. This isn't the same thing."

His fist slams against the flimsy paneled wall. "That's where you're *wrong.*" Wyatt's voice is booming, anger altering his former unflappable expression. "She's my fucking sister. She's held my hand my whole life, kept me outta trouble, risked her ass to keep me safe. She's my world, my goddamn twin, and you've tossed that sweet heart of hers into a meat grinder more times than I can count. Wendy is a good person, and she doesn't deserve the pain she's suffered at the hands of an asshole like you who could never love her right because he's already in love with his *fucking sister.*"

Deadly silence blankets us.

We're both breathing hard, violently, spitting through our teeth.

I say the only thing I can think to say: "I'll kill you if you touch her again."

Wyatt pauses. And it's that heavy kind of pause, the kind when you know something sinister lurks right around the corner. I brace myself for it.

His grin curls, brimming back to life, as he says to me, "Like father, like son."

I'm off my feet in an instant, my knuckles flying at his face, bones cracking with the gravity of my rage. I tackle him to the nasty carpet, and all I want to do is bury him under the floorboards.

Blood spills from his nose, misting me. His own fist slams against my jaw, sending shock waves of throbbing pain throughout my body. Clearly being the more efficient fighter, he gains the upper hand the moment he punches me, and I'm on my back, my hands going straight to his neck.

My fingers curl. A vicious noose.

He does the same to me.

We're throttling and strangling and gagging.

And then my mother's face flashes to mind, her eyes bugged out, mouth open wide. The life snuffed out of her. The hideous purple tie coiled around her neck, sealing her fate.

My hands release his neck, arms dropping to the floor with surrender. With submission. With the final threads of my humanity still intact.

If he still wants to strangle me, so be it.

I'd rather be dead than become my father.

Wyatt's teeth bare, his stubbled chin wet with strings of saliva. He looks at me, right in my eyes, and I guess he sees a sad white flag staring back at him because his grip loosens and he lets me go. He jumps off me, reeling backward onto the floor, where blood from both our faces stains the already mottled carpet. Inching back until his spine hits the wall, he slams his head against the panels with a final growl and closes his eyes. "She couldn't go through with it," he mutters, and I almost don't even hear him over the ringing in my ears. "She pussied out before I could sink my dick between her lips. Congratulations."

I lie there, staring at the dusty ceiling fan, letting his words sink in.

"Now get the fuck out."

His tone is quiet, calm.

Done.

I pull up on my elbows, still catching my breath. We glance at each other, just once, and there's a flickering of mutual understanding that hangs mutely in the air.

Don't touch June.

Don't touch Wendy.

And the damnedest thing happens—

We obey.

June is curled on her bed when I get home that night, knees drawn up, Aggie tucked tightly in her grip. I hover in the doorway, a broken shadow.

"June."

My voice sounds just as cracked.

But she doesn't take my splinters and holes as any sort of weakness. No, she takes them as an invitation to slip inside.

June jumps from the bed, clad in only an ivory nightgown. She races toward me, slowing to a stop in the center of the room. "Brant."

Her voice quavers. My name pours into the darkness like a plea, an apology, and a confession all at once. Just the sound of her so lost, so crestfallen, has my walls tumbling down for good, as if the last five weeks were nothing but a bad dream.

My legs start moving. I close the gap between us, catching her face between my palms. "Junebug."

She gasps a little, a burst of something. Relief or remorse, I can't tell. Tears glisten in her eyes, glittering with silver moonlight.

Her hands lift to my wrists, curling tight. Holding on. Like she can't believe I'm real.

"You called me Junebug."

My heart squeezes.

I know I've pushed her away; I know that. It's been killing me. But I promised her I'd always protect her, and as long as I'm alive, I will.

I knew it wouldn't be easy. I knew it would be a damn hard promise to keep, but *hell*...I had no idea it would be this hard.

I had no idea the one person I'd need to protect her from was me.

I cling tighter, the tips of my fingers grazing her hair. Silky soft, but not made for me. Not made for my hands to fist, or for my lips to kiss.

This is so wrong.

So, so wrong—and all I've wanted to do is protect her from these feelings.

These confusing fucking feelings.

Wendy poisoned my mind with crooked thoughts, and all I've done is let them fester. Every time I close my eyes, I think of that wretched dream.

I think of June, so sweet and perfect, naked in my arms, writhing, panting, begging me to take her.

It's sick.

I've been derailed. Possessed.

I'm losing myself...

I'm losing *her.*

"Please don't hate me, Brant," she says, pressing her face into the front of my shirt. She inhales deeply, then nuzzles her nose against the cotton. The gesture sends an illicit tremor through me. "Promise me."

I swallow back the poison and hope it doesn't choke me.

"That would be impossible," I say, and it's as honest as I've ever been. With her cheeks between my palms, I tug her head back gently, gazing down at her. My thumbs brush along her skin, collecting the new falling tears. "I can only love you. There's no other way."

"You mean it?"

"Of course I mean it."

A smile lifts on her pretty face, as porcelain as a china doll and just as delicate. But as she stares up at me, her eyes start to squint through the wall of darkness. And then they widen with horror, and her hands fly up to grasp my face. "Brant, you're hurt."

"I'm fine."

I allow her to graze her fingertips along my busted bottom lip. I shouldn't allow it, but I do. I've gone too long without her touch, and my willpower has shriveled up and died.

My heart will be next if I don't step away.

June traces two fingers along the ugly split, with nothing but affection and sweetness glowing in her eyes. Far from the corruption lacing my bloodstream, tainting me with impure thoughts. My eyelids flutter, and I pray she doesn't notice the way I sway, drunk on the feel of something so innocent. Something I never used to question.

I need to go.

I need to figure out a way to protect her from whatever the hell this is, this plague, this sickness, without pushing her away. Without breaking her heart.

Without making her think I don't love her because nothing—*absolutely nothing*—has been further from the truth.

"June." I take her wrist in my hand and lower her arm, catching the flash of worry in her eyes. "Junebug, you should get some sleep. We can talk more in the morning."

I don't let her question it or convince me to stay.

I just go. I walk out.

I can't be in here right now. She's too soft, too vulnerable. I'm still surging with adrenaline. I'm still suffocating on the awful awareness that the child I watched grow up, the angel I swore to protect, the little girl I craved in a million beautiful, innocent ways—is now becoming the girl I crave in the only way I shouldn't.

And it's not fair.

It's not fucking fair.

If my father hadn't murdered my mother, I would still just be the neighbor boy and she would be the girl next door. Instead, he branded us with a label, forced me into something twisted. He turned the only girl I've ever wanted into the only girl I can never have.

But I still love her.

I still love her in all those other ways—all those precious, pure, *good* ways.

And I just have to hope that the rotten love doesn't spoil all the rest.

Lines were starting to blur.

And if there's anything in this world that can mess a man up inside and drive him to the brink of insanity, it's a blurred line.

I did all I could to rid myself of the bad love, without ridding myself of June entirely. I truly did.

I tried to temper it.

Tried to bury it alive.

But here's the thing about trying to bury something that isn't dead—

Sometimes it comes back, madder than ever.

19

FIRST LAW OF NATURE

The first law of nature is self-preservation. Cut off that which may harm you. But if it is worth preserving, and is meaningful, nourish it and have no regrets.

—T. F. HODGE, *FROM WITHIN I RISE*

BRANT, AGE 24

It's June's eighteenth birthday.

The last nine months have blown by like a tumbleweed in the desert, leaving me burned out and sucked dry. We've gotten back into a semi-old routine, with June none the wiser about the insidious feelings that have attached themselves to me like a leech.

She's my Junebug again.

And that's because there's no other option.

There's no other way.

"Yo, Luigi!" Theo hollers, storming in through the back patio, already on his third beer. "Peach wants cake. Hurry it up or I'm gonna start calling you Toad."

My lips pucker as I crane my neck to glance at him in the kitchen. "Why?"

"Toads are slow."

An amused grin pulls into place, and I multitask with the final layer of fondant, while revealing the truth to Theo. "You might want to be sitting down for this, but I have some news. Toad is a mushroom—not a toad."

"What the hell?"

"Don't tell me you never knew this. He looks exactly like a mushroom."

Theo taps the half-empty beer bottle against his thigh, running a hand through his slightly grown-out sandy hair. "I always thought he was a weird-ass-looking toad. Why is his name Toad, then?"

"Because a toadstool is a type of mushroom," I say, unable to hold back my laughter.

"Shit. Shut up. Are you saying my whole life has been a lie?"

"Told you to sit down."

"Fucking hell, Brant."

Theo storms back out the way he came, his voice evaporating as he rambles off this new revelation to the guests outside.

Sorry about that, Mario.

June pokes her head inside a few moments later, her own laughter spilling into the kitchen, shooting straight to my heart. "Theo is losing his mind out there. How could you?" She breezes through the entryway, closing the door behind her, her smile wide and real.

I spare her a glance, popping the candles into the cake as my laughter meets hers. "The truth hurts sometimes." When my gaze dips to the way her stunning birthday dress hugs her curves, and when the scent of her sweet vanilla body mist floats over to me smelling like the cake that sits under my nose, my statement hits a little too close to home.

Luckily, I've mastered the art of disguise, so June is oblivious as she skips over to me perched at the counter, the hem of her shell-pink dress kissing her knees.

She hugs me.

She wraps her arms around my middle, her chin resting on my bicep as she gazes up at me with an innocent, charmed smile. "Mmm. You smell good."

I nearly choke, my hand starting to tremble as I insert the final candle.

Eighteen.

Eighteen.

"Um, thanks." I'm not sure what else to say. She smells good, too, but I'm certain I'd sound a lot creepier if I returned the compliment. "I showered. Works wonders."

June giggles a little, hugging me tighter. "Ivory soap. It's one of my favorite smells because it reminds me of you."

This is innocent. This is completely innocent.

I force myself not to voice aloud all of her wondrous smells that are practically ingrained in me. Lilacs, mostly, fused into the flowery notes of her shampoo. Her citrus body wash like lemon drops. Vanilla cake when it's her birthday, but only on her birthday, and sometimes Samantha's fancy department-store perfume when we go out for a nice family dinner.

Clearing my throat, I force a quick smile and only hold her eyes for a second. "Ready for cake?"

June only wanted a small family gathering for her birthday celebration this year. She's past the age of pony rides, bounce houses, and even giggle-infused get-togethers with her girlfriends.

She wanted something intimate, just her and her favorite people.

She nods, grinning as she speeds ahead of me. "I was born ready for cake."

As night falls, only Theo, June, and I remain on the patio, reminiscing around the firepit. Theo and I are sipping on beer, while June nurses her bottled iced tea. She pulls a lawn chair right beside mine, and Theo sits across from us, his features betraying amusement as he stares into the ambient orange flames.

"That did not happen," June squeals, wrought with giggles, almost as if she's as buzzed as Theo. "Take it back, Theo. You're a liar."

"I'm not a liar. I swear to God. You can even ask Mom. You thought this complete random stranger at the swimming pool was Dad. You tried to go home with him. Only, he was *covered* in chest hair. The hairiest fuckin' guy I've ever seen. And you take his hand and look up at him all innocent-eyed and you say, *'Why did the water turn you into an ape, Daddy?'*"

'She turns beet red, hiding her face behind her hand and curtain of long hair. "Lies. A web of lies." June shakes her head back and forth, insisting through an embarrassed laugh, "I'd recognize my own father."

A smile blooms on my face. "Are you sure it wasn't him?" I question Theo, an eyebrow arching.

Here it comes.

He frowns. "Obviously."

I almost don't get the words out. "I mean, he could've been a toad…or he could've been a mushroom."

June snorts, nearly spitting out her drink.

Theo's head whips toward me, the wound clearly still fresh. "Yes, Brant, I'm sure. And by the way, fuck you, and fuck mushrooms." His flash of teeth and burst of laughter softens his words. "I don't even like mushrooms. Now I'm pissed I always picked him in Mario Kart."

"Fuck mushrooms," June echoes, doubling over with laughter. She tips sideways, her temple falling to my shoulder as her hand cups her mouth.

"Seriously," he says. "Fuck a lot of things, but fuck mushrooms the most."

"Oh my God…that's our new catch phrase, Theo." Her shoulders are shaking, her nails digging into my forearm as she holds herself up. "When we absolutely hate something, we'll say 'fuck mushrooms.'" She can't breathe through her fit of giggles. My frame is literally keeping her from toppling to the patio pavers.

Theo isn't faring any better. He's hunched forward across from us, beer bottle dangling between his knees, his head down. His whole body vibrates with silent belly laughter. "Jesus, Peach." He finally lifts his head with a sigh, tears shimmering in his eyes. "That's gold right there."

I laugh with them, partly because it's funny but also because June has tears trickling over her cheekbones as she comes down from the high, hiccupping, with the side of her face smashed against my arm. "You good?" I grin down at her, nudging her with my elbow.

Nodding, she swipes at the tears tinged with mascara and sucks in a deep breath. She meets my eyes, hers still twinkling. "I think I'm good. Whew." June reaches over me and flicks her thumb across the corner of my mouth, her face mere inches from mine. Vanilla crème invades me. I inhale a sharp breath, noting the sweet smile still curving her lips. "You had a little dab of frosting," she says softly, her nose crinkling.

My mouth tingles from her touch.

Get a grip, Brant. Get a fucking grip.

"Thanks." I take a swig of my beer and look away, trying to ignore the feel of her shoulder still glued firmly to mine, as if she's cold. As if it isn't seventy degrees out, with a crackling fire only a foot away.

I sigh, lowering my beer.

When I glance up, Theo is staring at me. Watching me carefully.

Studying me.

His eyebrows are pinched together, the easy humor gone, his hand fisting the nozzle of his beer bottle in a tight grip.

What does he see right now?

Is there a spotlight on my heart?

Did I give myself away when my eyes dipped to June's mouth for the swiftest second?

I send him a small smile, tapping the side of my beer with my index finger. Theo hesitates for a moment, like he's lost somewhere in his mind, then blinks himself from the haze. He smiles back, but it doesn't feel as genuine.

Unless I'm imagining it all.

Maybe Theo is simply daydreaming about sports, or an inside joke with Kip, or what he wants to do to his girlfriend later.

Maybe I'm going mad, making up wild scenarios that hold no weight.

And that's the terrifying thing about keeping a secret that can rip your whole world apart. Sometimes you hold on too tight and spring a leak. Bits and pieces start to spill out, little by little, and before you know it all your ugly, shameful truths have been exposed.

There's no going back once there's a leak. All you can do is mop up the spillage and pray the damage isn't more than you can bear.

Theo slaps a hand to his thigh and rises to his feet, taking a final chug from his bottle and tossing it into the nearby recycling bin. "I'm gonna take off. I've got a shift bright and early, and you," he says, pointing at June, "have your last week of senior year starting tomorrow."

"God, I don't want to go. It's going to drag. I just want to fast-forward to prom."

"Don't blame you. School is the worst. Hated every second of it." He leans in to June, giving her a big hug, then whispers fondly, "Fuck mushrooms."

June laughs into the crook of his shoulder. "Do not get me started again. I almost peed myself."

"Don't want that. You're officially an adult now. Can't have you regressing already."

She swats at him. "Thank you for coming today."

"Anything for you, Peach. Happy birthday."

I stand from my chair, disposing of my own empty beer bottle. "Need a ride?" I offer.

Theo seems to falter a little. His eyes slide up to me in a slow pull, narrowing when our gazes meet.

My insides pitch with warning.

But then I convince myself I'm imagining things because his subsequent smile is easy and light. Like nothing could possibly be wrong. "Nah, I'll walk. Thanks, though. You still chaperoning Peach's dance thingy next weekend?"

"It's called prom." She sighs.

I nod. "Yeah, I'll be there."

"Cool. Kip and I are on duty that night. Maybe we'll stop by and make sure the princess isn't getting herself into any trouble." He looks pointedly at June, then winks.

She pales. "Absolutely not. That's humiliating."

"Why? One brother is going, why not two?"

His eyes glide back to me. Subtle, so subtle, but damn it, I swear there's something there.

Brother.

Brother, brother, brother.

Theo looks back at June, his smile returning.

June crosses her arms, acting pouty. "Principal Seymour personally asked Brant to be there. It wasn't my choice."

It's true. My old principal always had a soft spot for me ever since he found me crying in a bathroom stall one day after Wyatt and his mates tortured me on the playground.

Asshole.

Principal Seymour transferred over to our town's high school when I was in sixth grade, so he was a part of my life for the majority of my education. He was well aware of my story and frequently checked in on me, making sure I was okay, while sneaking lollipops into my backpack in my younger years.

I'd accepted the invitation to chaperone June's prom, and while I'm looking forward to seeing my old teachers and staff members, it wasn't the main reason I'd jumped at the chance.

June has a date.

A kid named Ryker.

And I plan to keep a close eye on this kid named Ryker, because anyone who has a name like Ryker probably also has a motorcycle, bad intentions, illegal drugs, and an executive suite booked at the Sunnyside Inn under his mom and dad's credit card.

Hell no.

Ryker can ride off into the sunset on his motorcycle all alone after the dance, while June comes home with me, safe and sound.

Theo stuffs his hands into his pockets with a sniff, shrugging. "We'll see how the night goes. Promise we won't embarrass you if we make a quick patrol."

"You'd better not," she says, her pout twisting into a farewell grin.

He smiles warmly, then gives me a short nod before heading back inside the house.

June turns to me as I'm watching Theo retreat, telling myself everything is fine. She gives my arm a little pinch. "Hey. There's something else I want for my birthday this year."

I blink. "What do you mean?"

"It's something you might not like."

My curiosity is piqued as I twist to fully face her. I fold my arms, my brow furrowing with confusion.

June smiles. She reaches out and squeezes my hand, her thumb grazing over my knuckles as the light of the fire dances in her eyes, causing them to glimmer with an orangey glow. "Let's go for a drive."

My feet stop at the gate, a deep-rooted sense of panic sluicing through my veins.

A cemetery looms before us.

"June, I can't."

Moonlight casts its milky glow on shadowy headstones, spotlighting my pain. June stands beside me in a navy-blue jumper, her hair piled up in a high bun, her shoulder pressed against mine. She slides our hands together, interlacing our fingers until I'm squeezing tight. So tight I'm afraid I might break her fragile bones.

Two big round eyes gaze up at me. "You can, Brant. I know you can."

I shake my head. "You shouldn't have brought me here. This isn't your decision."

"Sometimes we need a little push from the people who love us." June squeezes my hand just as hard, telling me I won't break her. She'll be as strong as I need her to be. "You just need to be brave that first time, then all the other times come easy."

My own words echo back at me.

I know I've been a hypocrite.

I'm twenty-four years old, and I haven't visited my mother's gravestone. Not once. When I was just a little boy, I was convinced she'd come alive, bust through the dirt and soil, and grab me with her skeleton hand. Foolish fairy tales, of course. Childlike excuses to get out of doing that hard thing. And the older I got, the harder it became. With every passing year, it felt like a greater distance grew between my mother and me. She slipped farther away.

Maybe there was a tinge of resentment there.

She promised me she'd always protect me. Those were her last words, and I believed them.

But where was she?

She was six feet underground. She was dead, and I was still here.

Somehow, visiting her gravesite would feel like a cruel reminder of that. A cold, bitter reminder of her broken promise.

"I don't think I can."

"I promise you can—"

"I don't want to!" I spin to look at her, my chest heavy with the weight of my buried grief. I'm white as a ghost and feel just as lost. "I don't want to."

If I startled her, she doesn't show it. June lifts her hand to my face, resting it against my cheek. My eyes close. "Yes, you do."

I swallow, nuzzling into her palm. It's an involuntary reaction to her touch. She touches me and I melt. I sink. Inhaling a shuddering breath, my eyes still closed, I freeze when I feel the sensation of warm lips grazing the side of my jaw.

"For comfort," she murmurs. Her lips slide to the opposite side of my face, where she presses a second kiss. "For courage."

My eyes flutter open, and I know it's a mistake. It's a mistake to look at her when she's standing on her tiptoes, one hand in mine, the other holding my shoulder for leverage, and the feel of her sweet kisses still burning my skin. But I do my best to quell the urge to take more than she's given—more than she'll *ever* give—and simply nod. "Okay."

June flattens her feet, a sigh of relief leaving her as she lowers to the ground. A smile stretches, a proud, thankful smile, and she leads me through the gate, our hands still entwined.

I stare at the grass as we wind through headstones, focusing on my swiftly moving feet.

Focusing on her hand tucked warm inside of mine.

Focusing on the cicadas singing to the ghosts.

I keep my mind busy until she slows down toward the middle of the cemetery, a shiny stone plaque moving into my vision. Significant, yet unfamiliar.

Precious, yet frighteningly intimidating.

Caroline Marie Elliott

Mother. Daughter. Sister.

Loyal Protector.

Her words thunder through me:

"I'll always protect you."

Something inside me breaks like a dam. My hands ball into fists and my throat tightens. My heart hurts.

It hurts.

I pull at my hair, spin in a circle, and stare up at the starry sky. "Where are you?" I shout, sounding like a madman, like an unhinged beast. "Where are you, huh? You said you'd always protect me. *Where. Are. You?*"

Silence answers me, as it always does, so I kick at the grass, at the mud, and I fall to my knees, growling my desperate pleas into my hands. "You lied." My voice cracks, quavers. "I trusted you and you lied…"

"Brant." I'm falling apart, right along with the bodies and bones, when June wraps her arms around me, crouched beside me in the grass. "She kept her promise."

I shake my head, tears spilling from my eyes. I'm crying. I'm fucking crying, and I can't remember the last time I cried. "She didn't."

"Shh…she did. She did." June strokes my hair, kisses my forehead, whispers her soft coos of solace into my ear. "She gave you to us, Brant." Her own tears get the better of her, and she chokes out, "She gave you to *me*."

My heart stutters.

My breath hitches, realization dawning on me.

Oh my God.

All this time…

All this time I'd been angry and bitter, thinking my mother had broken her promise. She'd whispered hopeful words into a little boy's ear that she couldn't possibly keep.

But June is right.

My God, June is right.

My mother never broke her promise.

She said she'd always protect me and she did.

Even in death.

She'd written me into her will. She'd written the Baileys into her will. Mom made sure I had a safe, loving home to go to if anything were to ever happen to her—and I think maybe deep down she knew. She knew what my father was capable of, so she took the proper precautions to protect me long after she'd left.

By sending me to live with Samantha and Andrew Bailey, my mother protected me from the legal system, foster homes, temporary families, and so many terrifying unknowns I can't even begin to imagine. How different my life would be right now if she hadn't done what she did. How frightening.

How lonely.

My mother's last wishes were *all about* protecting me, and I can't believe I never saw it.

Fresh tears flood me, and I collapse against June, her arms enveloping me as I bury my face into her neck. She holds me. She holds me so tight, keeping all my broken pieces from scattering.

"Thank you," I croak out, my throat raspy and raw, my voice tired but strong. My heart bruised but free of the heavy weights. "Thank you for bringing me here."

June pulls back, her hands clasped around my neck. Her own tears shine back at me. She feels my pain in the same way I feel it, and I'm not sure what that means. "You might not notice, but I always spritz myself with vanilla-scented body mist on my birthday," she tells me.

I notice.

I hate that I notice.

She continues, pressing her forehead to mine. "I picked it up at a bath and body shop years ago, and the bottle is still practically full. I only use it once a year. It's called Sweet Desserts." Her thumbs massage just below my ears, and her breath kisses my mouth as she speaks. "I bought it because you used to tell me that your mom smelled like desserts. I know my birthday is the same day she..." She swallows, glances up at me. "Well, you know. I wanted to give you a reminder of her every June first—a happy reminder. A sweet memory hidden in the sadness."

A sound falls out of me that I can't take back.

A choking, painful sound.

And if she'd listened close enough, if she'd just strained her ear, she would have heard exactly what that sound said.

I'm hopelessly, irrevocably in love with you, June Bailey.

The desperate, aching kind of love.

The kind there's no coming back from.

The kind there's no way out of.

The kind that's going to be the death of me one day.

I fall more in love with June than I ever thought possible as we clutch each other in a moonlit graveyard on her eighteenth birthday, with my mother on my mind and the scent of sweet desserts dancing in the air.

That night still stands out in my mind all these years later.

Maybe it was because of the closure I felt with my mother's memory, or the way June held me while I purged my ghosts. Maybe it was the vanilla breeze and singing cicadas, or maybe it was the profound knowledge that my heart would never come back from loving June.

But…maybe it was something else.

It was an end. A final chapter.

A swan song, of sorts.

You see, everything changed shortly after that night. Everything fell apart. Life as we knew it was forever altered.

I'm going to tell you about the second time Samantha Bailey ever cried.

It started with a kiss…

20

FIRST TIME'S THE CHARM

JUNE, AGE 18

"Oh, June, honey. Look at you!"

My mother gasps in awe, pulling a pen from her silvery hair then jotting something onto a note card. Dad strolls up behind her with tears in his copper eyes. He's always been the sappy one. Mom is steely and strong, while Dad turns to mush at the slightest sentiment.

"Look at my June," he singsongs, sniffling through his words. "Going to make the boys swoon."

"Dad, come on," I tease. My cheeks heat as I duck my head, landing at the bottom of the staircase. "You like my dress?"

I twirl the skirt, feeling like a true princess. Mom picked it out with me when we had our girls' day of boutique shopping and sugary treats at the pastry café. It's a pale crystal blue, and it reminded me of a radiant sky. In the sunshine, the tulle lights up like a prism, like a rainbow.

It's my "Over the Rainbow" dress… *Where skies are blue.*

Where dreams come true.

Dad swipes at his leaky eyes. "I love it. I love it, sweetheart." He paces forward, scooping me into his big bear arms. "You'll be the most beautiful belle at the ball."

My smile stretches over his shoulder. I feel beautiful—I truly do. My hair is curled into chestnut ringlets, partially pulled up on top with a rhinestone-studded clip. My skin shimmers with glitter-infused lotion, and my face is painted tastefully. I'm excited for Ryker and my girlfriends to see me. I'm the final stop on the limo ride over, giving me a little extra time for family pictures and last-minute preparations.

"Your brothers are going to blow a fuse when they see you. God help any poor boy who dares glance in your direction," Dad says, pulling back to drink me in with pride.

I chuckle, dipping my chin again. Mom fluffs my hair, adjusting a long ribbon of curls over my shoulder and sighing sweetly.

Theo is stopping by for photographs before his shift with Kip tonight and should be here any minute. Brant is outside on the patio.

"I'll be right back," I tell my parents, excusing myself from the living area, gathering my long skirt and making my way to the back door to surprise Brant.

I think he'll love my dress as much as I love it.

Will he think of bright skies and bluebirds flying high, just like I did?

Will our favorite song pop into his head, filling him with magic and warmth?

A smile blooms as I traipse through the kitchen and peek through the glass door. Brant is standing in the center of the patio, staring out at a big tree—the same one that used to hold our childhood tree house. Memories spring to mind of storybook games, grand adventures, and summer sleepovers with flashlights and buckets of popcorn as I huddled in my favorite place with Theo and Brant.

I hate that I fell.

I hate that Dad tore it apart the next morning, closing a chapter of my childhood that will always be near and dear to my heart.

Inhaling a deep breath, I tug open the patio door and step out onto the pavers.

Brant turns to me.

Everything about him seems to go still—his stance, his muscles, even his breath. He just stares at me across the patio, silent and unflinching. The emotion that crosses his face isn't what I saw when Mom and Dad saw me walk down the staircase. It's not the same at all.

He almost looks like he's in pain.

Does he hate my dress?

There's the heat of a thousand suns blazing in his eyes, and I worry that it's anger. "Hi," I say meekly. My lips feel dry even though they're bathed in cherry gloss. Clearing my throat, I take a hesitant step forward, pulling a smile to my face. "What do you think?"

I do a silly twirl.

When I curtsy, then straighten, Brant blinks, appearing to shake himself of whatever emotion stole him away from me.

He averts his eyes for a moment, then looks back at me. "You look stunning."

Warmth trickles through me like a sun-kissed stream. "You mean it?"

"Of course I mean it."

"I wasn't sure. You looked mad."

His gaze flickers over me, and when our eyes lock again, a shiver skips down my spine. His stare is so penetrative, it almost feels like he can see inside me—straight through to my furiously pounding heart. My hand instinctively presses to my chest, as if I can calm the beats.

Brant rubs at the back of his neck, a smile finally lifting. "I was a little mad."

My heart thumps faster. I press harder.

"I was mad I'd have to get this new suit dirty, fighting off all the boys tonight."

A sense of relief washes over me as I drop my arm, laughter slipping free. "It is a nice suit." I take a few steps forward, watching Brant's smile slip further with every step I take. When we're nearly toe-to-toe, I lift my hands to adjust the little blue bow tie, his Ivory scent mingling with a new cologne. Something woodsy and clean. "Your bow is blue like my dress," I note.

That wasn't planned. It makes me smile.

Brant's eyes are fixed away from me as he says, "It's a pretty dress."

"It reminded me of our song. Blue skies, bluebirds. When the light hits it just right, it glitters with every color of the rainbow. It reminded me of…"

It reminded me of you.

My cheeks stain with blush at the realization that it *had* reminded me of him. Brant's face had flashed to my mind the moment I saw it.

I lower my hands, sliding my palms down the front of his chest as my thoughts drift. He snatches them. "What did it remind you of?"

Our eyes pull back together.

I swallow. "My childhood. Lullabies and things like that."

I'm not sure why I lie, but thinking of my brother as I purchase a dress for prom—to wear for a boy who probably wants to rip the dress right off of me—feels...*strange.*

Wrong, somehow.

He'd likely be horrified by that response.

Brant blinks, releasing my hands and taking a small step backward. He scratches at his dark hair, glimmering with various flecks of golden highlights in the setting sun. "Well, I love it, Junebug. You look—"

"Hell no, Peach. Absolutely, no." Theo storms out onto the patio with a knitted shawl Grams made for Mom last winter. "You're wearing this."

I spin toward him as he drapes the scratchy cloak of yarn around my bare shoulders. My nose scrunches with distaste. "It itches. And it smells like ancient dust bunnies and dying plants."

"It smells like no one's gonna touch you tonight."

I glower at him. "It doesn't match at all. This isn't even a color, Theo." *Is it brown? Burgundy?* No one knows. "I'm not wearing this. Fuck mushrooms."

"You—" He falters, blinks...then bursts into laughter. His whole body shakes when he laughs, and that always makes *me* laugh. Theo sighs, adjusting the holster around his waist. "Touché, Peach. Touché."

Brant slips past us, giving Theo a smack on the shoulder as he sweeps by. His gaze trails to me for only a moment, and the smile I give him goes unseen as he disappears into the house. Swallowing, I return my attention to Theo. He's looking at me funny. "What?"

His lips twitch. "Nothing."

"You have a look."

"I'm just thinking about how I'm going to get out of an assault charge when your date tries to lay a finger on you tonight. Felonies don't mesh well with my line of work."

I snicker. "What on earth will you do when I get married one day? And have babies?"

He visibly shudders, and I flash back to my fever dream from years ago. I think about Theo and his speech I never got to hear, and how it was more than likely a laundry list of threats toward my future husband. A grin crests with amusement, only to fade the moment I remember who my groom was in the dream.

My cheeks burn.

So weird.

"Well…" He sighs, shoving his hands into the pockets of his slacks and glancing toward the sky. He taps at his holster. "It's a good day to save someone."

"It's always a good day to save someone." I smile fondly.

"Yeah, I guess it is." Theo's eyes glisten with affection when they skip back to me. "I'm proud of you, Peach. You know that, right?"

My grin grows brighter as I shuffle in place on bare feet, tiny pebbles biting into my soles. "Yeah, I know."

"You're smart and wise, and so fucking kind. I can't wait to see you light up a stage one day with your talent and with that big beautiful heart of yours. You're going places, Peach, you really are. And I'll be cheering you along, all the way to the top." He raises his hand, placing it atop my shoulder and squeezing gently. His dark-blue eyes glint a little lighter when the sunshine hits them just right. With a cheeky smile, he finishes, "And I'll kick the crap out of every single boy you try to take with you."

I rip off the shawl and chuck it at the back of his head as he bolts into the house, his laughter trailing behind him.

I cup a hand over my mouth in shock.

No way. There's no way!

Celeste fidgets in front of Mr. Kent, wringing her hands together, her skin flushed as red as her sheath dress. Overplayed pop music drowns out the sound of her voice as Genevieve and I sit shoulder to shoulder at a round table a few feet away, trying to hide our squeals of disbelief.

Mr. Kent takes a step back from Celeste, scratching at his neck and glancing around the room. He's even sweating a little.

"She's crazy," Gen whisper-shouts into my ear. "She's absolutely nuts."

I giggle under my breath.

When we entered freshman year, we made a pact. We each had to perform a spectacularly stupid dare on prom night. We don't get anything out of this, of course; no trophy or golden medal. Only our combined mortification, mutual respect, and a lifetime of "I can't believe we did that" giggles.

Honestly, I thought my friends had forgotten about our silly little pact, but Celeste brought it up the moment we gathered around the table and our dates took off to drink punch and talk sports.

Celeste's dare came easy. She's had a crush on her math teacher, Mr. Kent, since the moment she set foot into his classroom. Gen and I dared her to confess her deepest fantasies to him. The naughtiest of fantasies, the kind that would make a grown man blush.

It seems to be working.

He's blushing profusely.

Gen's elbow rams into me when Celeste turns and skips across the dance floor in her high heels, her face the deepest shade of fuchsia I've ever seen.

"Oh my God. Oh my God. Oh my God." She mumbles it over and over before she collapses into a chair and buries her face in her arms. She tosses her cell phone onto the table with a recording of the whole conversation—*delicious proof.* "I hate you both. I hate you both so much."

We nearly die of laughter.

Mr. Kent strolls by our table, exiting swiftly, clearly rattled and embarrassed.

"Don't hate us, Celeste. Retribution is so much sweeter." Gen waggles her eyebrows at me, our friend crumpled between us over the table. "Who's next? Me or June?"

Celeste sits up straight, blotches of red still painting her face. "God, my heart is beating out of my chest. Give me a minute to make sure it doesn't give out." I slide a glass of water over to her, and she takes it eagerly, gulping it down and collecting herself.

My attention wavers when Brant steps into the ballroom with my chemistry teacher, Miss Holland. I dart my gaze over to him, stiffening as my teacher laughs at one of his jokes. The sound of her cackle has my arm hairs standing at attention, and I don't know why. She's older than him—beautiful, sure, but at least a decade his senior. I frown, watching them interact. Brant leans back against the wall, folding his arms and looking light and carefree. He doesn't give her that same look he gave me on the patio when I debuted my ball gown, the look of fire and brimstone.

I pick at the sequins on my bodice, gnawing on my bottom lip as I watch them tease and tell jokes. At one point, Brant seems to check out of the conversation, as if he's distracted. He looks away from her to scan the room, glancing from table to table. He's looking for something.

And then his gaze lands on me, perched at the table on his right.

He smiles a little, his posture relaxing. His eyes fill with warm relief, as if I was what he was looking for.

My hand lifts in a small wave as I return the smile.

And when I glance back at Celeste, she's grinning devilishly. My insides pitch. "What? You've thought of my dare, haven't you?"

"Oh, yeah."

Her focus is pinned on Brant, causing my heart to flutter with worry. "You're not allowed to make a move on him. He's off-limits." It's a silly thing to demand, but he's my brother. It would be too weird.

The evil gleam in Celeste's eyes doesn't fade. "Not *exactly* what I had in mind," she says breezily, then leans in to Genevieve, shielding her mouth from me so I can't hear what she's concocting.

Gen gasps. "No way. She'll never do it."

"She has to. It's the dare."

My own heart is now beating so fast, I fear it might escape. "What? What is it?"

Gen pulls her lips between her teeth as she straightens, glancing over her shoulder at Brant, then back at me. "Oh, girl, prepare yourself."

"*What?*" I'll go mad if they don't tell me right now.

With a dramatic intake of breath, Celeste pivots toward me and announces my fate: "Kiss Brant."

The air leaves my lungs.

The room spins.

My skin starts to sweat.

"N-No... What? No." I'm shaking my head, horror drenching me. "Are you insane? He's my *brother*."

"He's not *really* your brother," Gen says. "He's not blood."

"It doesn't matter. That's sick! It's twisted. You're both out of your minds."

Gen shrugs, leaning in to me. "Listen, you can't tell anyone, but I have a huge crush on my stepbrother. It was super weird at first, but it happens, you know?"

My eyes pop. "I don't have a *crush* on Brant. You're acting crazy. This was supposed to be fun."

"It's supposed to be humiliating," Celeste intervenes, holding up her hand. "I can attest to that. Go on now, June. Don't disappoint us."

Both girls giggle at my impending doom.

I bite my lip, my objections all caught in my throat. Glancing over to Brant, I find him looking at me again, but he turns away the moment our eyes meet.

I gulp. "How can I? He'll be disgusted. Horrified. He'll hate me forever." I let the words rush out, hoping to change their minds. There must be something else I can do. *There must be.*

"He's not going to hate you. It's just a silly dare." Celeste stares at him from across the room, her smile wicked. "As far as I'm concerned, you have the easiest dare by far. Look at that man."

No. I won't look at him.

And if I do this, I'll never be able to look at him again.

"Come on, June. You can't chicken out on us." Celeste places her hand over mine, a gentle encouragement. "Everything will be fine, and you'll both laugh about this by morning."

My chest twists with terror. My stomach swirls with dread.

But...maybe she's right. If I don't accept this dare, I might be forced into something worse—stripping naked in front of my classmates, or coming on to a teacher far more appalling than Mr. Kent, or having to kiss someone else.

Someone awful, someone I don't even care about let alone love.

I love Brant. He loves me.

All will be forgiven.

Sucking in a deep breath of courage, I nod with flimsy resolution—but with resolution nonetheless. Flipping my hair over my shoulder, I rise from the chair, then smooth out the tulle of my skirt. "Fine."

"Fine? Shit, okay." Celeste pops up from her own seat, snatching Gen by the wrist. "Let's go."

"Wait, you can't come with me. I can't have an audience… This is unbearable enough."

"We have to see it, June. We need proof. Slip into the hallway behind the double doors and we'll just watch through the glass window."

"Kiss him in the hallway? Someone will see us," I snap back.

"The rest of the venue is all closed down. No one will be wandering on the other side of the doors."

Oh God.

I may vomit.

"Fine, okay, just…give me a minute, then come over once the door is shut." My heart is ricocheting off my ribs. "And I hate you both more than I've ever hated anything in my life. Remember that."

They just laugh at me.

Gathering my wits, I lift my chin with an air of conviction I absolutely do not feel. My mouth is dry, my palms sweating. I walk over to Brant, almost rolling an ankle in my dumb heels, and his attention pulls toward me as I approach. I wonder if he can see that I'm actually dying right now. I'm passing away and floating up to the clouds at this very moment because my spirit would much rather get the hell out of Dodge than go through with this.

I stop in front of him, picking at my freshly painted fingernails.

A smile brightens his face, and he pushes up from the wall. "Junebug. Having fun?"

"No."

He frowns.

I clear my throat, backtracking. "Yes. I mean yes… Um, can I borrow you for a minute?"

"Everything okay?"

"No." *Damn it, June.* "Sorry. Yes. I just want to tell you something."

He knows I'm acting like a true basket case, so he steps toward me, close enough that I can smell the soap on his skin. His eyes dance across my face, no doubt trying to figure out why my cheeks are redder than the punch and why my left eye is twitching sporadically. "Okay. Of course."

"This way." I force a weird semi-smile and stalk away, expecting him to follow. He does. *Damn him.* Coughing a little into my fist, I lead him down the long hallway and slip through the double doors. Then I stall my feet, spinning around to face him when he joins me on the other side.

Brant lets the door swing shut behind him, his brow furrowed with confusion. "Why are we over here?" He senses something off about me and moves in closer, his hand extending to my forearm. "You're scaring me a little."

It's so quiet on this side of the doors, and I fear he can hear my heart screaming in terror. I lick my lips. "I'm not trying to. I just...I have to do this."

He shakes his head, a baffled laugh slipping out. "You're not making any sense. Do what?"

Breathe in.

Breathe out.

Just get it over with, June.

"This."

I don't think. My hands lift, reaching up and pulling his face down to mine. His stunned breath is the last thing I hear before our lips crash together, and I'm inching up on my tiptoes, my palms clasped around his jaws, my mouth parting on instinct.

I didn't intend to part my lips, but I do.

We just hover there for a moment, our breaths heavy and unsteady, turning into pants the longer we linger, while our mouths connect in a way they never should.

And then something happens.

I don't know what happens, but *something* happens.

I feel his hand cinch around my waist, while the other drags up to my hair, tangling in the mound of loose curls. My pelvis jerks forward without warning.

Then he kisses me.

Truly kisses me.

An involuntary sound spills free when his tongue slips inside my mouth. A sound I'll never understand, could never explain away. A sound that has him making an identical sound. This isn't my first kiss, but *my God*...it feels like it.

My tongue flicks against his. I feel him shudder against me as his grip on my hair tightens. He groans, pulling me closer to him as our tongues touch and taste for the very first time.

Forbidden. Illicit. Scandalous.

Wrong, wrong, wrong.

But I don't pull back. I don't shove him away.

In fact, I move closer. Closer than I ever should be, my hands trailing from his face to his hair and fisting gently. He groans again as he deepens the kiss, sweeping his tongue over mine, over and over until I'm mewling and gasping and grinding myself against him.

Brant pulls back, breathless. His eyes are dark and stormy, brimming with lust and confusion. He doesn't let me go. He holds me tight, squeezing me as he says, "Why did you do that..." It's not even a question. He says it like a breathy growl of defeat, as if he just lost something he'd been fighting desperately for.

My lips feel puffy and swollen. Tingly.

I stare up at him.

I don't know what to say.

But I couldn't speak if I wanted to because his mouth crushes mine again in another bruising kiss. A moan pours out of me. A terrible, wicked sound that I wish I could take back. This is madness. Sinister madness that has me drunk and light-headed, scared out of my mind.

He nicks my lip with his teeth, then plunges his tongue into my mouth, both of his hands rising to cradle my face. He cherishes me as he ruins me. His fingertips burrow into my cheeks while we kiss each other desperately, faces angling to taste deeper, harder, my hands still pulling at his hair, nails digging into his scalp. Pants, moans, growls. His erection presses into me. My whole body hums and burns as I suck his tongue into my mouth and feel him tremble.

I'm wet.

My panties are soaked through, I can tell.

My God, what are we doing? What the hell are we doing?

Alarms begin to drown out the coil of hunger spiraling low in my belly.

Warning signs sweep across my mind, stealing my attention.

This is Brant.

This. Is. Brant.

Panic seizes me, and I find the strength to pull back, my startled cry hitting the air when our mouths part and I shove him away from me. Brant's chest is heaving, his eyes glazed and wild. Hair a mess. Skin flushed, lips kissed raw.

Oh my God.

I think I hear something in the distance, a plethora of footfalls, but I don't wait around.

I bolt.

With tears rushing to my eyes, I bust through the double doors, nearly plowing over Celeste and Genevieve who were watching from the other side. I don't stop to drink in their horrified expressions or see whose footsteps those were.

I just run. Fast and furious, all the way out the main entrance and into the parking lot where I can finally stop to catch my breath.

I don't look back.

21

FIRST RESPONDER

THEO, AGE 25

"YOU'RE SUCH A SUCKER, BAILEY."

I smirk as our cruiser rolls to a stop at the back of the country club, where a small group of dolled-up teenagers are sucking on cigarettes. "We'll just do a quick sweep and make sure these kids are being law-abiding citizens. Can't have any underage drinking or wild orgies commencing, eh?"

"Because you were such a saint at eighteen."

Kip throws me a knowing grin and kills the engine. I shrug, fondly recalling my own senior prom. Monica blew me in a utility closet.

It was great.

And it's the exact reason I'm here right now—can't have Peach finding her way into any sketchy closets, getting pressured into performing despicable acts with that son of a bitch, Ryker.

Dumbass name.

Kip follows me through the lot as the four teens toss their cigarettes to the cement, snuffing out the cherries with their shiny shoes and glittery heels. They look terrified, silencing their conversations and pretending to check their phones. I nod at them as we pass and enter through the back door, sighing at their reaction.

I hate it.

Most of the cops in my department love the power trip…the air of intimidation that comes along with a badge and a uniform. They plod around with puffed-out chests, somehow thinking the loaded weapon in their holster is making up for the inadequacy between their legs.

Not me—I really fucking hate it when people cower when I walk by, or avert their eyes when I try to send them a smile. I hate that they avoid me when I'm only trying to help.

Kip gets it. His passion for saving people is just as great as mine, ever since he lost his parents in a suspicious boating accident. He's not about meeting ticket quotas or terrifying civilians into submission. He just wants to make a difference.

This is why we make damn good partners.

The sound of shitty mainstream music fills our ears as we move through the rear of the venue, peeking into empty rooms, making sure there are no teen moms in the making. Static from our radios penetrates the otherwise quiet hallways.

Kip takes it as the perfect opportunity to ambush me with his unwanted advice about my sister.

"You'll need to start loosening that leash soon, so you don't lose your mind when she breaks away for good." Kip's words of warning trickle through me, and I respond with a grumble. He adds, "You can't keep an eye on her forever."

"Says who?"

"Says the guy who tried to do that very thing and failed. Jocelyn despised me for two solid years because I micromanaged her personal life and scared away her boyfriend at the time."

"Good for you. If the pussy ran, he wasn't good enough for her."

Kip lets a grin slip. "One hundred percent."

We fist-bump.

"But that's not the point," he continues, taking long strides beside me, his thumbs hooked into his belt loops. "The point is she hated me. Didn't talk to me for years because she was pissed off and resentful, and that hurt like hell after already losing our parents. I had nobody."

I rub a palm down my jaw with a sniff. "Yeah, well, Peach isn't prickly like that. She's too soft to stay mad at me for long."

"That's because she hasn't found a guy you actively want to murder yet. Wait and see how she reacts when you try to stick your nose where it doesn't belong, and the guy she loves breaks her heart." He spears me with a pointed look. "She's going to break your heart in return."

The thought sends a nasty shudder down my spine.

Glancing at my partner, I notice that his sharp, angled features seem to mellow at the flash of worry in my eyes. I clear my throat, trying not to appear ruffled. "I got it covered, partner. Peach isn't going anywhere, I can promise you that. Family is everything to her. Mom and Dad, me, Brant..." My skin hums with subtle intuition. An irritation, really, like tiny needles tiptoeing all over me.

I scratch at my arms.

"If you say so, Bailey."

The music gets louder as we round a corner then traipse up a staircase that leads to an upper level. I realize Kip is making some valid points, but I'm a stubborn bastard, and my stalwart love for June has always trumped reason. Ever since I was a rascally kid, I'd wanted a sister. A little princess I could protect. I thought it'd be easy to keep her safe from dragons and black magic, keep her tucked away inside a stone castle, but sometimes the enemy isn't always black and white. Sometimes the monster slips through undetected, disguised as things we don't expect.

Sometimes, the monster is already inside.

To this day, I still feel the guilt and sense of responsibility from when I discovered little June crumpled in a pile of dead leaves at the bottom of our beloved tree house. Those feelings tether me to my mission in a profound way. Bone-deep. I'd promised to always protect her, and I let her down the instant some immature girl batted her pretty eyes at me. June almost died that day, and I know I never would have forgiven myself.

So all I can do now is make up for it.

Every good deed, every life saved chips away at that hollow block of shame.

And Brant? Well, he's always been my trusty sidekick. My partner in crime, but more so in justice. A brother through and through, despite his inability to accept that title.

It bothered me.

It bothered me a whole hell of a lot as we were growing up, and I never understood why he ran from something most people craved.

Family.

It still doesn't make sense to me, but he suffered through a tragedy, and I don't think anyone can really make sense out of tragedy.

Only...something else has been bothering me lately. Something that's kept me up at night, made my wheels spin out until I hydroplane so badly that I pull myself from the ugly wreckage and convince myself that I'm seeing shit that isn't there. Shit that's too fucked-up to warrant even an ounce of speculation.

Something far worse than any monster, demon, or foul beast I could ever imagine or create.

"The dance is this way." Kip's voice breaks through my dark thoughts when I veer off in a random direction. He gives me a sharp smack on the shoulder, but it doesn't rattle me as much as my own inner workings. "You good?"

"Yeah, I'm good. I—" My cell phones buzzes in my front pocket. Veronica's name lights up the screen with a text message and I smile, a warm fuzzy feeling replacing the poison. "Hold up, it's the girlfriend."

Kip waves a hand at me as if to say "carry on."

Veronica: I have a surprise for you :)

Ooh. A surprise from Veronica either results in sexual favors or...

Actually, that's it.

She's pretty easy to figure out, but I'm sure as hell not complaining.

Me: New toy, new lingerie, or new position to try...? ;)

Veronica: *gasps with horror* How dare you assume that I'm only trying to get into your pants. Lingerie.

Me: Cheeky minx. I guess I might have to dip out of my shift early. Not feeling so well tonight.

Veronica: It's not flu season, but it could be flu season. Hurry home, Theodore. ;)

Ah, the full name.

She's definitely horny.

I send her a few suggestive emojis as Kip chuckles beside me. "What?" I'm still smiling when I glance up at him.

"Nothing. I just miss that."

"Sex?"

"That's not the issue. It's the other stuff." His finger circles in front of my mouth, where I'm still grinning like a lovestruck idiot. "The feelings. Being smitten. You know…love."

"I'm not in…" I stop short because I don't necessarily believe what I'm about to say. Maybe I'm in love. Hell, I'm not so sure I know what it even feels like, but it's different from my relationship with Monica. That was a roller coaster of toxicity and back-and-forth insanity.

This is…something sweeter.

Veronica is someone I'd draw my sword for in a heartbeat.

Maybe that is love.

My palm glides along the banister overlooking the lower level as I glance back down at the inappropriate meme Veronica just sent me. Laughter slips through as I tell Kip, "You know, I think I do lo—"

Two hands suddenly plant against my chest, shoving me backward.

My hackles rise, confusion blanketing me.

"What the hell are you—"

"Go. Turn around." Kip's face is pinched with distress. His voice is gravelly. His body blocks me from moving past him to see what the fuck is going on.

I shove him to the side, but he immediately swoops back into my line of sight. "Kip. Get the fuck out of my way."

"Turn around and walk, Bailey. That's a goddamn order."

Our eyes lock.

My heart pounds.

And then I hear something.

A moan, or a gasp. Something from right below us that has me glancing to my right, unable to see anything due to Kip's hulky frame. My gaze flicks back to his. A dark warning glints in his eyes, and I think I know. I think I fucking know.

A surge of adrenaline has me plowing past him until he stumbles back, and I storm over to the railing and peer down over the edge.

My veins freeze with ice.

Bile burns the back of my throat as my stomach churns, and I almost double over and retch.

Brant and June.

Brant and my baby sister.

Kissing.

Grinding.

Panting and moaning.

His tongue is down her throat.

His hands are in her hair.

His hips are thrusting against her as he desecrates the sweetest thing I've ever known.

I fucking fly.

I book it down the staircase, two, three steps at a time, nearly spilling down headfirst as June pushes Brant away, then makes a mad dash through the double doors.

"Theo!" Kip flies after me. I can hear him, barely, but it's hard to hear anything over the sound of my blood hissing, my heart exploding, and my sanity snapping in two.

Brant stares at me, unmoving.

Like he's in shock.

My fists turn to stones as I race toward him. "I'm going to *kill* you."

Inhaling a sharp breath, Brant shakes his head back and forth, his hand finally extending as if he's trying to slow me down.

No chance.

Fuck that. Fuck him.

He's fucking dead.

I tackle him, my knuckles flying at his face. "She's your sister." I punch him again, blood spurting from his nose. "She's. Your. Fucking. *Sister.*" My arm lifts again, angrier than the first two times, but it's stopped short when Kip grabs me by the wrist and yanks me off of Brant with some kind of superhuman force. "Let me go, asshole. *Let me fucking go!*"

Brant lies there, one knee drawing up, his hand cupping his face.

I think I hear something come through on our radios, but blind rage rings louder.

My arms are still flying, legs flailing, while Kip continues to drag me back in a deathlike grip. I'm snarling like a rabid bear, saliva dripping down my chin. I point at Brant, who's trying to pull himself up on his elbows as rivers of blood paint his face red. "That's it, isn't it? I finally fucking figured it out." My chest heaves with anger, madness, sorrow. "You never accepted me as a brother because that meant you'd have to accept June as a sister." Brant is breathing heavily, still swinging his head back and forth. Blood spills down his nose, jaw, mouth, staining his suit collar. "And you couldn't, could you? Because this whole time you wanted to *fuck her!*"

The last two words purge out of me in an animalistic roar.

"Theo, get a *fucking* hold of yourself." Kip still grapples with me, keeping me reined in before I let loose and kill the man I've considered a brother since I was seven years old. "We have to go. A call came in." He spins me around, fisting the front of my uniform with one hand as the other smacks against my jaw. "Do you understand me? We have to go. *Get it together.*"

He shakes me a little. The red haze over my vision starts to desaturate, and I blink, swallowing down the soot and squalor in my throat and nodding my head. "Yeah, okay…*fuck*. I hear you."

I shove his arms away, bending over to collect myself. I think I hear Brant behind me, pulling to a stand, his own breathing as ragged as mine. He doesn't say anything. There's nothing he could possibly say.

"This isn't over," I grit out through bared teeth.

Kip grabs me by the arm. "Let's go."

He's probably worried that I'll fly off the handle again.

He should be.

"You hear me, asshole?" I don't want to see his face. I don't want to look at him, but I do. I whirl around and find Brant staring off to the side, hands pulling at his hair, his hazel eyes wet with pathetic fucking tears, face smeared with blood.

He looks gutted.

Shaking.

Guilty.

I growl, my anger escalating. "This isn't fucking over!" My body moves to lunge at him again, but Kip whips me backward, practically dragging me down the corridor. My words echo through the hall as Brant stares after me, looking nothing like the brother I thought I knew.

We make our way to the scene with lights flashing, siren blaring, and tires squealing down congested streets.

My heart pumps viciously beneath my ribs.

I can't shake the image of Brant and June tangled up like lovers, their tongues twisting, bodies writhing.

It's nauseating.

Maddening.

Kip hasn't said a word from the driver's seat as we cruise at a breezy sixty-miles-per-hour, my fists squeezed white-knuckled in my lap. He just sits there in heavy silence, one hand on the wheel, and the other holding his jaw like he's deep in thought.

There's been an accident along Route 83, our main drag.

I wonder if it could possibly be any worse than the train wreck I just witnessed.

A sigh finally fills the space between us as Kip shifts in his seat, glancing in my direction. "Tell me you're good. If you're not, I'll get Mitchell on the phone right now and—"

"I'm good." My fingernails bite into my palms. "I'm good, Kip."

"You didn't know?"

My head jerks to the left. "Did I know what? That my adopted brother has been wanting to put his dick inside my little sister?"

Queasiness claims me.

I feel light-headed.

Dizzy.

I suck in a deep breath.

Kip is quiet for a few beats, leaning back, his fingers tapping along the wheel. "I just mean…you've had a front-row seat to their relationship your entire life. If anyone would have suspected anything, I figured it'd be you."

Suspected.

Yeah, sure, it's crossed my mind more than once lately—that dark shadow following me around, whispering down my back, filling me with nasty thoughts. There's been signs. Fleeting touches, heavy eye contact, long hugs that teeter along the line of innocent and illicit.

But I thought I was going crazy, losing my damn mind.

How could he…?

How could they…?

I swallow. Brant and Peach have always been close—extremely close. They've shared a bond so concrete, so unbreakable even I could never hammer my way through. I never understood it. I was never able to pinpoint what drove their mad affection for one another, what nourished it or, hell…what sparked it in the first place.

My relationship with June was built on loyalty, security, and a fierce, protective love.

My relationship with Brant was built on shared interests, respect, and a powerful common denominator—*June.*

But Brant and June? They were always something else entirely.

I asked Mom one day when I was just a little punk, pissed off because June wanted to ride her bike with Brant instead of have a sword fight with me in the backyard, why June loved him more than me. Mom told me I had it all wrong.

She didn't love him more. She just loved him differently.

I thought it was a stupid answer at the time, but now I can't help but spot those "differences" as my mind reels in reverse like a spinning time machine.

Was this inevitable?

If Brant had never come to live with us, would they have still gone down this same path?

It's too much to process right now.

My fists still tingle with suppressed rage.

My heart still feels galloped on by steel hooves.

"Talk to him. Fix this." Kip's voice is calm yet assertive as he sits beside me, as if listening in on all the things I'm not saying out loud. We pull up to the scene of the accident, my teeth grinding together as he finishes. "Life's too short to hate the people we love the most."

I sniff. "I'm not the one who needs to fix anything."

"Then allow him to fix it."

We spare each other a sharp glance as he veers off to the shoulder, where two mangled cars sit before us. "I don't know if I can."

"That's your ego talking, Bailey," Kip says, unbuckling his belt. He pauses for a beat. "Trust me on this. It's not worth it."

My jaw clenches.

"Listen…June is going to end up with somebody, right? It's inevitable. You can't keep her from falling in love, no matter how hard you try. At least you know where Brant stands. You *know* him. And you know he loves her."

It's too much.

It's too much to consider right now as I run a hand through my hair, shaking my head. "Yeah," I mutter. "I guess."

I unbuckle my seat belt and force the situation from my mind for the time being.

Time to be a saver.

Exiting the patrol car, we make our way toward the three pedestrians that are standing near the guardrail, one woman tending to a gnarly gash along her temple.

I make the rounds to check injuries and am taking statements when Kip says, "Bailey, there's a child over here."

I turn to the red sedan with the right end smashed up against the concrete barrier. The engine smokes as pungent fumes travel over to me, and I zone in on a little blond head whipping around in the back window. A girl.

My feet start moving.

Kip is already ripping open the back door as I glance into the driver's seat and discover an elderly woman slumped over the steering wheel, unconscious and unmoving, while her tiny lone passenger cries in the back seat, strapped to a booster. The girl is on the passenger's side, partially entrapped by the crumpled metal.

Pulling open the driver's side door, I dip inside to check the woman's vitals while the little girl wails in terror from the back seat. "Hey, hey. You're okay." I look back, taking in her tearstained face and bloody lip that looks like she bit right through it. "What's your name, little princess?"

The woman has a faint pulse. I breathe out a sigh of relief while we wait for the ambulance to pull up. We're trained not to move anyone who's been injured in an automobile accident, so we need to wait for the medics to arrive. All we can do is keep the little girl calm and distracted.

"How about that name?" She must be only three or four. Her golden ringlets remind me of June at that age. "My name is Theo. This is Officer Kip."

Kip has the back door open, one hand resting atop the hood, his head poking inside as he smiles at the preschooler.

She sniffles, her eyes wide and glistening with blue fear. "Anna."

"You're okay, Anna," I tell her, giving her a look of reassurance through the crack in the seats. "We're both here to help you. You're going to be just fine."

"Gamma fell 'seep."

The elderly woman in the driver's seat hasn't moved. I force a half smile onto my face, nodding at her grandmother. "She's just taking a little nap. Do you like naps?"

Kip adds, "I love naps."

Anna shakes her head, tears tinged with blood. "No."

"You will when you get to be old like us."

I swear I see a little grin stretch onto her face. It takes me back. It takes me way back to the days of imaginary fairy tales, tree-house sleepovers, and whimsical adventures in the backyard with Brant and June beneath cloudy skies and giant mulberry trees.

Innocence.

For a minute, I can see it. I can envision June's rose-stained cheeks and dark-blond curls as she ran as fast as her stubby little legs would allow, with me and Brant purposely trailing behind her. We'd let her think we couldn't catch her—that she was fast and clever, mightier than us both. We'd always catch her, though. Brant would tackle her to the ground and blow raspberries onto her belly, while I'd pretend to fight off the invisible goblins and warlocks until the sun began to set behind a crimson-orange horizon.

Then we'd pass out beneath the tree house in sleeping bags and ratty old quilts, sunburned and sapped, but happier than we'd ever been before.

I miss that.

Swallowing, I shake away the memories as an ambulance sounds in the distance. Anna stares at me from her half-tipped booster, her eyes big, filled with worry. "Do you have a big brother or sister, Anna?"

"Yes. A bwuva."

Kip's smile is laced into his voice. "Wow, a brother, huh? I bet he takes good care of you."

She nods.

"I'm a big brother, too. We both are. I bet he really misses you right now."

She nods again. "He call me Anna Banana."

I share a charmed glance with Kip, then reply, "I call my little sister Peach, so that's—"

And then I hear it.

Screaming.

Terrified screaming that sends a flurry of chills down my spine.

A shrieking voice behind me fuses with squealing tires, yanking me out of the car, and I spin around to find a flash of headlights careening right at us. Out of control. Erratic.

Destined to hit us.

It's one of those slow-motion movie moments that no one ever thinks actually happens in real life. But it does. It really does.

Your heart is in your ears, beating like a hollow drum.

Th-thump. Th-thump. Th-thump.

Your blood is pumping hot and fast, reminding you that you're still alive. For a few more moments, anyway. It's almost like an out-of-body experience, and it's so fast, so quick, just the blink of an eye.

You only have a split second to make a choice.

A decision.

And I always knew what I'd do if I was ever faced with a decision like this. Ever since I was a young boy. I just knew.

I wanted to be a saver.

So that's why I do it.

That's why I use that second to shove Kip into the back seat, knowing that it's the only second I have. I don't have another one.

I don't have two seconds because that next second has me pinned against the red sedan from the waist down as the vehicle slams into me, shattering my bones, devastating my insides, while a sharp, strangled breath is forced out of me.

The pain doesn't register right away. I'm not sure what exactly registers as my arms lay draped over the top of the sedan while my eyes glaze over. I'm slightly aware of the spattering of blood sprayed across the hood, the blood that came out with that rush of breath.

I'm partly aware of the ambulance that pulls up beside me as people gather and gasp, while a smoking hunk of metal is the only thing keeping my insides together.

I'm vaguely aware of Kip screaming at me from the back seat of the vehicle, trapped, unable to help me.

"Theo! *Theo!*" He's shouting at the top of his lungs, somewhere far away. Muffled, murky. "Fucking answer me, Bailey! Goddamn you!" His voice drowns out with radio static and a dull ringing in my ears. "Officer down..."

Officer down.

But it's not him who's down—it's me.

Kip is okay.

He's alive.

It's not him.

My lips quiver as I try to speak, too quiet for Kip to hear me. But I pretend he's right here, laughing with me, telling me this will be a good story to look back on one day as we reminisce over a beer. "I–I knew it was a good day...to save someone," I tell him in a choppy breath.

The thought brings me peace as my eyelids flutter, a dull, hot pain slicing through me. It's the kind of pain that sends you into a dizzying spiral, into a black abyss, where your mind shuts off because it just can't fucking deal.

Fuck, it hurts.

Cold sweat slicks my skin. My teeth start to chatter as everything around me blurs. Just a haze of shrill noise, undistinguishable words, and dancing tendrils of light.

I hate that it's going to end this way.

I hate that Brant's last memory of me is filled with violence and bloodshed after he's already experienced so much of that.

A tear slips.

A single tear trickles down my cheek, filled with so much regret that I'm not sure what hurts more—my pulverized insides, or my heart.

My shattered legs, or the heavy burden of grief resting on my shoulders.

And hell, maybe it's the Pale Horse galloping up beside me, or maybe truth shines a little brighter in the floodlights of mortality, but…*fuck*, I get it now.

I *know*.

I think I've always known.

A weighty sigh falls out of me as I blink through the film over my vision. And when I rest my cheek atop the hood of the car…I think I see her. Golden-blond curls bouncing behind her as she floats over to me, a picture of sweetness weaving through the chaos.

It's little June, small and young.

She's moving closer to me as my tension drains, my body going limp, and a smile lifts through the pain.

She looks like an angel, like the little princess I've always tried to save.

But not today.

Today, I think she's here to save me.

"Peach."

I know it's not her. I know she can't really be here, fifteen years younger. Everything is shutting down, and I'm hallucinating. Going into shock.

It's just a trick.

"Pretty as a peach, you are. You'll keep dancing, right?" Little June does a twirl, the pink skirt of her princess dress fluttering as her laughter tickles my ears. "You gotta…keep dancing."

Another face materializes in the crowd; a medic, I think, rushing toward me. Nothing more than a fuzzy shadow, saying things I can't understand.

He looks frantic. Trying to reach me. Desperate to help me.

But there's only one thing I need help with.

A message.

This paramedic is my only messenger.

"Tell Brant…" I inhale a slow, shuddering breath. My teeth are still chattering as I force out words. "Tell him…it's okay."

Darkness whispers down my neck, eager to swallow me whole, but I force it away. I fight it. I drown it out before it drowns me because I need to purge before I plummet.

"You have to tell him…June…it's okay."

I don't know if I'm making any sense.

Colors and noise swirl around me, and I think he's speaking to me.

Telling me not to worry.

It's not me I'm worried about.

"Please, tell him. Tell Luigi…" I shiver. I exhale. I use the last of my strength to give *Brant* strength.

To give him *peace.*

He can't think that I hate him. God, he can't think that at all.

"We came first…Mario and Luigi, right?" A nostalgic smile twitches on my mouth, and for a moment I pretend the paramedic is Brant. I picture his dark hair and dimples, his hazel eyes glimmering with grief. I turn this blurry stranger into my brother.

I pretend that he's Brant because I *need* him to be Brant.

"I need you…to be Mario, now."

I think I hear giggles.

Childlike giggles.

Calling to me, beckoning me.

Not yet. Not yet.

"Take care of Peach because…no one…" My eyelids flutter. My throat tightens. My heartbeats stutter and slow. "No one will ever love her…like we do."

I start to fade out.

Dizzying lights flicker in my mind's eye.

I think I hear something, a horrible cry, a ghastly moan, but it dissolves into the giggles still tempting me someplace else. "Promise me...you'll tell him, right?"

Tell Brant. Please, tell Brant. He has to know.

I'm not sure if the medic ever responds, but I think he does.

He must.

He must promise me because something inside of me releases.

A burden. A weight.

I feel free.

Sound evaporates as I drift away, clinging to those giggles I hear echoing in the distance. Just beyond the beacon of light.

I race toward them.

Peace blankets me as I run, my bare feet tickled by grass blades while I chase a ladybug through the backyard. There's a sword in my hand. A gallant sword, designed for battle.

Created for saving worthy things.

Those worthy things are sprinting beside me through the yard, young Brant on my right and a tiny June on my left. Her soft curls are glowing in the golden sunset, smelling of baby powder and lilacs. We collapse underneath our magical tree house with adventure in our eyes and innocence in the air.

Brant moves in next to me, and we sit shoulder to shoulder with a little princess tucked safely between us. He looks over at me with a watery smile. "I'll take care of her, Theo. I promise."

I smile back as the sun settles behind a fluffy cloud.

We're happy here.

We're untouchable.

We're forever young.

"I know you will."

22

OF THE FIRST MAGNITUDE

BRANT, AGE 24

PEOPLE MAKE SUCH A BIG deal about firsts.

First steps, first words, first kiss, first love. They're often celebrated and recognized. Revered. There's applause, fireworks, toasts, and smiles.

But here's the thing about firsts—

There's always a last.

Nobody likes to think about that. There's no joy in taking your last breath, saying your last goodbye, or whispering your last words.

And when I met Theodore Bailey for the first time in my driveway while my father arranged stones around our mailbox, I sure as hell wasn't thinking about the last time I'd ever hear his voice.

"Hey."

I glanced up from my chalk design on the driveway. I was trying to draw an elephant, just like Bubbles, but it looked more like the weird mole on my dad's leg. "Hey."

"I'm Theo."

"Yeah, I know."

"How do you know? I just moved here last week."

My tongue poked out as I tried to make the elephant's nose longer, but now it was too long. I'd ruined it. I sighed as I fell back on my heels. "Your mom is my mom's new best friend. They were drinking lemonade together and talking about stuff."

"What stuff?"

"Mom stuff. You know... like, recipes and the weather and cute babies."

Theo scratched at his mop of light-brown hair. The color reminded me of the shoreline at the beach when the sand got wet. "Want to be friends?"

"Yeah."

"Want to be best friends like our moms?"

"Definitely."

We smiled at each other as Theo sat beside me on the driveway, looking down at my drawing.

But when I went to stretch my legs out, he stopped me.

"Hey, wait!"

Leaning across my legs, Theo tipped his finger to a crack in the driveway with a wondrous, crooked grin lighting up his face.

"What? What is it?" I asked.

Then I saw it.

A squiggly caterpillar crawled onto the tip of Theo's finger, causing him to giggle. "He tickles."

Awestruck, I stared at the strange creature as it wiggled and wormed its way up his hand and onto his knuckles.

"You almost squished him," Theo said, glancing up at me. His smile brightened as he returned his attention to the caterpillar. He grazed a finger along its fuzzy body and whispered, "Don't worry, little guy... I saved you."

No, I wasn't thinking about our lasts.

I wasn't thinking about how he'd look dying in front of me, smashed between two vehicles as blood oozed from the corner of his mouth.

This can't be happening.

Hands are holding me back as I try to claw my way through the human barrier, looking on helplessly.

"Theo... Theo, stop. You're okay. Do you hear me?" I shove at the two police officers keeping me from diving into the scene, but they maintain their hold. "You're going to be *fine*."

He smiles a little.

I swear he smiles as his cheek rests against the hood of the red sedan, his eyes glossed over, fixed somewhere just beyond me.

He's limp. Helpless.

Paramedics surround him, but he doesn't notice.

Tears are crawling down my face, tunneling through the dried blood left by Theo only thirty minutes ago. He was full of life and hating me only *thirty minutes ago*, and now…now, he's giving me his blessing.

He's telling me goodbye.

"Take care of Peach because…no one…" He's fading. He's dying. He's fucking leaving me. "No one will ever love her…like we do."

"*Theo…*" A painful growl of penitence shreds me from the inside out, forcing me to my knees as the two officers loosen their grip. It's a wretched sound that tears through the night, echoing off the wall of sadness hanging heavy in the air, and thundering back into me like a wrecking ball of regret. "Don't do this. Please, don't do this," I cry. "It's you and me. It's always been you and me."

"Promise me…" I can hardly hear him. His eyes are glazed, looking at nothing, as he whispers his final words. "You'll tell him, right?"

Fuck.

Fuck!

I nod, despite the fact that I don't want to answer him. I don't want to give him any reason to fucking go. But I do because I have to, because it's important, and because he needs to know on his dying breath that I will *always* take care of June. "I promise."

My eyes burn with hot tears.

My whole body tremors with sickening disbelief.

"Theo…*please*…fucking please don't do this…" I practically moan from my spot in the middle of the road.

I don't think he can hear me anymore.

I don't think he ever knew I was even here.

"There's no Luigi without Mario," I croak out, my voice shaking.

I think he's gone.

I think he's fucking gone.

"No..." My growl escalates into a desperate roar. "Don't you dare fucking *leave me!*"

He's not moving.

He's not moving.

A woman in uniform with purple earrings appears in my line of sight, her hands extending toward me like she's trying to calm me down. Trying to keep me down. Trying to prevent me from *breaking* down.

Her mouth moves, but I can't hear her.

All I hear is a faraway voice slicing through my fog:

"I'm calling it. 9:03 p.m."

A time.

A time of death.

The officer in front of me tries to ease my pain as I release a strangled cry, but all I can see are her purple earrings. It's all I can focus on.

Purple.

The color of death.

I lurch forward onto my hands and vomit all over the cement.

A sob follows, pouring out of me, my body burrowing into the roadway, gravel biting into my skin.

The jaws of life work to remove Theo from the wreckage—Theo's *body*—and that's when I fall back on my heels, bile still stinging my throat, and I zone out. That's when everything turns into a foggy, slow-motion cloud of numbness. I can't watch this. I can't watch the boy I grew up with, the man who called me a brother, peeled off of a smoking piece of metal, reduced to nothing more than a hollow shell, while a woman with purple earrings tries to soothe my broken heart.

This can't be happening.

This.

Can't.

Be.

Happening.

I've lost my best friend—the Mario to my Luigi.

I've lost one of the only people in my life who's been by my side from the beginning, who accepted me, who offered me friendship in my loneliest hours and laughter in my saddest.

Who knew my deepest, darkest secrets and loved me anyway.

Who used his last moments on earth to forgive me for breaking a childhood promise.

Who told me it was okay.

But it's not okay… He's gone.

Theo is gone.

And now I have to go tell June that her brother is dead.

23

HEAD FIRST

JUNE, AGE 18

"ARE YOU SURE YOU'RE OKAY?"

Ryker holds me close as we sway to the romantic song, his hand pressed into the arc of my back. His opposite hand holds mine in a loose grip, while his eyes search my face with a hint of worry.

The dance is almost over.

Prom night is dwindling to an end, and instead of feeling fantastic and free, I'm feeling like a horrible traitor.

A traitor for kissing a man I had no business kissing.

A traitor for slow dancing with another boy after kissing that man.

I'm confused, disoriented, and terribly broken.

"I'm okay." The lie is muffled in the baby-blue corsage tickling my lips. "I don't feel very good."

Ryker stiffens a bit as his palm squeezes mine. "Do you…do you not want to go to the hotel with us tonight?"

The cautious disappointment in his tone is evident.

He was hoping to get lucky.

My friends and I all went in on a big hotel room for post-prom fun, but it will be impossible for me to have any sort of fun now after what transpired tonight—after that dare gone devastatingly wrong.

Stupid dare.

Stupid Celeste.

Stupid, stupid, stupid.

I swallow, shaking my head. "I'm sorry, Ryker. I think I need to rest."

He doesn't reply, but his whole body tenses.

And maybe I should feel guilty for backing out of our plans, but I already have far worse things to feel guilty for.

What happened?

What the hell was that?

Brant's face flashes to mind: the usual warmth of his earthy eyes blazing into fiery passion when he stared down at me, his fist tangled in my hair. My cherry lip gloss smeared across his mouth. The flush of his skin as he groaned with want.

My brother. *My brother!*

God, how could I? What on earth was I thinking?

And why…*why* did he respond like that?

It was only supposed to be a dare. A silly, immature dare. Instead, it became a death sentence that will hang over both our heads. Forever.

There's no erasing the way our tongues ravished one another's.

There's no silencing those awful, lustful moans.

There's no pretending he wasn't painfully hard and I wasn't humiliatingly wet.

There's no going back in time and taking it all back…and I'm sick—absolutely *sick*—that our beautiful, precious dynamic has been forever altered.

Tainted.

Hot tears blur my eyes as I nuzzle into Ryker's suit coat, searching for comfort that doesn't exist. He glides his hand up and down my back, unaware of my moral crisis. Oblivious to the destruction I've caused. Ignorant of the fact that I'm wishing it were *Brant's* chest my face is buried against while he soothes my ravaged heart and whispers into my ear that it will be okay.

We will be okay.

Sniffling, I force a smile, trying to shake away the sorrow. "Sorry, I didn't mean…" My words trail off when I pop my head up, and my peripheral catches a glimpse of something over Ryker's shoulder. Something alarming.

Brant.

His face.

He looks beaten. Brutalized.

Oh God, what happened?

I push away from Ryker, his queries of concern mere gibberish as my brain tries to process what I'm seeing.

Brant is hovering just inside the entrance of the ballroom, his jaw bruised, blood crusted on his skin. And I want to run to him, ask him what happened, tend to his wounds, but...but there's something else.

His eyes.

His eyes are pinned on me, glistening with pain.

Rivers of tears have sliced through the dried blood smearing his cheeks, and I'm desperately confused, taking a slow step forward and shaking my head.

Brant starts walking toward me, his hand lifting, cupping his mouth.

He shakes his head right back at me.

His face morphs with anguish, and I know.

I know something is horribly, devastatingly wrong.

My skin prickles with dread as I watch him approach me, and only then do my eyes slide over to his left, landing on a familiar man in uniform.

But it's not Theo.

It's Kip—wearing that same pained expression.

It's Kip.

Why is Kip here? Where is Theo?

Why is Brant walking over to me, tugging at his hair, still shaking his head with tears in his eyes, as if he's trying to tell me something that's too awful to be said with words?

The crowd seems to part as the two men approach me on the dance floor, while I just stand there, frozen like a statue.

Time stops.

Everything around me moves in slow motion.

A song is playing, something happy and upbeat.

And then it hits me.

It hits me.

My heart drops out of me, straight to the floor, and so do I.

I buckle.

I collapse before they reach me.

I collapse into a pile of horror, screaming with disbelief.

I'm screaming.

Brant races toward me, too late to catch me. But he still tries, sliding to his knees and wrapping his arms around me, holding me close as I disintegrate.

We sob and we shake, clutching each other while people gather around and the music cuts out, the happy song replaced by my horrible screams.

And it's there on the dance floor, amid balloons and ball gowns, that I have my first full-fledged asthma attack.

"You were unsure which pain is worse: the shock of what happened, or the ache for what never will."

—SIMON VAN BOOY, *EVERYTHING BEAUTIFUL BEGAN AFTER*

24

FIRST MOVE

BRANT, AGE 24

SHE HUGS ME FROM BEHIND as I wash the dishes.

Lilac and ambrosia waft around me when her arms encircle my midsection, linking in front of my chest. She presses her cheek into the arc of my back and lets out a heavy sigh that warms my skin through the thin layer of cotton.

There's nothing unusual about this hug. Nothing off. June always hugs me like this, and I've come to expect these hugs over the years—crave them, even.

But it's different now. Everything is different.

I drop a plate.

The white porcelain slips from my grip the moment she gives me a light squeeze, and while I try to catch it, try to keep my hold on it, I try too hard.

It falls harder than it would have if I'd just gracefully let it go.

Glass splinters into three jagged pieces at the bottom of the sink, causing June to jump back.

I swallow, my jaw clenching.

A weighty pause fills the air as my fingers curl around the edge of the countertop.

"Sorry," she whispers, fracturing the thick silence.

I turn to look at her. Her eyes are wide and glistening, her bottom lip pulled between her teeth. She stands only a foot away, wringing her hands together as she gazes up at me. Apology, longing, and grief tangle together, each one holding a different meaning for both of us.

My eyes pan to the floor as Samantha enters the kitchen.

"What happened? I heard a crash." Dark circles and a hollow blue stare fix on me, then on June. "Did something break?"

Her question hangs heavy between the three of us. June visibly flinches.

Pressing forward on the edge of the counter, I close my eyes.

Something broke.

Something broke twelve days ago when I bolted from that god-awful dance with blood pouring from my nose, the memory of June's tongue still wet and hungry in my mouth and her delicious moans vibrating my skin. I booked it with tears biting at my eyes as Theo's murderous threats still lingered in the air, his enraged fists causing my busted face to throb and tingle.

I told everyone that I'd slipped...

...and I suppose it wasn't a lie.

I slipped.

Slipped up.

Slipped into a dark, deadly void I may never be able to climb my way out of.

I lost my footing in the worst way, and it's the kind of fall you don't ever recover from.

Then I ran like a coward, drunk on grief, sick with disbelief, and drove right through the scene of a grisly accident.

A man in uniform, pinned between two vehicles. Blood spattered along the hood of a wrecked car, red on red. Another man, trapped inside, shouting with anguish.

Chaos.

Catastrophe.

A nightmare that would haunt anyone who had the misfortune of witnessing it.

But the worst part?

It wasn't just any nightmare.

It was *my* nightmare.

Theo was that man in uniform.

It was his blood decorating the red sedan, his body crushed between two pieces of unmerciful metal.

It was Kip trapped inside, begging for his partner to answer him.

It was me slamming to a stop, stumbling from my own vehicle and watching my world fall apart as my best friend, the man I'd just betrayed in the worst way, died before my eyes with forgiveness laced into his final words.

Forgiveness for me.

It was also me who buckled to the pavement when they announced his time of death, sobbing into my hands and begging for it to not be true.

9:03 p.m.

It was me who watched Kip get pulled from the wreckage, disheveled and devastated, along with a little girl and elderly woman, all alive—all destined to live another day.

Because of Theo.

Because Theo sacrificed his life for theirs.

It was me who cried harder after hearing those heart-wrenching details, and it was me who carried the painful burden of breaking the news to June.

It was June who watched me approach her on the dance floor, her face turning white, a mask of panic and confusion.

It was June who collapsed against me and had a blindsiding asthma attack when the realization sank in that her brother was gone.

It was Samantha and Andrew Bailey who rushed to the hospital.

It was Samantha and Andrew Bailey who met me in the waiting room, terrified for their daughter's well-being, only to be informed of even graver news.

Their son was dead.

It was me who caught Samantha as she fell, a scream tearing from her lips.

It was me who consoled her as she cried. She cried for just the second time since I kidnapped baby June on that terrible night, and she cried so hard, I wondered if she'd been saving all her tears for that moment.

It was Kip who comforted Andrew, filling him in on the harrowing details as they both wept in a quiet corner of the waiting room.

It was me who held June after her diagnosis and subsequent release. We broke down together in the middle of the hospital parking lot, clinging to each other as if we were all we had left.

And it's me, right now, a week after Theo's funeral, knowing exactly what broke, but only having the resolve to mutter, "A plate."

Silence festers around me, and I open my eyes.

Samantha looks haggard as she tinkers with the sleeve of her baggy sweatshirt, her eyes vacant. A chasm of bleakness.

A gaping, missing piece.

Blinking, she clears her throat and glances at June, who's standing idly beside me with a similar emptiness painting her face. "June, honey, maybe we can sit down and discuss colleges tomorrow. If you're up for it."

The dark cloud hovering over us sparks with a brewing thunderstorm as June tenses, her eyes flashing with lightning. "You want to talk about colleges?"

"Of course. You need to decide where you're going to go."

"No, I don't."

"June..."

She holds back a rainfall of tears, her hands balling into fists. A long, messy braid hangs over her shoulder, swinging against her T-shirt as she shakes her head with incredulity. "I don't want to go to college. I don't want to leave the town my brother took his last breath in."

Samantha gasps a little. Just a sharp, painful intake of air.

I blink out of my haze and reach out a tentative hand to June. My fingers lightly graze her elbow, and she startles for a moment, only relaxing when she realizes it's me. She softens as our eyes lock. The storm passes.

June finishes through trembling lips, "And I don't want to leave the only brother I have left."

I stiffen.

With a lingering look, she moves away, sweeping past her mother who stands rigid in the center of the kitchen, her skin pasty, her hair pulled up into a ratty mound of mats.

Samantha lets out the breath she was holding and finds me staring after June, probably looking as wrecked as I feel. "You'll talk to her?"

My gaze skips back to Samantha. "What?"

"About the colleges. It's important. She needs…she needs something to look forward to. A distraction. A purpose."

"She needs time to heal, Samantha. It hasn't even been two weeks."

"Mom." She worries her lip with her teeth, ducking her head away from my frown of confusion. "Would it kill you to call me that?"

My breath stops.

My heart clenches.

Samantha has never asked me that before. The Baileys have always respected my decision to address them by their names instead of Mom and Dad. They know it's not because I don't love them or appreciate their kindness and nurturing over the years. It's simply a deep-seated childhood response to what happened to me, and it's one I've carried with me all my life.

But now Theo is gone.

I'm the only son she has.

Guilt eats at me.

Stepping forward, I approach Samantha for a hug, for sympathy, for an apology that I'll never be exactly what she needs…but she steps away. She retreats.

She offers the apology instead.

"Forget it," Samantha mutters softly. "I'm sorry I said that."

She sighs, then spins on her heel and exits the kitchen without another word. Without a backward glance. She leaves me alone to finish the dishes, and I make my way back to the sink.

The silence is deafening, so I turn the faucet on full blast, hoping to drown out the memory of Theo's laughter, his jokes, the way June would squeal when he picked her up and threw her over his shoulder until she was dangling upside down. I zone out, trying not to think about the special moments we shared in this kitchen—disastrous cooking lessons, family dinners, comical bickering over chores, and late-night munchies when we'd stay up until sunrise engrossed in epic video game marathons. I sigh, wishing for June to return and wrap her arms around me again, and knowing I would hug her back.

I stare down at the broken plate, wondering how I can piece it back together.

The doorbell rings, pulling me from thc depressing cave of bedcovers that are well overdue for a wash. It's almost noon the following day, and I'm still buried deep inside my blanket fort. I had to take a bereavement leave from the restaurant, too scattered to focus, too broken to perform, so the days are all bleeding together and time doesn't seem to exist.

I traipse from my room in a white T-shirt and athletic shorts, my hair looking like a bird's nest made of grass and twigs. When I turn down the short hallway to the staircase, I falter. I pause, pivoting toward the opening of Theo's old bedroom, now a guest room.

Andrew is sitting on Theo's bed.

He's just sitting there.

Staring at nothing.

A deep ache hollows out my heart, and I have to look away. It hurts too much.

Ring, ring.

The doorbell chimes again, startling me back to the present moment, and I make my way down the staircase to the front door.

It's Wendy.

Surprise claims me for a beat. While she made an appearance at Theo's wake to pay her respects, we didn't talk much. We haven't talked much at all since she infected me with her depraved perspective on my relationship with June. A perspective I've come to internalize to the point of imminent annihilation.

Resentment bubbles to the surface, but I'm not sure if it's aimed at Wendy for digging up my buried feelings or at myself for allowing them to exist in the first place.

"Hey." I pull the door open wider, letting her inside. "What are you doing here?"

Wendy hesitates before stepping through the threshold, her burgundy hair pulled up into a loose bun and a purple silk scarf around her neck.

My eyes narrow at it, my teeth clinking together.

"Sorry to bother you," she says, dangling a little gift bag from her fingers. Her copper eyes are wide and glossy, shimmering with sympathies. "Chef Marino wanted me to bring this by for you. He sends his condolences."

She hands me the bag, and I peek inside. "Chocolates?"

"His renowned hazelnut truffles."

A smile lifts. Pauly sent me a handwritten card after hearing about Theo, telling me to take off as much time as I needed—that there would always be a place for me when I was ready to return.

It meant a lot.

For as prickly as Pauly comes across, there is something genuine about him. Something sincere.

"Thanks," I murmur.

She nods. "Of course." Wringing her hands together, Wendy clears her throat, glancing down at her sandals. "How are you, Brant?"

The truth?

The watered-down truth?

A blatant lie?

I've never understood that question in the aftermath of grief and loss—especially when it comes from people who aren't equipped to handle the truth.

And if a lie is what they're after, why bother asking?

"I'm not good, Wendy." The truth wins out, causing her head to snap up, her brow furrowing with worry as if she anticipated the lie. "In fact, I've never been worse. I can't remember the last time I showered or dragged myself out of bed before noon, and I don't really know how to move on from any of this. I'm not okay. And mostly, I wish I could go back in time and take Theo's place."

Her lips part, but no sound passes through. She takes a hesitant step forward, her hand extending for a hug, or a touch of comfort, but she's stopped short when a new voice sounds from behind me.

"What is she doing here?"

I swivel around, spotting June at the bottom of the staircase, her hand curled white-knuckled around the railing. A hardened look is etched into her typically soft features, and she's dressed in nothing but one of Theo's old T-shirts, the hem skimming her thighs.

She looks at me, then at Wendy, her eyes squinting with distaste. "You're not welcome here. We're grieving."

"I was asked to stop by." Wendy glances in my direction, a silent plea for help, before addressing June. "Brant's boss wanted me to bring him a gift."

"Brant's boss has his phone number and address. Why send his ex-girlfriend?"

"I offered."

The two women silently stare at each other, the air charged with animosity. June is hardly ever combative, so her disposition jars me. Clearing my throat, I take a tentative step toward June. "It's fine, June. It's just chocolates." I hold up the bag for emphasis.

"It's not fine." June crosses her arms, her shirt inching upward. Her eyes darken to blue coals as she keeps them pinned on Wendy. "She's using your trauma to try to win you back."

"That's ridiculous," Wendy cuts in, moving forward.

"Why are you wearing that?"

"What?" Wendy looks down at her outfit. "What are you talking about?"

"That scarf. It's purple." June stalks toward her, her eyes full of spite and sorrow. "Why would you wear that?"

"You're acting craz—"

June rushes at Wendy, yanking the scarf from around her neck, tears leaking, body trembling. It flutters to the wooden floor. "If you actually cared about Brant, you wouldn't wear that," she spits out. "Just go! You're not welcome—"

"Whoa, hey." My shock dissipates, and I jump between the women, my attention on June as I grip her upper arms and walk her backward, away from a stunned and wide-eyed Wendy. My voice is low, gravelly. Infused with concern. "What are you doing?"

"I..." Her cheeks are flushed pink, lips quivering, as her gaze skates from me to Wendy, then back to me. "I'm sorry..." She swallows, shaking her head. "I'm sorry, Brant."

The anger dims from her eyes, replaced with only grief. Soul-shattering grief. When my grip on her loosens, she pulls free and spins around, dashing back up the staircase.

I'm compelled to chase after her.

I stall briefly, turning to watch as Wendy picks up her scarf and spares me a wounded glance before slipping out the front door. Then I make my way to June's bedroom.

Andrew is still sitting on Theo's bed as I pass by.

Still staring at nothing.

Fuck.

Fuck.

Choking back a lump of sorrow, I find June curled up in the corner of her bed, legs drawn to her chest, face buried. Aggie is tucked inside one arm as she sniffles into the valley between her knees.

While I stare at her from the doorway, I'm drenched in a familiar sentiment, and a single word slips out before I can think it through. "Junebug."

She freezes, the word echoing all around us.

Junebug.

I haven't called her that in weeks. How could I? That nickname was born from innocence and purity. Unsullied love.

But now I know the sound of her desire. I've memorized the way her curves melt into me when I tug at her hair and make love to her mouth. I've witnessed the blue flames in her eyes when she looks at me in a way she should *never* look at me.

God, why did she kiss me?

Why did she have to go and do that?

And why was I not strong enough to resist her?

The name causes her eyes to flare when she lifts her head, a softness trickling in for a split second.

A flicker of…relief.

She looks at me. She looks at me and in the single heartbeat that skips between us, I know we're both thinking about that kiss.

We haven't talked about it. Haven't even mentioned it.

If it hadn't burned its way through my skin, sizzling my bones and scarring the marrow, I'd have wondered if I imagined the whole thing.

When June and I walked out into the hospital parking lot the night Theo died, June held a prescription for an inhaler in one hand and my trembling palm in the other. It had only been hours since our lips tangled, our tongues twisted, and our bodies rocked against each other, shamefully tempted by something we should never think to crave.

But a lot can happen in a few hours, and it did.

The unthinkable happened.

At the end of the day, two tragedies occurred that night—and when placed together side by side, a forbidden kiss was nothing but a small crime.

So when June let go of my hand as our feet stalled beside my car and raised her chin, finding my eyes with a look of pure devastation, I gave her what she silently begged me for.

A mutual understanding.

An absolution.

A shared promise that we'd sweep it under the rug for good.

Erased.

And then we both shattered, falling apart in each other's arms, rocking against one another in a completely different way. I peppered kisses into her hair with apology instead of want. I held her with comfort instead of passion. Our moans bled into the night with loss instead of lust.

June curls a piece of unwashed hair behind her ear, her grip tightening on the childhood elephant.

I dip my eyes.

She can't see the truth hiding behind the wall of grief; I can't let it free. I can't let it whisper in her ear and spill my dark secret—that kissing her fundamentally changed me, and there's no erasing it.

There's only pretending.

Pressing forward, I keep my head down. "I'm not going to ask you if you're okay," I tell her, stepping up to the edge of the bed and placing my hands in the pockets of my shorts. "I'm only going to ask you what I can do to help ease even a fraction of your pain."

A small sound breaks free. Angsty and raw.

I brave a glance at her still huddled in the corner, her bare legs stretching as she clings to her stuffed animal. Tears continue to track down flushed cheeks as her swollen eyes search my face. June slicks her tongue over her lips as she whispers, "A lullaby."

A lullaby.

Our lullaby.

"I can do that." My voice sounds frail. Far away. "Anything you need."

She scoots over, gesturing for me to join her on the bed, inhaling a shuddery breath as she reins in her emotions. Her eyes don't leave my face. Her clutch on the toy only strengthens.

Chewing on my cheek, I move toward her.

One leg raises, my knee pushing into the mattress, then the other. I crawl my way over to her until we're shoulder to shoulder, side by side, and June instantly presses into me like I'm her personal cocoon. My arm lifts to wrap around her shoulders, tugging her closer, feeling her shake with a new wave of tears. She nuzzles her face to my chest, and I prop my chin atop her head.

We sit like that for a while, my back against the wall and June molded against my torso, a moment made of lilacs and melancholy.

And then…I sing.

I sing her favorite lullaby, partially off-key, nearly cracking on my own remorse, and June continues to cry until her body goes still and her breathing steadies. I sing about rainbows and blue skies, and I wonder if that's where Theo is right now. Somewhere over the rainbow, a happy little kid again, laughing and loving, rescuing things in need of saving.

Only, the things in need of the most saving are right here—nestled together like two lost creatures sheltering from the cold.

June lifts up slightly when the song fades into silence, dragging Aggie over my hip and placing him in my lap. Her voice is scratchy as she says, "Take him, Brant. He's a good friend."

I look down at the well-loved toy with ratty fur and wrinkled ears. Some of the plush is rubbed raw, the white inner stitching peeking through from where June gave him one too many kisses or held him a little too tightly. I shake my head. "No, he's yours."

"I want you to have him. You already lost Bubbles, and I broke my promise. I never found him for you."

"I don't need Bubbles anymore," I tell her softly, pressing a kiss to her hair. "I'm okay."

Her eyes draw up to mine, wide and watery. "You only say you're okay so you can be strong for me. But I know you're not. You're in need of comfort, too."

"I have comfort, June," I say. Cupping the back of her head with my palm, I pull her back down to my chest and braid my fingers through her long, limp hair. I sigh, a smile breaking through as she curls back in to me. "I have you."

I should have known she'd find her way into my bed.

Vulnerable, teary-eyed, and wracked from nightmares, she crawls in beside me, stirring me from my own restless slumber. "Brant."

My name is whispered on a broken breath as fingers slide their way through my hair and a warm body presses to mine.

Alarm bells sing as my eyelids flutter open.

She shouldn't be here.

Not now. Not anymore.

She's too fragile, too lost, too pliant.

And so am I.

Backing my hips away from her warmth, I let out a sigh: equal parts turmoil because she shouldn't be here, and solace because she is.

"June," I murmur, loathing the shakiness in that single word. "Go back to bed."

I see her head shake back and forth through the dark room while moonlight illuminates her falling tears. "Don't make me, Brant. Please."

"You shouldn't be here."

"Why not?"

This time I can justify it. This time I have a reason. Swallowing, I grit out as gently as I can, "You know why."

Her breath hitches, her fingers still twining through my hair.

I know it's harmless.

Innocent. Pure comfort.

But now all I can feel are her hands in my hair, tugging at it desperately, like when our mouths were locked together as moans poured from her lips.

My nether regions begin to rouse at the memory, and I inch backward. "Please. Go."

"I can't. I had a horrible nightmare." She moves closer. "You died. I lost you. God, I can't lose you..." June buries her face against my bare chest, her body tremoring with quiet sobs. "Let me feel you. Please...let me know you're alive."

My heart cracks, right along with my resolve. I let out a hard, painful exhale, and gather her in my arms, yanking her as close as I can. Her left leg lifts, wrapping around my hip until we're impossibly tangled.

Too close. Way too fucking close.

She's breaching my barriers. Burrowing inside.

Her hands are all over me, my hair, my jaw, my neck, my shoulders. Her breathing is heavy and ragged as she presses a kiss to the curve of my neck, and I feel sick.

I feel absolutely sick because all she needs is comfort, and I'm getting hard.

"God, June, please go." My words are laced with desperation, and even though I'm telling her to go, I still hold her tight. Instinct drags my hand to her knotted hair and I fist it, crashing my forehead to hers. "Please."

She makes a gasping sound. "I need you."

"Why?"

"I–I'm scared."

"*Why?*"

Her breaths come quick and shaky. Our lips are so close, nearly grazing. "I..."

"Why did you *kiss me*?" I blurt out, tugging her hair harder, forcing a whimper from her lips.

Time stands still. Blue eyes lock with mine, our mouths hovering only a hairsbreadth apart. Just the slightest motion forward would sink us into another corrupt kiss, a kiss I'm confident would lead to something far worse, here in my bed, insatiably entwined, with darkness and desire fueling us—something we'd never recover from.

June inhales a sharp breath, her gaze dipping to my mouth, then back up. Swallowing, she answers in a shivery voice, "It was a dare."

I blink.

My hand relaxes in her hair as I frown.

A dare.

She kissed me on a dare, and I thought it was more.

I thought it was so much more.

Letting her go, I jump back and sit up straight, running a hand across my mouth as if I'm trying to wipe away the taste of that kiss.

A kiss she never wanted in the first place.

It was just a dare.

She senses the dramatic shift in mood and sits up, scrambling toward me. "I–I'm so sorry, Brant. It was stupid of me to do it, but I made a pact with Celeste and Gen, and we all had to do something awful, and—"

Something awful.

Something. Awful.

"June."

Her rambling ceases as she leans into me, chest heaving with worry. There's a long pause before she continues. "I'm sorry. Please, don't hate me for it. You're the only brother I have left, and I won't survive it if you hate me—"

"Go," I say, my tone eerily low and firm.

"I promise I won't—"

"You need to go."

"But you're my brother, and I—"

"I'm not your fucking *brother*!" Something inside of me snaps. That flimsy thread I've been holding onto since prom night, when my entire world crashed and burned at my feet, filling my lungs with soot and turning my heart to cinders. June stares at me, staggered, lips parted with the remnants of her unsaid words. "I'm just an orphan," I continue. "Life's forgotten transient. I'm the by-product of a man who didn't give two shits about me—who killed my mother, then killed himself.

"I'm the leftovers of a tragedy, like that steak you forgot about in the fridge, the one you really wanted to eat. It had so much potential to be good, but you spoiled it. And you don't want to throw it away because that would be such a damn waste, so you just let it fester, stinking up everything around it that's healthy and thriving, wishing you had gotten to it in time. It's futile, though... You always end up tossing it."

My chest heaves with heavy weights as I purge my guilt, my self-loathing. My sickly fear that I'm going to infect June and drag her down into the waste with me.

Her gaze scatters across my face, glossed with tears. She's breathing just as hard as I am, drinking in every rotten word while she shakes her head to counter my tirade. "You don't really think that," she mutters gently. "You couldn't possibly."

I clench my jaw, pinching the bridge of my nose. "Just go, June…please."

"You're the strongest person I know. The bravest. When life knocks you down, you keep getting back up again. No one in the world has that kind of resilience—no one." She's still shaking her head. "You're a true fighter. A hero. My rock."

"Stop. You don't know what you're talking about."

"Of course I do. I'm not stupid, Brant."

I spear her a sharp glance. "You're naive."

She has no clue. She has no idea that only moments ago I was imagining how my name would sound on her tongue when I made her come.

It's sick.

It's fucked.

It's going to ruin us both.

June looks wounded, her face flashing with subtle pain. "Don't," she whispers. "Don't be cruel. We need each other right now."

"I can't be what you need." Averting my eyes, I shut her down. I have to. She's the only good, pure thing I have left in my life, and I refuse to pollute her with these poisonous feelings that I don't even understand. "You have to go. Don't come back in here."

My eyes remain fixed on the far wall while she processes my words beside me, still and quiet. While she absorbs this new energy swirling between us. While she cuts herself on the rusty razors hidden within my command.

I don't wait for a reply.

I just lie back down, roll away from her, and pull the blanket up to my chin.

A blatant dismissal.

June never does respond…not with words, anyway. Her response is in the small cry of anguish that breaks free, the one that haunts my dreams that night.

It's in the shift of the mattress as she abandons me alone on the bed and retreats from the room, leaving only her sweet scent behind.

It's in the starkness of her absence.

And it kills me, it does.

It absolutely destroys me.

But, ultimately, I know it's for the best—

Better me than her.

I thought that losing my parents would be the worst thing that ever happened to me. True tragedy can't be topped, right? There's only so much trauma one person can suffer through…right?

Well, Theo's death proved me wrong, and to this day I still feel the ripple effects of that catastrophic blow. I'm still picking up pieces of debris.

The only sliver of peace during those awful, soul-crushing months after he died?

Practice.

I'd had practice with tragedy. I'd been there before, and I'd seen what the darkness could do.

I'd lived inside it, and I'd crawled my way out with teeth, claws, and blood. I knew that darkness wasn't permanent—just as the sun sets, the sun always rises.

And so do we.

But June didn't know that. In her whimsical eighteen years of life, she'd been untouched, unscathed, a stranger to true darkness.

Until the day Theo died.

Tragedy changes people. It alters them permanently.

And June manifested her grief in an overabundance of unhealthy love…for me. She clung. She squeezed. She traded in her devastation over losing Theo for an obsessive fear of losing me.

Maybe I should have tried harder. Perhaps I should have stayed just a little bit longer, to help her heal. But I truly believed I was the one thing standing in the way of her healing.

So I did what I thought I had to do.

I did what I thought was right.

One month later…

I moved out.

25

IF AT FIRST YOU DON'T SUCCEED

BRANT, AGE 24

Andrew scratches at his silvery hair, glancing around the cheerless apartment.

Sounds of traffic permeate the wall of silence stretched between us as he parks his hip against the couch we just hauled over from Theo's old place. Veronica was moving into a new complex, too grief-ridden to stay in the apartment she shared with Theo, and asked if I needed any of his furniture.

I did, technically.

I've been living in my new two-bedroom unit for three weeks now, sans a couch. My move out of the Bailey household was abrupt and unplanned, so I wasn't exactly prepared to furnish a space, and I'm short multiple paychecks thanks to my leave of absence from work.

I've been eating my meals at the small laminate kitchen island and hardly have anything in the living room aside from a rocking chair and television I don't use.

Most of my time has been spent in the barren bedroom, or out on the balcony that overlooks a populated downtown street. I purposely chose a noisier unit, leaving the balcony door cracked open regularly so the hustle and bustle seep inside.

The quiet is where I overthink.

The quiet is where I backslide.

The quiet is where I second-guess everything.

"This could be a remarkable place," Andrew murmurs, nodding as he gives the nine-hundred-square-foot unit a quick sweep. White walls, outdated fixtures, and hardly any character make it underwhelming at best—hardly remarkable. "It has potential."

I stuff my hands into my pockets, rocking on the heels of my feet. "Yeah. I'll spruce it up."

"I can help if you want. God knows I need a distraction."

My mind takes me back to watching Andrew sit like a stone on Theo's old bed as he stared out into space. Focused on nothing. Focused on everything that is now nothing. Clearing my throat, I say, "I'd like that."

"I know Samantha was reluctant to see you go, but I think you're right. It's for the best," Andrew continues, still nodding. Still looking around, drinking in the proclaimed potential. His receding hairline emphasizes the wrinkles and sunspots etched into his prominent forehead. He's aged. And I wonder if he's aged more in the last two months than he has over the last two years. "Moving forward is the only way to keep from slipping back. The timing was hard for her, but it's right for you. This has been a long time coming."

Tentacles of guilt coil around me.

The timing was shit.

The timing was callous.

But it was also born out of a blinding desperation to protect June at her most vulnerable. To protect her from *me*—from whatever the hell happened that night at the prom, because as much as we want to, we can't possibly sweep something like that under the rug. Not now when it's so fresh, so raw. That kiss went beyond dust and crumbs.

It's a roaring beast that can't be tamed, and all I could do was run.

"I'm not far," I tell him, riffling my overgrown mop of hair. "I'll visit. You're in walking distance."

He smiles, just a slight smile. "That's what I keep telling June."

My muscles tighten at the sound of her name.

She didn't take the news well.

She said I was deserting her. Abandoning her.

And I get it, I do, but I wasn't abandoning *her*; I was abandoning what my presence under that roof was *doing* to her. June was spiraling. Clinging to me so tightly, it was as if she thought my very existence could heal her broken soul, that if she could burrow far enough inside of me, she could make a new home for herself. A new life.

A reality where her brother wasn't gone.

But I knew better.

I *know* better.

Swallowing, I ask softly, "How is she?"

Andrew glances at me, his sad smile still in place. "She misses you. She misses both of you," he says gently, holding back his own anguish.

I close my eyes, inhaling a deep breath through my nose.

"She's been waking up in the middle of the night with nightmares. Having panic attacks. Using her inhaler more often." He looks off over my shoulder. "I found her curled up in the fetal position where your bed used to be one night."

A strangled little sound escapes me, like I've been physically struck. "What?"

God.

No.

My resolve starts crumbling at my feet until I'm questioning everything.

Am I making it worse?

Is she deteriorating without me?

Holy shit…*am I killing her?*

Nausea swirls in my gut as I watch Andrew's expression carefully, trying to discern the truth. Trying to figure out if my plan to protect June and help her heal is backfiring.

Maybe I'm wrong. Maybe I *don't* know better.

Maybe she *needs* someone to cling to, to help her over that salient pinnacle of grief. Hell, I know I did. The Baileys were my rock, my only hope of recovering from the loss of my parents, and if they had turned their backs on me, I'd be irreparably shattered.

Andrew is still zoned out, staring at a cobwebbed corner of the ceiling, so I approach him with a furiously pounding heart. "Andrew."

He blinks, canting his head toward me.

My dry mouth tastes like cotton balls and decay. There's a catch in my voice as I wonder aloud, "Did I make a mistake?"

The steady stream of traffic continues as we stare at each other, a heaviness wafting through the air, the silence between us thickening.

It feels like an eternity passes us by before he shakes his head. "No, Son. You didn't make a mistake."

I'm not entirely sure I believe him.

All I can envision is June sobbing on my bedroom floor, clutching her elephant, her chest caving in while she tries to breathe.

My chin dips, my gaze landing on the floor. Fixating on the blotchy carpet riddled with old stains, vacuumed over in an attempt to appear new.

This is what I traded June for.

Four hollow walls and discolored carpeting.

A new beginning, tainted with the stains of the spills I left behind.

She's outside tending to the lilac bushes and foliage that line the front of the house when I park my Highlander beside the familiar vehicle sitting idle in the driveway.

Her back is to me, a wide-brimmed hat shielding her from the scorching August sun.

I watch her for a few minutes. She has earbuds popped into both ears, making her unaware of my arrival. Dirt from the garden smudges her cotton shorts and tank top while a flush of pink stains her porcelain skin.

I'm transported back to summers long ago when she'd be sunburned and filthy after hours of playing outside beneath the heated sky, her light-brown hair shimmering golden when the light hit it just right. I can almost hear her childlike laughter.

The screen door claps shut, loud enough that June pokes her head up and yanks out her earbuds. A smile stretches on her face as Kip steps onto the front porch, wearing his everyday attire.

He smiles back at her.

My teeth scrape together.

She saunters toward Kip, lifting a hand to hold her hat in place when a warm breeze floats by, then falters midstep. June pauses before spinning to face the driveway.

Our eyes lock through the windshield. Swallowing, I muster the courage to push open the driver's side door and make myself known.

Kip offers a friendly wave as he moves down the cobblestone walkway. "Brant. Hey."

"Hey." I slip my keys into my back pocket. "What brings you by?"

My gaze must shift pointedly to June because he hesitates for a beat, reading me, then issues a reassuring smile. "I'm helping Andrew with a kitchen project. Refinishing the cabinets. He needs something to keep him busy…keep his mind busy."

June fidgets, then turns away, tinkering with a pair of gardening gloves.

I skate my attention back to Kip, guilt snagging me. "Can I help?"

"Nah," he says, giving me an amiable smack on the shoulder. "You've got enough on your plate. I'm just trying to be useful where I can—and that goes for you, too. I'm just a phone call away."

My lips twitch with gratitude.

Kip has been a beacon of strength over the last two months since Theo died, and honestly, I don't know how he does it.

He was the one Theo saved.

Theo sacrificed himself…for him.

The weight of a burden like that sounds backbreaking, so it boggles my mind that Kip manages to still stand tall, taking on our added weights and offering his heartfelt support when his own heart must be suffocating.

And then there's me.

The guy who deserted his family during their time of need. The asshole who ran away like a coward.

The self-proclaimed protector who abandoned the girl he vowed to take care of.

I abandoned her.

"Brant."

Kip's worried voice pulls me back to the front lawn. My eyes are blurred with tears as I blink at him, inhaling a shuddering breath of regret. "I think I fucked up, Kip."

Empathy shines back at me, and I'm so glad there's no trace of pity.

I couldn't handle it.

"You did what you needed to do," he says.

My head whips back and forth. "For myself. I was selfish."

"*Grief* is selfish. There's no shame in that." Kip sighs, his shoulders relaxing as he takes a small step forward. "Listen…everyone reacts to trauma differently. There's no right or wrong way to heal. Some people need time and space to process, to grieve alone, and some people, like me, need to stay busy. Social and useful."

"There is a wrong way," I counter, my eyes panning back to June, who is kneeling in the grass, bent over a flower bed. "The wrong way is the way that drags other people down with you."

"No." He shakes his head. Adamantly. "You're not responsible for the way others react to what *you* need to do to get better."

I allow his words to sink in, giving me the smallest pocket of peace.

My intentions were pure.

I wasn't actively trying to hurt anyone. I was doing what I thought I needed to do to keep June from careening into a downward spiral because I wasn't mentally strong enough to fight my grief over losing Theo *and* my grief over loving June in a way I should never dream of loving her.

It was too much all at once.

It was too fucking much.

Kip follows my stare to where June sifts the parched soil with gloved hands, rubbing the back of his neck. "She'll be okay. She's stronger than you think," he tells me gently.

"Have you, uh…" I scratch at my hair, shuffling my feet. "Have you been spending a lot of time with her?"

I hate that my knee-jerk reaction is jealousy when it should be appreciation.

Kip is here, and I'm not.

That's *my* fault.

He senses the underlying question and quickly dismisses it. "I wouldn't do that." When I look back at him, he's frowning a little, almost hurt by the subtle insinuation. "I wouldn't do that to you, or to Theo. Please know that."

"I didn't mean—"

"You did," he says, but he's not mad. Just firm. "You did, but it's okay. As long as you know I'd never cross that line. I'm here to help, not make things worse."

I swallow. "Sorry."

"Don't be." Kip inhales deeply, ducking his chin to his chest. "I know you two have a lot of…history."

There's a word for it.

Shame engulfs me, knowing Kip saw what we did in that country club hallway. He knows my dirty little secret.

Still, there's no judgment pouring out of him.

No sense of disapproval.

He continues. "I don't blame you for moving out and getting away after everything that happened. I think you had to. For your own well-being, and for hers, too…even if she doesn't see it."

I glance at him, waiting.

"What happened between you both was big." Kip meets my eyes. A beat passes. Then he finishes, "Be bigger than it."

Inhaling a sharp breath, I blink as he sends me a supportive smile, gives my shoulder another slap, then moves around me toward his vehicle.

The sound of his car door slamming shut has June's head popping up as she glances back at me, biting her lip when she discovers Kip has left and it's just me staring at her from across the yard.

She looks away, pretending to go back to gardening.

Be bigger than it.

I muster the strength to traipse across the lawn toward June.

Once I'm in earshot, she mumbles over her shoulder, "Dad's working in the kitchen. Mom is grocery shopping."

"I wanted to talk to you," I say, stopping once I'm standing over her. June stills for a moment before continuing her task. "Please."

"I'm busy, Brant. I told Mom I'd help with yard work today, so maybe another time."

"Junebug." She freezes again, her hand tightening around a tool. She doesn't look up. The large hat masks whatever emotions are dancing across her face. I whisper softly, "I'm sorry."

I'm sorry for leaving.

I'm sorry for shutting you out.

I'm sorry for kissing you back.

I'm sorry for loving you all wrong.

June clears her throat, falling back on her haunches. "I'm doing okay. You don't have to worry about me."

"I always worry about you." Her long hair whips around the edges of her hat. I wish I could see her face. Read her. June wears her heart in her eyes. She always has. "You know I do."

"Well, that's not necessary. I'm fine."

"Are you?"

"Yes."

I pull my lips between my teeth, debating my next words. Sighing, I say, "That's not what your dad told me yesterday. He said you're having panic attacks. Nightmares. Your asthma is flaring."

"He said that?" June gasps a little, finally rising to her feet. She doesn't turn around right away. She ducks her head, drops the gardening tool, then wraps her arms around herself like a hug. When she pivots to face me, she pulls the hat off her head until her hair flutters free and her eyes shimmer with a glaze of tears, glowing light-blue in the summer haze. "He's exaggerating."

"He told me he found you crying on my bedroom floor, curled up in the fetal position."

Her breath hitches, eyes widening. She shakes her head back and forth. "No, that's… That was weeks ago. I'm better now. I'm fine."

"June…" My hands reach out to cup her face, but she steps back. She retreats from me. "June, please. I only left because I thought I was hurting you by staying. I thought it's what you needed, but..." I blow out a hard breath, dropping my arms to my sides. "I said I couldn't be what you needed, but I lied. The truth is, I didn't *want* to be what you needed. I didn't think I was strong enough. And I'm sorry. I'm so sorry for that."

June's bottom lip trembles, but she doesn't reach for me. Even as a tear slips, she remains rooted in place. "I'm fine," she repeats, like she's trying to convince herself.

"Okay." I nod. "But if you're ever not fine, I promise I'll be there for you. I'll be stronger next time." My eyes rove over her face, her cheekbones tinged with sun, her full lips still quivering as she processes my words. "I'll be as brave as you need me to be, June."

She bites at her lip to stop the tremors, then shifts her attention away from me.

A thick silence falls between us as I gaze down at her. As she looks everywhere but at me. As she hugs herself again like she's cold, but it's eighty-five degrees out.

June finally nods her head, just slightly. "Thanks."

Then she leans down to scoop up her hat and abandons her yard work, sweeping past me and heading into the house. She doesn't say goodbye. She doesn't say anything else.

I resist the urge to chase after her, to pull her into my arms and kiss away her tears.

I let her go.

I'll accept that she feels angry and betrayed, and I'll give her the space she needs.

I'll be stronger than my feelings.

I'll take care of her like Theo asked me to.

I'll be bigger than that kiss.

26

FIRST OF NEVER

JUNE, AGE 18

My heart feels scorched and tangled as the door shuts behind me, and I lean back against it, cool metal pressing into flushed skin.

Flushed from the sun.

Flushed from the look in his eyes.

Flushed from the memory of our kiss that still tingles my lips, regardless of how much I try to pretend it never happened.

I told him it was a dare, and it was. It started as an innocent dare.

But we both know it became so much more.

It grew wings.

And the only way to prevent wings from soaring, from flying too high to where danger is imminent, is to clip them.

"June Lampoon, my darling daughter," Dad says, stepping out of the kitchen with paint-smudged overalls and sawdust in his salt-and-pepper hair. "Want to help your old man with these cabinets?"

I straighten from the door, tossing my hat in the foyer and slipping out of my flip-flops. "You're running out of decent rhymes, Dad." A forced smile pushes through the tears, despite my grievance that my father told Brant about my struggles. I can't blame him for being concerned.

I can't blame him for anything right now.

"Nonsense," he says, scratching at his stubble and leaving a smear of white paint behind. "I have a whole arsenal of them waiting for their remarkable debut."

"You have them all documented in a spreadsheet on the laptop, don't you?"

He winks. "Nope. They're hidden away with my trove of amazing animal-themed slippers that I'm dying to showcase."

My smile turns genuine for the first time in two months.

Two months.

The last time a real, sincere smile graced my lips was at prom when I caught Brant's eye from across the ballroom, sent him a small wave, and smiled at him with my whole heart.

Then everything fell to pieces, starting with a kiss and ending with a funeral.

Dad smiles back at me, his silly grin softening with a trace of sadness, almost as if he just remembered Theo is gone and that smiles aren't something we do anymore.

I jolt in place when my cell phone rings from the elastic band of my shorts. Shooting Dad an apologetic glance, I snatch it from my hip and trudge my way up the staircase to my bedroom. It's Celeste trying to video call me.

I decline it.

Celeste is leaving for New York this week to live with her aunt, eager to jump-start her dancing career. She wants to be a backup dancer for performers and musicians.

My own legs tickle with the urge to tap and twirl, but I dismiss the sensation.

I'm not sure I want to dance anymore. To dance is to flourish, to release, to thrive—and I'm not that girl anymore. I'm just a poor imitation of her, a gloomy shadow.

I rely on an inhaler and a man I crossed a deadly line with just to breathe. Without either of those things, I would wither away into nothing.

Collapsing onto my unmade bed, I reach for Aggie and pull him to my chest. Tears begin to sprout when the silence settles in, my smile long gone.

I think of Theo. I think of how he'd react to the knowledge that I kissed our beloved brother—that I didn't just kiss him with innocent lips. I kissed him with clenched thighs, wicked thoughts, and a blazing fire smoldering low in my belly.

Then, I almost kissed him again—last month, before he moved out. I crawled into his bed, vulnerable and desperate for comfort. Any kind of comfort.

My heart raced with turmoil.

My hands roamed with recklessness.

My core ached with…*something*.

And when he grabbed my hair, pulled my mouth a centimeter from his, and demanded why I'd kissed him, I froze up.

A different need took over—a need to replace the gaping hole in my heart.

I'd already lost Theo. If I kissed Brant again, there would be no going back, no stopping the runaway train, and no pretending there wasn't a terrible, forbidden spark crackling between us.

I'd lose him, too.

I'd have no brothers left.

My eyes dart around the cluttered bedroom as I suck in a shaky breath, landing on the framed canvas painting on the wall above my dresser. Theo picked it out for me at a flea market two years ago when he went furniture shopping with Brant and Veronica. It's an abstract painting of a bluebird with rainbow wings taking flight toward a sky made of funny-looking clouds.

He said it reminded him of me.

A soaring bluebird, destined for great heights.

Theo told me on the patio before I left for prom on that god-awful night that he'd be cheering me on, all the way to the top.

But he's not here. I've lost one of my stalwart defenders, and I've pushed away the other with a kiss that never should have happened.

A kiss that grew wings.

My cell phone vibrates on the mattress beside me as I slide beneath my comforter and reach for the phone, expecting to see an aggravated text from Celeste. She's been trying to convince me to join her in New York, to move in with her and her aunt and pursue our dreams together.

Only, my dreams died the day Theo died.

And if I leave Brant behind, far more than just my dreams will die, too.

Swiping open the notification, my belly flutters when a different name flashes on the screen. It's a message from Brant.

My mouth goes dry.

Brant: I know you're not okay. I know you were lying, and I know that because I know you better than anyone else in this world. You wear your heart in your eyes, Junebug, and I can see that your heart is torn apart. Mine is, too. Over Theo, over abandoning you, and over what happened between us at the dance. It may have started with a dare, but that's not where it ended. We both know that, we were both responsible for letting it escalate, and we've both thought about doing it again.

A breath catches in my throat as another message comes through.

Brant: I know that scares you. I know you're afraid and confused, but you don't have to be. We're not going to do it again. I'm not going to risk losing the most important thing in my life over a moment of weakness. An indiscretion that, right now, can be filed away as a lapse in judgment. It was just a blip. We're still the same people. I'm still Brant, and you're still June.

Tears trickle down my cheeks, recalling the night I said those very words to him as I crawled into his bed, desperate for him to chase my nightmares away.

Brant: I'm still that same boy who loves you with everything he is, who wants to be your comfort and your courage, and who would use his dying breaths to sing you your favorite lullaby. That kiss meant something, but it wasn't everything. We're going to move past it. We're going to be bigger than it. We have to be...because we've already lost too much.

Three last words pop up, and I break down.

Brant: I love you.

Falling sideways onto my bed, I pull the covers up to my chin and squeeze Aggie tight, my heart seizing with both relief and fear.

Relief because we're going to forget about it.

Fear because I'm not sure we can.

I stare at the bluebird on my wall with blurry eyes, thinking about that kiss, thinking about the wings it grew and how I tried to clip them.

Realizing and knowing that they may not rise…

They may not soar…

But clipped wings can still fly.

PART III

THE THIRD TRAGEDY

27

FIRST FIDDLE

JUNE, AGE 19

MY TIRES ROLL TO A stop in front of the chic nightclub on the other side of town called the Black Box. Brant is standing outside the main doors, leaning back against the iron-gray bricks, laughing with a cute blond with cat-eye glasses and an impressive figure. The woman looks like she's laughing so hard she can't catch her breath, doubling over with her palms clasped around black-leather-clad knees.

I bite my lip.

Pauly Marino opened the posh club a few months ago, determined to bring an air of decadence to our northwest Chicago suburbs. The club features renowned DJs, a magenta-lit bar, upscale appetizers made from scratch, and well…my brother, the lead bartender.

While Brant still works full-time at Bistro Marino as head chef, he offered to help Pauly out on the weekends slinging drinks and partaking of a semblance of a social life for once. I was surprised when he volunteered for the position, since Brant is all about food. But apparently, cocktails and culinary cuisine aren't too far off. Brant says it's all about nailing the flavor fusions, and if you can do one, you can do the other.

This has been good for him.

He's been happier lately, smiling more, joking with me. His touches and hugs aren't filled with doubt and disintegration like they were in those dreary autumn and winter months, as we fought to get back on track to who we used to be.

It feels like we're finally "us" again, and I couldn't be more thrilled.

So I'm not sure why seeing him so happy and carefree right now, lost in laughter with one of his coworkers, is causing my stomach to twist with knots.

I'm being foolish.

Shaking the weirdness away, I turn the car off and hop out, finally catching Brant's attention.

His eyes glitter at me beneath the neon lights. "June."

I feel as drab as can be in my baggy hoodie and leggings, my hair pulled up into a messy bun, and hardly any makeup painting my face. I look like a troll compared to the blond, who spins around, gifting me with a flash of perfect white teeth and an adorable crinkled nose.

"Oh, hey! Are you Brant's sister?" She shakes off the remnants of her laughter as her light-blond hair is swept up in a sharp breeze. "He's told me so much about you."

"Good things, I hope?" I laugh lightly.

She taps her index finger to her chin. "Define 'good.'"

Brant gives her a gentle nudge with his elbow, chuckling under his breath. "C'mon, Neville."

She giggles, ramming him right back with double the force.

I blink.

"Ack, sorry," she blurts out, skipping forward and extending her hand. "I'm Sydney. Brant's favorite coworker."

"My favorite pain in the ass," he corrects in jest.

Chewing on my cheek, I return the handshake and force a smile. My eyes skip between them as a stab of jealousy punctures me. Brant looks so happy right now.

But it's not me who's putting that smile on his face or adding that bounce to his step. He's not laughing over a joke I told, or partaking in affectionate banter with me.

And I have no idea why that stings.

You're being ridiculous, June. You should be happy that he's happy. Period.

Clearing the senseless emotion from my throat, I wring my hands together and fidget in place. "Well, I'm ready when you are," I say to Brant, sending him another tiny smile that took far too much effort to produce. Brant's Highlander is in the shop until Monday, after the alternator died, so I offered to be his chauffeur for the weekend.

He studies me for a moment, the sienna flecks in his eyes darkening to umber, as if he can sense something off about me. "Yeah, I'm good."

Sydney pipes in, waving her arms back and forth. "I'm going to take off, too. I have a date with a riveting book of smut and my vibr—" She wheezes a little, catching herself. "Vibrant imagination."

Brant laughs.

And I can't help it. I laugh, too.

"Have fun with that," I chuckle, pacing backward. "It was nice meeting you."

"Likewise." She waves us off with a toothy grin, then wanders toward the parking lot.

Brant's smile lingers as he pivots to face me, his hair looking darker than ever. Almost black. But his eyes have a light I wasn't sure I'd ever see again.

Tipping my head to my car parked behind me, I gesture to it. "Ready?"

He nods, and we both pile into the dated sedan that Mom and Dad bought for me for my nineteenth birthday. The mileage is high, and it smells like Sharpies, but I'm grateful for my own set of wheels—mostly because I don't have anywhere close to the funds I'd need to purchase one on my own. It's embarrassing, really, but my dreams of becoming a Broadway dancer shriveled up and died last year, and leaving to go off to college was too painful to even consider.

So I enrolled in a few community college courses to keep myself busy until I fully decide what I want to do with my life, while waiting tables four days a week at Barnaby's diner.

Truly pathetic.

I've considered picking up more shifts at the diner and moving in with

Genevieve, who also decided to stay local and share a place with her stepbrother right after high school. But he's entering the military, so she asked me if I'd be interested in taking his place and splitting the rent.

I am. I really am.

But my paychecks are going entirely to car insurance, gas, and my cell phone bill, and I have pennies left to spare.

Sighing, I close the car door and sit quietly for a minute, fiddling with my keys. A cloud of Ivory soap and spearmint fills the small space, causing me to gnaw at my lip as I lift my gaze to Brant. He's already looking at me. Probably wondering why I seem so glum after spending a fun, exciting day at the beach with him just two days ago.

Before he can interrogate me, I twist a piece of loose hair around my finger and blurt out, "You should go out with her."

He frowns, his neck craning back slightly with bewilderment. "What? Who?"

"Your coworker. Sydney."

I'm not sure why I say it.

Queasiness claims me the moment the words tumble from my lips.

Brant swallows, facing forward for a moment before looking back to me. "Why?"

Yes, June, why?

"Because…you haven't gone out with anyone since Wendy. You must be lonely, right?"

He fidgets in his seat. "I'm fine. I keep busy."

"Well, you deserve to have fun and be happy. You're young, and good-hearted, and sexy, and…" I stutter over my words, wondering why I chose one of them.

Sexy.

I gulp.

Sexy?

He blinks at me because I've clearly gone mad. His Adam's apple bobs in his throat as his gaze dips to my mouth for the briefest second. "You think I'm sexy?"

I flush with embarrassment, shoving the key into the ignition and turning it until the vehicle roars to life. "I just meant…she thinks you are. Surely."

"Why would you assume that?"

Flustered, all I can think to do is twist the rearview mirror in his direction until he's staring at his own reflection. Then I put the car into drive and take off, wishing I could leave my humiliation behind to choke on the exhaust fumes.

A burst of laughter escapes him as he clips his seat belt into place beside me. I'm certain he's about to probe and tease me, but all he does is prop a foot up on the dashboard and change the subject. "So, did you decide if you're moving in with Gen or not?" he asks as I turn on the radio, allowing an ambient song to drown out my lingering shame. "Might be good for you to get out of your parents' place. Get a taste of independence, you know?"

I spare him a quick glance as we pull out onto the main road. We had talked about my desire to become more independent at the beach this past week as we sprawled out on beach blankets and counted the clouds. "I'm not sure if now is the right time. I don't have a steady paycheck."

"Smart. You're still young."

"Young and goalless, sure."

"You could start dancing again." Brant removes his attention from the passenger window and looks over at me. "I wish you would."

My chest aches with nostalgia. With disappointment. With regret for giving up on something I cherished so dearly and worked so hard for.

Swallowing, I nod. "Maybe one day. My asthma makes it tricky."

"A lot of people with asthma have labor-intensive jobs. You just need to be careful. Aware."

"I suppose."

"Think about it, Junebug. Please."

The sound of my special nickname sends a tickle to my heart. Brant doesn't say it as often as he used to, and I'm confident it's because of our reckless kiss. He associates the name with innocence, and what happened between us was anything but.

Lord, that kiss.

It's been a year since it happened, but it still haunts me.

Still clings.

Brant hasn't brought it up since his text messages to me shortly after he moved out, and I haven't brought it up either. I think that was the point—we were going to move past it. Acknowledge that it happened, and put it behind us.

And we have.

Things are better now. Good, even.

Brant comes over and cooks us family dinners at least once a week, and we often spend one-on-one time together grabbing coffee, riding our bikes at the forest preserve, or lounging on the beach. Kip joins us for family barbecues on occasion, having formed a deep bond with my parents, ignoring the fact that our lips have locked, lips have locked, that our tongues have tasted.

It was just a blip in our ever-complicated history.

In terms of outward appearances, at least.

We may have put it behind us, sure…but it followed me.

It nibbles at my ankles every now and then when Brant looks at me a certain way, his eyes hooded, or when he holds me for a beat too long as he hugs me goodbye, or when his knuckles graze my own while we walk side by side, his soapy scent enveloping me in a heady cloud.

A sigh leaves me, and it must tremble slightly because Brant notices.

"You okay?" he asks, reaching across the center console and cradling my unoccupied hand that has balled up in my lap. "You seem on edge."

"I'm good." My tone is strained despite my attempt to sound perky, and my hand pulses with warmth inside his grasp. "Just thinking about my dismal future, as usual."

He hesitates for a moment. "You know, you could…" His voice trails off.

Turning onto the familiar street that houses his apartment complex, I shoot him a quick look. "I could what?"

"Never mind. Not a good idea."

I frown. "Brant, tell me. You must."

"I just…" He resituates in his seat, blowing out a hard breath. Another few beats go by before he finishes. "You could move in with me…if you want."

My heart stops.

A strangled sensation inches its way up my chest and into my throat.

"Like I said—bad idea." He tries to recover. "I just figured…a year's gone by, we're in a better place, and you deserve a taste of independence. But maybe—"

"No, you're right." Swallowing, I start nodding my head. "I'll think about it. If you're sure."

Move in with...*Brant*?

Brant...as my *roommate*?

I'm not sure if the idea is preposterous or strangely compelling.

We lived together under one roof for most of our lives, so this wouldn't be much different.

He has two separate bedrooms.

Plus he works almost every day of the week, so we'd hardly even see each other.

My hand that grips the steering wheel goes white-knuckled as the invitation processes. Brant lets go of my other hand, scratching at the back of his head and murmuring, "Yeah, I'm sure."

I don't say anything as I pull into the complex's parking lot and stop the car. The air feels thick and heavy, hardly enough to breathe off of, so I roll down my window and drink in a few deep breaths as the evening breeze filters through.

I'm about to say my good-nights when Brant speaks first. "Do you want to come inside?"

That lump returns to my throat as I glance at him. I'm unable to pinpoint the sentiment gleaming back at me, but it feels different. It feels...*charged.*

His hazel eyes are glowing in the muted moonlight, earthy and electric.

I'm tempted to say yes; so, so tempted.

But I have plans already.

Shaking my head, I smile with apology. "I can't. I have a date tonight."

Brant stiffens. Everything about him goes rigid as he looks away from me, the cords in his neck prominent as his muscles twitch. He stares out the windshield in silence.

No reply.

Desperate for some kind of response, I begin to stammer, "I–I'm free tomorrow from—"

"I probably shouldn't be saying this, but the thought of another man putting his hands on you makes me borderline murderous."

I almost choke.

Canting my head in his direction, I watch as he rakes his gaze over me, his jaw clenching, before his eyes slide back up to mine. I heave in a precarious breath and squeak out, "Another?"

A beat passes. "What?"

"You said *another* man. Did you mean someone other than…you?"

Oh my God.

I can't believe I just asked him that.

What the hell is wrong with me tonight?

Delete! Delete!

My cheeks flame with mortification as I quickly look away, ducking my chin to my chest, wondering if I should start chanting in Latin and maybe the ground will open up and swallow me whole.

The silence is horrifying as I sit there, squeezing my eyes shut and biting my lip. Waiting for him to scold me, or laugh at me, or tell me I'm being a silly girl.

When the silence becomes too much to bear, I press my palms to my heated cheeks, inhaling a shuddery breath. "God, I'm sorry. That was really—"

"Yes." His voice is low and husky. He stares at me as my head pops back up, his eyes alight with wild embers. "That's what I meant."

My throat feels tight and full of grit. I'm not sure what to say or what to do. How to react. Luckily, Brant breaks the tension with a heavy sigh and glances away, rubbing at his chin. "Well, good night," he mutters, unbuckling his seat belt and reaching for the door handle. "Come by this week. I'll cook for us."

I nod swiftly. "Okay. Sure."

I'm this close to becoming a statue as I sit there with both hands curled around the steering wheel, my spine straight, my chest feeling stacked with weights. Brant's shoes crunch along the gravel as he gets out of the car and moves around the rear, stopping at the driver's side. I see him in my peripheral vision, hesitating, debating his next move.

And then he sweeps over to me in a quick blink and leans in through the open window, his hand extending, cupping my face until I turn my head and we're eye to eye. "My offer still stands. About moving in with me," he says gently, his thumb grazing my jaw. A smile whispers on his lips, and his eyes twinkle with genuine affection. *With love.* "Be safe tonight. I worry about you."

Before I can respond with more than a pathetic little whimper, he pulls back and walks away.

He disappears into the apartments, and I'm left clutching my chest, wishing I hadn't been so vague. Wishing he wasn't worrying.

The truth is he doesn't need to worry—

My date is with the dead.

The following Saturday, I'm pacing around my bedroom with packed bags and an anxious heart.

We had plans tonight.

I told Brant I wanted to talk to him about something, so we decided to grab a late dinner after he got off work at the nightclub.

I wasn't expecting his latest text message.

Brant: Hey Junebug, I'm sorry to do this. Sydney's sister had an emergency come up and had to bail on her, so I offered to drive Syd home tonight. Can we reschedule our dinner? You don't need to wait up for me.

As I scanned it, my insides instantly pitched with a horrible, ugly feeling.

You don't need to wait up for me.

That's code for he's staying the night.

That's code for sex.

And hell, I told him to do it.

I told him to go out with her.

So I have absolutely no right to feel like my organs are suffocating and withering to dust right now. It's embarrassing. It's weak and pitiful.

And for what?

Why do I even feel this way?

Brant deserves to find happiness with someone. I have no claim over him, even though it feels like he's tethered to me in the most profound, all-consuming way. I love him more than I love breathing. He knows every dent and divot in my heart, and he knows how each one got there. He's tasted my tears and silenced my fears.

But he's not mine.

I have no reason to feel jealous.

And yet hot tears slice at my eyes as I shove my cell phone into my back pocket.

I'm a hypocrite, too, because I kissed a man over Christmas break when Celeste came into town to visit her family. She hosted a holiday party, and I made out with her cousin Aaron in the upstairs bathroom.

It wasn't enjoyable.

His tongue was sloppy, his hands clumsy.

He smelled like fried fish.

And the moment he tried to sneak his fingers into my underwear, I shoved him away, lying about being on my period.

The truth was I just wasn't into it. I tried to be, but ever since the prom, my body hasn't responded to men in the same way that it used to; my sensuality has dwindled into ash.

I'm broken.

A knock sounds on my bedroom door, startling me. I swipe the remnants of tears off my cheeks and move to open it.

Mom stands on the other side, hair in her typical messy bun with a pen stuck inside, and wearing white robe. Her eyes pan to my overnight bags that are brimful in the center of the room. "Where are you going?"

"I, um…" I fluster, sweeping my hair over to one side. "Remember how I told you I was thinking about rooming with someone?"

She frowns. "Yes. You told me Genevieve asked you to move in with her, but you couldn't afford it."

"Right. I can't…so, someone else offered."

Her "Mom eyebrow" rises.

I bite my lip. "Brant offered."

"Brant?" Mom tugs the ties of her robe, then crosses her arms, leaning against the doorjamb. Her blue eyes flicker with confusion. "When did this happen? Why are your bags already packed and I'm just now hearing about it?"

Because I'm being dramatic and impulsive. "I'm just going to stay for a couple of nights to see if it's a smooth transition. I was going to talk to you before I left."

My mother has always had that uncanny sense of something not being right. She calls it a motherly intuition, while I tend to lean more toward the voodoo or witchcraft angle.

She has a lot of crystals, and her favorite movie is *Practical Magic*.

When I kissed Marty Buchanan by the mulberry tree, she knew. Instantly. After releasing my wrath upon Brant, I stalked inside—and Mom twisted around on the couch, raised that infamous eyebrow, and told me I was too young to be kissing boys.

When I fell through the ice, she knew. She said the moment it happened her skin chilled and her blood froze. She obsessively called my father, insisting something terrible had happened.

The night of the prom…she knew.

Mom told me there was a pang in her chest all night, from the moment we stepped out the front door. She couldn't stomach dinner. She couldn't concentrate on her crochet work.

She sat on the couch with her cell phone in her lap all evening, until she got that call from Brant. The one that informed her I was in the hospital after collapsing at the dance from an asthma attack.

She never expected Theo, though.

She just knew *something* was wrong.

Like right now.

Something.

Her lips purse with concentration, as if she's trying to pull brain waves out of my mind and pick them apart with her sorcery.

Good luck, Mom. I don't even know what I'm thinking.

Unable to get a read on me, she sighs heavily. "You seem flustered. What are you not telling me?"

I hope she's not shining a light on my inner psyche with her laser-beam eyes, because I'm currently replaying that kiss over and over, detail for detail. My cheeks redden like traitors. "Nothing, Mom. I was on my way down to talk to you, and I was nervous. I thought you wouldn't approve."

"Why wouldn't I approve? He's your brother."

I falter. I don't have an answer for her that doesn't implicate us for our indiscretion, so I focus on the situation itself instead of Brant. "I didn't want you to feel abandoned. If I leave, it would just be you and Dad, and it hurts my heart to think of you both all alone in this quiet house."

Tears blanket my eyes as my own words sink into me.

My mother lifts up from the doorframe with a sympathetic smile, stepping toward me and curling my hair behind my ear. Her hair shimmers with a sprinkling of silver threads beneath the hall light. "All birds have to leave the nest eventually, June. There's no good time or right time. They simply fly when their wings are ready."

I shift my gaze to the bluebird canvas above my dresser, sniffling through a nod.

"Take a few days to feel out the situation, and if it's a good fit, I'll talk to Dad and we can help move your things over."

"Are you sure?"

"I'm sure." Mom lowers her arm, her smile still in place. "If you're going to stay with anybody, I'm glad it's Brant. He's always had your best interest in mind."

My hand slips into the pocket of my hoodie where one of the spare keys to Brant's apartment rests. Mom and Dad have the other.

I send my mother a strained smile, gripping the key in a tight fist. "Okay… thank you," I tell her, stepping backward and bending down for my two bags, jam-packed with clothes and toiletries. "When Dad gets home from trivia night, can you fill him in for me? I'll stop by and talk to him tomorrow."

"Of course, sweetheart."

"I love you."

She returns the sentiment and leaves me to finish gathering my belongings. Before I retreat from the room, I hesitate briefly, my eyes skating up to the bluebird painting.

I worry my lip between my teeth.

Then I snatch it off the wall and stuff it into one of the bags.

Two hours.

I'm sitting on the bright-blue sofa in Brant's living room for two hours before the sound of jingling keys pulls me up straight and sends a colony of butterflies to my belly.

Will he be mad?

Will he be happy to see me?

He doesn't know I've decided to move in with him yet. That was the purpose of our dinner meeting tonight.

I watch nervously as he pushes over the threshold with a weary sigh, tossing his car keys to the countertop and kicking off his shoes. He doesn't notice me at first. He has no reason to think his sister would be standing in his living room after he returned home from a one-night stand.

My palms start to sweat.

Brant falters in the entryway for a beat, tousling his dark hair that's clipped shorter on the sides but wild and untamed on top. Slightly curly. He looks tired as he stands there, just staring down at the small patch of ivory tiles that house two pairs of shoes.

I clear my throat.

His head shoots up, eyes squinting through the dim lighting, then widening when he registers my presence. He sucks in a breath, and we stare.

We stare at each other in silence, my heart in my throat.

My heart in his hands.

"June?"

Brant poses my name like a question, as if it could be anyone else but me. "Hi."

"Hi," he says softly. He shakes himself from the daze, taking slow steps forward and ruffling his hair again. "What, uh…what are you doing here?"

He wipes at his mouth.

My stomach pitches, envisioning that mouth on hers. "My answer is yes."

"Your answer?" Another step forward. "To what?"

"Moving in with you."

Dipping his gaze lower and to the left, he finally spots my overnight bags, still zipped and full. Still waiting for permission. He swallows, glancing back up at me. "Okay. Right."

"Okay?" I nibble my lip, my fingernails leaving tiny crescents on my palms. "You're not mad that I just showed up unannounced?"

"You're always welcome."

My throat feels like I swallowed needles as I take a few tentative steps toward him. "This was what I wanted to talk to you about," I say. "At dinner."

A flash of guilt lights up his eyes, and he ducks his head. "Sorry about that. I didn't mean to stand you up, I just felt obligated to give her a ride home and—"

"Did you have sex with her?" I blurt out.

The air leaves the room as my cheeks flood with heat.

My knees are quivery, hardly stable.

My chest hums with prickling anxiety.

Brant is silent as the question echoes off the unfurnished plaster walls, his chin lifting back up as his eyes settle on me. It takes an eternity for him to reply. "No. It didn't go that far."

"You…you stopped it?"

I'm beyond pitiful. His sexual conquests are not my concern.

He's. My. Brother.

He pulls his lips between his teeth, shaking his head. "She did."

Jealousy thunders through me—the most loathsome, most venomous of all the human emotions. Tears rush to my eyes as my hands curl into fists.

"June…" He descends on me, concern radiating from his worried eyes. "June, talk to me. You look like I just ripped your heart out."

My bottom lip trembles, so I chomp down on it, flicking my head back and forth.

"I don't understand," Brant murmurs, moving in until we're toe-to-toe. His hand raises, his knuckles skimming my flushed cheek. "You told me to. You said I should go out with her."

"I–I know… You should. I'm sorry." I'm not sure what to say or how to explain away this ridiculous reaction. All I can think to do is run from it. "I should go. I didn't mean to just show up like this. It was rude and presumptuous."

Pulling away from his touch, I sweep around him and march my way to the front door. I don't grab my bags, but I'll come back for them. It's fine.

I just need to go.

When I reach the door, I twist the brass knob and tug it open, prepared to dart into the hallway and escape this mess of confusion.

Only, I'm stopped short when a hand plants against the door right above my head, slamming it shut. I draw in a sharp breath. He's right behind me, his chest brushing along my back as he cages me in. Swallowing hard, I squeak out, "Brant..."

Electricity hisses all around us.

My hand squeezes the doorknob, more for balance than for reprieve.

Brant leans in, his lips caressing my ear and sending a shiver up my spine. "Tell me why the thought of me having sex with someone else bothers you."

I inhale another choppy breath.

He remains flush against me, his warmth causing me to overheat.

"Else?" I mutter, licking my lips. The word comes out shaky. Everything is shaky. "Did you mean someone other than...me?"

A sigh leaves him. A sigh that sounds like want and yearning.

A sigh that sounds like I should go.

"Yes," he whispers, his head drawing up. Another few seconds pass before he moves back over me, resting his forehead on the crown of my head. "That's what I meant."

We remain in that position for a long time, his hand pressed to the wooden door above me, his body leaning forward, blanketing me with his hard frame and spearmint scent. His breaths tickle the nape of my neck, causing my hair to flitter and dance.

His command hangs in the air, but I don't have an answer for it.

Only the sad truth: *I don't know.*

Brant finally moves away, pulling his hand from the door and taking a step back. My palm is still fisted around the doorknob, clammy and trembling.

He sighs again, this time with an air of defeat. "Stay."

The word reverberates through me.

Leaves me conflicted.

Leaves me rattled.

Leaves me dropping my hand from the knob and saying the one word I probably shouldn't say: "Okay."

I stay.

And I wonder if I'll ever leave.

28

FIRST DESERVE, THEN DESIRE

BRANT, AGE 25

"Let's play shoulder wars." Her face glistens with water droplets, her long hair soaking wet and draped down her back. June's arms rest along the edge of the inground pool, her chin propped up on top of them as she sends me a stunning smile.

I try to ignore the way she looks at me like I'm the only one here, even though there's a sea of people mingling around me. "You mean a chicken fight?"

"No...shoulder wars. You know, when someone is on your shoulders fighting another person on somebody else's shoulders."

"So, a chicken fight."

Kip speaks up beside me in his wooden lawn chair, nursing a beer. "It's a chicken fight."

"You're both crazy," June says, jumping out of the water and trailing over to me in the grass. "It's literally a war battled upon shoulders. There are no chickens."

My muscles lock up as she approaches, clad in only a pink polka-dotted bikini as rivulets of water trickle over her skin, causing her to glisten under the sun.

I chug my beer.

When Kip invited us to a pool party at his new place, it was a welcome reprieve from my seven-day work stretch between the restaurant and the club.

A Saturday off? Almost unheard of these days, which hasn't exactly been a bad thing. Working myself to utter exhaustion has kept me sane. Kept me progressing, moving forward, one chocolate soufflé and lemon-drop martini at a time.

But the long hours on my feet have been getting to me, so when Pauly ordered me to take a weekend off, I humbly accepted. My bills are paid, my savings account is growing, and I honestly couldn't think of a good reason to say no.

Especially today, when the late summer sun is shining hot and bright, music and laughter are serenading me, and my good friend Kip is seated beside me, filling me in on his latest drug bust.

The grill is hot.

The beer is cold.

And then there's June—

In a barely there bikini.

She appears oblivious to her own perfection as she rings out her sopping hair, her light skin already pinkening beneath the unforgiving sun.

Kip has his phone pulled out and is aimlessly scrolling, head down.

Good.

I'd probably club him if I caught him gawking at her.

Taking another sip of beer, I try to keep my eyes from dipping below her face. "I don't know why it's called that. It just is."

"Well, do you want to play? You and me versus Kip and Celeste."

Kip's head snaps up. "Oh…uh, I'm good. I think I aged out of that about ten years ago."

Celeste is in town for two weeks for something family-related, so June invited her to the pool party with us. Kip was fine with it as long as the girls didn't drink.

I shake my head, in agreement with Kip but for entirely different reasons. June squirming atop my shoulders in her tiny bikini bottom sounds catastrophic. "Sorry, but I'm going to pass, too."

"You're no fun. How about—" June is closing in on me, smelling of chlorine and coconut sunscreen, when Celeste steals her attention from the edge of the pool.

"Let's dry off and grab food!" she calls out, dangling a beach towel from each hand.

June nibbles her lip, sending me a quick glance that holds more than it should, then turns to head in the other direction. I can't help but watch her float away for a beat too long, transfixed by the way she moves, inciting inevitable commentary from Kip.

"How's that going?" he murmurs around the opening of his beer.

Clearing my throat, I lean back in the lawn chair, twirling my own bottle between my fingers. I glance at him in his white T-shirt and swim trunks, his coppery hair grown out more and highlighted by the late afternoon sunshine. "It's not going anywhere," I lie.

It's gone too far already.

His eyebrow arches with doubt. "You know I'm a cop, right? I can spot deception from a mile away."

"Nothing's happened."

He nods, then takes another sip. "That I believe."

Sighing, I place my quickly warming beer in my chair's built-in cup holder, my eyes trailing to June as she wraps a colorful beach towel around her slim waist. She chose the rainbow print. "She moved in with me last week."

"Are you serious?"

"Yeah, I'm serious," I mutter, already knowing what a huge mistake it was. Already knowing that while I've been safely wading in the shallow end for the past year, stupidity and weakness pushed me into deep waters, and now I'm flailing. "She wanted a taste of independence, so I offered."

"Independence. Right." He ducks his head, lips pursing with thought. "You're playing with fire, Brant. If you're looking to get burned, have at it, but those flames are going to spread… You have to be okay with letting the things around you burn, too."

I swallow. "It's complicated."

"Fire is pretty straightforward. You light a match and shit burns down."

My gaze lingers on June as she wrings more water from her hair, then disappears around the side of the house with Celeste.

He's right. I know he's right.

And I've tried—I've *tried*—to keep my feelings bottled up, to fight this tooth and nail, to be stronger than whatever this is. I've been seeing Dr. Shelby again, my childhood psychologist, hoping for advice. For guidance.

She told me, "Out of sight, out of mind—and if you can't do that, set your sights on something else."

I tried that, too.

Hell, June *encouraged* me to try that...so I did. I kissed Sydney. I kissed Sydney knowing it would likely lead to more, knowing she could be the perfect cure for this disease.

I haven't been with a woman since that final time with Wendy, on the night she brought my fucked-up feelings into the harsh light of day. I haven't had sex in *years* because I'm in love with someone I shouldn't be in love with. Someone I can't have.

And that's not healthy.

June is dating, and I'd be lying if I said it hasn't been tearing me up inside. Every Saturday evening she disappears into the night with some mystery man she won't tell me about, probably too afraid I'll track him down and show up at his front door like I did with Wyatt.

Valid.

She's probably having sex.

She's probably having wild, raunchy sex with someone who isn't me, and that thought shouldn't sicken me the way it does.

Kip interrupts my reeling thoughts, sensing that he touched a nerve. "Hey, wherever you are right now, I didn't mean to send you there." He elbows me lightly on the shoulder. "I support you. Both of you. And you can take my unsolicited advice or leave it—you're both adults—but I just want you to tread carefully, okay?"

I glance at him. "Yeah, I hear you."

"You've lost a lot already, and I'd hate to see you lose even more."

Theo springs to mind.

His last words.

His dying blessing.

My chest tightens at the memory, and I inhale a pained breath as I nod. "You know, I wish I could tell you this was just some fleeting fixation, something perverse and temporary…an itch I want to scratch," I tell him, my tone low and gritty. "Would that make me a twisted creep? Probably. But at least it wouldn't hurt half as much as it does right now, being desperately in love with her, unable to see a future with anyone *but* her…not being able to live a normal, healthy life as a single man because I already belong to someone I can't even touch."

A lump thickens in my throat as emotion floods me.

When I look over at Kip, he's staring at me. His brows are pinched together, his jaw twitching with a similar sentiment. My words hover in the air, sounding louder than the aimless chatter and seventies music playlist filtering around us.

"My real name isn't Kip," he finally says.

I give him a curious frown, not expecting that reply. I blink. "What?"

"It's Lance. Lance Kipton." He looks away, pinning his eyes to the grass beneath our bare feet. "Before I became a cop, I worked as a mental-health case manager. I was on call a lot, visiting different psychiatric units, substance abuse clinics, in-home care. There was a hospital I visited frequently…and at that hospital there was a woman. A nurse." He smiles with whimsical affection. "Her name was Elloine—pretty name, huh?"

I fold my hands together in my lap, giving him a small nod.

"Anyway…she called me Kip. A nickname I grew to crave almost as much as I craved my visits to that hospital. She was beautiful, of course. Black hair the color of coal, and pale-green eyes. She had a softness to her—an aura you just wanted to keep and protect. The patients were drawn to her, the staff was drawn to her…and so was I."

"You…fell for her?" I deduce, noting the hint of torment in his tone.

He nods. "I did. Easily. Effortlessly," he says. "Unfortunately, everything past that was anything but. She was married."

"Shit."

"Yeah," Kip murmurs, rolling his tongue along his teeth. "He was an abusive son of a bitch, so I felt like that gave me some kind of permission to get involved with a woman who wasn't mine. A woman I couldn't have. She was off-limits…forbidden."

He looks at me pointedly, and the correlation sinks in deep.

"But we fell in love. We fell madly in love, and once it starts, it's really damn hard to stop." Kip takes a moment of silence, tapping his index finger against his beer bottle, his muscles tight and twitching. "I told you that my parents died in a boating accident years back. It's what gave me a new purpose, a new direction, and drove me to become a cop. I wanted justice. I needed it…and not just for them." He glances my way, his eyes glazed with deep pain. "For her, too. For Elloine."

My breath stalls as his words settle in, sluicing me with daunting realization. "She was on the boat?"

Kip pulls his lips between his teeth, holding back tears. "Yeah, she was. It was my boat, and I took Elloine out on the water with my parents that day, introducing them to her." He closes his eyes, dipping his head. "A fire broke out near the engine. Detectives found it suspicious—discovered evidence of tampering. It reeked of arson, and I knew it was her piece-of-shit husband. I *knew* it…but I could never prove it, and the case went cold," he says. "I was the only survivor."

Jesus.

My heart thunders with grief. Kip has lost so much. He's been through absolute hell. I run a hand down my face, sighing heavily as his story reverberates through me, sticking like sap. "God, I'm sorry. I can't even imagine."

"Yeah…it's hard to imagine that I've lived through the unimaginable," he replies, biting his lip and shaking his head. He takes another moment, then glances back up at me. "So…when I tell you to be careful, I'm telling you that from my own very relatable and very tragic experience. Be really fucking careful. I understand that need, that all-consuming fire that turns all good reason into ash. I've been there, right in the hot center of the flames.

"But I've also been there when everything burns down and you're standing all alone amid the devastating ruin, when all that's left is soot and kindling and billowing smoke. I've breathed in that smoke. I've choked on it. And I'm not saying your situation is the same… I'm not saying you're destined for tragedy." A smile blooms on his mouth, a little trace of empathy through the agony. "I'm just saying, friend to friend, that there *are* worse things than loving the wrong person."

I stare at him, waiting, my stomach twisting into knots.

"And that's losing them."

An hour goes by of stewing in Kip's words, picking at my burger, and mingling mindlessly with an assortment of Kip's friends and coworkers, and then I realize I haven't seen June since she disappeared with Celeste to grab food.

The girls rode over with me, so I know they're around somewhere.

Excusing myself from a casual conversation, I toss my empty beer bottle into a trash can and saunter into the older trilevel house, recently upgraded on the inside. The screen door slides open, leading through a quaint kitchen and dining area, and I'm instantly flooded by the sound of June's laughter trickling up from a downstairs den.

My feet carry me to the doorless doorway, then down the stairs and into a furnished den, where I discover June and Celeste chatting with two male friends of Kip's.

I stop at the bottom of the staircase, watching for a moment as one of the men curls his hand around June's hip, a gesture of flirtation. She's wearing denim shorts over her swimsuit bottom, but she's still only clad in her bikini on top.

And that's exactly where his eyes are fixated.

A fierce sense of possession funnels through me despite the logical truth that June is a grown adult. June is allowed to flirt with men.

June. Is. Not. Mine.

Did I retain nothing from Kip's warning?

She sways a little, looking unbalanced. And when she responds to something he says, her words slur together.

Shit. Has she been…drinking?

I clear my throat aggressively, garnering the attention of four heads twisting in my direction, and June lights up when she sees me, ignorant of the venom racing through my blood.

"Brant! My brother…" she singsongs, stumbling toward me as I approach. "My brother is here, you guys! He's just the *best*."

June slings her arms around my neck, nearly collapsing into me as the rest of the group looks on, probably wondering why it looks like she's trying to climb her brother like a tree.

I peel her off of me, then lift her chin with my index finger. Her eyes are glassy, her smile lopsided. A pang of worry stabs me. "Are you drunk, Junebug?"

The sound of her nickname brings a flicker of reality to her eyes. She swallows, then pinches her fingers together to signify a teensy amount. "Little bit."

Celeste pipes in, strolling over to us with a panic-stricken expression. "I'm so sorry, Brant… It's my fault. I brought those miniature liquor bottles, thinking we'd just get a little buzzed, but June drank two and now she's drunk a-and—"

"Jesus," I mutter, swiping my palms over my face. "Kip is going to kick my ass."

The two friends of Kip offer a sympathetic smile, then sweep past me and the girls, disappearing up the staircase. Celeste wrings her hands together. "I'm sorry. I'll grab our stuff and we can go."

June pouts. "I don't want to go. I'm having fun." She storms over to Celeste, pleading, "Let's stay a little longer. I want to swim."

"Celeste, can you give us a minute?" I intercede.

She looks at me, fiddling with her dark-blond braid and nodding her head with apology. "Sure. I'll wait out back."

"Thanks."

When she heads up the stairs, leaving us alone, I wait for June to turn around and face me. I'm disappointed that she was drinking when she hardly drinks at all, at a cop's house no less, and I'm even more disappointed that she almost just fooled around with a stranger twice her age.

Disappointed, or jealous?

I ignore my subconscious buzzing in my ear and watch as she clumsily pivots around, her hand reaching for the armrest of the couch to steady herself. Her eyes bat in my direction, her full lips parting as she says, "It's been hell living with you this week. Even though we've hardly seen each other…" She swallows, taking a step forward. "It's been hell."

My fingers curl at my sides, tension rippling through me. "Why is that?"

"You know why, Brant."

Of course I know why. It's almost as if I took in two roommates last Saturday—June, and the tangible sexual tension that came along with her.

It was a stupid idea.

I'm not exactly sure what I was thinking, especially after working so hard to put space between us, so I've concluded that I wasn't thinking at all. June was struggling, and I swooped in to save her. June wanted to leave the nest, so I offered her a safe place to land.

Unfortunately, the arrangement is backfiring, so I purposely put in long hours at work this week in order to avoid some kind of imminent explosion.

Seeing her so upset over what happened with Sydney confirmed my worst fear…

She feels it, too.

This is a mutual thing, and mutual things are ten times harder to ignore.

But I'm still trying. I'm still trying so damn hard to be strong, to do what I know is in her best interest—to keep us from going up in flames and singeing everything we hold dear.

June takes another step forward, her eyes glazed with more than alcohol.

I shake my head. "I'm not talking about this with you right now. Not when you're inebriated."

"Maybe we should. Maybe we have to."

"Maybe. But not now."

"But you look upset, and I hate when you're upset. You can talk to me."

My teeth grind together. "I'm upset because one minute you're calling me your brother, reminding me of how *wrong* this is, and the next minute you're looking at me like you want me to tear that bikini off of you and cross a line we can't come back from."

June slicks her tongue over her lips, inhaling a quick breath. Then she nibbles that lip, conveying innocence but looking like pure sin.

She teeters as she moves closer toward me, circling her finger around my face with a long, weary sigh. "It's not fair."

"What's not fair?"

"Your face."

I frown. "My face isn't fair?"

"No. Not at all."

"Why?" I almost laugh, watching as she continues her wobbly trek forward. My gaze dips south for the tiniest moment, landing on her ample cleavage, before sliding back up.

Pure sin.

June lands toe-to-toe with me, her partially dried hair cascading over bare shoulders in thick sections, the ends still wet and tickling the swell of her breasts. She sucks in a deep breath. "It's not fair that your face is so perfect, a piece of art on display that I'm not allowed to touch. I should only adore it from afar, even though its beauty calls to me. Even though I'm convinced it was created just for me." Her eyelashes flutter as she sways, as if she's drunk on more than rum or whiskey, as if she's drunk on her own words. "It's not fair that it holds two eyes that look at me the way they do, like they were made for seeing only me. It's not fair that it has lips that I've memorized, that I can't forget, and a tongue I've dreamed about tasting me over and over again." June lifts her hand, pressing the pads of two fingertips to her mouth. She adds huskily, "And not just here."

Any trace of humor lingering in the air pulverizes into dust as raw hunger takes its place.

My molars scrape together, my cock twitching at her implication.

June's hand extends from her mouth, planting against my chest as her eyes rove my face with bold lust. She's never come on to me like this before, and I think that's the only goddamn reason I haven't turned us into something criminal.

Her innocence tames me.

Her naivety grounds me.

Her sweetness buries the rotten thoughts.

But this?

This girl has the power to unleash the hibernating beast.

She's drunk. She's not thinking clearly. You'll regret this for the rest of your life.

I'm about to tell her to put some clothes on and collect her things when her hand slowly travels down my chest, over my abdomen, then grazes the swollen bulge between my legs. "I bet this isn't fair either," she whispers, her voice full of smoke. "I bet it would wreck me."

Holy shit.

I audibly groan, my better judgment snapping in two as I lean down and snatch her up by the thighs, coiling her legs around my hips. She squeaks in surprise as I carry her to the nearby couch and collapse backwards with June in my lap. She falls against me while I fall further under her spell.

June continues to rub my erection, her breaths morphing into quick pants and her skin flushing pink before me. She writes a little, seeking friction, then uses her opposite hand to shove my face between her bikini-clad breasts.

Another moan pours out of me, and I'm certain I'm going to come in my pants in about five seconds.

My brain starts trying to think ahead.

Is the door locked?

No, there is no door.

Do I have a condom?

No, I haven't had sex in two years.

Is this a one-way ticket to hell?

Yes.

June's movements are languid and lazy as she swivels her hips on my lap, her fingers gliding through my hair while she strokes me with her other hand. "Maybe we don't need to talk at all. If you want me," she says breathily, "you can have me."

As she gives me permission to fuck her on Kip's couch, in his den, while dozens of party guests who see us as brother and sister are above us thinking we're down here playing fucking checkers or something, a whiff of alcohol on her breath infiltrates my lungs.

It chokes me.

It wakes me the hell up.

With my face smashed against her cleavage, I breathe into her skin, "You want to know what's not fair?" One of my arms wraps around her back, drawing her closer, while the other palms her breast. My thumb brushes over her pebbled nipple as I tug down the thin slip of bikini, then I drag my mouth over to it until I'm sucking it between my teeth. June whimpers desperately, squeezing my rock-hard erection with one hand and gripping my hair with the other. I lave my tongue over her breast, savoring the taste of her skin fused with salt and chlorine, before situating her bikini back into place. I glance up at her through hooded eyes. "It's not fair that I can't have the woman I'm madly in love with, who's wriggling around in my lap, stroking me through my jeans, telling me that my cock would fucking wreck her."

June stills, her forehead falling against mine. Inhaling sharply, she inches her hand away from my groin, breathing heavily, her skin prickled with goose bumps and painted in sunburn. Glazed blue eyes open slowly, almost as if she had been sleeping. Groggy, glimmering with confliction.

"I can't have you," I repeat.

I repeat it for her. I repeat it for me.

I can't have you.

She swivels her forehead, reining in her feelings, trailing her hands up my chest until they rest on my shoulders. The tips of her wet hair chill my heated skin. "If I forget this by tomorrow, can…can you remind me? I don't want to forget this moment," she rasps out, curling her fingers around my T-shirt. Then her forehead slips from mine, and I'm worried she's going to kiss me—I'm worried because I'm not sure I can stop it if she kisses me—but instead, she drops her head to the top of my shoulder, becoming deadweight in my lap. "Please remind me."

June passes out almost instantly, and before someone can walk downstairs and discover us precariously entwined, I twist her off my lap and lay her on the couch, pulling an afghan off the back and draping it over her. Bending forward, I push a piece of hair out of her eyes and kiss her temple, whispering, "I won't."

29

FIRST TIME

BRANT, AGE 25

There's something different about her tonight.

June stands before a full-length mirror just inside her parents' bedroom, wearing a silky, baby-blue slip dress while clipping an earring back into place. I'm perched in the doorway, watching with measured fondness, when she tilts her head toward me.

A smile stretches, tender and real.

Her eyes glitter with unmistakable affection.

A piece of freshly blow-dried hair slips into her face, captivating me.

My hands are stuffed into my dress pants, my chest humming with something I can't exactly pinpoint, as I murmur, "We're about to sing 'Happy Birthday.'"

It's Andrew's fifty-seventh birthday.

Naturally, he's positioned at the grill in a full-on suit with a metal spatula in his hand and platypus slippers on his feet.

June's smile only brightens, a flash of teeth following her hair flip. "Be right there," she tells me. "You look really handsome, by the way."

"Oh…thanks, Junebug." Instinctively, I glance down at my classier attire, from dark-gray slacks to a white dress shirt with navy pinstripes. The curls in my mop of hair are tamed with a little bit of gel as a I run a hand through them. "So do you."

"Handsome, huh?" Her nose crinkles with amusement as she tips her invisible hat to me. "I do look rather dapper."

I laugh, ducking my head and mussing my hair again. "Pretty…you look really pretty."

When I glance back up, she's glowing.

Our eyes ignite with more than a flame, with more than the smoky tension filling the space between us.

I see dancing clouds and bright blue skies.

Rainbows and lullabies.

Toy elephants and kindred promises.

Deep within her crystalline stare, I see a love that burns stronger than any wicked firestorm threatening to torch us into cinders.

Maybe that's what's different tonight. Our desire to maintain our precious bond feels bigger than our *desire*. That could be because we're back in our old house, surrounded by wholesome memories, reminded of our childhood when we sweep down every hallway and turn every corner. Photographs litter the walls. Nostalgia thickens the air.

Theo feels closer than ever.

In the five days following our brush with temptation the prior weekend, I've been reflecting on Kip's words of caution, advice born from his own terrible tragedy:

"There are worse things than loving the wrong person. And that's losing them."

I'll lose June by loving her the wrong way.

She'll slip through the cracks of my fingers like gunpowder.

And Kip is right… I've lost too much already.

Luckily, June doesn't recall our heated rendezvous on Kip's couch—and if she does, she's been faking it well. I kept my promise and haven't dared remind her of the way she brazenly came on to me with lust in her eyes and wicked words on her tongue.

Words that have filtered through my brain on repeat all week…and are reappearing right at this very moment.

Damn it.

Doing a little twirl in front of the mirror, June curtsies before me, still smiling wide. "Okay, let's go," she says, floating over to me in her ballet flats and linking our hands together.

I try to ignore the heat that creeps up my arm when our fingers interlock, and I try to suppress the fuzzy feeling that zaps my heart when she glances up at me with that same sweet smile and doe eyes. Clicking my teeth, I ruefully pull free of her hold the moment we're within eyesight of her parents.

It's not really a party—it's just the four of us. That's what Andrew wanted for his birthday this year. He asked us to dress up, put on our "boogie shoes," and leave our frowns behind.

When we glide out through the patio door, he's already boogying.

The song "September" by Earth, Wind, and Fire is blasting through the speakers as Andrew and Samantha hop around the brick pavers, her in a red satin gown and him in his ridiculous slippers. He twirls her in a circle as she throws her head back with a laugh, then reaches for the discarded spatula and brings it to his mouth like a microphone. "Do you remem-ba?" he sings dramatically on the dip.

June cups a palm over her mouth, giggles spilling out and blending with the song. She grabs my hand again. "Dance with me," she commands through a grin.

I'm pulled to the center of the patio along with the Baileys as June wraps an arm around my midsection and tucks her hand into mine. Yoshi sprints out behind us, hobbling on his old, stubby legs, barking up at us like he's trying to sing along.

"You know I can't dance, Junebug," I tell her, my charmed smile letting her know that I'm still going to try.

Andrew sends us a wink as he dips Samantha again, almost dropping her.

We all laugh.

We all laugh so hard our bellies ache, and June collapses against my chest, squeezing my hand as she clumsily shimmies us around the patio. Her muffled laughter vibrates through my dress shirt, sending warm tremors to my heart.

She looks up at me, chin propped against my chest. "I miss dancing," she murmurs, her tone a little sad. A little wistful.

"I know."

"Sometimes I think about when I was a kid, dancing on the big stage at all those spring recitals. No asthma, no heartbreak. It was only dancing."

My hand splays along the middle of her back as I dip her. "It still can be."

A smile creeps in as she swoops back up, our palms clamped together. Her eyes twinkle in the early evening haze. "Too many bad things have happened. There's this black cloud following me around, and it's not the same anymore..."

"Dancing is dancing, June." I spin her in a clunky twirl.

"The black cloud is too big."

She spins herself with far more grace, and as she falls back against me, her chest to mine, I whisper down at her, "Be bigger than it."

June parts her lips with argument, but her words dissolve away when mine sink in. She blinks, her gaze fused with something hopeful.

"Honey, it's one of your favorite songs," Samantha pipes in, shaking us from the moment.

I let go of June, wondering if we were too close. Replaying the moment, questioning if we were looking at each other in all the wrong ways or pressed together too intimately.

I wonder if the Baileys saw that look of longing in my eyes I'm certain I forgot to hide.

God, I hope not.

I scratch at the nape of my neck as June eases backward, pulling her attention off of me and zoning in on the song. Her face lights up with recognition.

"Stand by Me" by Ben E. King.

June danced to a rendition of it a few years back as she was just entering high school. It was always one of her favorite performances.

"I think I still remember the routine," she says, skipping off into the grass and getting into one of her ballet positions.

When the next verse starts, she moves.

She floats and glides.

She dances.

The song drowns out, and all I see is June—a vision in baby blue, skipping across clouds like a melodic bluebird.

Like she never lost her wings.

I inhale a choppy breath, clenching my fingers at my sides as my eyes drink her in. Her body bows, her legs leap and sway, her arms arc in the shape of a rainbow. She moves like pure poetry, and the smile etched onto her lips is the exclamation point.

June is so much more than a dancer.

She's nature's most exquisite choreography.

When the song ends, Andrew and Samantha clap joyously, their faces pinched with pride. Andrew whistles with his thumb and index finger, while Samantha clasps her hands in front of her, beaming with maternal admiration.

I know they saw what I saw—that reemerging spark.

And I hope she stokes it. I hope she keeps it warm.

June takes a dramatic bow, twirling one arm in a circle, then flipping her hair back with a bashful burst of laughter. Her gaze trails to me, eager for my reaction.

I clap.

I smile.

But everything she's searching for is in the way I'm looking at her, like the whole world has fallen away, swallowed up by the love I feel.

She ducks her head.

"I'm not sure about you kids, but I'm ready for cake," Andrew pipes in. He shoots me a quick glance. "Strawberry rhubarb, right?"

"Always," I confirm. "With cream cheese frosting."

I was in charge of his birthday cake this year.

I'm in charge of everyone's birthday cake every year.

"I'll never take Brant for *grant*-ed," he winks, sweeping past me.

Wow.

I'm pretty sure the joke itself has secondhand embarrassment.

We all groan simultaneously as Samantha trails after him, giving my elbow a tender squeeze along the way. "I'll fetch the plates."

As they step into the kitchen through the sliding door, closing it behind them, June startles me by reaching over and wrapping her arms around my middle for a tight hug. Her cheek plants against my chest, and I hesitate briefly before stroking my fingers through her hair, hoping the Baileys aren't watching through the drapes.

It's just a hug, I tell myself.

Lilacs invade my senses, sweet and fragrant.

Soothing and healing.

I'm not sure if it's coming from the bushes that line the back of the house or from the woman in my arms, soft and delicate like a flower petal. "You always smell like springtime and lemon drops," I say gently, kissing the top of her head. My eyes close with contentment as I breathe her in.

She sighs, her breath warming me through the fabric of my shirt. "You always smell like spearmint and Ivory soap."

Songbirds serenade us as we stand in the center of the patio, enmeshed in a potent embrace, breathing in perfect time and swaying lightly, as if nature is singing just for us.

Then we say it at the same time: "Like home."

We enter our shared apartment a few hours later, our bellies full of birthday cake and laughter still ringing in our ears. June tosses her handbag to the countertop and slips out of her ballet flats. There's a strange energy in the air hovering around us, and I wonder if she notices it, too, as she straightens in the entryway, lifting her eyes to me. She fiddles with her hair, twisting it over one shoulder, a tentative smile touching her lips.

I stare at her for a few beats, not really sure what to say. All I know is that I'm not ready to say good night yet. "Do you…" I swallow, popping my thumb over my shoulder. "Do you want to watch a movie or something?"

She doesn't hesitate, still playing with her hair. "Sure."

"Okay." My smile claims me, something almost shy, like I'm inviting a girl inside after a first date. Shaking my head, I clear my throat and saunter into the adjoined living room, sifting around the cushions for the remote and taking a seat.

June sits right next to me on the couch, her bare thigh pressed against my slacks as her slip dress rides up. I only spare the image a fleeting glance, refusing to recall the way her thighs were linked around me just five days ago as she whispered delicious, forbidden things in my ear.

Flustered by the memory, I shift away from her and start aimlessly scrolling through Netflix.

June inches closer. "Remember when Theo would recite movie lines before they were voiced, pissing everyone off, because he'd seen almost every movie ever created?"

Genuine laughter rumbles through me. "Yes. Drove us all nuts," I recall fondly, leaning back against the cushions and ruffling my hair. "We'd always get up and leave halfway through the movie because it was so annoying. I think it was his way of secretly hoarding all the popcorn."

"Oh my God, I bet you're right." June giggles, her temple falling to my shoulder. She pulls her feet up beside her until she's pressed fully into me. "He was such a rascal."

"Yeah…I'd give anything to have him here right now, ruining whatever shitty movie we're about to watch."

"Me too." She sighs softly.

Instinct and an inherent need to feel her even closer has me wrapping an arm around her shoulders, tugging her to my frame. June curls into me with effortless ease, as if it's where she's always belonged. Her fine wisps of hair tickle my chin, her curves molding against me.

"Thank you for tonight," she tells me, her voice muffled by my shirt. "I needed that. The dancing, the laughter, the family time. I can't even remember the last time I felt so…burdenless." She glances up at me. "You know?"

I nod as my fingers braid through her mane of hair. "Yeah, I know. I think we all needed it."

"And this is the perfect end to a perfect day. Cozied up on the couch with you as we scroll through hundreds of different movies, finally deciding on something after we're too tired to even watch it anymore."

Another laugh slips out. "Happens every time," I say, nuzzling in to her. "Remember when our Netflix binges would always end in a tickle fight?"

She pinches my thigh, as if retaliating to the mere memory. "Yes. You were terrible. You knew all of my sensitive tickle spots, and I'd laugh so hard I'd almost pee."

"Not my fault you're so ticklish." I give her arm a pinch.

June feigns pain. "Ouch."

"You pinched me first."

"I'll pinch you again." She does.

My hand travels down her arm, to her ribs, my fingers dancing lightly over her silk dress. She tenses up in anticipation, pressing further into me like she can crawl inside and escape the inevitable. "Don't fight it, Junebug. You're long overdue."

"Brant, I swear—"

I tickle her. Hard and furiously, until she's squealing and squirming, desperate for reprieve. As she nearly breaks free, my other hand grabs her by the waist and tosses her backward onto the couch, her hair splaying around her like a russet halo. High-pitched squeals morph into belly laughter as her legs try to kick me away, but I hold them down with my torso, trapping her beneath my weight. My fingers continue to dance and roam with the perfect amount of pressure, digging into her sensitive spots until she's sliding down the edge of the couch, her dress riding up when my hands dip higher.

"Stop, stop, it's too much," she says, laughing, tears leaking from her eyes.

My own grin is wicked as I hook one hand around her waist to keep her steady while the other tickles her opposite side.

As her foot pulls free and presses against my outer thigh as a means to push herself away from me, she slides back even more, still squirming and breathless, until her bare stomach is level with my face.

I notice.

The levity leaves me on a sharp breath.

Her dress is rolled up to just below her breasts, her lacy white panties exposed and only inches away from me. June stills, winded as she comes down from the adrenaline high, glancing south to see why my roving fingers have stalled and are now curling around her hip bone.

I look up at her, and her smile fades, both of us absorbing the compromising position we're in—June spread out beneath me, half-naked, one foot propped along my thigh while the other dangles off the side of the couch. Me on my knees between her legs with my mouth hovering over her belly button, my hands latched around her hips. My fingertips dig into her, nearly bruising.

The mood shifts in an instant.

Dark, crackling tension swoops in, and June releases a little gasp laced with something dangerous. Her head falls back to the armrest, her body heaving below me with labored breaths. She doesn't move. She doesn't try to escape.

She just waits.

She waits, nearly trembling, as I lower my face to her creamy white skin, my eyelids fluttering closed as I inhale her citrus scent. My nose grazes the expanse of her stomach, skimming downward, over the hemline of her underwear, until the smell of lemon drops is replaced by the feminine musk between her legs seeping through the thin lace. A gravelly groan leaves me as my nose nuzzles into the juncture between her legs. Damp and hot. I breathe her in, still clutching at her hips so hard I'm afraid I'm going to hurt her.

June whimpers as her shaky hands make their way to my hair, fingers sifting. Nails grazing my scalp. Her pelvis jerks up, just slightly, like it's instinct, like she's silently begging me to sample her.

Her legs spread farther apart.

And I lose it.

I fucking lose it.

I trail my fingers underneath the hem of her panties, yanking them down past her knees.

Then I bend over and bury my face between her thighs.

June cries out.

She lets out a sharp, primal moan as her hips thrust up against my mouth and her nails carve into my scalp.

I feast on her.

Untamed. Untethered.

Hungry.

Her wetness rolls across my mouth as I plunge my tongue deep inside her, in and out, my groans mingling with her desperate mewls. After tugging her underwear all the way off, I glide one hand up her body, beneath the silk fabric of her dress, until I'm cupping her breast, while my other hand holds her firmly to me.

"Brant, oh God…oh my God…" she chants, panting and writhing beneath me. She hooks one leg along my upper back, the other dangling off the side of the couch.

I grab it, wrapping it around my shoulder until her bottom half is lifted off the cushion, her thighs clamping my face as she tugs at my hair.

As I palm her breast, tweaking her nipple, she arches into me, and I drag my mouth to her clit, flicking it with my tongue and sucking it between my teeth.

"Ooh," she moans, thrusting harder against my face. "Oh, Brant…Brant… oh, shit…"

Jesus Christ, the noises she's making. The way she's panting my name as her body shamelessly thrashes and throbs under my tongue. The way she grips my hair, her spine arching, her skin flushed bright pink while I eat her out.

I'm eating her out.

I'm eating her out like a fucking animal on my living room couch.

My cock is rock-hard and raging in the confines of my pants as her sweet nectar fills my mouth, her wetness pooling. I push two fingers inside her, pumping furiously while my name spills from her lips over and over, my tongue still working her to climax.

Still fucking her with my fingers, I use my other hand to unbuckle my belt and yank my zipper down, my erection aching for freedom. My tongue continues to pleasure her, laving and licking, as I wrap my hand around my dick and jerk myself while she unravels.

Her body tenses, bracing for release, and a tapered groan falls out of me as I murmur against her, "*Fuck*, June…you're going to come all over my mouth, aren't you?"

She shudders, bucking upward. "Y-Yes…God, yes…please, Brant, don't stop…"

I stroke myself harder as she begs me, my own orgasm building. "Fuck," I repeat, my body trembling with need as I curl my fingers inside her, still sucking her clit until I feel her peaking.

She's gasping and panting. Clenching her thighs. Riding my face as I feast and suck and ravish her with my tongue and fingers.

And then a sharp cry catches in her throat, her breath hitching, her body vibrating with the swell of orgasm. I let go of myself to palm her outer thigh, holding her firmly against me as I continue to work her. She fists my hair at the roots and throws her head back over the armrest, a moan pouring out of her as she breaks.

As she comes.

June is coming on my mouth, on my fingers, drenching me with her release. Singing my name like it's her favorite song.

When she deflates with a soft whimper, collapsing beneath me and draping the back of her arm over her forehead, she sucks in long, deep breaths, her body going limp. I raise my head, my lips and chin glazed with her climax. She's never been more gorgeous, half-bare below me, her hair in disarray and her skin painted in blotches of pink flush.

She lifts up a little, our eyes locking.

The realization sinks into both of us that we just crossed a very dangerous, very intoxicating line, and I have no idea where to go from here.

June bites at her lip. Her glassy eyes travel south, to where my pants are pushed down my hips, landing on my red and angry erection. It hangs heavy between my legs, the tip glistening with precum. Pulsing with the need to be inside her.

I'm not sure if I should apologize or kiss her.

I'm not sure if I should take this further or lock myself in my bedroom and jerk off with her honey still on my tongue.

Unrehearsed words start to spill out of me as I lower myself over her, until we're face-to-face and I'm brushing a piece of knotted hair from her eyes. "Shit…June, I—"

"Make love to me."

Her words whip through me like a windstorm as our eyes tangle together, her hand trailing downward and wrapping around my cock. My eyes snap shut, forcing back the wave of pleasure that floods me the moment she fists me. I grit my teeth through a groan, then tug her dress all the way up her body, over her head, discarding it to the floor.

Moving back up to my knees, I gaze down at her.

Completely bare. Utterly vulnerable.

Her full breasts heave with each breath, her nipples pebbled and wanting. Lust glitters back at me in pools of light blue.

June.

My sweetest blessing and greatest sin.

I start unfastening my dress shirt, one painful button at a time, while June watches, her gaze dancing between my fingers and my thick erection. When I shrug the shirt off, I drape myself back over her, pressing our foreheads together as our lips hover a hairsbreadth apart. June's arms link around my neck, her knees spreading like an illicit invitation. "I should look for a condom," I mutter, my voice full of grit.

She shakes her head. "No. I want to feel you…" Her hands rove down my shoulder blades, as if soaking up the feel of my bare skin, then travel back up to muss my hair. "All of you."

"Fuck, June…" I cradle her cheeks between my palms, my thumb dusting over her lips. Wide eyes stare back at me, gleaming with hunger and nerves. She's nervous, I can tell. "Are you sure? We don't have to—"

My words are cut short when she lifts up and crushes her mouth to mine. I melt into her, my eyes closing as a groan rumbles in my throat. Our tongues instantly twist and twine, delicious familiarity spurring us both, wrapping us in a blanket of lust and misdeed. Her release still coats my lips as I angle my face, tasting her deeper, my tongue filling every inch of her mouth. I only pull back to whisper raggedly, "Can you taste what I did to you?"

She whimpers, her legs coiling around my hips, then she sweeps her tongue along the roof of my mouth. "Yes," she says in a squeaky breath. "Do it again."

God.

My dick twitches at her command to make her come again, eager to slip inside. I drag my hands down her body, over her breasts, until I'm gripping her slim waist. Then I reach for my cock and slide the head over her wetness, still slick and needy. A moan slips out of me as my face falls into the crook of her neck. June's hands make their way down my spine and land on my ass, squeezing hard, and it's all I need to push inside, just a torturous inch. Just the tip.

She squirms beneath me, panting, her mewls vibrating in my ears.

Holy shit—she's tight. So fucking tight. Fisting her hair and dragging my tongue up her collarbone to the sweet curve of her neck, I shove all the way inside with a satisfied moan.

Then I freeze with stunned shock.

A strangled gasp escapes her, and she bites down on my shoulder to stifle the pain.

No way.

I lift up as her head falls back.

Our eyes lock.

No fucking way.

I felt that.

I. Felt. That.

Like I just tore through a precious barrier that I had no right to breach.

An avalanche of conflicting emotions chokes me—

Horror.

Confusion.

Relief.

A sickening, animalistic rush that has my blood pumping hot and my hips starting to move as if of their own volition, despite the knowledge that I just stole June's virginity.

June was a virgin.

Our eyes are still holding tight as I rasp, "How…"

She shakes her head a little, like she doesn't want to address it. She doesn't want to talk. She doesn't want to stop.

My forehead drops to hers again as my teeth clench. "I'll go slow."

"No, don't," she squeaks out.

Fuck. She shouldn't say that when I'm sheathed inside her—knowing I'm the *only* man who's ever been inside her. I rock my hips, forcing myself to go slow despite her request otherwise, then cup her face between my palms with our foreheads melded and noses kissing. My fingertips slip into her hair, my thumbs bruising her cheeks while our bodies move together. "Am I hurting you?" I muster, trying not to lose all control.

"No. Keep going." Her nails are digging into the skin at the nape of my neck, her legs wrapped around me, tugging me close.

"God, you feel so good…"

I pick up speed. I can't help it.

June's body bows, her head dipping back, hair spilling over the side of the couch like a chocolate fountain. She pushes my head down toward her breasts as I pump into her faster, my lips locking around a dusky nipple and sucking it into my mouth. She moans. She begs me to keep riding her. We're dancing with the devil, yet she's the purest thing I've ever savored. A sweet, forbidden fruit.

And I'm drowning in her.

I'm succumbing to everything we are, and everything I never thought we'd be.

I clutch her hips for leverage as I rut into her, my teeth clamping around her breast and causing her to shudder. She's mewling and scratching me, dragging her nails up and down my shoulders. I move back up, nibbling her earlobe and whispering, "Were you saving it for me, June?" My hand dips between our joined bodies, my fingers finding her clit. "Were you saving this for me?"

She cries out, thighs clenching tight. "Yes."

"Fuck…"

My cock thrusts into her, our skin slapping together, our mutual moans growing louder as my mouth finds hers for a sloppy kiss. I curl a hand around the ivory expanse of her throat, squeezing gently, like I'm claiming what's always been mine. My other hand still works her clit, guiding her to another orgasm—desperate for her to dive over this jagged, fucked-up cliff with me.

I should be making this magical for her. Carrying her to my bed and worshiping her beneath cool, clean sheets until she's sleepy and satiated, until sunrise douses us in a red-orange glow, until she's wrapped up in my arms while divine deities sing her to sleep.

But this isn't a watered-down fairy tale.

This is messy, urgent…*fucking hot.*

I'm wrecking her with every furious thrust, my tongue knotting with hers, one hand wrapped around her throat as the other pulls another orgasm out of her.

My own release is mounting as I slam into her tight heat, grunting against her mouth, "I'm going to come in you."

"Please," she whimpers.

I tug her hair back. "You want my cum?"

Her body tenses, legs squeezing me with a viselike grip. She starts to tremble with the onset of her second climax. "Yes, Brant, please…"

Smashing my lips to hers, I continue to rub her clit until she explodes underneath me: fireworks, embers, falling stars. She breaks apart, gasping and chanting my name, and I break right along with her. A moan of pleasure pours out of me and into her mouth, our tongues clumsily moving together as I ride out the ripples, emptying into her. My hands rise up to hug her face as my body shudders, finding more than just relief, more than a temporary satisfaction, as I sink unconditionally inside of her. Inside every immaculate inch of her: heart, body, soul.

And I don't just *sink*.

I catapult headfirst into the deep end.

June grazes her fingertips up my back, over my shoulders, and cradles them around my neck as her toes tickle down the underside of my legs. I collapse onto her with a frayed breath, catching myself on my elbows so I don't crush her. Our lips are still hovering together, my eyes closed as I gather the courage to look into hers.

She gently presses a kiss to my mouth, our bodies slick and sticky. "Look at me, Brant," she says, her voice cracked and worn from her cries of pleasure. "See me."

My eyelids flutter, mimicking my worried heart. I hold her tighter. "Did… did I hurt you?"

"No."

Opening my eyes all the way, I search for the truth in her wide-eyed gaze. But all I can focus on is the lone tear trickling down her cheek, collapsing onto the armrest of the couch. A frown claims me, my body tensing with concern, and I lift up.

She hisses a bit as I slide out of her, and the sound is like a dull dagger to my chest. The blinding desire dwindles into dread when I glance down to where our bodies were just joined, seeing my cum pooled between her legs, tinged red with her blood.

Horror sinks me.

I'm also coated in red, as if I'm spotlighted in sin.

Branded with crimson shame.

Pulling up all the way, I tug at my pants that are bunched around my calves, fastening them back into place. My face twists with guilt and apology as I gaze down at her, her knees still spread, thighs smeared with blood, body heaving with arduous breaths. "Hold on…I'll–I'll be right back," I force out, forgoing my shirt as I sprint toward the single bathroom.

I return moments later with a warm damp cloth.

June is sitting up, her knees now pressed together, lips trembling. "I'm okay, Brant," she tells me as I approach. "I'm fine."

"You're not okay. God, I wrecked you…" Falling to my knees in front of her, I use one hand to gently part her legs. I swallow. "I'm sorry."

"Please…don't be sorry. I wanted it as much as you did."

As her thighs spread before me, revealing the evidence of my crime, my ribs ache with the weight of my grief. "I wasn't gentle. I wasn't kind." I dab the damp cloth to her juncture, wincing when she hisses again. "I did this to you."

She asked me to make love to her, and instead I fucked her raw and dirty on my couch. I made her bleed. I came inside of her with no protection, and I growled filthy things into her ear.

I'm a monster.

"Brant…" June leans forward, her eyes glistening, hair a matted mess. Mascara is streaked above her cheekbones. She clasps my jaws in her trembling palms as she pleads, "Don't regret this. Don't regret me."

"I regret how it happened," I confess, still blotting the cloth to her tender core. Trying to erase my infraction. "I should have made it special for you."

"It was special." Her fingertips graze along my stubbled jawline, whispering over my lips. "It was with you."

With *me*.

Her adopted brother.

This is beyond fucked.

A lump sticks in my throat as I pull to a stand, taking her with me. June rises on wobbly legs, her eyes glazed with worry as she steps forward and presses herself against my bare chest. Skin on skin. My heart gallops as I cup the back of her head, her floral scent mingling with sex and sweat.

She whispers softly, "It was everything."

Emotion races through me. Every emotion—regret, bliss, self-hatred, fear, and untouchable love. A love that has gone frighteningly off course, one that I'm not sure how to get back on track before we suffer an inevitable crash and go up in flames.

Kip's words of warning follow me like a dark cloud as I guide June to my bedroom and slip into the bed beside her, pulling her close, spooning her tight, and falling into a tumultuous sleep.

"Those flames are going to spread... You have to be okay with letting the things around you burn, too."

30

FIRST TASTE

JUNE, AGE 19

I'M AWOKEN BY AN ACHE between my legs and empty sheets.

Both left by him.

By Brant.

Sunlight filters in through the crack in his pale-blue curtains, the only color pop in an otherwise sterile, barren room. A chill whispers down my spine as I sit up straight.

I can't help but wince.

I'm sore and bruised all over, but his absence hurts the most. Maybe it was my own idyllic fantasy that we'd wake up gloriously entangled, whispering words of love against swollen, kissed lips, and begin a beautiful new chapter together. Surely, it was. But I thought at the very least he'd still be lying beside me when the sun breached the morning sky.

Inching my way from the bed that smells of his favorite soap, I search the dimly lit room for a spare T-shirt I can slip on until I make it to my own bedroom to change. I fell asleep naked in his arms last night, safe and satiated, not regretting a single moment of what happened between us. I fell asleep with a smile.

How many people experience their first time with someone they love so purely? So unconditionally? So *entirely*?

Not many, I'd reckon.

Unfortunately, by propriety's standards the tradeoff is that my first time *should* have been with anyone other than him. And I know that's probably eating at him right now.

I shuffle from the bedroom in one of Brant's T-shirts and crack open the door. Brant is perched in front of the living room couch, scrubbing away at the cushions with a rag and cleaning supplies. He doesn't notice me right away as I slip from the room and tiptoe closer, fidgeting with the ends of my hair. He's too focused, too absorbed in his task. When I'm only a few feet away, I squeak out, "Good morning."

He startles, his head popping up. Brant straightens as his arms drop to his sides, one hand fisted around a sudsy washrag. He pulls his lips between his teeth while tortured tawny eyes give me a quick sweep. "Hey."

I stare at him, unblinking. Waiting for more.

He remains silent, then looks away.

"What are you doing?" I force out, my breaths sticking to the back of my throat like paste. I take a step closer to him. "I, um, didn't expect to wake up alone."

Silly girl fairy tales.

"Oh…" A doleful look crosses his face. Something penitent. "Sorry, I–I didn't want to wake you. You looked peaceful." When I glance down at the washrag, he gives it a light squeeze and follows my stare. "I was just cleaning up."

Cleaning up.

My eyes trail to the soapy stain on the couch where Brant was trying to remove a blot of blood left behind. Blood as a result of my severed virginity.

He's cleaning up the mess we made.

Emotion swells in my chest, causing it to feel tight and smothered. "I'm sorry. I didn't mean to ruin your couch," I say softly. Meekly.

Pathetically.

Brant sucks in a sharp breath, his expression turning even more haunted. His gaze flicks over me, like he's taking a moment to absorb my words. He's letting them in, letting them fester.

Then he drops the rag and closes the gap between us, reaching for me. He pulls me straight to him until our foreheads crash together and he's holding me in a stormy grip. "Don't," he whispers, his hands clinging to my waist. "Don't you dare apologize for anything."

"I feel like I need to. You're upset… I can tell."

"I'm upset because of what *I* did—not you. Never you."

My hands lift, settling on his denim-clad hips. "You did exactly what I wanted you to do," I confess in a soft breath.

"Hurt you? Steal away your innocence? Make you bleed?"

"Heal me. Accept my innocence as a gift I gave you. Make me come… twice." His eyes darken, flashing with lingering heat from the night before. "I wanted you to make love to me, and that's what we did."

"That wasn't…" His eyes squeeze shut as his fingers tighten around my waist. "I lost control. Your first time is supposed to be slow and sweet, tender and kind. I took you like a fucking animal, June. I couldn't stop, and I hate myself for it." He blows out a breath. "Are you on the pill?"

"Yes. Mom got me on a prescription a few years ago, just to be proactive." Tears prickle my eyes. My heart aches seeing him so fractured. So conflicted and torn. I raise a hand, cupping his jaw as I brush my thumb over his bottom lip. "And I wish you wouldn't feel that way. It was perfect."

"Don't say that," he rasps out. His tongue pokes out, tasting the pad of my thumb, sending shivers down my back. "Don't allow me to believe you wanted it like that. Especially when you're standing in my arms, dressed only in my T-shirt, still smelling like last night's sins."

I arch into him, a whimper slipping out when he catches my thumb between his teeth. "Believe it," I tell him. "It's the truth."

Brant groans as his hands start to move, grazing up the back of my thighs and palming my bare bottom, our foreheads still melded together, our lips a mere whisper apart. He pulls my pelvis flush against him as he says, "Then lie to me."

Lie to him?

Lie to the man who has only ever shown me truth?

True strength…true meaning…true love.

No.

I can't. I won't.

Biting my lip, I shake my head.

His grip on me slackens with a defeated exhale. Brant takes a sizable step back and dips his chin, looking like he's lost a battle he already knew he couldn't win. When our eyes meet on a somber beat, he asks, "Why didn't you tell me you were still a virgin?" The question sounds pained. It sounds as if my choice of chastity has physically wounded him.

My shoulders shrug with an air of flippancy, even though I feel anything but. "I wasn't aware you didn't know."

"I heard you, June. I *heard* you tell your friends you were having sex three years ago."

"I…" My mind reels back in time, trying to pinpoint his reference. A hazy memory of sitting in a three-way circle with Celeste and Gen on my bedroom floor on a summer afternoon comes into focus. I had lied, of course. All of my friends were having sex, so I wanted to jump on the bandwagon. I wanted to feel mature and important, just like them. "I made up a story to fit in. I didn't know you heard me."

He stares at me like that trivial moment has ruined his whole life.

"Brant…" I step forward, trying to close that gap between us again, but he backs away and my heart sinks. "It's not important, okay? It's not."

"How can you say that?" He swallows, shaking his head. "Were you… actually saving it for me? Because a bombshell like that sounds a hell of a lot different today than it did last night in the heat of the moment."

I curl my fingers into fists and drop my eyes to the floor. "I don't know, Brant," I murmur. "Maybe. But it wasn't something I was ever consciously aware of. All I knew was that no man ever made me feel the way you have, so it never felt right. I wanted to wait for someone special."

"But why would you give it up to *me* when you know we can never be together? That's not special, June. That's heartbreaking."

Now I'm the wounded one. A breath catches, and I swallow it down. "I know it's complicated, but—"

"Complicated?" Brant exhales a deep breath, linking his hands behind his head. He spins away from me, then pivots back. "This is more than complicated. This is impossible."

"Nothing is impossible when two people love each other."

"You're not supposed to love me like that," he says, breathing hard, jaw clenching. "It's different for me. I entered your life already knowing you weren't my blood. I conditioned myself to believe you weren't my sister for dark, painful reasons—for *survival*—but you..." Brant's eyes glaze over with his own grief. "You were born believing I was your biological family. You had no reason to feel otherwise."

"You don't know how I've felt. You couldn't possibly."

"You've spent your entire goddamn life calling me your *brother*," he argues, tone escalating.

"Because I had to."

"No. Because it's true."

I shake my head. "Stop trying to pick apart my feelings like they're yours to dissect," I say through the lump in my throat.

"Stop trying to twist this into something acceptable when you know damn well that I'm your broth—"

"You've never felt like my brother!" I shout, temper flaring, cheeks burning hot. I stare at him with a heaving chest, balled fists, and swiftly falling tears. "Theo was my brother. You've only ever felt like...mine."

He opens his mouth to speak, but only silence kisses the air.

It amplifies with each strangled breath we take, with every word still dangling carelessly around us.

The balcony door is cracked open, inviting in the songs of sparrows, the chatter of passersby down below, and the rumble of street traffic, but it's all drowned out by the sound of my heart begging a boy to hear its truth.

Brant deflates before me, rubbing his hands up and down his face with a ragged sigh. He glances at the couch, then at the wall clock over my shoulder. Then back at me. "I have to leave for work," he says simply. I'm not sure if he's putting the conversation on hold or eclipsing it indefinitely.

He finally looks away and moves around me, traipsing to the foyer area to slip on his shoes. I watch him. I watch him through bleary, puffy eyes, wondering if he heard my painful truth.

I receive my answer seconds later.

"June…" Brant hesitates with the door cracked open, glancing at me over his shoulder. He taps at his pocket, his keys jingling. He falters. And then he says, "I wish you would have lied to me."

He walks out and shuts the door, and I collapse with tears onto the stained couch.

"Come to New York with me. Please?"

I sit across from Celeste at the ice cream parlor as we lick our respective cones at one of the outdoor patio tables. The request turns the warm summer breeze into icicles. "You know I can't."

This is Celeste's final day in town before she flies back to her shiny new life in New York City. We wanted to get together one last time before we go back to texting and FaceTime.

"Why not?" She swings her braid over her opposite shoulder with a frown. "I know you needed some time off last year after everything that…happened." A sympathetic smile peeks through. "But I think it's time, June. Dancing has an expiration date, and it would kill me to see your dreams expire."

I look down at the small puddles of melted strawberry ice cream that dripped onto the wooden table. "I'm not that girl anymore. I don't know what I want to do."

"That's bullshit," she counters, leaning back in her plastic chair. "You were born for this. You were by far the most talented performer in our class, and everybody knew it. Camilla wrote you a shining recommendation letter."

"Yes, well, Camilla didn't bury her brother, then fall for…" I trail off, choosing my words wisely. "Someone she shouldn't have."

Celeste nibbles on her lip, her eyes squinting in my direction.

She knows about Brant.

She saw that wanton kiss at prom with her own eyes, and so did Genevieve. We've hardly spoken about it since, but they both grilled me relentlessly that night.

I'd shut down, though.

I hadn't known what to think.

And clearly, I still don't.

"This is about Brant, huh?" Celeste deduces, licking around the edges of her cake cone. "You have feelings for him?"

My cheeks flush. "You could say that."

"Is it mutual?"

I hesitate.

Is it?

It sure felt mutual on Thursday night when he made a woman out of me, brought me to two orgasms, then held me in his strong, loving arms as I fell blissfully to sleep.

But it's Sunday now, and we've hardly spoken since our heated morning-after discussion. Brant has been working grueling hours at two separate jobs, and in the passing moments between us, there have only been casual pleasantries that border on avoidance.

I worked yesterday at the diner, schlepping around hot plates of food along with my miserable personal baggage. I did the bare minimum for tips because smiles are hard to muster when it feels like your whole world is weighed down by melancholy.

I opt for "It's a mess." Truly a mess. "I love him, Celeste…I love him so much, but I don't know how to love someone I'm not allowed to be with."

Empathy shines back at me as she tilts her head. "No one does, girl. They don't write manuals or offer college courses for that kinda thing."

A sad chuckle slips out. "You don't seem too horrified by this development."

"Oh, please. I've spent the last year talking Gen off an emotional ledge after she hooked up with her stepbrother, Colton. Her family basically disowned her, then shipped Colton off to the military."

My blood runs cold.

I knew about their relationship, but not about the family fallout.

When she sees my face go white, Celeste adds, "Not that your situation is the same or anything. I'm sure your parents will be cool…assuming they don't know yet?"

"No, they don't know. I'm certain they'll be anything but cool. This only started to escalate a few days ago, so I've hardly processed it myself."

"Escalate?"

Her sandy-blond braid catches a sunbeam when she shifts in her chair, and I zone out for a moment, lost in the golden glints. I shake my head, blushing. "Well, um, we sort of, uh…"

She raises a perfectly shaded eyebrow.

"We slept together," I choke. "Thursday night."

Celeste's lips pucker and she mouths a silent "*oh*."

"I–it was completely unplanned. Shocking, really. He feels awful, and I feel…well, awful that he feels awful, and I suppose—"

"Was it good?"

Her words cut me short. I stare at her for a quiet moment, blinking, and I lick my lips, dipping my chin to my chest. "It was incredible."

A smile spreads on her pretty face. "That's my girl."

I can't help but laugh, while also dying inside of embarrassment.

"Listen, June…I've been a big part of your life for a while now, and trust me when I say that Brant is one in a million. He's protective, he's loyal, he's kind. He would literally do *anything* for you. Plus he's smokin' hot." She pops the final bite of cone into her mouth, taking a moment to chew. Then she finishes, "Honestly? The smartest thing I ever did was dare you to kiss him."

"I'll never forgive you for that." I glare.

"Not only do you forgive me, but you thank me daily." She winks, sitting up and leaning forward on her elbows. "Tread carefully. Delicately. Gen said her parents walked in on them having sex, so that sort of set the stage for an ugly breakdown. Don't recommend that route."

I cringe. "I assure you that's not in the plan."

My phone buzzes beside me on the table, and it's almost as if my mother knew I was thinking about her.

Witchcraft.

Mom: Let me know which days you're working this week. I'd love to schedule a shopping and lunch day! Xoxo, Mom

My stomach roils with dread as I swipe away the message.

"Brant?" Celeste inquires.

"My mother."

Her nose scrunches up. "Well, I wish I had better advice for you. All I can say is follow your heart—knowing that there might be a few casualties along the way. You have to weigh the good and the bad," she tells me. "No relationship comes without a fight, but it *has* to be worth fighting for. It has to be worth all the sacrifices you'll inevitably have to make."

Ice cream drips onto my hand, and I realize the whole thing has turned into a melty mess. I toss it into the trash can beside me and lick away the sticky remnants, stewing in Celeste's words.

She interrupts my thought process a final time. "Tell me, June…do you actually want to give up on dancing, or does pursuing your dream make you feel like you're giving up on *him*?"

My chest squeezes. "I miss dancing," I admit, swallowing down the sting in my throat. "But…I know I'll miss him so much more."

"Maybe you need to fly free for a little while. You've spent your entire life tethered to him, too afraid to spread your wings. Maybe distance would be good for both of you."

Anxiety pools in my gut at the mere thought of moving nearly one thousand miles away from Brant. "I can't, Celeste. Brant and my parents are all I have left… I can't just leave them."

"They're not *all* you have left." Her hand reaches across the table, landing atop mine. She sends me a tender smile. "You still have *you*. And you matter, too. You matter a whole hell of a lot, okay?" Giving the back of my hand a gentle squeeze, she concludes, "Don't forget about that girl I've grown to love like a sister. She has big dreams, and those dreams deserve the same consideration."

I wipe my sticky hands along my denim shorts, sending her a small smile.

I do have big dreams.

I'm just not sure which one is bigger.

After spending the afternoon with Celeste, I made a pit stop over at my parents' house for dinner, still too on edge to face Brant. It was a nice visit, despite the fact that I literally had to practice every sentence that came out of my mouth in fear of accidentally spewing out *"Brant and I had sex!"*

I came close to overstaying my welcome, lollygagging until nearly 10:00 p.m. when my father did his dramatic yawn and slapped his knee—a gesture we've come to decipher as "I love you but please leave now."

As I shuffle into the apartment after ten, I notice Brant's shoes in the entryway, alerting me he's home from work. My stomach pitches. He's not in the main living area, so he must be hiding in his bedroom, knowing I've gone directly to my own room the last two nights.

But tonight will be different.

Tonight we're going to talk.

When I'm finished sucking down the contents of a water bottle, I trek the short distance to his closed bedroom door and tap lightly on the frame. I hear him moving around on the other side until his footfalls approach and the door pulls open.

My eyes flare with authentic joy when I see him—from his tired hazel gaze to his mop of dark curls to his plain white shirt and navy athletic shorts. Regardless of our predicament, regardless of the messy web we've gotten ourselves stuck in, he's still Brant.

And I'm still June.

"Hi," I murmur softly, wringing my hands together. I monitor his expression, studying him for a reaction—hoping I don't see disappointment or irritation shining back at me. But all I see is that same troubled look I saw on Friday morning, and I have no idea what's worse. "Are you busy?"

He shakes his head after a long beat. "No. I was about to text you to see where you were... I was getting worried."

A smile crests. "I had dinner with Mom and Dad. I figured you were working late."

"I just got home a little while ago." He leans against the edge of the door, giving me a once-over. "Everything okay?"

"Yes. Mostly." I'm fidgety and restless as I shift my weight from one leg to the other. "Can I come in?"

He swallows. "Sure."

Stepping aside, he allows me room to enter, and I send him a grateful nod as I pass through. "I hope I'm not inconveniencing you. I don't mean to intrude."

"You never inconvenience me, June."

I dally nervously near the edge of the bed, sparing it a quick glance that reminds me of the last time I was in it.

Naked. Entangled.

With him.

My smile is strained when I pop my head back up, finding his eyes from a few feet away. He's searching me for clues. He's drinking me in as the muted lamplight illuminates my jitters. "I don't like the way we left things on Friday."

Brant's eyes flicker across my face for a moment before he dips his head. "I don't either."

"So let's pick up where we left off."

"It's not that simple."

"Sure it is. I'll go first." I clear my throat with a dramatic flair. "Hi, Brant. I love you. I think we should be together," I say, lifting my chin with as much resolve as I can muster. "Your turn."

He blinks.

His fingers splay at his sides, then ball into fists. Tension ripples off him as he takes a step toward me. "Hi, June," he says back. "I love you, too. I want nothing more than to be with you, but that's not possible because we were raised by the same parents and everyone we've ever met sees us as siblings. And that kills me. It absolutely guts me. So I'm trying to figure out where to go from here, after succumbing to a weak moment we can't take back, and it seems like every single scenario I come up with ends with me hurting you. And that kills me, too. I'm trying to figure out which scenario hurts less than all the others, and I haven't been able to do that yet."

His eyes are latched on mine as he stops to take a breath, his feet still moving forward. "On top of all that, I can't stop thinking about that weak moment. I can't stop replaying every shameful, delicious second of it—the sounds you made, the way you tasted on my tongue, and how it felt being inside you for the very first time." I remain frozen to the mottled carpeting, my whole body trembling as he inches closer. He's toe-to-toe with me when he finishes. "It felt like I'd give my dying breath just to have one more weak moment with you."

Everything goes still as I digest his words. I'm afraid that if I breathe, I'll choke. The way he's looking at me sends goose bumps down my spine and butterflies to my belly. The hazel of his irises gleams bright in the tungsten glow of the room, a conflicting mix of love, anguish, and immeasurable heat. They remind me of warm apple cider with a shot of bourbon.

We don't speak.

We let the tension swirling around us fuel the flame.

But when I gather the courage to reach for his hand and sweep my thumb along his knuckles, I might as well have tossed a bucket of ice water over us.

Brant looks away.

He takes a step backward, and I drop my hand.

Rubbing a palm to the nape of his neck, a sigh of defeat falls from his lips as he closes his eyes. "That's not what I meant to say," he murmurs under his breath.

"Maybe it was what you wanted to say."

Brant slowly lifts his eyes to mine, his hands fisted at his sides like he's trying so hard not to touch me. His nostrils flare. "We have to stop, June. I can't do this to you," he says. "I think it's for the best if you move out."

No.

No, no, no.

"You won't break me, Brant," I insist. My feet inch forward, desperate to shatter his walls. Desperate to change his mind. "I'm not as fragile as you think I am."

"That's not what I'm afraid of."

"What are you afraid of? Hurting me?"

"Worse."

I frown, trying to read between the lines. "What's worse than hurting me?"

He swallows, shaking his head a little, inhaling a troubled breath. Our eyes lock as he replies, "Ruining you."

A gasp leaves me.

"I'm terrified of ruining you for the poor bastard who has the unfortunate burden of loving you after me, that when you finally let him kiss you all he'll taste is my ashes. When he brings you to his bed, it's *my* name you'll scream. And that's not fair. You deserve so much more than to live your life in the shadow of this…*curse*."

My eyes water as my legs start to shake. Every word slices through my skin, detonating just beneath the surface until I'm burned out and broken down. A little cry spills out as I say in a strangled voice, "Brant…it's too late." I watch as his forehead wrinkles, his brows pulling into a frown. He waits for my next words, eager and anxious. "You've already ruined me."

"Don't…" His own eyes glisten with painful tears as he whips his head back and forth. "Don't tell me that."

"It's the truth," I confess. "I've always belonged to you. *Always.* I was still a virgin because I was waiting for a man who had the ability to even come *close* to the way you make me feel. Someone who could chase away my fears with a forehead kiss. Who could sing away my nightmares with a lullaby. Who was both my comfort *and* my courage, who held my heart in steadfast hands, and who looked at me like I was the most precious thing in this world." I watch his tears fall as freely as my words. My heart pounds and aches as I step right up to him, clasping his hands in mine. He doesn't pull away this time. He just stares at me with a tight jaw and wet cheeks. "But you see…he doesn't exist. There is only you," I say, squeezing his palms. Pulling him closer. "You ruined me the day you met me, Brant Elliott. I was born yours."

His hands lash out, gripping me around the waist and yanking me to him before I can take my next breath. "Jesus, June," he grits out. "You have no idea what you're asking of me." Bruising fingers dig into my hips as his face lowers to mine, our lips a centimeter apart. "Once I get a taste of what this could be, I won't be able to stop."

I arch into him, my palms rising to cup his cheeks. The heat from his body burns into me, making my skin flush. Turning any remaining sensible logic into kindling. "Good."

"You're going to regret this one day." Brant drags his fingers up my spine, fisting them in my hair as he tugs my head back, towering over me, eyes blazing. "And that's going to be such a damn tragedy."

I cry out when his hot mouth steals mine and his tongue plunges past my teeth. He walks me backward until my calves meet the bed frame, our tongues twisting as we moan together. His T-shirt crinkles between my hands as I cling to him, one of my legs lifting to curl around his thigh.

He grabs it, holding me flush against him as he kisses me with fevered urgency. Then he lets me go, giving me a light shove until I collapse backward onto the mattress. Reaching behind his back, Brant gathers his shirt in one hand and pulls it up over his head, tossing it to the floor.

My eyes round at the sight of him: sleek and rigid, muscled and defined.

Strong arms that have kept me safe my whole life.

Broad shoulders that have carried my added weights.

A chest that holds a warrior's heart.

Our eyes remain tethered as he crawls over me, and my hands slink around his back, grazing his shoulder blades. When he dips his head, his mouth finding the tender curve of my neck, I arch into him, my fingers crawling up to his hair. His erection grinds against me while his tongue laves up my neck, teeth nicking my skin until I whimper.

"June," he whispers on a ragged breath, his mouth moving up to my ear and nibbling the lobe.

I wrap my legs around his hips and buck upward, seeking more friction. "Junebug," I correct. "Call me Junebug."

Something in the air shifts, and he stills. An angsty sigh hits my ear, sending a shiver through me.

"Brant…" I keep writhing, my body pleading. "Don't stop."

He doesn't move right away. He just hovers over me, his warm breaths tickling my ear as his chest rises and falls against mine. Then he slowly lifts up on his elbows, his eyes hooded as he stares down at me.

I blink. "What is it?"

"I can't call you that anymore."

My grip on him tightens. His words slice into me one by one, piercing my skin and bruising my heart. "It's what you've always called me."

"I know." He swallows, his gaze agonized. "That's why I can't."

"You don't mean that."

"Yes, I do." He rolls off me, landing on his back beside me on the bed. His shorts are still tented with the evidence of his arousal. "You don't understand what this is doing to me. It's tearing me apart."

A lump rolls down my throat, and I lean over, tentatively running a feather-light touch over his erection. "Brant, please..."

Brant snatches my wrist and in a quick flash is on top of me again. The agony in his eyes shifts to something almost volatile. "I called you Junebug beneath our childhood tree house as we played with ladybugs and read storybooks," he growls out, his voice low. Laced with warning and a tinge of self-loathing. "I called you Junebug at your first dance recital when you could hardly pronounce my name and kissed my cheek, leaving your mother's lipstick behind.

"I called you Junebug when I cradled you in my arms after a nightmare, and when I gave you piggyback rides through the backyard, and when I sang you sweet lullabies as you bounced innocently in my lap, your pigtails tickling my chin." His teeth clench and bare as he stares down at me, my wrists clasped above my head, tucked inside his unyielding grip. "And you want me to call you that now? When I'm about to fuck you?"

I suck in a shallow breath, my fingers curling as he presses me into the mattress. My chin lifts. "All of those things share one thing in common," I murmur as tears gather at the corners of my eyes. "And it's not what you think."

He shakes his head, rejecting the very notion.

I sigh. I'm not sure what else to say because I see it in an entirely different light.

All I do is raise my hips, rubbing against his erection until his eyelids flutter with the prelude to surrender. And when my head pulls up from the bed to steal a kiss, catching his bottom lip between my teeth, his lust-laced groan is the sound of defeat.

Brant dives into me, ripping my shirt over my head and fumbling for the button on my jean shorts. I squirm beneath him, wriggling free of the denim when he yanks the zipper down, and then I curl my fingers into the hemline of his shorts and tug them over his hips. His boxers follow, then my underwear, and we're just a heap of desperate, shaky limbs, exposed skin and bare bones, clinging and stumbling as we tangle further into this web.

He fists my hair again, my neck and breasts arching into him as his mouth finds both. I gasp and mewl beneath his hot tongue, my hand reaching between us to grip his cock and guide him into me. I can't wait. I need him to fill me.

"God, June," he moans, his teeth nipping my jaw as he slips an inch inside. Then with one hand in my hair and the other dragging downward to clutch my hip, he slams into me all the way.

I cry out, biting my lip.

He starts thrusting.

Hard, fast, punishing.

He fucks me like he's trying to wash away everything sweet and good between us, until we slip into the darkness where our sins are overlooked.

Where permission lies in wait.

Where we fit in.

Our bodies are half draped over the bedside, my feet scraping against the carpet for leverage until Brant slides me up the bed and climbs to his knees. My hips pop up from the mattress as he spreads my thighs wider and pounds into me, his fingertips bruising as they dig into my skin. The box spring squeaks in time with my shameless whimpers. His own moans fill the room as our skin slaps together, his cock ramming into me over and over.

"*Fuck*," he grits out, one hand slinking up to rub my clit, the other still wrapped around my thigh. "I want you to come. I want you to come so fucking hard."

"Brant…God…" I cry, my body angled so he's hitting me just right. So deliciously deep.

"You're so wet. You're soaking me."

My hands clutch at the bedsheets, fisting them in my palms. "Ohhh…" I've been reduced to unintelligible sounds and whines as my body shakes and trembles with need, the swell of an orgasm building. I can hear how wet I am as he ruts into me with reckless abandon.

I glance down to where our bodies are pounding furiously together, watching him slide in and out of me, his muscles flexing, a look of savage possession glowing in his eyes.

My orgasm unravels in an instant.

I arch and bend and break, scratching at the bedsheets then at his arms as I moan his name with my release.

Brant collapses over me, his hips still pumping hard and fast, hands grasping my cheeks. He buries his face into the crook of my neck, groaning against my sweat-slicked hair, chanting my name as his own orgasm claims him. His thrusts become clumsy as he empties into me with a satisfied grunt of pleasure, filling me in every possible way.

I hold him as he comes down.

I wrap my arms around his back, link my wrists, and just hold him.

I'm not sure if it's the gesture itself or the aftershocks of his climax or the heaviness of it all—but Brant breaks down. He falls on top of me, slightly to the side so I don't bear the brunt of his weight, and lets out a ragged, painful sound near my ear. He gathers me into his arms, so close, so vulnerable, and he trembles beside me as emotion funnels through him and warm tears rain down on my shoulder.

"It's okay," I whisper, my fingers twining through his air. "I love you, and I promise it's okay."

He inhales a shuddering, tearful breath, pressing a kiss to the tender skin just below my ear, riding out the final waves of grief. We stay like that for a while, Brant still sheathed inside me, as our bodies remain fiercely entangled.

"When the day comes and you regret this," he murmurs softly into my neck, his voice cracking, "I pray you can forgive me."

My chest tightens. My muscles lock up, and all I can do is cling to him tighter. "I'll never regret this," I tell him. I kiss the top of his head, his damp curls tickling my nose. "Never."

I'll never regret you.

31

FIRST GLIMPSE

BRANT, AGE 25

SHE'S ON MY MIND AS I accidentally bump into Sydney, nearly spilling my Long Island.

"You okay?" Sydney wonders, arching a worried eyebrow in my direction. "I'm supposed to be the flighty one here."

I regroup quickly. "I'm good." Reaching for a top-shelf bottle of liquor, I twirl it in the air and catch it with ease just to prove how "good" I am.

She narrows her eyes, jabbing me in the chest with her long fingernail. "Nice try. I'm the master of the smoke show. You can't fool me."

This time I'm the one raising an eyebrow. "You're the master at being attractive?"

"What?"

Sydney's sister, Clementine, is perched on one of the barstools, slurping on a daiquiri and nearly choking at the look on Sydney's face. We both start laughing.

Sydney blinks rapidly, her eyes flaring with bewilderment. "What? What did I say?"

"Smoke *screen*," I correct her, still chuckling as I toss some olives into a martini glass. Clem drops her head to her arms as her shoulders shake with laughter, her blue-streaked hair bouncing. "You're right, though. I did need the laugh."

"Wow, I'm a fucking idiot," Sydney says, smacking the underside of her palm to her forehead. "Sorry. I have a boy on the brain. It's a legitimate impairment, you know…very serious."

"*Oliveritus*," Clem chimes in, snickering under her breath. "Maybe Brant will grant you medical leave so you can take some time off to *recover*. I think we both know where you can find the cure."

"You, shush. I'm charging you double for that daiquiri."

"Brant said it was on the house," Clem sniffs.

Sydney glares at me. "Traitor."

My cheeks fill with air as I blow out a breath, accepting a generous tip from a middle-aged couple as I move down the bar to serve the next customer. I needed the distraction tonight. After five days of highly emotional, mind-blowing sex with June, where we skirted around the difficult logistics of our predicament, I'm feeling tapped out and run down.

Every morning this week, I've woken up with my arms full of June.

My *heart* full of June.

And two of those mornings, my body full of June when she decided to wake me up by sliding between my legs and wrapping her mouth around my cock.

It's impossible to be strong in those moments.

Then again—I'm not sure if I even grasp the definition of that word anymore.

What is strength when it comes to *us*?

Is there strength in fighting for this fucked-up, taboo relationship that absolutely nobody will embrace let alone accept, and that will force us to lurk in the shadows for the rest of our lives?

Or is strength in letting June go, because I know—*I know*—she's meant for so much more than a shadowed existence.

She's meant to fly free. She's meant to burn bright.

She's meant to outshine every shadow.

Strength, by definition, is overcoming that hard thing…but what happens when every avenue is equally, painfully hard?

It's a mess.

It's a mess I'm determined to dig myself deeper into because every time she looks at me with those hopeful blue eyes, and every time she whispers words of adoration in my ear when I'm inside of her, nothing else seems to matter.

I don't care about being strong or brave or righteous.

All I care about is loving her.

Lost in my wayward thoughts again, I don't even notice a familiar figure gliding up to the bar and sitting right in front of me. He smacks a single penny and a five-dollar bill onto the counter. "Penny for your thoughts, and a five for whatever you've got on special tonight."

Startled, I glance up.

Kip.

He's taken a seat beside Clem, watching me with a friendly smile. I smile back. "Jägerbombs," I inform him.

"Ouch. Pass." He cringes, then says, "These better be some damn good thoughts, then."

Clem does a double take as she sips delicately on her beverage, her eyes scanning the man next to her, their shoulders grazing as he resituates on the stool.

Kip glances at her, folding his hands atop the bar counter. His smile stretches. "I like your hair."

She falters as she instinctively fiddles with a piece of bright-blue hair, then takes a generous final slurp through the thin straw. Swallowing, she pulls back from the empty glass and gives him another once-over. "I like your…face."

Her eyes widen with mortification.

"Wow," Sydney chimes in, eavesdropping as she sweeps a rag down the counter. "You just out-lamed me, Sis. Super impressive."

Clem blushes, pushing away from the bar and snatching her purse. "That's my cue," she says, flustered, shooting me a quick smile. "Thanks for the drink, Brant."

"You got it."

"Nice meeting you." Kip grins at her, hands still folded in front of him.

"Oh, right… You, too." Clem gulps. "Thanks for the…" Her voice trails off.

Kip circles a finger around his face. "Anytime."

I can't help but laugh. Sydney snorts.

Clem flushes with embarrassment, then bolts in the opposite direction.

"You'll have to forgive her," Sydney cuts in, passing out a round of tequila shots as she whizzes around behind the bar. "She's going through a divorce. She doesn't know how to flirt yet."

"Forgiven."

Chuckling under my breath, I whip a rag over my shoulder and pop open a beer, setting it down in front of Kip. I lean forward on my palms. "What time are you and Andrew stopping by tomorrow?"

We scheduled a "guys day."

It's my only day off this week, and June has to work at the diner. Andrew has been wanting to set something up before summer passes us by, and we all desperately need the R and R.

So we're packing up some beers and lunch and going tubing up in Wisconsin.

I'm looking forward to it.

I'm looking forward to everything but having to make eye contact with Andrew Bailey, knowing that I'm sleeping with his daughter behind his back.

Kip doesn't know this either. The last time we spent any time together, he was filling me in on his own tragic, forbidden love story, trying to convince me to run from mine.

Clearly, I learned nothing.

Kip tips his beer to me in thanks, then takes a swig. "Probably around eight or nine."

"Perfect."

I'm about to further the conversation when I feel a presence sidle up beside me, my nose filling with bergamot cologne.

"Mr. Elliott. A word, if you will."

Pauly gives my shoulder a slap with his meaty paw, and I excuse myself for a moment, making sure Sydney has it covered. Trailing Pauly into the kitchen behind the bar, I scratch at the coarse bristle on my chin, feeling like I'm in trouble. I always feel like that when Pauly wants to talk to me, even though he's only ever shown me kindness and respect. He has that way about him.

"Everything okay?" I wonder as we come to a stop in a quiet corner.

"Yes, of course. I have a proposition for you." He smooths out his beard, black with a smattering of silver flecks, striking against his light-olive skin. He regards me with umber eyes. "My restaurant in Seattle. I would like you to work at it."

I frown, my arms crossing. "Seattle?"

"Yes. An executive chef position has opened up, and you are more than qualified. You would receive double the salary you are currently making," he explains, watching my reaction. Studying me. "Mr. Elliott...you are one of the best culinary artists I have had the pleasure of working with in all of my career. I fear you are not living up to your full potential. It would be a great honor if you would consider my offer."

Swallowing, I exhale a tapered breath, glancing down at the tile floor. I'm speechless.

"You would have more responsibility, of course. Staffing, budgeting, managing ordering... However, you are very smart. Quick on your feet. I believe you are more than capable."

I glance back up, noting the hint of a smile that crosses his lips. It looks like pride. It almost looks like I would be doing *him* a favor by saying yes.

My mind reels.

Double the pay.

A new, exciting city.

A huge career advancement, doing something I love.

But...

A breath leaves me as I deflate, and I see the way his eyes flicker with disappointment. He knows my answer before I say it out loud. "I'm extremely honored, Pauly. Humbled. It's just..." Folding my lips between my teeth, I try to piece my words together in a way that makes sense—in a way that doesn't sound like *"I can't because I'm in love with June."*

"This is about your family, yes?" Pauly questions. His dark eyebrows crease studiously as he reads me, slipping his hands into his pockets.

My teeth clack together as I nod.

"Your sister."

I nod again. "Yes," I admit. "We're...close. Even more so since we lost Theo, and I just don't think I can leave her. She still needs me."

His head bobs up and down ever so slowly, drinking in each word like an aged wine. Then he leans back against the wall as kitchen commotion clatters behind us. "When I was just a young boy, I found a bird with a broken wing," he says in a wistful voice, his gaze locked on mine. "My mother let me nurse it back to health. It was a white-breasted nuthatch—a brilliant little bird with blue and gray wings and a snow-white underbelly. I bonded with it, keeping it tucked inside a wire cage close to my bed. I named it Annalise because I fancied a schoolmate with the same name." He chuckles, his eyes glazing with old memories. "It began to fly one day. Its wing healed nice and strong, and even though I had promised my mother I would let it go the moment it could fly, I could not seem to part with it. The bird had become my friend. I loved it."

I stare at him, my jaw tense. My heart patters with anticipation as I hang on every word.

"One day, the bird tried to fly through my closed window. It dazed itself on the pane of glass. I cried myself to sleep that night, whispering apologies to the little bird, saddened I had caused it pain. And yet…I still could not part with it. I could not let the bird go." Pauly's smile returns, but it's a watery smile. A smile weighed down by remorse. "The next day, it tried to fly through the window again. One final time," he tells me. His voice cracks on the last word. "It did not survive that final time."

A lump forms in the back of my throat. My skin feels clammy, and my eyes mist over as the story resonates. As it digs into me, burrowing deep.

"I still think about that bird, Mr. Elliott," he says, his Adam's apple bobbing as he lifts up from the wall. He stares just over my shoulder for a moment before meeting my eyes. "I think about where it could have flown, and the life it could have lived…if I had just had the courage to let it go."

Our gazes linger and hold, tangling with double meaning.

Then Pauly reaches out and squeezes my bicep, giving me a light slap as he moves past me. "My offer remains," he says, his voice fading as he strides toward the double doors. "If you change your mind."

I stand there for a while, hands clenching at my sides.

Eyes clouded over, zoned in on the white plaster wall.

Head spinning.

I stand there thinking about my Junebug and all the places she could fly.

When I step into my apartment at nearly midnight, my senses are assaulted by the scent of chocolate baked goods.

June stands in front of the stove with an oven mitt, her long brown tresses bouncing down her back as she waves the mitt back and forth as if she's trying to cool something down. She spins around when the door clicks shut.

"Brant!" Her face brightens upon seeing me, her eyes shimmering beneath the brassy yellow ceiling lights. "I know you're the master chef around here, but I couldn't sleep so I thought I'd whip up some dessert for you."

A smile crests as I stare at her, my entire body warming.

She jumps to the side, showcasing her creation. "Ta-da," she exclaims. "Brownies. And not just any brownies… These are extra special. I added those little caramel candies for some added sweetness." June grins, crinkling her nose. "Which is basically a nicer term for calories."

The scents of milk chocolate and warm caramel float over to me as I hover in the doorway, my feet frozen to the grubby tiles. June is a picture of perfection, wearing the chef apron she bought for me a few years back, tied around a modest sundress.

I can see it.

I can see it all in that moment.

A future.

June as my wife, baking brownies when I return home from a long day of work. The kitchen alight with sweet smells, the house a mess of toys and living, maybe a happy-go-lucky dog circling my ankles, and the chatter of our children, the ideal soundtrack to our life of bliss.

I can see it so fucking clearly.

And it hurts my heart that the things I see, the things I crave with everything I am, aren't necessarily the things that are right.

I heave in a frayed breath, my eyes glazing with unshed tears as I slip out of my shoes and step toward her. June's smile fades slightly, sensing the heaviness radiating off me. I force a smile, not wanting to worry her—not wanting to be the reason her smile fades. "Hey," I greet her, my hand extending to clasp hers. "They smell amazing."

Her joy flickers back to life. "Yeah? I'm a little impressed I didn't burn them," she says, ducking her chin to her chest. "I used Grams's recipe. I always thought they were the best."

June's words hardly register. The brownies are forgotten as I lift both hands to cradle her cheeks, moving in to her until our chests kiss. "Are you happy?" I ask softly. There's a catch in my voice, sounding louder than my words.

Worry claims her pretty features, and she reaches up to hold my wrists. "Of course I'm happy. I'm so happy."

"Even though you're not dancing? Even though you're not in New York?"

She falters.

It's only for a second, only for the briefest, tiniest moment, but I see it.

I see it.

"Yes," she nods, squeezing me. "I'd rather be here with you."

I press our foreheads together. "What if you're missing out? What if you always regret not chasing your dreams?"

"Brant…I love you. I'll never regret choosing love."

"Your dreams have an expiration date, June. Love doesn't. I'll *always* love you," I murmur, bringing her closer. Breathing her in. "You know that, right?"

She pulls back a little, licking her lips. "What's wrong?"

"I'm afraid you're making a mistake."

"We're not a mistake," she insists. Her nails dig into me, carving little crescents into my arms. "We were written in the stars. Stars don't make mistakes."

My eyes close tight, my body swaying as if it's being pulled in two different directions.

Dancing and distance are what's best for June.

No, I'm what's best for June.

Fuck.

I don't know.

I don't know, so I just kiss her, because nothing is scary or messy or wrong when I'm kissing her.

She arches upward, sinking into the kiss, her hands gliding up my arms and landing on my shoulders. Her lips part, pleading for me to slip inside, and when our tongues touch, I groan, gathering her closer and melting.

The urgency swells between us, as it always does. I lift her up by the thighs, wrapping her legs around my waist. When I pull back from her mouth, I breathe out, "I want to make love to you."

"Okay." She nods eagerly, arms linked around my neck. "Bedroom."

I kiss her again, then start walking the short distance to my room. "I want to make *love* to you, June. Sweet and slow and soft. The way it should have been that first time."

"It was perfect," she rasps out, clinging to me as I carry her into the bedroom and set her on the mattress. "It's always perfect."

"It's always rough. Dirty." I pull off my T-shirt, then start unfastening my belt and slacks. My eyes heat as I watch June shrug out of her cotton sundress, her hair splaying around her on the white sheets. "It's like I'm trying to bury us deeper into the dirt, until we sink, until there's no way out. Because I don't want to find a way out."

Crawling on top of her, she immediately coils her legs around my hips and tugs me close, inching up to kiss me. Her hands sift through my hair as she murmurs, "I don't either."

"God, June… I don't want you to be my filthy little secret. You're better than this."

"I'm *meant* for this."

My fingers weave through her soft hair as I pepper her face with kisses, from her forehead to her nose to her perfect parted lips. "I want to treasure you. Cherish you. Adore you."

Her back arches as I trail my mouth down her neck. "You do that every time."

I slip down her body, worshiping every freckle, every crease, every birthmark. I spread her thighs and feast on her, taking my time, bringing her to the edge of orgasm then pulling back and doing it again. Exquisite torture. I make love to every inch of her until she's writhing and sweat-soaked, moaning my name and tugging my hair, desperate for release.

And when I finally sink my cock into her, my own desperation blinding me, I gather her closer than ever, our faces a whisper apart, our bodies slick and tangled. She whimpers as I move, slow and deep, rocking against her as our eyes remain locked.

Then I say it: "Junebug."

Her whimpers morph into a startled cry. Something like disbelief.

Glorious disbelief.

My arms cage her in as I hover over her, fingers twining through her hair, my hips pumping, languid yet fervent. "You were right," I confess, my lips caressing hers as I feel her thighs cling tighter around me. "That name didn't come from innocence or some kind of familial connection. It was born out of *love.* My love for you." Her eyes glaze with tears, her hands gripping my shoulders. She nods as breathy little sounds spill out of her. "And maybe that love has evolved and blossomed over the years, but it still comes from the same place. And that place is beautiful. That place is pure."

Wetness stains her cheeks, her lips trembling.

"You're my Junebug," I tell her, sweeping back the strands of hair matted to her forehead. I kiss her hairline. "You'll always be my Junebug."

She sniffles, sucking in a shuddering breath. "You mean it?"

"Of course I mean it."

Releasing a tiny gasp, she kisses me hard.

I groan against her sweet mouth as our tongues take over the conversation, and our bodies continue to move together. I thrust into her with lazy, delicious strokes, clutching her in unwavering arms and whispering words of endless love into her ear. I grip the headboard above her while my other hand cradles the top of her head, and my speed picks up as the mattress squeaks and our skin slaps. June pants and moans, craning her neck back, her body quaking with her climax.

And as I follow behind, releasing inside of her, sinking and falling and melting, I know I've never felt more alive, more at peace, more *grateful* than I do in this moment.

For all the tragedy I've witnessed, for all the heartache…

I'm lucky.

I'm lucky to have something so good in my life washing away all the bad.

I'm awoken the next morning by a strange, muffled sound as I'm pulled out of a dream.

A nightmare, really.

Every now and then I'll have a vivid, bone-chilling nightmare about that night. About the night my father woke me out of a sweet sleep where my mind had me dancing on rainbow clouds. Those clouds morphed into black storm clouds the moment my father shook me awake, begging for forgiveness. I still see that manic, desperate look in his eyes. I feel the sweat on his skin. I hear his broken voice telling me to cover my ears.

One more thing, Brant. Cover your ears.

In my nightmares, I do. I always think that if I can't hear the sound of that gun going off, then maybe it never went off at all.

Rousing groggily, I hear the muffled noise again.

But it's not June.

It's not June perched between my legs, sucking me off as the sun spills in through light-blue curtains, glinting her eyes while she peers up at me.

June is still nestled in my arms, naked and fast asleep.

I stir, my eyelids fluttering.

And the sound repeats itself.

"Oh…oh God, no."

It's a string of sounds—of words…of…*horror.*

My eyes snap open and I sit up straight, craning toward the wide-open door.

Andrew Bailey and Kip stand at the threshold, staring at me. Andrew cups a hand over his mouth, the color draining from his face as he witnesses his daughter, completely bare, intimately entwined with the man he considers a son.

June rouses beside me, lifting up on her elbows.

She gasps. "Dad?"

"No…this isn't real," Andrew mutters, his eyes huge and full of sickening outrage. He stumbles backward, bumping into Kip. "Please, no…*no*."

I'm frozen. I'm speechless.

June starts to cry as she yanks the bedsheet up to her chin.

Andrew shakes his head, looking like he's about to be ill, then clumsily retreats from the room.

Kip stares at me.

I stare back.

Disappointment dims his eyes as he swallows, rubbing a hand down his face and pivoting away from the door.

Everything else is a blur as June continues to sob, scrambling for her clothes, while I just sit there.

Numb.

Sad.

Done.

Last night I was lucky…

But not today.

Today is just another tragedy.

32

FIRST CRACK

JUNE, AGE 19

THIS ISN'T HAPPENING.

My father staggers away, hand clasped over his mouth as if he's trying not to vomit. Tears pour out of me, desperate, ugly tears, and I search for my dress as Kip moves out of frame.

Brant sits beside me, breathing heavily and totally silent. He looks like he's in shock.

It wasn't supposed to happen like this.

Locating my dress peeking out from under the bed, I throw it over my head and whip off the covers as the front door claps shut. "I–I have to go talk to him…" I mutter through my tears. "God, Brant…"

Brant doesn't respond.

He just sits there, glassy-eyed and void.

"What should I say? What should I do?" My whole body is shaking as I stand beside the bed on trembling legs, fists balled like stones at my sides.

Nothing.

He doesn't even blink.

"Brant," I choke out, leaning over the bed to shake his shoulders. Panic tightens my chest. "Please. I need you."

After a long moment, he finally cranes his head toward me, his jaw rippling with tension. "I forgot to set an alarm. I didn't mean to sleep in."

My fingers curl along his shoulders, my lungs feeling wheezy. I drink in a few choppy breaths as our eyes meet. "Th-that doesn't matter. How do we fix this?"

"Fix this?" His dark eyebrows pinch together, his muscles stiffening as his gaze tracks my face. Then he murmurs in a low, defeated voice, "There's no fixing this, June."

I shake him again with flared emotion. "Stop. There must be."

"No."

"Stop!" I shriek, drawing back from the bed. My ribs ache from the weight of my breaths as I glance around the room for my purse and car keys. "I–I need to talk to Mom. She'll understand. She'll understand…" I pant out, my thoughts scattered while I idly step into a pair of house slippers. "I can fix this."

Before I stumble out of the bedroom, I look back at Brant who is still rooted to the mattress, frozen. His face falls into his hands. "You can't fix it."

I choke on a strangled cry, gripping my purse strap.

I have to.

As I spin around, he says to me as I retreat, "We were broken before we even began."

Dad's car is in the driveway when I pull in.

My heart thunders as my tears fall like a violent rain shower. He's probably telling my mother the sordid truth right now.

I squeeze the steering wheel, my forehead collapsing against it as I let out a hopeless sob, wondering what the hell I'm going to do.

How can I explain the inexplicable?

How can I excuse the inexcusable?

How can I justify the unacceptable?

With all the words in existence, I can't seem to piece together any that will make this sound even remotely reasonable.

We were careless.

We were reckless and foolish, and my worst fear has come to life.

Instead of me sitting down with my parents with a laid-out plan, a well-rehearsed explanation, my father walked in on us spooned together like lovers, naked in Brant's bed.

Humiliation warms my skin.

And then a sharp tapping at the window pops my head up from the wheel.

A gasp escapes me when I lock eyes with my mother through the glass. She's waving at me with a smile, but that smile slips the moment she notices the torment gazing back at her.

She doesn't know.

She doesn't know yet.

My hand quivers as I twist the key out of the ignition and push open the driver's side door. Two slipper-covered feet meet the cement, but they are not enough to hold me upright. With knees made of jelly, I buckle, falling at my mother's ankles with an anguished cry as tiny pebbles dig into my palms. Tearstained hair curtains my face, my shoulders heaving with grief.

"June? Dear God… What's wrong, honey?" Mom drops beside me, immediately pulling me into her arms as we huddle on the driveway. "What happened?"

I can hardly speak. I shake my head back and forth as she combs loving fingers through my hair.

"June, please talk to me. Is someone hurt? Is it Brant?" Mom's comforting touch turns tense, wrought with fear. She pulls back, clasping my face between her hands. "June. Is Brant okay?"

My stomach roils. I'm sure she's flashing back to that hospital right now.

Hearing the devastating news.

Finding out that she just lost a son.

She's about to lose another.

Blinking back the wall of tears, I manage to croak out, "D-Dad saw us."

"What?" Her deep-blue stare is full of bewilderment. "Sweetheart, you're scaring me."

"Please…" I choke, sniffling and gasping. "Please don't hate him."

Mom frowns, inching backward as her hands fall from my cheeks. "Why would I hate your father?"

I swing my head back and forth, a piece of hair catching on the wet tears pooled along my lips. "No…not Dad," I rasp, still trying to catch my breath, trying to keep an asthma attack from overtaking me. "Brant."

Confusion clouds her eyes. We both face each other on the pavement, our knees touching, while the humid late-summer breeze seems to go still. The air turns stale and stifling, like it's waiting for the next moment to unfold.

Expectancy hums all around me.

My mother licks her lips, inhaling a slow breath. "What would make me hate Brant?"

She asks the question softly, so softly, almost as if she doesn't want me to even hear it because she's terrified of what the answer may be.

Only…I think she already knows.

She knows the answer.

It lights up her eyes like a bushfire.

How does she know?

Her head shakes slightly. She pats at her loose hair bun, like she's searching for the pen that usually resides inside it, but it's not there today. Mom pulls her lips between her teeth, falling back on her heels and gazing off over my shoulder at a bicyclist riding by on the sidewalk. A long, quiet moment stretches between us, causing my skin to prickle with anticipation.

Then she cups a hand over her mouth and sighs. "How long?"

Pushing my hair back with my fingertips, I stare down at the cracks in the driveway, hoping one of them will suck me in. I can't seem to muster a response.

She repeats louder, "How long have you been sleeping with him, June?"

I squeeze my eyes shut and let out a shuddery breath. "A week," I confess, mortification heating my face. It's horrible enough talking to my mother about having sex, but *this*?

Her daughter is admitting to a sexual relationship with the man she deems a *son*.

Cowering on the pavement, I wish I could shrink away into nothingness.

"A week," she clarifies.

"But…it's more than that," I say, lifting my chin and braving a glance at her. My voice breaks as I repeat meekly, "It's so much more."

Teardrops fall hard, disappearing into the stone cracks, but they don't take me with them.

Mom's hand is still clasped over her mouth, her eyes shimmering with debilitating disappointment. Her crow's-feet crease as her head bobs slowly, absorbing my words—*my sins*. Then she blows out a breath and pulls herself to her feet, swiping grit from the driveway off her khaki pants. "This is going to destroy your father."

I crumble as I watch her march toward the house. "Mom, please…" Rising to unstable legs, I chase her through the front door, begging for pardon. "Please understand. Please…I *love* him."

"I know you love him, June." She storms through the house, then plants her palms facedown on the kitchen table, leaning forward. "That's not the point."

Stopping a few feet away, I wipe at my falling tears. "Of course it's the point. It's everything."

She whips back around. "It's *not* everything. Have you fully grasped the severity of this situation? You're a smart girl, June. *Think.*" My mother taps her index finger to her temple. "Think long and hard about what you're doing."

"I am thinking." My right hand presses against my chest, fingers twisting the fabric of my dress. "I'm thinking with my heart, and that's what counts."

Her arms drop to her sides with added frustration. She heaves out another big breath. "You think I haven't seen it?" she asks me, eyes trailing back to my startled expression.

My insides buzz.

What?

A glimmer of tears reflects back at me, but they don't fall. "You think I haven't noticed the signs?" she says softly. "I watched you grow up with Theodore, and I watched you grow up with Brant. And let me tell you…it wasn't the same."

I swallow, fisting my dress in a clammy palm.

"I've seen the way you look at him," she continues. "With curious eyes as a small child. With possessive eyes as you got older. You always needed to be near him. And when you weren't near him, you were talking about him. You've held a torch for Brant your whole life, and I just *prayed* it would burn out before it burned you both."

I lick away a stray tear, trying to find my voice. "You…you never said anything."

"Because he's your adopted brother!" she bursts out, temper flaring, arms lifting at her sides. "There's a legal document upstairs in my closet that confirms that fact. My God, June… I thought you'd have the common sense to not pursue him in that way."

"There is no sense in love," I counter, swiping away more tears. "It's a senseless thing."

Mom pauses, pinching the bridge of her nose, chin tucked to her chest.

I forge ahead. "And I didn't pursue him. He didn't pursue me. It just… *happened*. Because that's what love does. It happens. It sneaks up on you, and then it burrows. It festers in your blood. And once it's in your blood you can't just flush it out. It's a part of you. Trying to get rid of it would be like cutting off a limb or carving your heart right out of your chest."

She looks up, her brows knit together.

"You love Dad, right?" I ask gently. "If you love him, *really* love him, then you understand." I press my hand to my heart again as I step closer to her. "And I hope you do. I hope you know exactly what I'm talking about."

Swallowing, my mother straightens as she shakes her head. "Of course I love your father, but this is different. I fell in love with the right person at the right time."

"I completely disagree," I contest. "When you find the right person, there is no 'right time.' There's only right now because that's all we ever have." Tears blot my vision as I inhale a quick breath and finish. "I bet Theo would agree with me."

Mom's eyes round with pain.

With warning.

But her words are cut short when the front door bursts open, and I spin in place.

My father stands in the doorway, his cheeks rosy red, with bloodshot eyes to match. He tousles a hand through his graying hair and pins his stare on me.

He must have been riding with Kip this morning.

Through trembling lips, I whisper, "Dad."

"You're going to New York. I'm booking your flight," he says in a grief-ridden voice, storming through the foyer, not bothering to close the front door.

Panic sinks into me. "What?"

He looks disheveled and lost as he winds his way to the study where his laptop resides. "I already spoke with Celeste's aunt. You're more than welcome. I'll pay your portion of rent until you secure a job and—"

"Daddy, stop!" I rush toward him. "I want to stay here."

"I don't care."

"Please!" I plead to his quickly retreating back. "I don't want to go to New York."

He flies around with fury in his gaze. "And I don't want my daughter fooling around with her goddamn *brother*!"

Both of our chests heave with labored breaths. I've never seen my father so upset. So riddled with emotion. He's always been the more sentimental parent, as Mom is the voice of reason, but his temper has never gotten the better of him.

I broke him.

My tears keep falling as my mother sidles up beside me with her arms crossed. She keeps her voice level. "I agree with your father, June. I think it's best if you go to New York."

I'm flabbergasted. Outraged. My own anger heightens as I look between them. "So this is how you choose to deal with me? Ship me off to a new state?"

"It's not like that," Mom says.

Dad intercedes. "It's exactly like that. Distance is the best way to handle this situation."

"I'm nineteen years old. You no longer need to *handle* me," I bite back. "I'm a grown adult, and I don't live under your roof."

His jaw tightens. "Is that why you moved out? So you could gallivant around with your brother in private?"

Fisting my hands at my sides, I snap, "Stop trying to cheapen this. He's not my real brother… We're in love."

"Damn it, June!" he shouts, slicing a hand through the air. He moves in closer—close enough that I can see the stress lines etched into his features. I can see the desperation glinting in his eyes. "Listen to yourself. You're trying to justify a crime. You're defending a predator."

Mom jumps in, holding out her hand. "Whoa, hey… Andrew, don't go there."

A horrified cry escapes me.

He can't think that. He can't possibly think that of Brant.

This was *mutual*.

"No," I squeak out. "That's not true at all. He's a good man…he's your *son*."

My father's face contorts with disgust, a finger pointed at me. "He stopped being my son the moment he chose to put his dick inside my daughter." Then he turns around, disappears into the study, and slams the door behind him.

His hostility vibrates the walls.

The picture frames rattle.

A photograph slips from its place above the doorframe, shattering on the wooden floor beside my feet. My hand flies to my mouth as I realize it's a picture of me, Brant, and Theo on prom night when we stood in front of the bay window, our arms linked around each other. We're slightly silhouetted, but our smiles glow bright. And even though my head is tipped to Theo's shoulder, my bottom half is pressed into Brant.

My right arm is draped casually around Theo's neck, but my left arm is curled intimately around Brant's waist.

I suck in a quivering breath, bending down to pick up the photo sprinkled with shards of glass. Memories of that night race through me as I trace a finger over Theo, raking my eyes over his police uniform and knowing it would be the last time he'd ever wear it. His grin is cheesy and wide, and I recall Mom telling us to think about that time we dressed up Yoshi like a UPS man for Halloween. All three of us started laughing, and Mom snapped the picture, catching the precise moment when Brant looked down at me, his face lit up with authentic joy.

I start to cry.

Hard.

Painfully.

My mother moves in and collects me in a warm embrace, stroking her hands through my tangled hair and pulling me close. The picture falls from my fingertips and floats down to the pool of broken glass. She whispers in my ear, "I love you. And I love Brant." Her chin rests atop my head as I fall against her chest. "But I don't love this."

I don't love this either.

I don't love that I fell for the one person I shouldn't have.

It's not fair.

It *hurts*.

Wrapping my arms around my mother, I sob quietly into her shoulder, wishing I could jump into the photograph and change our fate.

Theo wouldn't go to that accident scene, and I wouldn't kiss Brant on a silly dare.

My eyes land on the photograph, lying amongst the jagged pieces of the picture frame.

Fractured.

Cracked.

I think back to seven years ago when I was standing on the frozen pond. I can still hear my pounding heart. The cruel laughter coming from Wyatt and his friends. Brant calling my name as he raced toward me, his face a mask of blind fear. And then…that sound.

I heard it, louder than all the other sounds.

We all heard it.

That first crack.

I'll never forget the feeling that shot through me when the ice split. It was only a tiny fissure—a chip in the surface. But it was a catalyst for the big break. The ultimate collapse.

The end.

I'd gone completely still, weighing my options as I held Brant's horrified gaze from across the pond, knowing that one wrong move could kill me.

And now, as I cling to my mother, a crumpled mess of grief, that same feeling ripples through me. It's like ice in my veins.

We're that first crack.

Me and Brant.

One wrong move, one misstep, and we're going under.

We're going to drown.

And I don't know what to do.

33

FIRST GOODBYE

JUNE, AGE 19

It's a good day to save someone, Peach."

Joyous disbelief washes over me when his voice meets my ears, and my head pops up as I sit cross-legged in a golden field of tall grass and wildflowers while fluffy white clouds dance overhead.

There he stands.

Backlit by the bright sun that's illuminating his head like a halo.

Like an angel.

"Theo!" Leaping to my feet, I race over to him with outstretched arms and a wildly beating heart. "You came."

"You think I'd pass up an opportunity to dump my semi-passable advice on you? Hell no." He grins, hefting me up in the air when I land in his arms. "You're way overdue."

Warmth encases me as I hold on to him, and all I want to do is soak up his sunshine, storing it inside all my empty holes and pockets so I never grow cold, so he's always near. "I miss you so much," I murmur into his shirt collar. "I hate that you left me."

"I didn't leave you, Peach. I'm here, aren't I?"

I let out a huff as I pull back, gazing into his steely-blue eyes. They twinkle with a galaxy of stars. "You're just a manifestation of my subconscious."

He scratches the nape of his neck with an acquiescent shrug. "I didn't realize they made subconsciouses this witty and charming." As he swipes his hair back, a small mirror appears in his hand and he gazes into it with a smile. "Wickedly handsome, too."

A tearful laugh spills out of me. "Where are we?" I wonder as I let him go, memorizing the way his sandy freckles decorate his cheekbones.

"You tell me. This is your brain," he replies, quirking a smile.

I look around.

The sunlit field appears endless, and the tepid breeze kisses my face just right. A rainbow arches overhead, playing peekaboo with silly-shaped clouds. They look like Super Mario characters. I smile. "I guess it doesn't matter, as long as you're here."

When I glance back at Theo, he's sprawled out on a bright-blue couch with a video game controller in his hand. His thumbs tap away at the buttons while he stares at a television that appeared out of nowhere. A grin curls in my direction. "Rainbow Road," he says. "My favorite level."

Mario Kart lights up the screen.

I saunter toward him, collapsing at his side and resting my head atop his shoulder. Sighing heavily, I murmur, "Everything is a mess. I'm lost without you."

"You're not lost," he counters. "You're finding your way. There's a difference."

"How do I know which way is right?"

He cocks his head as the game flickers across from us. "There's no right way, Peach, and there's no wrong way. There's only the way you choose and what you decide to make of that choice."

"That sounds terribly vague," I groan.

"I told you my advice was only semi-passable."

My muffled laugh meets his shoulder as I shift beside him. The sky starts to dim, the sun dipping behind a downy cloud, causing me to snuggle closer to Theo. "Mom and Dad are so angry right now. They're angry at me, they're angry at Brant. And Brant is angry with himself," I ponder miserably, picking at the fringe on my Technicolored romper. "And the only thing I'm angry about is that everyone is so damn *angry*."

"Anger is nothing but misplaced passion."

My eyes narrow with thought. "Passion is trouble. Passion only leads to heartache."

"Passion is meaning, and it would be a hell of an empty life without it."

Quiet reflection passes through me as I internalize those words. I think back to all of life's heartaches, all of life's most trying moments, and I know exactly what sits at the root of them all.

Love.

So much love.

And for as heartbreaking as those trying moments are, I would never in a million years forfeit the love that spurred them.

I wouldn't give up knowing Theo to spare myself the pain of his loss. I wouldn't give up meeting Brant to prevent the fallout of our love story.

Yes.

Passion is meaning.

Passion is purpose.

And tragedy is simply the risk we take in order to experience it.

Swallowing, I nod, reaching for Theo's hand and squeezing. "I'm faced with a choice, Theo. Do I pursue my lifelong dream, or do I stay right here with the man I love?"

Theo turns to look at me, the video-game controller vanishing from his grip. We're both lying on our backs now, grass blades tickling our skin as we stare up at the rainbow-spun sky. Shoulder to shoulder. Heart to heart. "Maybe it's not a matter of choosing one or the other," he tells me. "It's just a matter of which one comes first."

I don't hesitate. "Brant will always come first. But...how do I know what's best for him?" Tears wet my eyes, and my chest aches with conflict. "Oh, Theo, this is so hard. This is impossible."

"When you wake up, you'll know," he says gently. "You'll have your answer."

Our fingers interlace between us in the grass, and when I glance at him, he's a young boy again. Small but mighty. My fierce protector.

My big brother.

His freckles spread and scatter as he sends me a lopsided grin, his eyes glinting with gallantry. "Don't worry, Peach... I'll save you."

And in a flash he sits up with a wink, lifting his hand filled with sparkling pixie dust and blows it right into my face.

I inhale a sharp breath.

My eyes ping open.

Thunderous heartbeats reverberate through me, and my skin feels damp and clammy as I sit up straight in bed.

Blinking, I grip the front of my nightshirt, fisting the cotton between shaky fingers while new daylight spills in between cracked drapes. And when my eyes adjust from the sleep fog and the dream haze, my gaze lands on the far wall, fixing on the canvas perched above my dresser.

The painting of a fearless bluebird with rainbow wings, soaring skyward, daring to dream.

The one Theo bought for me.

"You're going places, Peach. You really are. And I'll be cheering you along, all the way to the top."

I cup a hand over my mouth as emotion sluices through me. As awareness flows through me. As my vivid dream with Theo both guts me and pieces me back together.

I feel him with me.

Right here, right now.

I feel him.

Whipping off the bedcovers, I slip into a pair of shorts and throw my hair up into a sloppy ponytail, then look around for my shoes and purse.

I race out the front door of the apartment, already knowing Brant isn't sleeping in the room beside mine. He hasn't come home yet. It's been four days since my emotional showdown with Mom and Dad, and I haven't seen Brant since I left in a tear-filled rush that morning.

No phone calls. No checking in.

Only a single text message that first night:

Brant: I need to clear my head. Kip is letting me sleep on his couch for a few days. I'm sorry, Junebug. I'm sorry I'm not strong enough right now. I'm sorry I let you down, and I'm sorry for loving you in the worst possible way. I failed to protect you, and it's killing me. I need to figure out what's best for us—for you. I just need some time.

I cried myself to sleep that night, and then again the next night.

And not out of anger. Not out of resentment that Brant allowed me to deal with the fallout with my parents all on my own. I didn't cry because of him.

I cried *for* him.

He shut down.

He's hating himself right now, and I can't think of a sadder thing.

Tugging at my ponytail, I traipse through the parking lot and hop into my car, pausing to pull out my cell phone before I start driving. I shoot a quick text to Brant as I fend off tears.

Me: We need to talk. Today. It's important. Meet me at the apartment when you get off work. I hope you're okay...I love you. <3 Junebug

He reads it right away, but he doesn't reply.

And fifteen minutes later, after I pull into the familiar parking lot and exit the car, he still hasn't replied.

A hard lump stings the back of my throat as I shove the phone into my pocket and trek through the maze of graves and headstones. I fit in here. I'm as haunted as these sacred grounds.

But I'm setting myself free.

I make a beeline to the headstone I know all too well—the one that steals my breath every time I see it.

The one I spent every Saturday night with for *months*.

The one that listened to me vent, sing, cry, and purge as I sprawled out across the grave site.

Theo.

Dropping to my knees beside the stone, my lips tremble as I read the familiar tribute.

Son. Brother. Friend.

Saver.

My chest hurts. It hurts so bad.

"I had a dream about you last night," I say, wiping away tears with the back of my wrist. "I dream about you a lot, but this one felt so real. It's like you were really speaking to me, from wherever you are. Over the rainbow, up in the sky, maybe even on the moon..." Pressing a hand to my heart, I smile. "Or from right here."

Birds chirp and chatter in a nearby tree, and I think about the bluebird painting.

"I just wanted to tell you that I won't be coming back here for a while, but I promise to take you with me. I'm going to soar, Theo. I'm going to spread my wings and fly, and you're going to cheer me along, all the way to the top. I know you will." I sniffle, my hair floating around me as a breeze sweeps through. It's warm and safe, and I pretend it's Theo letting me know he's listening. "I'm going to be brave like you. I've learned from the best, after all." I squeeze my eyes shut, the tears trickling down my cheeks and landing in the precious soil. "It's time."

The birds stop singing, and the breeze goes still.

It's just us.

It's just me and Theo now.

"It's a good day to save someone," I whisper, my fingertips skimming along the carving of his name. "And I think in the end...it might just save us both."

My chin lifts, my tear-glazed eyes peering up at the sky full of clouds as I inhale a tattered breath. But that breath catches in my throat, manifesting into a startled gasp, and my tears fall harder, my heart galloping. Goose bumps prickle my skin as a knowing smile paints my lips.

I blink up at those clouds.

And I swear...

I swear...

The cloud that dances right above my head is shaped just like Mario's hat.

The suitcases are heavy as I lift them off the floor, but not as heavy as the weight of my heart. That weight is backbreaking.

He didn't show.

I try to force back the sob climbing its way up my throat as my fingers curl around the suitcase handles, but it pushes through anyway. Ugly and mean.

Devastating.

My arms start to shake, and I drop the suitcases back to the floor, dragging them across the carpet as more awful cries pour out of me. Dad booked a one-way ticket to New York City the day I confronted them at the house, and I'd had no intention of setting foot on that plane. I'm an adult, after all. Just because my father wanted me to leave didn't mean I had to.

But I changed my mind.

And Brant has no idea. He has no clue that my father is driving me to the airport in an hour and I'm not sure when I'll be back.

I don't know when I'll ever see him again.

The pain is wretched. Truly excruciating. This decision was hard enough, but not having a chance to say goodbye to the boy I've loved since my heart learned how to beat?

Tears stream down my flushed cheeks. Aggie is tucked under my right arm while I pull the suitcases toward the front door.

And that's when the key jiggles the lock, and I freeze.

The door pushes open.

Brant.

It's Brant.

"Oh..." I'm not sure if it's a word or a sound or simply pure relief. I drop the luggage and my stuffed elephant and dash into his arms, nearly knocking him off his feet. "God, Brant...I didn't think you'd come. I almost couldn't go through with it."

Emotion seizes me. My arms cling and my chest squeezes.

"Where are you going?" His voice is frayed and broken as he lifts his arms to envelop me in a gentle embrace. "Your bags are packed."

He sounds so distant and far away, like he's already checked out. I draw back, my face a mess of grief. "I–I wanted to talk to you about that. You're usually off at four on Wednesdays, and it's almost seven. I don't have much time."

Brant swallows, drinking in my tears and packed suitcases. A frown mars his brow. "You're moving out?"

My head shakes slightly. "I–I'm moving to New York. Indefinitely." I watch his eyes flare with a mix of astonishment and dismay. "My flight leaves at ten fifteen."

Silence coils around us, thick and suffocating.

Brant just stares at me as if he's waiting for the punch line. His hands curl at his sides while his jaw grinds, but he says nothing.

A panicked whimper tickles my throat. "Say something, Brant. Talk to me."

He blinks, then refocuses his gaze to the left. His expression is pure heartbreak.

"Brant, please—"

"Okay," he whispers softly, nodding his head as his eyes glaze over. "Okay."

My breath hitches. "Okay?"

"Yes. It's the right call." He clenches his fists, staring off over my shoulder. "You should go."

Tremors ripple through me, causing my limbs to tremble.

It's so easy.

He's letting me go so easily, like I'm nothing more than water in his palm.

"That's it, then?"

He still won't look at me. His Adam's apple bobs in his throat. "I've been spinning my wheels trying to figure out what's best for you, June, and I keep coming back to the same conclusion," he says. "And it's not me." He glances down at his feet, his biceps twitching and flexing, riddled with tension like it's taking all his effort to remain composed. "I just… I thought we'd have more time."

"I'm sorry… I know it's sudden, but Dad booked me—"

He closes his eyes with a sigh, dipping his head. "Don't do that. You don't need to justify something I already know is right."

"I–I don't know what to say," I admit on an anguished breath.

Brant stands a few feet away, looking tortured beyond belief. His complexion is bloodless, his stance defeated. I want to hug him again, but I'm afraid I won't ever let go. "There's nothing left to say, Junebug. This is the way it needs to be, and anything else is just going to sound like…*stay*." His voice cracks horribly, but he regroups. "And that's the last thing you need to hear."

That's the only thing I want to hear, my mind screams.

He inhales a shuddering breath and glances up at me with eyes like those of a wounded soldier. "I stayed away because I'm completely defenseless when I'm around you, June. Logic flies out the window, and all I want to do is whisper pretty lies into your ear, telling you we're going to be okay. I can't be around you without touching you, and I can't touch you without wanting to keep you."

Touch me.

Keep me.

Never let me go, Brant.

My brain is a traitorous beast. I run shaky fingers through my hair and squeeze my fists. "This feels wrong. It feels awful."

"It only feels wrong because I'm standing right in front of you, trying so damn hard not to break," he murmurs. "When you're on that plane and your head is clear, you'll know it's right."

He's right.

I need to go.

It's for the best.

But I still can't bring my feet to move.

"Go," he chokes out. Brant spins away from me, linking his hands behind his head, as if it's far too painful to watch me walk away. The muscles in his back ripple with agony. "Please."

My head bobs as my tears continue to spill out of me, trailed by more heart-wrenching whimpers. Turning quickly, I place a hand over my mouth, and my long shirtsleeve dampens with sorrow. I trudge over to the discarded bags, bending over to grasp the handle of one.

With one hand still holding in my cry, I use the other to drag a bag as I move backward. It scrapes along the floor, mimicking the sound of my shredding heart.

That's when I feel him.

That's when he comes up behind me and wraps his arms around my waist, burying his face in the crook of my neck. "I'm trying to be strong because I know this is what's best for you," he confesses, his voice cracking on every word. "But I'm not built for this, June. I'm not built for a life without you."

My stifled sob falls out, and I spin around in his arms, collapsing against his chest. He holds me so tight, crying right along with me as we shake and mourn and grieve.

"You've always been here," he says through gritted teeth, cradling the back of my head. "It's always been you and me, and I'm going to be so fucking lost without your hugs and the sound of your voice and your sweet smiles." He squeezes me in his steadfast arms. "But I've been selfish for too long. I need to let you fly."

"Come with me," I weep into his T-shirt. "Fly with me."

"I can't, Junebug. You know I can't." Brant twines his fingers through my loose hair, kissing the top of my head as he shudders against me. "You need this. You've lived your whole life in my shadow, and it's time for you to find your place in the world."

He's right.

I hate it, but he's right.

We've grown codependent. We're addicted to each other. And until I learn how to live without him, I'll never be able to live with him in a healthy way.

Sniffling, I murmur, "What if my place is with you?"

"Then I'm here. I'll be waiting."

A gasp leaves me as I press my cheek to his chest. "You mean it?"

"Of course I mean it."

I can't stop crying. Even though I know in my heart that I need to do this, it's the hardest decision I've ever had to make. I want to prove to my parents that this isn't a temporary lapse in sanity, or a dirty little consequence of our tight-knit bond, and I can only do that through time and space.

This decision is about more than just dancing.

Our future depends on it.

Glancing at him with swollen, puffy eyes, I reach up and clasp his face between my palms. "I know we'll be miles apart, but…" My lips quiver. My hands shake. "You're still Brant…and I'm still June."

His eyes close, and he says in a strangled breath, "That's right."

I pull up on my tiptoes to kiss him. "You told me one year on Christmas Eve that sometimes a lot of love can make you cry," I whisper, pressing a kiss to the little freckle that dots his lower lip. "I didn't understand it then. I didn't even want it." I kiss him again, lingering longer. "But I wouldn't trade it for anything in the world, Brant. Loving you is worth every single tear."

His forehead crashes against mine as a gut-wrenching sound passes through his lips. "A lot of love…is a good thing to have," he says, his voice worn and raw, echoing his past words. "The downside is the more love you have, the harder it is to lose it."

"We'll never lose it. I've been yours since the day I was born and I'll be yours until the day I die. Distance doesn't change destiny."

Brant scoops me into his arms as our mouths collide and our tongues seek. The kiss is desperate and frenzied, full of salt from our tears and mournful moans. I feel him breaking down the longer our mouths remain fused, the longer he touches me, longing to keep me. His grip tightens, his fingers fisting any place he can reach—my waist, my neck, my hair. He devours me, angling his mouth to taste new places, hoping to unlock one where we can both escape to.

His resolve is disintegrating.

He's cracking.

And I'm on that frozen pond again, needing to make a choice that will change the course of my life.

With a strangled cry, I pull back, shaking my head, knowing I need to be the strong one now.

Brant has spent his entire life being the strong one.

He's taken on my added weight, my heavy burdens, and he's carried them with dignity. With pride. Brant has always gone out of his way to protect me, and now it's my turn.

It's my turn to be brave.

His mother's last words to him filter through my mind, tightening my chest with sentiment. I heave in a rickety breath, taking a small step back. "I'll always protect you."

I watch him carefully as a beat passes.

As he absorbs my words.

His kissed lips part with a sharp inhale.

"Now…cover your ears," I tell him gently.

Brant's eyes flash with memory. With painful familiarity. A single tear makes a languid, agonizing descent from the corner of his eye, down his cheek.

But he does it.

He obeys.

His hands lift slowly as his eyes close tight, more tears pooling and falling, and he cups his ears, exhaling a long, tapered breath.

"I don't want to leave," I begin, placing my own hands over his, keeping my voice low. Tears pour down my face like a fractured dam. "I want to stay and build a life with you—a beautiful life I know we deserve. I want to marry you, Brant Elliott, and I want to make love to you every night beneath rainbows and stars. I want to have children with you. I want to raise them strong and brave, just like their father, and I want to sing them lullabies by the light of the moon." My words clip with grief, and I take a moment to find my voice again. With a sorrow-filled sigh, I finish, "I don't want to chase my dream because it's not a dream without you in it."

I stare at him.

Exposed, vulnerable, so beautiful and broken.

His palms are pressed against both ears as wetness streaks his face like sad, falling raindrops. His eyes are still squeezed shut as his body shivers with emotion.

I pull away, letting go of his hands and waiting.

A few heavy moments stretch between us before Brant's eyes flutter open and his hands slowly drop from his ears. He licks away the tears at the corner of his mouth and whispers raggedly, "What did you say?"

Closing my eyes, I gather my courage.

And I lie to him.

"I said…this is for the best. It's better this way," I murmur, trying to keep my tone level. Strong and fearless. Then I step in to him one more time, lift up, and place a final goodbye kiss to his lips. "Look for me over the rainbow, Brant. This Junebug will be flying high."

BRANT

She's gone.

June is gone—and now the only comfort I have left is the hope that all of her dreams come true.

I sit collapsed on the floor with my head in my hands, hating the sob that pours out of me. I don't want to hear it.

I don't want to hear my chest caving in, because there's no sound more painful than a breaking heart.

So I cover my ears.

I cover my ears and let myself break.

A tragedy occurred, that much I know.

I just don't know if the tragedy was in her leaving me…

…or loving me.

34

YOU FIRST

BRANT, AGE 25

IT TAKES THREE MORE DAYS for me to muster the backbone to knock on the Baileys' front door.

Normally, I'd walk straight inside. I used to live here, after all.

But I don't live here anymore.

My hands are stuffed into my jeans pockets to keep them from shaking as muffled footsteps approach on the other side of the threshold. I try not to think of June when a breeze carries over the flowery scent of lilacs.

The door pulls open.

Andrew stares back at me, his eyes sunken in, his skin pallid.

Surprise steals his expression for the briefest moment before loathsome disgust takes its place. Angry fingers curl around the doorframe, his knuckles going white. He clenches his jaw as he seethes, "Get the hell off my property. You're not welcome here."

And then the door slams shut, rattling the hinges and nearly cracking the frame.

I close my eyes, holding my breath as I work to keep my emotions in check.

I'm exhausted.

I'm bone-weary, having spent the last seventy-two hours working double shifts to keep my mind distracted. I haven't slept, I've barely eaten, and I'm shocked my legs are even functioning enough to keep me upright. All I've done for three days is work and miss June.

She texted me a picture from the JFK airport, letting me know she'd landed safely. Seeing the name Junebug pop up on my cell phone screen felt like a sucker punch to the gut, but I was grateful for the communication. I hope it continues. I hope she calls me, texts me, video chats me. I hope she shares her life with me because mine is numb and uninspiring without her in it.

Which only confirms the fact that this was for the best.

Who am I without her?

Running a hand over my face, I debate my next move, glancing down at the happy welcome mat decorated with frolicking dachshunds.

I realize I've been a coward. I've kept my distance from the Baileys, and I didn't back up June when she confronted them about our relationship. The guilt still eats at me. She was so brave, so full of conviction as she stormed out of the apartment that morning whereas I had completely shut down. I was blank. Catatonic.

Useless.

And I feel just as useless right now as I stand here wondering what the hell I'm going to do.

Luckily, a decision is made for me when the door cracks open again.

This time, it's Samantha on the other side of it.

I swallow, meeting her eyes—blue like June's. She's frumpy and makeup-less, looking like she's slept just as little as I have over the last few days. I heave in a frail breath, and all I can manage to spit out is "I'm sorry."

I'm sorry for tearing the family apart.

I'm sorry for ruining your daughter.

I'm sorry for betraying the two people who gave me a second chance at life.

I wonder if she can see everything I'm sorry for shining back at her as she pulls the door open a little bit more, taking a step toward the screen. Her face is a mask of remorse paired with indecision. She doesn't know what to do. Her feelings aren't as black and white as Andrew's.

Inhaling deeply, she moves away from the screen. "Come in."

Those two words sound like more than I deserve, but I let them inside; I let them burrow. I let them fill me with the only semblance of relief I've felt since the last time I fell asleep with June tucked in my arms, warm and soft and mine.

It's not forgiveness, but it's something.

A crumb.

And when you've lost everything that matters, a crumb might as well be a four-course meal.

Stepping into the house, I let the screen shut softly behind me as I stop just short of the living area. Samantha stands a few feet away, her arms crossed, her back to me. She pulls a pen out of her bun then clicks the end of it like a nervous habit.

When she spins around to face me, her arm drops to her side as she shakes her head. "I lost one child, but it feels like I've lost all three."

My muscles contract, and my jaw clenches. I stare down at my shoes guiltily as a horrible, insidious feeling coils through me. I feel sick. "Samantha, I never meant to hurt anybody. You have to believe that."

"Of course I believe that," she says, still clicking her pen. "I raised you, and I know I raised a good man." She pauses, letting out a long sigh. "But good men can still do really stupid things."

When I glance up, she's watching me with measured disappointment. I scrub a hand down my face again. "I fell in love with her," I mutter softly. "And it never felt like a choice, it was just…effortless."

"Loving someone may not be a choice, but acting on that feeling when you know it's wrong *is*."

I open my mouth to speak, but nothing comes out.

She's right.

She's absolutely right.

Hanging my head again, I plant my hands on my hips and close my eyes. "I realize this may not be fixable," I say, sorrow lacing my words, "but you have to know that I did everything I could to prevent this from happening. I fought it, and I fought hard—but for all the stigma surrounding our relationship, for all the fucked-up technicalities that shadowed us, my *feelings* for her never felt wrong. *She* never felt wrong." I'm breathing hard, my heart pumping fast. "And it's really hard to keep fighting something that feels so goddamn right."

Samantha stares at me, her expression softening just slightly. She stops clicking her pen to drink in my words, searching for her own.

But our conversation is interrupted when the patio door slides open and Andrew makes his way inside. He does a double take when he spots me, his eyes narrowing to pointed slits. "What the hell are you still doing here?"

Samantha answers quickly. "I let him in. He deserves a chance to explain himself."

"He doesn't deserve anything. An explanation that justifies what he did does not exist." Andrew's face is angry and red, the veins in his neck popping. I watch as he storms over to us through the kitchen and into the living room with indignation in his gait. He raises a finger to my face, moving in closer. "We took you in when you'd lost everything. We *raised* you."

My blood swims with ice and shame. I look down, too conscience-stricken to meet his eyes.

"We paid for your years of therapy, we gave you an education, we packed up everything and *moved* just so you wouldn't have to grow up living next door to that house of horrors."

Tears sting my eyes. My heart grows heavier with every word.

"And how do you repay us?"

Samantha steps forward, the steady voice of reason. "Andrew, calm down. I'm handling this."

He ignores her. "Answer me," he spits out.

"Please," I muster, lifting my hand like a prayerful white flag. My voice shakes. "I didn't mean to—"

"You son of a bitch." His teeth are bared, his finger jabbing at me as he stands toe-to-toe with me. "You desecrated our daughter!"

We all go silent.

I look up, my gaze shimmering with penitence.

I don't know what to say.

I don't know how to excuse this, or argue my case, or latch onto the smallest thread of sympathy and make him understand.

All I have is my pathetic truth, so I let it fall out of me: "I'm in love with your daughter."

He responds by slamming his fist at my face.

Andrew slugs me in the jaw, bowling me over until I stumble back against the wall.

"Andrew!" Samantha shrieks.

I don't have time to recover or process the hit before he's on me again, snatching my shirt collar in a deathlike grip and shaking me. "You're not in love with her. You *preyed* on her. You groomed her." His spittle mists my face as he growls through clenched teeth. "How long were you fantasizing about my little girl? How long were you *violating* her under my goddamn roof?"

No.

I'm floored, stunned, heartbroken.

A breath leaves me as my stomach roils with sickness and I feel like I'm going to puke.

That's what he thinks?

That's what he believes?

I whip my head back and forth, choking on my own air. "Andrew…no. God, no, it was never like that." Bile climbs up my throat as my body quakes with disbelief. I'm like a rag doll in his grip, listless and stripped of fight. "*Fuck*…no…"

Andrew shoves me away, and my knees buckle.

I collapse.

"Andrew, damn it, get ahold of yourself," Samantha says, her voice hoarse and pained. She races over to me, crouching down to inspect my face that's oozing with blood from a split lip. She grazes her fingertips to my jaw with a mother's touch.

I'm still shaking my head back and forth, my breathing escalating. It feels like I'm about to have a panic attack. "You don't think that…" I rush out, looking up at Andrew, my limbs trembling. "You can't possibly think that of me…"

A brief moment of regret flickers in his eyes, but he slips the mask back on. "What am I supposed to think? You were having sex with your sister."

"No…"

"Your *sister*, Brant!"

"She was never supposed to be my sister!" I burst out, my head falling back against the wall as venomous tears drench my eyes. My chest caves in, my ribs burn, my breath hitches. "And it's not fair. It's not fucking fair," I chant, broken and hopeless. "She was supposed to be *Theo's* sister and we were going to grow up together as *neighbors*. I would've just been a regular boy who had a crush on a regular girl, and that boy would have fallen in love with that girl the *right* way."

Samantha stills beside me, her own eyes watering.

Andrew goes silent. Watchful. His face untwists as he listens.

A growl funnels through me, and I slam my fist to the floor. "It's not fair that my father had to lose his fucking mind and ruin my life, taking my mother away from me while also destroying any chance I had of a future with that girl—that amazing, *incredible* girl with the purest heart I've ever known."

My own heart feels strangled and smothered as I push out more words. Sweat dots my brow while adrenaline courses through me. "The girl who removes all the purple taffies out of the bag because she knows I don't like purple, and who wears perfume that smells like desserts because it reminds me of my mother, and who bakes me things even though she doesn't like to bake because she knows I love sweets, and who's brave and kind and so fucking *good* it's impossible to see any other girl but her."

Wetness trickles down my cheeks as I crumple, defeated, against the wall, breathing hard. "I love June. I'm *in love* with June…madly, completely, infinitely. I'm in so deep, there's no way out. And I'd love her no matter what, regardless of the circumstances, regardless of if we were neighbors, friends, classmates, or strangers. I was always meant to love her." I swallow and close my eyes. "But these are the cards I was given. These are the shitty, unfair circumstances I was forced into, and instead of a blessing my love for her is a curse. And I'm sorry… I'm so fucking sorry for that."

My chest aches from my tormented breaths, and my jaw throbs from Andrew's fist.

Samantha places a tender hand along my shoulder, a small comfort.

And as I sit there with my eyes squeezed shut and my fists balled on the floor at my sides, Andrew's voice breaks the silence.

"I'm sorry for striking you."

I open my eyes, his haggard stance barely visible through my blurred vision. But I see the contrition in his eyes. I see his own guilt.

Andrew takes two full strides backward and lets out a harrowing sigh. "But I still can't look at you," he finishes, running both hands through his salt-and-pepper hair. "I don't know when I'll ever be able to look at you."

Andrew spins around and stalks away, disappearing up the staircase, his footsteps mimicking my thunderous heartbeats.

My eyes close again.

The man who raised me as his own son, who gave me shelter and love and unconditional support, sees me as a monster.

A traitor.

Samantha squeezes my arm, likely trying to cease my tremors.

I shrug her away. "Don't. You don't have to pretend to still love me just because a piece of paper says you should."

Just hate me.

Hate me like he does.

Hate me like I hate myself.

"That's absurd and you know it," Samantha says softly but firmly. She moves in closer, wrapping her arms around my shoulders and tugging me to her. "This has been a shock, that's true. It feels like a boulder in the pit of my stomach, and I've hardly slept in days. I'm not sure when, or if, I'll ever be able to accept it."

My head falls against her chest as I exhale slowly.

"But I understand it," she says.

She takes my hand in hers and squeezes, and I'm thrown back to my early days of childhood with the Baileys, when I was six years old and all I needed was a mother's love. I'd been caught in June's nursery, trying to comfort her with a toy.

Samantha had ushered me toward her on the rocking chair, telling me that I'd done a kind thing.

"I'll love you like my very own, Brant. I'll love you like Caroline loved you. You have my word."

The memory shoots more tears to my eyes because I don't know if I ever returned that promise.

She loved me like I was her own son, yet I could never call her "Mom." I refused to take their last name because that would make me *theirs*—and I belonged to Caroline Elliott.

But still, even now, she comforts me like I'm hers, despite the fact that I've betrayed her in the worst possible way.

Pressing her palm to my jaw, she holds me close, with tenderness and protection. "Nineteen years ago, I was drinking lemonade on my front porch with your mother…with Caroline," she says, stroking my face as I go still. "She'd caught you feeding the neighbor dog pieces of your pancake through the fence in your backyard that morning, petting its nose and giggling. She'd scolded you, of course—told you it wasn't safe and that the dog could bite your hand." Nostalgia laces her words. "But you didn't care. You said the dog wanted love… and if you got bit, that was okay. At least you gave it love."

I vaguely recall that moment.

It was only days before my world unraveled.

She sighs, still holding me close. "You've always put love first, Brant—regardless of the consequences. Regardless of the fact that you might get bit." Her tone shifts, riddled with a tinge of grief. "Three days later, Caroline stopped by again, hysterical. She had bruises all along her abdomen from where Luke had kicked her in a fit of rage. She begged me not to call the cops, fearful of what he might do…but she was finally done. She was going to leave him."

An icy chill sweeps down my back.

"Tomorrow, it will be June. June always feels like a new beginning."

My mother's words echo in my ears—words I didn't understand then.

Words that hold such a double meaning now.

And it kills me that she never got her new beginning, the one she was finally brave enough to take. She never got to leave.

He wouldn't let her leave.

"Caroline told me that if anything ever happened to her, she wanted us to raise you," Samantha continues, brushing her fingers through my hair. "She'd watched Theo grow up, she'd witnessed the bear hugs and piggyback rides from Andrew, T-ball in the front yard, endless barbecues and laughter, the bike rides and picnics in the sun…and she wanted the same thing for you. A *good* father, a loving home." She swallows. "I think she knew, Brant… I really think she knew her time was running out. A mother's instinct."

I wipe the emotion from my eyes, sniffling into the front of her blouse.

"Just like my own instincts told me that my daughter was never going to be your sister."

I go still, lifting my head a little. Inhaling a shaky breath, I ask, wondering, "How did you know?"

"Moments," she says quietly.

"Moments?"

Samantha nods, then scoots away, forcing me to sit up straight. "I'll be right back." She pops the pen back into her hair and makes her way down into the basement.

When she returns minutes later, her arms are full of shoeboxes, all stacked on top of each other.

I frown. "What are those?"

She moves toward me as I straighten more, my back flush with the wall. She plops the stack of boxes beside me, lowering herself to her knees. Black permanent marker is scribbled along the side of each box, the ink smudged and worn.

Numbers.

Years?

Reaching for the first box, my heart beats swiftly as I read off the number. "Two-thousand-and-three." I pull off the top, my nose assaulted with must and age. Inside the box rest dozens of index cards. Hundreds. I glance up at Samantha, my frown deepening with unspoken questions.

She smiles. "Moments," she repeats.

My teeth scrape together as I pluck a card from the box.

March 4, 2003

Theodore got an A+ on his science project. He made a solar system and named the planets after video game characters.

June fell asleep in Brant's lap watching *The Little*

Mermaid. She slept for three hours, and Brant refused to move from the couch because he didn't want to wake her. He told me his legs felt like a mermaid fin later that night, but that it was worth it.

September 16, 2003

June had a nightmare about a giant bug that tried to eat her. Theodore and Brant spent an hour calming her down and telling her funny stories. When I checked on them the next morning, I found them all curled up together, fast asleep.

Popping the cap off more boxes, I keep digging. Keep reading.

May 10, 2005

Brant went to a birthday party today. He was given a chocolate cupcake, his favorite flavor, but he didn't eat it. He brought it home and gave it to June because she skinned her knee this morning and he thought it would make her feel better.

April 5, 2006

Theodore wanted to have a sword fight with June in the backyard, but June wanted to ride her bike with Brant. Theodore thinks she loves Brant more than him, but I told him he was wrong. She doesn't love him more, she just loves him differently. I'm glad he didn't ask me what that meant because I don't know.

June 23, 2008

June told me she wants to marry Brant one day. I told her she couldn't because he's her brother. She said,

"Theo is my brother. Brant is my handsome prince."

This kid watches too many Disney movies.

January 2, 2011

Brant canceled his plans with Wendy because June fell ill. He made her soup and suffered through a Hannah Montana movie with her. Whoever he marries one day will be a lucky lady.

Emotion is clogged in my throat as I reach for a more recent box, both eager and terrified.

May 11, 2019

June picked out her prom dress. It's gorgeous. The first thing she said? "I think Brant will love it." I had no idea what to say to that.

June 7, 2019

June just walked down the stairs in her prom dress. She's absolutely glowing. Andrew is tearing up like a giant sap. I love this man.

Brant can't keep his eyes off of June. I guess he loves her dress.

Theodore looks so handsome in his uniform. I'm very proud of him. He hugged me a little harder before he left for his shift tonight, and he whispered in my ear, "You've raised us right, Mom. You've done a damn good job."

He's gone. Theodore is gone. My baby boy is gone.

Fuck, I can't do this.

Cupping a hand over my mouth, I shove the box away and drink in a deep, anguished breath. Samantha hesitates before pushing more boxes toward me across the floor. Older boxes, where sweeter memories lurk inside.

I gather my courage and pop off the tops, and then I lose myself.

I read through more cards. So many cards. Hundreds of cards.

Each one houses precious moments. Forgotten moments.

Glimpses into the future.

Foreshadowing.

And above all...*love.*

May 2, 2004

The boys gave June the cutest nicknames. Junebug and Peach. This little girl is so loved.

June wanted to draw on her new coloring pad, so Brant drew with her. She scribbled a bunch of colors onto the paper and said it was a secret magical place over the rainbow. She asked Brant if he would live there with her one day, and he said yes—but how will they get there? June already had the answer. "I'll fly us there because I have wings!" she said. Brant told her he couldn't wait to go. Then June said it might be a long time because she still has to grow up a lot more (aww). Brant said, "That's okay, Junebug. I'll wait forever." My heart!

The angry adrenaline leaves me as I deflate, running a hand through my hair and finding my bearings. I glance up at the pen sticking out of Samantha's bun, finally knowing why it's always in there. She's been documenting our life's moments—turning them into something tangible.

Small ones, big ones, forgettable ones, devastating ones, cherished ones.

Our entire lives are in these shoeboxes.

It takes my breath away.

And at the center of it all, one thing stands out.

One thing is crystal clear.

"You've always put love first, Brant," Samantha says, her blue eyes glimmering with awareness. With knowing. With a mother's instinct. "You've always put June first."

Five days later, I get a text from June while I'm making a pot of stew on the stove.

My heart leaps.

June: It rained all day in New York City, but I'd relive every gloomy minute just to see this again.

A picture loads, and when it pops up on my screen, I almost collapse.

It's June, glowing and happy, standing in front of the most beautiful rainbow I've ever seen. She's smiling. She has color in her cheeks.

She outshines every rainbow.

A final text comes through.

June: Pretty, huh? It's fitting, too—because I sent you a package, and the tracking shows that it just arrived at the main office. I was missing you a lot today, and the rainbow gave me so much comfort. I hope this package is able to bring you comfort. I kept my promise, Brant. <3 Junebug

Confusion trickles through me as I read over her message, but I slip the phone into my pocket and make my way down to the apartment complex's office.

Sure enough, the receptionist hands me a package addressed from June Bailey.

I smile my thanks and finger the gift, unsure of what hides inside.

As I tear open the plastic outer casing, shuffling distractedly back to my room, I peek inside to see something wrapped in tissue paper with a little envelope attached. I open the note first, stepping into my apartment and closing the door behind me.

It's a sheet of baby-blue stationary stamped with birds in flight.
I smile.
And then I read.

> Dear Brant,
>
> Comfort and courage
> Help keep us from sinking.
> But for you,
> I am both,
> So I had to start thinking.
> When I was a girl
> I made you a promise.
> A hard one,
> Indeed,
> But that's never stopped us.
> He's silver like a sword
> Yet soft like cotton.
> Both courage and comfort,
> And never forgotten.
> You see,
> I have Aggie
> To keep me safe from my troubles.
> And now,
> An old friend has returned.
> You know him as
> Bubbles.

The note slips from my fingers, fluttering to my feet.
I feel like I can't breathe.
What?
It can't be.
It's not possible.

It's not fucking possible.

The room starts to spin.

I'm shaking as I sift through the package and pull out a plush object wrapped in tissue paper, my chest weighed down by emotion-steeped bricks.

How?

How, June?

With trembling fingers, I carefully unpiece the tape from the thin white paper, uncovering an irreplaceable token from my childhood. Something I never thought I'd see again.

My cherished stuffed elephant.

Bubbles.

It's Bubbles.

I fucking break down like the child who used to clutch this elephant tightly in his arms beneath colorful bedsheets while his mother sang him lullabies and smelled of candy and cake.

A devastating, joyful sound creeps up my throat, and I cover a hand over my mouth as my whole body shakes with tears.

It's Bubbles.

"I'll find him someday for you, Brant. I promise."

She found him.

June found him for me.

Squeezing the worn, stuffed toy in my hands, my tears dampen his gray fur. He looks the same as he used to, only dappled with blotches of bleach from where stains were removed.

I bend over to pick up the note, remembering there was a final paragraph at the bottom.

My eyes skim over the remaining words.

> PS:
> He's had plenty of baths,
> So he shouldn't be smelly.
> But for more of the story
> Contact Aunt Kelly.

All my love,
Junebug

Still trembling, I reach into my pocket for my phone, set Bubbles on the kitchen counter, and snap a photograph. I send it off to June with the following message:

Me: I love you so fucking much it hurts.

She reads it right away and texts me back.

June: How much? :)
Me: To the moon and back.
June: That's not enough...
Me: Over the rainbow and back again.
June: That's better.

With tears on my cheeks and my heart in my throat, I think about that final note card I read from the shoebox, and I send June one final message.

Me: We'll fly over the rainbow together one day. Just you and me. I'll wait for you, Junebug. I'll wait forever.

I've always put June first.
She's always put me first.
And I hope,
I pray,
I *beg*,
That someday…
We'll finally be able to put *us* first.

35

FIRST THINGS FIRST

BRANT, AGE 26

It's my first June first without her.

Aunt Kelly sits beside me in the spongy grass, her cheeks streaked in tears. The sun sinks behind a blood-orange horizon, casting an ambient glow atop the staggered headstones.

"I've been visiting your mother's grave every year on this day," she murmurs, dabbing her cheekbones with a handkerchief. "This is only the second time I've cried."

My heart races as I sit beside the grave site, cross-legged. "This is only the second time I've visited her grave, period," I admit guiltily.

She smiles. "I appreciate that you came with me today. I think it's why I'm extra emotional."

A warm breeze kisses my face, and I close my eyes with a mix of melancholy and peace.

It's been nine months since I reached out to Aunt Kelly, reestablishing a relationship after years of bare minimum contact. She's always been kind to me; she's always been good. And she's the only person left linking me to my mother.

I'm not sure why I grew so distant.

Sad reminders, maybe.

Fear.

She looks like my mom with her coppery hair like maple syrup and melted-chocolate eyes. She still smells like her cat, but sometimes when the breeze blows just right, I'll get a hint of the same sweet scent of my mother. They're imprints that used to make my skin prickle and stomach pitch, but now they bring me a semblance of comfort.

Just like Bubbles.

As it turns out, Aunt Kelly had Bubbles tucked away inside a box in her attic this whole time. The stuffed animal was taken into evidence by the detectives on the scene, but when the crime was pieced together fairly quickly and the case was closed, the few belongings collected that night were given back to Aunt Kelly, the next of kin.

She'd nearly tossed him.

The plush toy had partially fallen into a puddle of blood, staining the elephant's leg. But Aunt Kelly decided to wash it instead, cleaning the toy thoroughly with bleach and peroxide, knowing how important it was to me.

Only, by the time it was returned to her, she'd already bought me a new elephant, thinking Bubbles had been thrown away.

I was finally acclimating to my new life with the Baileys. I was in therapy. I was trying to forget.

And she feared that if I saw the old toy it would set me back and hinder my healing.

So she sealed him up inside a box, along with an assortment of other childhood trinkets. Books and special outfits. A few art projects I'd created in kindergarten made of molds and clay.

She'd planned on giving me that box when I had my own children one day, to pass the treasures down to a new little boy or girl.

Bubbles sat inside that box in Aunt Kelly's attic for twenty years.

Until there was June.

She'd contacted my aunt on a desperate whim, shortly after arriving in New York. June eventually told me that she'd simply woken up with a feeling one morning. She couldn't explain it. She said she'd been missing me a whole lot, crying herself to sleep with Aggie in her arms, wishing I had my own special elephant from childhood.

While June had begged her parents for information about the lost toy over the years, they never had any answers for her. She'd even called the police department one time, but they had no idea what she was talking about.

She never thought to ask Aunt Kelly.

Not until that morning.

My aunt shipped the toy off to New York the same day, then June shipped him to me, wanting to personalize the gift with her poem.

And hell, I'm grateful.

I'm so fucking grateful.

Bubbles was returned to me at the perfect time, helping to fill the gnawing void as well as the multiplying holes in my heart. I'll never know what prompted June to call my aunt, but I'm convinced she saved my life that day.

I let out a sigh and glance up at the cloudless sky, grazing my fingers along the blades of grass. Turning to Aunt Kelly, I murmur, "I'm sorry it took me so long to come with you. I saw how much it hurt you every time I said no."

Aunt Kelly sniffles, sticking the handkerchief back into the front pocket of her peachy blouse. "I understood, Brant. I was never angry or resentful."

"But it still hurt."

The sun sets a little lower, shadowing my words.

She glances my way. "It hurt that we lost her. It hurt that asking you to visit your mother's grave with me was even a question—not that you said no."

I bite my lip, skimming over the carving of my mother's name. "Well, thank you for waiting for me. Thank you for giving me time."

"Sometimes that's the greatest gift we can give someone," she says. "Time."

Her words tickle me as I internalize them.

Time can be the most painful thing in this world, but sometimes it's the only way to heal.

"A memory found its way to my heart today," Aunt Kelly says to me, wiping a stray tear from her cheek. Her voice is soft and willowy, and her eyelashes are clumped with mascara as she blinks in my direction. "Caroline was pregnant with you…eight or nine months, I think. She was about ready to pop." She smiles wistfully, the hazy sunset bringing out the orangey tones in her hair that mingle with silver and white. "She was stressed because she couldn't decide on what to name you. It's a huge responsibility, after all—naming a human. We'd taken a walk through the park that day, sipping on hot cocoa as winter melted into spring, watching the children scatter around the playground."

My eyes water, thinking about my mother so content and carefree as she prepared for an exciting new life chapter. I swallow, leaning back on my palms as Aunt Kelly continues.

"We took a seat on a park bench, catching up on life. People-watching. She was so happy in that moment. I don't think Luke…" Her jaw tenses as she glances away. "I don't think Luke had become violent at that point. Controlling, yes, but…"

I glance down at the grass, hating him more than ever.

"Anyway…" She swallows, inhaling a choppy breath. "There was a little boy across the park, maybe seven or eight. He was the cutest little kid with shaggy dark hair and a crooked smile. But what stood out the most was the girl."

Our eyes meet, and my brow furrows.

"There was a little girl in the sandpit," she tells me. "She was younger. Tiny. She'd arrived with her own parents a few moments earlier, and the second they plopped her down into the sand, she started crying. Awful, terrible screams." Aunt Kelly smiles again through her welling tears. "The girl made the whole park go running for the hills…except for the boy. He stayed. And while everyone else packed up their things to leave, he ran straight to her, patting her back. Comforting her. Telling her she was going to be okay.

"He calmed the little girl down, then sat beside her in the sand and played with her for the next hour until her tears were replaced by laughter and joyful squeals. They made sand castles. They made moats. And let me tell you it was the sweetest darn thing I'd ever seen."

Chewing on the inside of my cheek, I clear the emotion from my throat. "What happened?"

Aunt Kelly's smile widens with memory. With sweet nostalgia. "Your mother walked over to the boy before he could leave. Well, she hobbled, really. Her belly was enormous." She laughs. "She went to the boy, and she asked him what his name was."

My breath hitches.

"He said his name was Brant."

A lengthy silence stretches between us for a moment, only fractured by the sound of singing cicadas. I run a hand through my hair, sitting up and watching as she stares off between the headstones, the heartwarming memories lighting up her eyes.

"She told me she'd finally decided on your name, and that any boy with that name was destined to become a good, honorable man," she explains. "And then when she got home, she researched the meaning behind the name, just out of curiosity. Do you know what it means?"

I shake my head. I never bothered to look it up.

"Sword," she tells me. "Brant means 'sword.' Brave, gallant, a stalwart defender." Aunt Kelly reaches into her purse and pulls out an opened bag of Skittles, quirking a smile as she tips the corner toward me.

Cupping my palm, I hold it out to her.

She pours the candies into my hand, the purple ones already plucked out. Just like she'd done when I was a small child.

"You've lived up to your name, Brant. More than you know." We both glance at the headstone, feeling my mother's presence swirling around us, wrapping us up in a warm hug. "I know she'd be so very proud."

"Let's go, June!"

Her smile lights up my phone screen, complementing the glitter in her silvery eyeshadow. She calls over her shoulder to an unknown female, "One sec! I'm on a call." Then she faces me again, her smile widening the moment our eyes lock through the video chat. "Birthday adventures," she says in a breathy voice, sounding apologetic.

"Go," I tell her lightly. "Have fun."

June glances behind her again to where a group of friends laugh and loiter near a storefront building, then walks with her phone to a quieter corner. "They can wait," she tells me, sucking her bottom lip between her teeth. A tension-filled moment lingers between us, our connection still palpable despite the fact that we're staring at each other through my cracked cell phone screen and June is nearly eight hundred miles away.

I clear my throat, breaking the silence. "You look really pretty."

Ducking her head, I swear she blushes as a bashful little laugh slips out. June sweeps her long brown hair to one side as it glints with streaks of golden highlights beneath the lamppost. She's wearing something that looks like an old-fashioned flapper dress, pearly and infused with gems, and her lips are cherry red. "Thanks," she says softly, glancing back up. "I just got done with a performance. Nothing major, just a background dancer. Celeste has had some really great connections for me out here, and…" Her voice trails off, her eyes turning haunted for a moment. Another life reflects back at me. "And I miss you."

My throat tightens as that tension flares again, riddled with poignancy and unsaid emotion. I swallow. "I miss you, too, Junebug."

"I'm doing really good," she tells me, tucking a thread of hair behind her ear. A silver hoop earring glimmers in the muted lighting. "I'm thriving, Brant, I really am. I feel so independent and alive and…" She hesitates, licking her lips. "And if you ever wanted to visit me, I think…I think that would be okay. It would be really good to see you."

Christ, I want to cry.

She's telling me she's thriving. She's flourishing.

She's living on her own, chasing her dreams just like she'd intended to do.

She's telling me she still loves me, and maybe we can make it work.

I love you, too. I love you so goddamn much.

It would be so easy to pack my bags and fly across the country to sweep her off her feet. It's what I want to do with every fiber of my being. Images of doing that very thing heat my blood as I think about our first meeting. Our first hug. Our first kiss.

I wonder how long we'd last before she was naked and moaning as I sank deep inside her.

But it's only been nine months.

And judging by the love-laced look twinkling back at me like bright blue skies, I don't think she's ready yet. I don't think *we're* ready.

My relationship with her parents is still rocky. Andrew hasn't spoken to me since his fist landed on my jaw and his words sliced me to the bone. Samantha has been more merciful, checking in on me and emailing me family updates.

But I haven't seen them since that day. I haven't seen them face-to-face, and if I can't even look them in the eyes yet, I have no business pursuing their daughter.

I refuse to set us up for failure.

She must notice the way my face falls, and the way my eyes dim as I fumble for a response that doesn't sound completely hopeless. June lets out the barest sigh, just a little breath of disappointment. She nods, a silent response to my own, and is then interrupted by a slender redhead.

"June, you're taking forever. Our ride is wait—" The woman does a double take into the phone, her eyebrows arching with interest. "Oh, hello," she says to me, an appreciative grin curling.

I blink. "Hey."

She nudges June with her shoulder. "Who is *that*?"

"He's…" June's voice trails off, fading into the night.

And I wait.

I wait for her answer because I have absolutely no idea what that answer is.

I'm not her brother. I'm not her boyfriend.

To most, I'm nothing but a mistake.

June glances at me in the screen, her smile flickering. "He's important," she settles on. "I'll be right there." The girl shrugs and tosses her purse over her shoulder, skipping out of frame.

Before I can reply, someone else pops into the camera. A man, probably the same age as June. He's lanky with shoulder-length black hair and a beanie on his head. He grabs June by the wrist, trying to tug her back to the group. "C'mon, Bailey, we miss you."

His bold eyes case her gorgeous face, trailing her curves as flirtation glimmers in his stare. As he sweeps his hand up and down her arm, she throws him an awkward smile and pulls free.

He wants her.

I wonder if he's had her.

And the thought makes me want to fucking die.

Traffic and car horns mingle with static as June walks farther away from the group, holding the phone closer to her face. She nibbles her lip again. "Sorry about that. I, uh… I should get going. The gang is waiting."

"Of course," I say, hoping I don't sound as pathetic as I feel. "Happy birthday, Junebug. Be safe, and send me a text in the morning so I know you got home okay."

"I will." She smiles warmly. "Thank you." June falters for a moment, her gaze slipping to the right, then back toward me. "Celeste made me a birthday cake. And when I blew out my candles, I made a wish. It was the same wish I made on my ninth birthday and every birthday since."

I stare at her, my chest swelling with emotion—burning, aching, stinging, as if that emotion is trapped inside with no way out. Heaving in a hard breath, I nod. "Good night."

"Good night, Brant."

A ribbon of hair floats into her face, catching on her ruby lips, and it almost looks like she's about to cry.

But she doesn't.

She clicks off the call just as her name is shouted from behind her, and my screen goes blank.

I sit on my couch for a few minutes, missing the sound of her voice.

Missing everything.

Then I drag myself to bed and prepare for another day without her.

"I wish that we can be together forever."

"Forever, huh?"

"Forever and ever."

I bet you're still wondering if June's wish came true.

Well, we're not quite to the end of the story yet.

But we're getting close.

Things were looking pretty grim at this point, and for as much as I wanted June to thrive and prosper, the more she settled into her exciting life in New York City, the more I felt like she was slipping through my fingers.

We still talked regularly, sometimes daily.

She sent me selfies in front of every rainbow.

We still looked at each other with that same potent mix of longing, pain, and heartrending love.

But it wasn't enough.

It would never be enough.

And as the days bled into months and another year passed us by, I wondered if I'd missed my chance. I wondered if our forever was just out of reach.

Luckily, things started looking up shortly after June's twenty-first birthday. I had my first brush with hope.

That hope came in the form of forgiveness.

And that forgiveness came in the form of Andrew Bailey.

36

FIRST LIGHT

BRANT, AGE 27

My lips stretch with amusement as I watch Wendy walk out of the restaurant kitchen, her hips swaying, her burgundy hair swinging.

"I wish Miss Nippersink would funnel her fiery tenacity into her hostess duties," Pauly mutters under his breath. He's talking to me, but he's really talking to Wendy.

She stops, spins back around, and marches over to where Pauly and I are standing. She jabs a long nail at Pauly's chest. "You think you're such a big brute, you know that? Everyone here is afraid of you, but not me. No, sir, I can see right through your surly exterior and…" Her finger snaps up to his eyes. "And furrowed brow of scorn."

I hide my laugh.

If Pauly is entertained, he doesn't show it. His stance remains surly. His brow remains furrowed. "You underestimate me, Stellina."

"You have a parakeet named Petey. Only softies would name a bird Pe—" Wendy falters, her head cocking to the side. "What did you call me?"

"Nothing of consequence." He shoos her away with the flick of his wrist, almost looking like he might smile. "Carry on, now. I am not paying you to ruffle my feathers."

"Ooh, so you feel ruffled," she snipes, planting both hands along her hips. Wendy's eyes cut to me with a haughty smirk. "Did you hear that, Brant? He's admitting to having actual feelings."

"Feelings of contempt, yes," Pauly corrects.

I lift both hands, palms forward. "I'm staying out of this."

"You're frazzled right now. I can see it," she claims, taking a step closer to Pauly and squinting her gaze. "Look, your left eye is twitching."

He frowns. "It is merely an instinctive reaction to your irksome personality. I cannot help it. Just as you cannot help being irksome."

"I am not irksome."

"You are a bother, I assure you."

Wendy's lips purse. "Fire me, then. I dare you."

"I will not. The customers tolerate you for unknown reasons, and it is simply not worth the time it would cost me to find and train your replacement."

I watch as they stare each other down, Wendy holding her own and Pauly towering over her with two muscled arms crossed over his sizable chest. He's lost quite a bit of weight over the past year after joining the gym with me. I'm there every morning as a way to keep myself distracted, because mornings are hard waking up alone—especially once you've experienced how it feels to wake up beside the one you love.

Pauly told me he needed to start putting his health first. He's forty-five years old and lost his older brother to a heart attack this past winter. We grew closer after that, as I could relate to his loss on a highly personal level.

Honestly, I consider him a friend.

And as an observant friend who's pretty damn good at reading the room, I'm almost positive he has the hots for my ex-girlfriend.

Interesting.

With a dramatic sigh, Wendy takes a step back, rolling her neck. "Face it, Pauly. You'd miss me."

"I absolutely would not."

"Keep telling yourself that," she says, floating away in her black pantsuit and silver name tag, then waving her hand dismissively. "And don't call me spirulina. That stuff smells like fish."

"Stellina," he chides to her retreating back.

Her response is muffled by the two double doors whipping shut.

Pauly and I glance at each other.

"She is quite incorrigible, yes?"

His tone is unmoved, even though I recognize the charmed flicker in his eyes. "You like her." I chuckle, readjusting my apron.

"I tolerate her. She keeps me on my toes and smells like my nonna's Italian bake shop." He runs his fingers and thumb along the inky scruff lining his jaw, his watch catching the light from the fluorescent kitchen lights. "Perhaps I should fire her after all. She is trouble."

"Or maybe you should ask her out."

Two dark eyes slant in my direction. "I am twice her age, Mr. Elliott. That would not be wise." As he says this, he drifts away for a moment, almost as if he's considering the notion of doing something unwise. He shakes his head with a gruff cough. "Enough bumming around. We will be opening shortly," he tells me, pausing for a fleeting moment before he disappears around the corner. "By the way, have you considered my proposal?"

Tightening my apron, I tense.

Since I turned down the Seattle offer, Pauly has been relentless in trying to secure me a higher paying position at a different restaurant location.

The restaurant just happens to be in New York.

I shuffle my feet, reaching for a towel. "I'm starting to wonder if you're just trying to get rid of me," I tease, dodging the question.

He doesn't know. He doesn't know about June, so he doesn't understand why I'm not jumping at the chance to further my career and relocate closer to my "sister."

I told him I didn't want to leave the Baileys behind, even though they're two people who would probably love to see me gone...*to any place but there.*

But he keeps poking me about it. He said he'll move staffing around to accommodate me the moment I say the word.

Pauly pivots toward me, still stroking his short beard. His expression hints at a trace of levity. "Nonsense, Mr. Elliott. I'm hoping to join you there."

My brows knit together, and I drop the towel to the counter. "What?"

"It is my home," he tells me, nodding his head. "I grew up in Tarrytown, just north of Manhattan. I have been considering moving back, and I think you may be the final push I need." A low chuckle rumbles in his chest as he turns away from me again, lifting his hand with a curt wave. "No pressure, of course."

I stand there for a moment, watching him move around to the back of the kitchen as my heart picks up speed. The transfer offer hasn't strayed far from my mind since Pauly brought it up over Thanksgiving week this past year as we lifted weights together.

June had video called me that day, a few hours before her parents arrived to spend the holiday with her. Pauly was near, so I tried to keep my longing in check. I tried to be aware of the way my eyes danced with love as I stared at her through the phone in her brown sweater dress, just a shade darker than her hair. I tried to prevent my mouth from spewing out foolish things that would give us away. And I feel like I'd succeeded, for the most part.

But Pauly noticed *something*.

"Anima Mia. It is my Manhattan location," Pauly had said, his workout tank drenched with sweat as his muscles flexed and his neck corded. "You should work there."

I bent over, stretching my legs. "That's a very generous offer. I'll think about it."

He grunted at me. "You will not. I know when you are lying, Mr. Elliott."

Chuckling, I approached the weight bench, trying to ignore the way my skin hummed with the desperate yearning to say yes. To be close to June. "You can call me Brant, you know. I think we've reached a first-name basis at this point."

"I will call you Brant when you become my executive chef at Anima Mia."

Fair enough.

He's hounded me ever since, bringing it up almost daily…and every day it gets harder and harder to say no.

Letting out a sigh, I press my palms to the metal countertop, a thought trickling back to my mind. Curiosity nudges me, so I pull out my phone and do a Google search for the Italian word *stellina*.

Then I smile.

"Little star," I murmur aloud.

Yep…Pauly's toast.

When a knock sounds on my front door the following day as I'm lounging on the couch after a run, I figure it's probably Ethel, the next-door neighbor, wondering if her cat wandered into my unit again. "Coming," I call out, sweeping back my sweat-damp hair and traipsing over to the door. I pull it open, about to tell Ethel that Blinkers isn't here, when my words fall off.

My breath catches.

"Andrew."

Andrew Bailey stands right outside my door, with eyes rimmed red and hair looking grayer than ever.

He's aged.

And I can't help but feel responsible for that.

Swallowing the brick in my throat, I curl my fingers curl around the doorframe as I stare at him, slack-jawed and shaken.

His throat bobs, his stance weary as he gestures past me into the apartment. "Can I come in?"

I nod instantly.

It's been two years since I've had any real interaction with the man who raised me as his son. Aside from seeing him at the grocery store one time, where we locked eyes then sped our respective carts in opposite directions, I only received a letter from him in the mail last fall.

Well, it wasn't really a letter; it was only two words.

"I'm trying."

I wasn't entirely sure what it had meant.

I'm trying to forgive.

I'm trying to forget what happened.

I'm trying to forget *you*.

Samantha and I have met up for coffee and lunch a few times since everything unfolded—since she held me on her living room floor with a mother's love after I'd failed her as a son. And I've looked forward to those dates. They've been critical in keeping me moving forward, because if someone I betrayed so severely, so wretchedly, can still care about my well-being, then maybe I should care about it, too.

While that first year without June was one of the hardest years of my life, this second year has brought about a semblance of healing. I'm accepting that what happened *happened* and I'm learning to live with it in a way that doesn't eat me alive and hollow me out. I've stayed busy with work, but more as a means to nourish my creative passion for cooking versus using my job as a way of forgetting. I've maintained friendships with Kip and my coworkers and with Aunt Kelly, and I've fostered those relationships, letting them restore the rotted parts of me.

People talk about rehabilitation all the time. Broken bodies learning to walk again. Impaired minds fighting disease, addiction, and dark thoughts.

But have they ever had to rehabilitate a heart?

Hearts fall apart, too. Bodies crumble, minds fail us, and hearts turn hopeless. They can deteriorate if we're not careful, and for all the tragedies I've suffered through, for all the tears and pitfalls, I can't think of anything more tragic than a hopeless heart.

The heart is the crux of life itself, and once it starts to wither, everything else starts to wither, too. And that's a damn shame. That's a devastating injustice to everything we've fought so hard to overcome and to everything still worth fighting for.

And there's always something. There's always a proverbial light at the end of the tunnel, waiting for us to turn that corner.

I wasn't ready to give up; I didn't want to wither.

But for all my progress, for all my mending, there's still been a dark cloud lurking overhead, keeping me from chasing that light.

It's a cloud that goes by the name of Andrew Bailey—the man trudging past me with a nearly grown-out beard steeped in silver, heavy wrinkles, and a defeated glaze in his eyes.

It looks like he's checking his own heart into rehab.

I watch as he slinks past me, running his fingers through thinning gray hair, then plants his hands on his hips as he lets out a long sigh. He just stands there for a while with his back to me, a few feet away, while I linger by the open door, clinging to it as if I might need something to hold me upright.

Moments pass.

Silent but deafening moments.

Then he pulls something out of his pocket and tosses it onto my kitchen counter. "I'm done," he says softly.

My grip loosens on the door. Scraping my teeth together, I glance at the index card sitting on my counter scribbled with familiar handwriting.

"I'm done trying to fight this," he confesses, his tone full of remorse and acquiescence. "I'm done living in the past, wishing I could change it. I'm done ostracizing my son when I already know what it feels like to lose one. I'm done being angry and hateful when I have so much to be thankful for. I'm done *trying*," he tells me, finally meeting my eyes. Finally seeing me for the first time in two years. "I want to start *doing*. I want to start living again."

Emotion swells in my heart and stings my eyes. I drop my hand from the door and close it behind me—as if I know, without a doubt, I won't be needing to run. I take a few careful steps forward, turning my attention to the index card, trying to read it through blurred tears.

Andrew follows my gaze. "I've reread that damn card every single morning since Samantha wrote it," he says painfully. "It's haunted me."

My eyes trail back to him as I come to a full stop.

"I ran into your boss last week when I went golfing," he continues. "Pauly. He told me he's been trying to convince you to go to New York—to take a job transfer that would better your career and potentially change your life. He doesn't understand why you won't do it."

I drop my head and close my eyes.

"But I know why." Andrew runs a palm down his face, shaking his head. His cheeks fill with air as he blows out a breath. "I've lost so much, Brant…so much," he murmurs, voice hitching. Grief steals his words for a moment as he tries to regroup. "But so have you. And because I'm choosing to wallow in this limbo of wishing I could change the past and wishing I can shape the future, all I'm really doing is *not* choosing what's right in front of me. I'm not choosing what matters, and that's my family. That's my children. That's *you*." Tears pool in the corners of his eyes, then track down his cheeks. "Yes, we've all lost, but until I choose forgiveness, until I choose healing…we're all just going to keep on losing. And I'm real damn sick of losing."

I inhale sharply, my chest constricting and my heart racing. "I'm sick of losing, too."

He swipes away the wet tears, nodding his head. Then he lets out a broken sound—or maybe it's a healing sound—and closes the gap between us, pulling me into a bone-crushing embrace.

My eyes squeeze shut as I hug him back, wrapping my arms around the man I've missed for two long years. "I'm sorry," I say. "I'm sorry for everything I've put you through."

Andrew breaks down. He drops his forehead to my shoulder and sobs, and we linger like that, as if we're making up for all the hugs we've missed out on. "I'm sorry, too," he whispers raggedly, still holding me tight. "I'm not saying everything is fixed or erased, and I'm not saying this will be easy for me. I can accept things for how they are while still struggling to understand them. Just bear with me, Son."

Hearing him call me "son" pulls hot tears from my eyes, and my throat stings with sentiment as I ask, "What are you saying?"

"I'm saying...go to New York, Brant." Andrew gives my back a sharp smack, then pulls away, still gripping my shoulders. He looks me in the eyes, and for a swift second I see Theo. I see their paralleled blessing shining back at me. "And whatever happens after that, happens. It's what's meant to be."

Hope blinds me like the first light of day—a light in the form of forgiveness.

A second chance.

We don't specifically mention June, but I know exactly what he's telling me: *Go to New York for your career, even if you end up staying for my daughter.*

He doesn't stay long after that.

Emotions are high, and we've said what we needed to say.

As Andrew steps out my front door, I run a hand down my face, letting out a deep breath, and I glance down at the index card still lying atop my counter.

My heart gallops.

And then I pick it up and read it.

September 13, 2020

Vilomah. I've never heard of this word before, but apparently, it's what they call a parent who has lost a

> child. It means "against the natural order." Only...it feels like I've lost so much more than that. I've lost three children, and I'm losing my husband in the process. I don't think they make a word for someone like me. The only word I can think of is...sad.

I drop the note card back to the countertop…then I quickly change my mind.

Instead, I shred it.

I tear it into tiny pieces and toss it into the trash can, wishing I had a match to set it on fire.

I'm done being sad.

We're *all* done being sad.

It's time to chase our light.

Do you want to know exactly what's hiding in that light at the end of the tunnel?

Well, I'll tell you.

That's your legs working again after months of physical therapy.

That's the medication readjusting the chemicals in your brain after you took a razor to your wrist.

That's the bronze AA chip after a year of painful sobriety.

That's the warm tickle in your stomach when you find love again after a messy divorce.

That's forgiveness after you've hit rock bottom.

That light shines differently for everyone, but at the end of the day, it all amounts to the same thing. It's the better version of yourself, the person you've been trying to get back to.

It's your healing heart.

And a heart can only heal if you choose to let it.

That same night, I packed my bags and booked a flight to New York City.

37

AT FIRST SIGHT

JUNE, AGE 21

My face feels stiff from the costume makeup as I tuck stray strands of hair back into my bobby pins. I feel lighter without the enormous animal prop secured around me, but the bright lights and cramped space always have my chest squeezing during intermission.

Delicious nerves sweep down my spine and tickle my tummy as my reflection stares back at me. I look different these days. I'm a dancer now—a Broadway dancer, living my dream—and aside from the elaborate makeup caked all over my face, the real difference is in my eyes.

I've grown up.

Beatrice bumps into me, curling her fingers into cat claws as she winks. "Where's Celeste?" she asks. She fans herself with one of the programs as dark strands of hair stick to her forehead.

"Smoking," I reply, smiling at her as I collapse into a chair and roll up to the vanity counter. Illuminated mirrors line the walls, decorated with those vintage Hollywood light bulbs and scattered photographs from the performers.

I only have one photo taped to my personal mirror space—the prom picture of me, Brant, and Theo.

It brings me good luck and placates my nerves.

I spoke to Brant before the show today, but he sounded busy. Distracted. Static and background noise stole most of our conversation, as if he were taking a walk or out in public. I wondered if he was with someone and my call was putting a damper on his plans.

He told me he had a present for me, though, so curiosity has prickled me all afternoon and into the evening. *What could it be?* As much as I want to know what it is, what I want even more is for him to deliver it in person.

The distance is hard.

It gets harder every day, and even though my life is exciting and my career is thriving, I will never truly feel fulfilled. I'll always be missing a giant piece.

I'll always be missing him.

"She's smoking without me? Wench." Beatrice pushes through a wall of dancers that are all chatting loudly and sucking down liquid from water bottles as they regroup from the arduous first half of the show.

Time to focus.

As I'm reapplying setting spray, I hear my name echoing through the sea of people.

"June!"

My head snaps up and I glance around, trying to pinpoint where Celeste's voice is coming from. I'm surrounded by hyenas and lions.

"Holy shit, girl, look what the cat dragged in…literally!"

Celeste is costumed as a lioness. Leaning back in my chair, I crane my neck and spot her beelining toward me. "What? What are you…"

My voice trails off, and then I rise from my seat like I'm being yanked up in slow motion by an invisible force.

It can't be.

My heart starts to race with recognition and coursing adrenaline.

I nearly choke on a stunned sob.

Celeste's fingers are curled around Brant's wrist as she tugs him forward, zigzagging through the crowd. "I'm not sure if he's technically allowed in here, but I had to borrow him for a minute," she says to me, her grin wide, her teeth looking even whiter against the dark orange face paint. "Surprise!"

Sweat dots my brow, and my lungs feel tight.

Brant.

Brant is here.

He's here in New York City, standing in the middle of my backstage dressing room, staring at me in glazed, wide-eyed wonder.

And I'm dressed like a zebra.

I blink, making sure he's real. Making sure I'm not having another delirious dream.

"Junebug," he murmurs, saying my name like it's a sacred thing.

Tears stream from my eyes. I think I might faint.

My black-and-white-striped legs pull me toward him, and Celeste slips out of the way to avoid being sandwiched between us when I inevitably catapult myself into his arms.

Only, I stop just short, afraid to touch him.

I'm terrified to feel his arms around me because I might just break apart.

"Brant," I whimper, my bottom lip trembling. My entire body trembling. "You're here…"

He's wearing a cream-colored button-down with the sleeves rolled up past his elbows. It's striking against his tanned skin and dark, unruly hair—the hair he's sweeping fingers through right now as his eyes twinkle beneath the fluorescent lighting. They twinkle with relief, with want, with sweet reunion.

This isn't a phone call or a video chat. This isn't a letter or a text.

I could reach out and touch him if I wasn't about to topple over.

He's really here.

His lips stretch into a smile, causing his dimples to pop. His hand falls from his shaggy hair, then extends toward me, reaching for my face. I'm bathed in familiar scents: Ivory soap and spearmint and *home.*

Everything around me falls away.

I close my eyes when his knuckles lightly graze my jaw, absorbing his touch for the first time in two years. Memories inundate me: good, bad, beautiful, painful. Desperate kisses and warm hugs. Tears, lovemaking, grief, and sad goodbyes.

God, it's too much… It's so unexpected and powerful and…

My lungs collapse.

I feel my chest start to wheeze as my breathing comes undone.

Oh, no.

A familiar overwhelming infiltrates me—the lights, the crowd, the heat… *him.*

It's him.

Brant is here.

How can he be here?

A stampede of emotion tramples through me as my knees wobble and my lungs fight for satisfying breaths. Brant's look of awe slips away, replaced with worry.

"Whoa…are you okay?" He steps closer to me, his palm cupping my cheek. "June."

I'm nodding even though I can't breathe.

"Shit," Celeste says, jumping into action and snatching my purse tucked beneath the beauty counter. She pops my inhaler into my hand. "Let's get you to the bathroom."

"No, I–I'm…o-okay…" I take a few puffs on the inhaler, closing my eyes as the medicine eases the tightness in my chest. I feel Brant's hands brush up and down my arms, languid and firm. A calmness seeps inside, and my frenzy morphs into a slew of hot tears biting at my eyelids. "Brant," I squeak out, my eyes fluttering back open. "I can't believe you're really here."

His brow is creased with unmistakable concern. He squeezes my upper arms, swallowing hard. "I'm here."

Celeste rubs my back, then whispers into my ear. "Go get some air. We still have a few minutes."

I nod.

Brant guides me through the dancers to the backstage door that leads outside, and the moment we step into the muggy August air I launch myself into his arms, my airways finally stretching with reprieve. The chaos in my chest dissipates and all I'm left with is profound relief.

I try to keep my tears from falling so I don't ruin my makeup but they slip out anyway. They dampen his shirt, ivory like his soap, and I feel two steadfast arms wrap around me, his palms sliding up and down the center of my back.

One of his hands moves around to my front and lands against my chest, his fingers splaying over my ribs like he's trying to soothe my faulty lungs. "Don't cry, Junebug," he whispers, leaning down to kiss my hair. "You scared me."

"I'm fine," I tell him, sniffling. "It was just a shock."

When I pull back slightly, my eyes lift to his, catching the sentiment glowing back at me. Feeling him in my arms, inhaling his scent, watching his expression flicker and burn has my mind spinning and loopy. I squeeze his shoulders to steady myself, still not convinced I won't topple.

"God…let me look at you." Brant inches back farther and takes my chin between his thumb and fingers. His gaze rakes over me, remnants of worry lingering from my brush with asthma.

"Don't," I beg. New tears rush out of me as I shake my head. "I'm a zebra."

His lips finally quirk into a smile. "You're a dream."

"A nightmare, honestly." I sniff. "What are you doing here?"

He steps back more, his hands finding their way into the pockets of his dark slacks. The streetlight casts a yellowy warmth upon him, highlighting the bronze flecks in his hair. Two earthy eyes find mine, glinting with more than he can say right now. "It's a long story, but maybe we can grab a drink and talk after the show?"

How did you find me?

How long will you be in town?

Do you still love me?

My mind races with questions but I simply nod, knowing I'm running out of time. I have a performance to finish. I have a small role in the acclaimed *Lion King*, and that's no small feat for a newer dancer like me.

"Of course." I nod, licking away the paint-tinged tears tickling my lips. I need to hurry inside and fix my makeup with only moments to spare. "Do you have a ticket? Will you be in the audience?"

He shakes his head ruefully. "This was sort of last-minute. I got Celeste's aunt's number and she said you guys were performing tonight. I was just waiting out here until you were done." Brant dips his head with a light chuckle. "Celeste caught me."

"Well, I'll meet you out here after the show," I say as a smile pulls on my awful zebra lips. I'm certain I look like a buffoon, and any attraction Brant still held for me has exploded into dust. "You'll wait for me?"

Brant's eyes squint toward me like my question is absurd. "You know I will."

"You mean it?" My smile blooms. I can't help myself.

"Of course I mean it." He steps forward, clasping my neck with both palms and pressing his forehead to mine. He inhales sharply, as if he's drinking me in. "I told you I'd wait forever."

With a kiss to my hairline, Brant pulls back and lets me go, leaving me with a smile and the remnants of his promise.

It almost feels like a first date as we stroll through the doors of the Rum House, a swanky bar located in the Theater District of Midtown Manhattan, and take a seat at the bar.

I suppose I don't really know what a first date feels like.

Aside from a few awkward kisses and house parties with classmates, the only man I've ever been with is Brant—and our relationship has been backwards from day one.

But if I could picture a first date, it would be something like this. Piano music, candlelight, classic cocktails, romantic ambience, and the man I love unable to keep his eyes off me.

He sips his scotch on the rocks like a red-blooded male, while I suck down a Cherry Upside-Down Cake Martini like a juvenile girl who's only been able to legally drink for two months and has limited knowledge of alcoholic beverages.

I send him a shy smile over my glass.

Brant returns it, spinning his glass between his fingers and letting the ice cubes clink. When he sets the glass down on the counter, he sighs, swiveling on his barstool to fully face me. "It's crazy to see you in a bar," he says, his gaze scanning my face, dipping briefly to my mouth. I nibble on my bottom lip. "It's been so long since I've seen you."

"I haven't changed, really," I confess, tucking my drab brown hair behind my ear. "I'm still terribly boring and as plain as can be." Chuckling with a bit of self-deprecation, I glance down at the change of clothes I'd brought to the stage performance. I hadn't expected a surprise visit from the love of my life, so I'm only wearing a pair of blue jeans and a loose-fitting *Wicked* T-shirt that I've tied at my hip with a scrunchie. My face is red and blotchy from removing my costume makeup, and my hair is still caked in hair spray, riddled with dents and bumps from being pulled back beneath a zebra head.

My appearance is appalling, and I'm shocked I was even allowed into such an upscale place. I'll bet Brant's swoony smile and Thomas Beaudoin eyes gave us the golden ticket in.

But as I take another drink of my frilly cocktail, I watch as that smile slips and those eyes dull.

Brant frowns, reaching for his scotch and fingering the glass. "You're not plain, Junebug," he tells me, looking away and taking a small sip. "There's nothing plain about a masterpiece."

A lump swells in my throat, clogging my response.

He says it so casually, so effortlessly, like he didn't just move me to tears.

"I'm really proud of you, you know," he says after a quiet, poignant moment stretches. "Whatever happens between us…I hope you know that."

That lump grows bigger. I try to swallow it down.

I pick apart his words, wondering why he says them like he's uncertain of our future. "Why did you come here?"

He's silent for a beat before he looks back over to me. "Pauly offered me a job in Manhattan. An executive chef position at his restaurant."

My instinctive reaction is pure joy. Pride. I lean in and throw my arms around his neck, squeezing him to me. "Oh my gosh, Brant. I'm so happy for you." But as I hold him, my fingertips grazing the soft curls at the nape of his neck, feeling his breath against my ear, his answer fully registers. I close my eyes and squeak out into the crook of his neck, "You didn't come for me?"

I still hold on to him, unable to look him in the eyes as I ask my question.

Too afraid to see the truth glimmering back at me.

Brant's hands lift to clasp my hips, holding me in a loose but intimate grip.

The breath he releases near my ear is shaky, and I wonder if our lingering proximity is having the same effect on him as it is me. "I didn't want to assume anything, June," he admits softly, canting his head so his lips brush the lobe of my ear. "It's been years. You have a whole new life."

"You're my whole life." I say it as if I've been waiting years to say it.

Another shuddery breath hits my ear. He finally inches back, his hands still glued to my denim-clad hips. His eyes lift to my face. "Just because I said I'd wait for you doesn't mean I expected you to wait for me. There's no pressure. I wanted to discuss the transfer with you before I took it."

"Take it."

His forehead wrinkles. "Are you sure you don't want to discuss—"

"There's nothing to discuss, Brant. Take the job."

Piano music sounds around us as Brant's hands slide down my hips and land atop my upper thighs. He sighs deeply, provocatively, his gaze skimming me as his thumbs brush over the faded denim, shooting goose bumps across my skin. The pianist behind us starts to play the Elvis song "Can't Help Falling In Love," and my insides pitch.

I close my eyes, homing in on my other senses, like the feel of Brant palming my thighs, his touch electric. His body heat emanates into me as his fingers trace down my legs, then back up again, as if he's re-memorizing my shape. The music pulses through my blood, turning my heartbeats into melodies, into beautiful love songs. I smell a hint of cigar smoke mingling with expensive liquor and something woodsy.

And if I zone out hard enough, I can still taste his kiss.

When my eyelids flutter back open, Brant is staring at me, the golden heat in his eyes outshining the muted greens. There's a fire brewing. A familiar flame crackling to life.

We're both breathing heavily, perched in this intimate position with his hands on my thighs, while my feet rest on the rung of his stool, my knees between his legs.

The silence thickens, the tension swells.

Brant's gaze settles on my parted lips. He clenches his jaw as he says, "I have a present for you."

"Oh, I..." I lick my lips, watching as he tracks the gesture. "I thought *you* were my present."

His eyes flick back up, a smile hinting. But it fades as the heady fog grows thicker, swallowing both of us. "Turn around."

I feel hypnotized, practically drugged as I stare at him, letting his words register. Blinking through the haze, I nod, twisting around on my stool until my back is facing him.

My skin hums with anticipation as I squeeze my eyes shut, feeling him inch closer to me after a few beats pass. The warmth of his skin radiates through my cotton shirt, and then his hands are reaching around me, equipped with a golden chain. He clasps the jewelry behind my neck.

Brant gathers up my long hair in his hands, pulling it out from the necklace and pooling it over my right shoulder. His lips dip down to my ear again as he whispers, "It made me think of you, Junebug. Finally spreading your wings." A kiss finds the curve of my neck, and I shiver. "Flying free."

I glance down and finger the pendant attached to a delicate chain. My breath hitches, emotion battling it out with the desire I feel as Brant continues to kiss my neck, his hands sliding down my body and curling around my waist.

It's a tiny bluebird.

"I–I love it," I manage, involuntarily leaning back, my spine flush with his chest. Goose bumps scatter along my skin when he drags his nose up the side of my throat, then kisses the shell of my ear. "Th—thank you."

His grip tightens on my waist, his fingers biting into me as he breathes out, "I'm staying at a hotel."

My thighs automatically clench.

I feel myself grow wetter as my skin crawls with a hot flush.

I imagine him taking me back to his room and showing me exactly how much he's missed me over the last two years.

My voice sounds small as I twist around on the stool and find his eyes over my shoulder. "I'm ready when you are."

His hands give me a hard squeeze as my response registers, his eyes lighting up with blatant arousal. He pulls his bottom lip between his teeth, his gaze flickering across my face, landing on my parted lips while he considers the implication.

Then he pivots away from me, swallowing back the last sip of his scotch. Brant slaps a few bills on the bar counter and stands, turning to me, his gaze still alight with hints of what's to come.

He takes my hand.

He takes my whole life, too.

38

US FIRST

JUNE, AGE 21

THE MOMENT THE HOTEL ROOM door shuts, Brant spins me around until my back is pressed up against it. A squeaky gasp falls out of me. His one hand is planted on the door right beside my head, while the other trails up my body, from my thigh to my hip, skimming over my breast, and settling along the expanse of my neck. He tugs at my bottom lip with his thumb, his eyes fixed on my mouth.

I thrust my pelvis forward, my body arching into his.

"June…" He whispers my name on a ragged breath, his thumb sinking between my lips. "I've missed your fucking mouth."

All I can do is whimper as I grind against him, the ache between my legs pulsing and needy.

"I've missed the way you say my name, and the way you laugh," he says, leaning in to pepper kisses along the side of my throat, then up my jawline, until his mouth is hovering a centimeter from mine. "I've missed the way your lips taste, especially when you're wearing that gloss that tastes like cherry pie. I've missed the sounds you make when you come."

He draws his thumb from my mouth, and before the desperate begging can spill out of me, he kisses me. My lips are his again, as they have been ever since we stood in that hallway at the prom and I opened a doorway to the inevitable. A prelude to *meant to be*.

Fate disguised in sinful wrapping paper.

But it doesn't feel wrong anymore. His hands on my body don't feel criminal, and his lips on mine don't feel like a fluke.

Brant seems to melt, deflate, as he presses a soft kiss to my bottom lip, just lingering for a pause as if he's accepting the moment—this inevitable, meant to be, fateful moment. A moment that confirms that *we* were never wrong. Our *love story* was never wrong.

We were simply waiting for the timing to be right.

He sighs against my mouth and it sounds like longing, like pure relief, then he tugs my bottom lip between his teeth with a groan. And when he dives back in for another taste, his hands grip my cheeks in a possessive, desperate clutch and our mouths both open at the same time, tongues colliding. I shiver at the contact. His tongue slides over mine as we moan together, and I suck on it, reveling in the way his hips jerk against me, his erection stabbing my lower belly.

He pulls back to grip the edge of my T-shirt and yank it up over my head, until my bra-covered breasts become the new prize for his tongue. The robin's-egg-blue lace is tugged down in one quick motion, as if taking the two seconds to unhook the clasp would be an eternity.

Brant sucks on my nipple as my whole body arches upward, seeking his hot tongue, and my hands hold the back of his head to my chest. As he nicks me with his teeth, one of his hands drops to his belt buckle and he clumsily begins to unfasten it.

"I need you," he murmurs against my cleavage, laving his tongue upward until he's decorating my throat in future hickeys. "I need you now."

"Take me," I say, my hands shaking as I reach for the buttons on his shirt.

With his belt hanging loose around his hips, he takes over for me, hastily pulling apart each button, his eyes blazing into mine. The moment the last button is undone, I push the dress shirt off his shoulders and graze my palms over his hard chest.

He's brawnier, more filled out. Rippled planks of muscle flex and twitch beneath my touch as my hands slide down his torso, landing at the button of his pants.

"There's something I need to know," he says breathlessly, flipping me around until my breasts are pressed against the hotel room door. I squeak in surprise as his mouth draws close to my ear and his strained breaths mingle with the sound of his zipper sliding down. "Tell me how many other men have been inside of you. I need to know, even if it kills me."

Reaching around my body, Brant unhooks my jeans and shoves them off my hips, my underwear following. Two fingers slip inside me, hard and sudden, causing us both to moan. I'm so wet, the slippery sounds echo all around us, nearly wiping his question from my mind.

"How many, June?"

He picks up speed, fucking me hard with his fingers and nudging his erection between the back of my thighs. I feel like I might come, and it's only been ten seconds. "Only you," I manage to pant out. "No one else."

He stills for a moment, slowing down. A long breath hits my ear, and his forehead falls to my shoulder briefly, like he's trying to process my response. He's savoring it.

Then he spins me back around, grabs me by the thighs, and hoists me up into his arms. I'm carried to the bed and dropped onto the mattress, but before I can situate myself, Brant is tugging my pants and underwear off my ankles and flipping me back over onto my stomach.

He climbs over me, covering me with his broad frame, his chest flush against my back. Taking me by the wrists, he extends my arms over my head, clasping them together with one hand as he uses the other to position his cock between my slick thighs.

Yes.

I need this.

I need him.

It's been so long.

He doesn't make me wait. Brant shoves into me from behind with a groan, and I cry out, squirming beneath him as his opposite hand glides up my body until he's fisting my hair. He tugs my head to the side and captures my mouth over my shoulder in a sloppy, lust-laced kiss.

"Oh God..." I whimper as his hips start bucking. Our tongues tangle wildly and without direction, as if we picked up a guitar and just started playing, unskilled and unprepared yet knowing it will still make music.

With fingers knotted in my hair, his forehead crashes to mine; he has a look in his eyes that's pure possession. Primal heat. "No one else," he rasps, mimicking my words. "Only you."

I think he's telling me he hasn't been with anyone else either, but I'm too drunk on the feel of his cock sliding in and out of me to question it. I cry out with each thrust. He's hitting such a delicious spot from this angle.

But as the tingles swell and crest, he slows to a stop. He pulls out and moves off me. "Come here."

As I lift up, my hair is in disarray, curtaining my eyes, and my cheeks feel hot and flushed. Brant scoots backward until he's backed up to the far wall. My gaze settles on his rock-hard erection as he strokes it, waiting for me to shake off my haze and climb back on.

I move forward on my knees, unclasping my bra as I join him. The moment I'm within reach, Brant grabs me and pulls me onto his lap so I'm straddling him, my hands planting on his shoulders for steadiness. His cock teases me, and I rock against it.

His eyes flutter closed. "It's always so urgent between us," he murmurs, hissing through his teeth as my hand reaches between us to grip his cock. "So hard, so dirty. I always fuck you like it's going to be the last time I'm ever going to fuck you."

"Maybe I like it a little dirty," I confess, rubbing the pad of my thumb over his wet tip. "It's hot. You make me come so hard."

He groans, then snatches me by the hips and lifts me up until I'm level with the head of his cock. Then he pistons into me and I sink down, throwing my head back with a sharp cry.

Brant wraps his arms around my back and tugs me close, his face buried between my breasts. His nose tickles the chain of my necklace as he murmurs, "I want to go slow. Adore you. Fuck you for hours, like we have all the time in the world because we do…" I grip his hair, his tongue dipping out to taste me. "We do, Junebug."

"I missed you," I whimper. "I missed you so much."

"I'm done missing you. I'm done sleeping alone. I'm done wishing for a future with you when you're still here." His head falls back against the wall as I ride him, swiveling my hips and leaning forward, our lips touching. "I…" He thrusts up. "Am…" He thrusts again. "Done."

I kiss him hard, frenzied, full of passion and need, holding his face between my hands as I bounce in his lap, emotion fusing with lust. A potent combination. When I pull back, I ask, "You…you haven't been with anyone else? In two years?"

"No."

"But you're…"

"What? A man?" He peppers kisses down my jaw and nibbles my neck, his fingers raking through my hair as our bodies slap and grind together. "And men have needs?"

I nod, tilting my head to the side to give him better access.

"I'm *your* man, June. And the only thing I've ever needed is you." Kissing and biting his way up the side of my throat, he nips my earlobe and says, "Never underestimate a man willing to wait forever for the woman he loves."

I want to cry.

Cupping his face between my hands, I move his head back until we're eye to eye. His pupils dilate, the browns and golds and greens of his irises swirling with faithful devotion. "I love you, Brant. I love you…over the rainbow and back again."

A smile paints his lips as he moves in for a kiss. "I love you, Junebug. More than you'll ever know."

We go slow.

We go hard.

We go fast, brutal, sweet, and kind.

We make love for hours, savoring, cherishing, appreciating, until we're sore, bruised, and satiated. We come. We cry.

We heal.

He breaks me apart and puts me back together again.

And then we fall asleep, tangled and spent, knowing that for the very first time, we don't need to fear what comes next.

Dawn spills in between the hotel curtains, spotlighting the man sprawled beside me. He's on his back with a knee drawn up, head tilted slightly toward me. His bottom half is only partially covered by a rumpled bedsheet, while one arm is draped over his middle and the other is propped above his head. The epitome of sexy bedhead draws my hand to his mop of hair, my fingertips dancing through the soft strands. He doesn't even stir as I gaze down at him, coiling a curl around my index finger.

He looks so peaceful, so innocent.

For a moment, he's just a boy again. He's the boy who stole my heart before I was old enough to even consider giving it to anyone else. With floppy bangs, knee-weakening dimples, and a stalwart soul, he's fighting off invisible monsters in our backyard, tucking me into bed with a lullaby, and reading me storybooks beneath our childhood tree house.

In a lot of ways, he'll always be that boy.

But he's also a man. He's the man who fought for my dreams, who never stopped waiting for me, and who made love to me all night long, cherishing every single piece of me.

I loved the boy, and I'm in love with the man.

Brant Elliott lays claim to all of my most precious memories of the past, and I know without a doubt he'll claim my future as well.

Finally he's stirring beside me. Brant's eyes flutter open as he stretches, a smile stealing his yawn when he registers my presence.

I continue to play with his hair, sliding in closer. "Good morning, handsome."

"Morning." The smile grows brighter as he wraps his arms around me and tugs me against his bare frame. "How do you still smell like lilacs after last night? You should smell like sweat and sex and…" Nuzzling my hair, he inhales deeply. "Very bad things."

I clasp his face and force his eyes on me. "There was nothing bad about last night," I say, crinkling my nose.

"Fine." He grins. "Naughty things. Dirty things." Two fingers trail down my middle, landing at the juncture between my thighs. "Things that are making you blush right now."

My breathing becomes unsteady. "It's warm in here. It's August."

"I recognize that color in your cheeks, Junebug," he rasps near my ear, curling his fingers inside me. "That's all me."

I arch my spine with a little whimper, grinding against his hand. "We—we should probably talk, don't you think?" He pumps in and out of me, slow at first. Languidly delicious. "Discuss things?"

Brant's right leg wraps around both of mine, trapping me to him as his fingers continue to ravage me. He buries his face in the crook of my neck, sweeping my hair back until he's nibbling down my throat and collarbone. "Ask me anything."

His fingers quicken their pace. "Why…why are you really in New York?"

"You." He nicks my shoulder with his teeth.

"Do Mom and Dad know?"

"Yes."

I feel his erection pressing into my abdomen as he continues to finger me, his own breaths unraveling. A gasp laces my words. "A-Are they okay with that?"

"Tentatively."

My hips meet his thrusting fingers as I feel the pressure building. "Only one-word answers?"

"It's really hard to string sentences together when you're about to come on my fingers, June."

The logical part of my brain says to put all orgasms on hold until we've had a proper discussion, but my body overturns rational thought so I continue to ride his hand until I shatter blissfully, wildly, and collapse against his chest as two strong arms hold me as I come down.

Brant's lips tickle my ear while he peppers me with kisses, and I can feel him smiling. My chest deflates with a long, satisfied breath. "Where were we?" I murmur.

"I'm not sure where you were, but I was right here…wishing I could be wherever you were." When he pulls back, a flash of teeth lights up his face.

It takes my breath away.

I nearly choke because I can't remember the last time I saw Brant smile like this. Untethered from grief and perfectly present.

I return his smile with my own as joyous tears shimmer back at him, knowing it's been a long time since I've smiled like this, too.

It's been years.

And I've been happy. Yes, I've been happy pursuing a lifelong dream, making new friends, dancing and working, experiencing my first foray into independence.

I've been happy.

But I haven't been *truly* happy… There has always been a hole. An absence.

True happiness is a puzzle. It's a jigsaw puzzle we're all carefully putting together, searching for those pieces that link and connect, that allow us to move on to the next part of the puzzle. Some puzzles remain incomplete, and I think that's because many people don't *know* what makes them truly happy. Or… they're unwilling to take the time to find those other missing pieces first. They just want to squeeze the last piece into a space it won't fit.

Those other pieces are integral, though.

They are the stepping stones for the finished puzzle.

And as I lie here beside the man I love, watching his organic, soul-deep smile put light back into his eyes, I'm thankful we both took the time to find those pieces.

I reach out and graze the pads of my fingertips down his stubbled jaw, sighing with gratitude. "You're smiling."

"I am," he confirms.

"You look truly happy."

"I am."

Licking my lips, I wonder, "Are Mom and Dad happy, too? About us?"

A little wrinkle mars his brow as his eyes glitter gold and green. "I think they're done being unhappy." His knuckles graze along my cheekbone as he bites his lower lip with consideration. "I think it's going to be a long, sometimes painful road. I don't think it will be easy or quick. But…I think they're ready to move forward. To start healing. I think your dad is ready to make up silly rhymes again and wear his ridiculous slippers. And maybe he's not there yet, but he gave me his blessing to move to New York, knowing what that would mean, and…" His eyes slant, gaze skimming over my face. "I think he'll get there…

and we're all going to feel pretty damn remarkable one day. And when that day comes, every unremarkable minute will have been worth it."

I sniffle through a wave of tears, nodding my head. "True happiness is worth every sad, unremarkable minute," I tell him, my smile lingering. "It's been worth every night sleeping alone, every tear spilled without you here to wipe it away, every rainbow I've watched paint the sky only for it to fade like it was never even there, all while I begged for it to come back. While I ached for one last glimpse." Pressing a tender kiss to his mouth, I tell him, "It's been worth the wait just to see you smile like that."

He smooths back my hair with both hands, pressing his forehead to mine. "I would've waited forever, Junebug...but I'm really glad we didn't have to wait that long."

"You mean it?" I whisper.

"Of course I mean it."

I kiss him again—hard, messy, and painfully beautiful.

Just like us.

Never underestimate a man willing to wait forever for the woman he loves, for there is nothing he's not capable of.

Noble to some.

A fool to many.

But to that woman?

He

is

everything.

39

GOOD NEWS FIRST

BRANT, AGE 28

I REALLY, REALLY MISSED HER MOUTH.

"Jesus, June…" My back is pressed against the bedroom wall as my hands fist her mane of silky hair. I watch as her head bobs up and down on my cock, her moans making it sound like she's enjoying this even more than I am.

Literally impossible.

I shut my eyes and throw my head back to the wall because if I keep watching her, I'm going to come. And it's only been thirty seconds since she ripped off my belt and dropped to her knees in front of me. "Fuck, that feels good," I practically hiss through my teeth. She replies with something like "mmm" and digs her fingernails into my ass.

Christ.

I realize guests are on the way over to celebrate June's birthday in our tiny, cramped one-bedroom apartment and the cake might be burning, but I'm pretty certain the whole apartment could be burning and I still wouldn't move from this spot.

June strokes the base as she tries to deep-throat me without gagging.

She gags.

And it's so fucking hot.

Still gripping her hair as she sucks me, I give it a tug until her eyes lift up. She releases me with a *pop*, leaving my dick rock-hard and glistening as I pull her up to her feet, then march her backward toward the bed. As much as I'd love to finish in her mouth, I need to be inside her. She's wearing a little black dress I've been wanting to strip her out of ever since she put it on thirty-one seconds ago.

She glances at the open bedroom door, then back to me. Her lashes flutter and her eyeshadow glints as she nibbles her lip. "We don't have much time…"

"I promise it'll be quick." I waggle my eyebrows. Grinning, she hikes up her dress, and I bend her over the foot of the bed. As I slip inside from behind, I lean over and whisper against her ear, "I want to put a baby in you."

Her gasp morphs into a needy cry when I push all the way inside, filling her completely, and start thrusting.

"Oh God, Brant…"

In and out.

"Do—do you really mean it…?"

Faster.

"Are y-you sure…?"

Harder.

I slam into her, the mattress squeaking, the headboard smacking against the wall in perfect time, likely pissing off our crotchety neighbor. Then I pull out of her for a second, flip her around, and link her legs around my waist. "I'm sure," I grit out, sliding back home.

It's probably not the smartest choice, but there's nothing I want more.

We've only officially been together for a little under a year, even though it feels like a lifetime. Our apartment is not ideal for a growing family with its creaky wooden floors, an obnoxiously loud air conditioner, and a dollhouse-sized kitchen with the distinct charm of 1987. It's dated and smells like the Chinese buffet down the street, but I'm still in love with all 610 square feet of it because it's ours. We've laid roots here.

But the more those roots thrive and grow, the more seeds I want to plant.

Particularly one seed.

Sliding my hand up her belly, I picture it plump and swollen, filled with our beautiful child. "God, I want a baby with you, June." I breathe out raggedly, slowing my pace and stroking her clit. She writhes and buckles beneath me, draping the back of her arm over her forehead, while her other hand squeezes the bedspread. "But I can wait."

She unravels quickly, arching her back while she comes and crying out my name as I lean over her. I grip her by the hips and pump into her a few more times, seized by a violent orgasm, and I groan with satisfaction as I empty inside of her.

She's on the pill, anyway.

It's a moot point.

June catches her breath, her breasts heaving. One of them pokes out of her slip dress, and my hand glides up to palm it, tweaking her nipple as I bend down to kiss her. "I missed you."

Her eyes blink open—her beautiful sky-blue eyes—and she gifts me with a magical smile. "Missed you more."

"How much?" Pulling out of her, I tug her dress back down, then tuck myself into my boxers, hoping I have five minutes to freshen up before guests arrive.

"Over the rainbow and back again," she says, lifting up on her elbows. Her hair is a mess. It's infused with static and sticking up in a hundred different places.

I'm pretty sure we both look like we just rode each other hard.

We had to, though. June was away three days for a traveling stage performance, and she only just got home while I was pouring batter into cake pans.

I was so distracted by the smell of her hair and the warmth of her skin when she came up behind me and wrapped her arms around my middle that I don't actually remember if I put the cake in the oven.

Maybe it's not burning at all.

Maybe it's not even cooking.

Shit.

My cell phone vibrates from the front pocket of the trousers I just pulled back up, so I tug the zipper and fish it out as June runs a comb through her hair. I smile when I glance at the screen.

Pauly: Hello, Brant. Buon compleanno to June. May all of her wishes be fulfilled and all of her blessings be noticed. My Stellina and I are looking forward to visiting you in the fall. In the meantime, continue to impress the great state of New York with your legendary beef Wellington.

A picture comes through of Pauly and Wendy standing in the middle of Chicago's iconic Millennium Park.

My grin widens.

Yeah, so—*that happened.*

I can't say I'm surprised, but…okay, I'm a little surprised. Wendy's been working for Pauly for years, and their combative bantering always teetered on the line of flirting, but I honestly never thought Pauly would take that next step, considering he's eighteen years her senior.

But oddly enough, they just *work.*

And they're happy. They're really damn happy, and if I've learned anything over the years, it's that happiness always perseveres over societal conventions.

Although Pauly planned to move out to New York with me last year, he chose to stay in Illinois with Wendy—as their relationship had just started blossoming—overseeing his beloved Anima Mia from afar. I'm basically in charge of the place, and while it's been a huge learning curve in management and workload, I'm creatively fulfilled in the best way. The restaurant is thriving. The food is garnering attention from food blogs, television shows, and even renowned chefs.

I'm living my dream.

I'm living my dream with the love of my life.

And Pauly is finally calling me by my first name.

As I ponder sending Pauly a selfie of June and me, I notice that her boob is still precariously poking out of her dress, and I don't seem to have the willpower to tell her to fix it, so I settle on a quick response instead.

That's when the buzzer rings.

Rushing over to June, I unwillingly adjust her dress and plant a kiss to the tip of her nose. "Happy birthday, Junebug," I murmur, lingering for a second kiss.

Her lips are shimmering with my favorite cherry gloss as her smile blooms.

I'm about to race to the front door when she stops me. "Brant," she calls out. When I pivot, she sweeps her hair to one side and bites at that delicious cherry lip. "I want a baby, too."

My eyes flare, stinging with sentiment.

A tickle shoots straight to my heart, filling me with a feeling I can't even explain.

Buzz.

Jolting in place, I shake myself from the haze—from the vivid daydream of newborns and nurseries and lullabies and precious stuffed elephants—and I nod, grinning like a fool. All I want to do is ravage her again, hoping she missed one of her pills.

Her birthday feels awfully inconvenient right now.

I jog to the front of the small apartment that's humbly accessorized with streamers and partially deflated balloons, and pull open the door to see a familiar face shining back at me.

"Kip."

Ah, Kip. I really miss Kip.

He hands me a terribly wrapped box, taped up with what looks to be menus from one of the local delis. "Don't say anything." He laughs lightly, sweeping past me with his suitcase and shrugging out of his jacket. "I panic-bought you something as soon as I flew in, grabbed a roll of tape, but forgot the actual wrapping paper."

I blink. "These are menus."

"The restaurant is next door."

"Okay, but we would have been totally fine with a gift card. They fit right into your wallet." Laughter spills out of me when he freezes in place, then pinches the bridge of his nose, shaking his head with a sigh.

"Well, I didn't think of that, Brant."

"Kip!" June darts from the bedroom off the living area, her shiny threads of hair fluttering behind her. She's buttoned a navy cardigan over her chest, likely fearful of another wardrobe glitch. She leaps into his arms for an enthusiastic hug, smiling at me over Kip's shoulder. "I'm so glad you could make it. I haven't seen you since the move."

Kip helped us move in last October, taking some time off work to sightsee in the big city and say his final goodbyes while we transitioned into our new life.

He's been a rock for us both, a loyal friend—and if one good thing came out of Theo joining the police force, it's that he brought Kip into our lives.

Because he doesn't have a lot of family back home and his sister is studying abroad in Switzerland, we invited Kip out to New York to celebrate June's birthday with us. He's sleeping on a futon in our living room for the next five days.

And because I don't plan on being celibate for the next five days, I'm really hoping he brought earplugs.

"Shit, it's great to see you," he tells her, setting her back down on her bare feet while she does a modest twirl. "How's life on Broadway?"

"Difficult. Incredible. Exhausting. Magical."

His lips twitch with a smile. "Sounds like my love life."

"Oh! Weren't you going to bring her?"

Swiping the beanie off his head, Kip scratches at the nape of his neck, his expression doleful. "We're currently in the difficult phase, unfortunately."

"I'm sorry." June pouts. "Truly."

Interestingly enough, Kip has been involved, off and on, with the sister of one of my old coworkers at the nightclub. Her name is Clementine.

From what I've heard, it's been a bumpy road, with a coupling of respective past traumas, along with the fact that Clem is a single mom to a young daughter.

It hasn't been easy, but hell, when he talks about her, when things are good…I recognize it.

I recognize that spark.

I know what it's like to fight for something that feels impossible, even when you *know* it could be so fucking perfect.

Kip takes his shoes off in the miniature foyer space and clears his throat, slipping his hands into his pockets. "It's all good. It'll be nice to spend some time away and clear my head." He twirls a finger in the air. "Absence makes the heart grow fonder and all that."

June and I share a quick, poignant look.

I wink.

"Is that a gift?" she wonders, her eyes trailing to the menu-wrapped package still in my arms. A giggle falls out of her, and she cups a palm over her mouth. "We were running low on takeout menus. Very thoughtful."

Kip's head swings back and forth through an embarrassed laugh as he runs his fingers through short, cropped hair. "It'll be a gift card next time, I promise." As he glances into the kitchen, a frown unfurls, and he points his finger toward the oven. "You know, the menus might actually come in handy if you're not able to salvage whatever's burning in there."

Ah, crap.

Plumes of smoke billow out from the stove as I race into the kitchen.

I guess I remembered to put the cake in after all.

"Kip heard us, didn't he? Nobody sleeps all night with earbuds in."

"With only a paper-thin wall separating us? Nah." We walk hand in hand through Central Park, munching on blueberry scones as the drizzle fades and the clouds clear. I glance upward, scanning the blue-gray sky, our feet sinking into the soggy grass. "He just likes music. Everyone likes music."

"God, Brant. Surely he was blocking out the sounds of my banshee wails as you brought me to ecstasy three times."

"You can ask him when we get back."

"I'd rather die."

"I'll ask him, then." I pop the last bite of scone into my mouth and start to chew. "For my own research purposes. I'd love an outsider's perspective. You know… were we actually at banshee-level wailing, because that's impressive, or was it more subpar moaning?" She narrows her eyes at me, swallowing the rest of her breakfast. "Is there something else I can do? A unique angle, or a tongue trick, or—"

Laughing, she leaps onto my back, and I hook my hands beneath her thighs. "You're humiliating."

"I just want to learn, June."

"You're a brilliant lover and you know it. You've left no room for improvement."

"Sounds like a challenge to me."

I carry her around the park, piggyback style, reclaiming my boyhood title of World's Best Piggyback Giver. My eyes are still casing the sky, where a golden haze is peeking through the clouds, when June's phone starts to sing.

"There's something I wanted to tell you, but..." She slides down my back. "One sec, Mom is video calling me." June accepts the call, then extends her arm until she's centered in the frame. Both Samantha and Andrew wave through the screen. "Hey!"

"Show Tunes June," Andrew quips, waggling his brows. "How's my dancing queen?"

Her eyes roll back. "Mildly horrified by your rhymes."

"Then I owe myself congratulations."

I slip on a smile then slide into view, lifting my own hand with a wave. "Morning."

They both smile warmly.

And I'm so goddamn grateful for that.

I'm grateful for every single smile they gift me with—because that's what it is. A gift. I'm beyond thankful for the birthday card I received in April, and the occasional phone call or email just to check in on me, and for the fact that they didn't turn their backs on me after I flipped their world upside down.

They could have. They could have so easily.

So I'm grateful. Every moment that they trust me with their daughter is a precious gift.

Samantha beams, sitting beside Andrew on the living room couch. She twirls a coffee mug between her hands. "Good morning, Brant. How's the weather over there?"

Not going according to plan, as usual, my mind replies. Instead, I say, "Rainy, but the sun is trying to poke through."

Andrew nods. "Same here. Did Kip make it into town safely yesterday?"

"Yep," June answers. "He was still sleeping when we snuck out for scones. Brant has this thing about going for walks together after rain showers." She sends me a quizzical side-eye. "It's refreshing, I guess. And the park is quieter."

"That sounds lovely, sweetheart," Samantha says. "We won't keep you… We just wanted to see how your birthday went last night…"

Samantha's voice trails off as something catches my eye just above the treetops.

A flash of pigment.

A swirl of color.

Holy shit, this is it.

I quicken my gait, marching ahead of June as she hangs back to finish her goodbyes. Rounding the corner with my head tilted up, I nearly lose my breath when a majestic rainbow comes into full view. My blood races with adrenaline. My heart skyrockets with relief.

I spin around, watching as June clicks off her call and glances at me across the way. She pauses, her forehead wrinkling as if she's wondering how I got so far ahead of her. Or maybe she's just confused by the giddy smile on my face and the tears in my eyes.

June paces forward, slowly at first. And then she stops again, doing a double take to the sky. Her eyes round into sapphire spheres, her lips parting with awe. "Brant…look!" She points as if I hadn't already seen it.

As if I could miss it.

As if I haven't been waiting for this moment for months.

With her gaze transfixed to the rainbow sky, she jogs toward me as a breathy, joyful sound spills out of her. "It's so beautiful. We had so many rainbows in New York when we were apart but none since you've been here with me, and I've been wishing for one so badly, ever since winter faded, and—" She spins around to face me.

But I'm already on one knee.

June's words fall off, her lips frozen into an O shape. Her hand flies up to grip her chest, right over her heart. "Brant…?"

"June Adeline Bailey." I gaze up at her wide, glistening eyes as I dig the ring box out of my front pocket. I bought it in March and have been carrying it with me every single day, waiting for a rainbow. "Junebug."

"Brant," she repeats, choking on my name.

"Twenty-two years ago, I tossed a toy elephant into your crib, trying to give you comfort in the only way I could. And I knew in that moment as you gazed at me through the crib slats with your big blue eyes… I knew you were destined to become *my* comfort." Emotion sweeps through me, stealing my words for a moment. I swallow. "That's exactly what you became. You were the laughter on the other side of my tears, the solace to quell my nightmares, and the rainbow after every storm. You saved my life, June Bailey."

Both hands cup her mouth as tears collapse onto her fingers. She squeezes her eyes shut.

"And I can't think of anything sweeter than to spend the rest of that life with you." Rising to my feet, I pluck the ring out of the box, holding it up between my thumb and forefinger.

She lets out a gasp when she looks at it. A breathtaking sound of disbelief.

"It's rimmed with tiny sapphires. Blue like the eyes I fell in love with. Blue like the sky that gives us rainbows, and the bluebirds that fly over them." I quirk a smile. "Blue like the prom dress that brought me to my knees." I take her shaking hand in mine, then slide the diamond over her ring finger. It's a perfect fit. Blowing out a heavy breath, I lift my eyes to hers. "I want to dare to dream with you forever, Junebug. On top of being my best friend, my lover, my soul mate, my comfort and my courage…will you be my wife?"

She nods.

She nods and sobs and whimpers into her hands. But when she drops her arms and sniffles, inhaling a choppy breath, she asks, "Do…do you want the good news or the bad news first?"

My heart nearly stops. I blink rapidly, trying to read her.

These are happy tears.

Right?

Shit…was this too soon? Is she not ready?

Trying not to black out, I choke out, "Good news first."

June doesn't hesitate.

She leaps into my arms, coiling her legs around my hips and linking her hands behind my neck. She kisses my shoulder, my collarbone, all the way up to my ear, and whispers, "Yes…*yes*. God, Brant, all the yeses. I'd marry you today, a thousand times over, in every version of every lifetime."

Relief swims through me and I squeeze her tight, finding her mouth as I spin her around in clumsy, happy fucking circles, kissing her breathless until we don't know whose tears we're tasting anymore. We cling. We sway.

We dream.

The rainbow fades into the sky, but we don't.

We're shining brighter than ever.

As I pull back to wipe the tearstains from her cheeks, I kiss her forehead, setting her back down on her feet. A thought stumbles back to my mind, and I frown. "Wait…what was the bad news?"

June sniffs, inching backward and drinking in a big breath. She places a flat palm over her stomach. "We'll really need to start saving, Brant. I might need to pick up a second job."

I glance down at her belly.

I look back up.

"Weddings are expensive." She moves her hand in a circular motion as a smile blooms to life. Then she says, "And so are babies."

40

FIRST COMES LOVE

JUNE, AGE 23

The gems on my tulle skirt twinkle like tiny prisms as the sun streaks in through the pop-up tent. I stand before a full-length mirror while my mother bounces one of my long curls inside her cupped palm, her eyes also twinkling. Incandescent blue. "You look like a dream," she murmurs to me.

I smile, fingering the bluebird pendant around my neck.

Celeste pops her head up from her bottle of nail polish as she glides it over a long fingernail. Her baby-blue dress sparkles in the afternoon sunglow. "I feel like I'm in a game of Candyland. I'm Queen Frostine."

Giggling, I realize that I did go all out with the rainbow theme. I'm wearing a white lace leotard with a magnificent skirt infused with Technicolor silk and tulle. A rainbow train spills out the back, and I'm quite an eccentric sight for a bride, but…

Still a step up from a zebra.

Wendy chuckles, sitting at the same small table as Celeste and scrolling through her phone as we count down the final minutes before the wedding begins. Her dress resembles Celeste's, the icy-blue color a striking contrast against Wendy's fiery red hair. "I sent Wyatt a selfie. He told me I look like a Smurf."

I chuckle. "How is Wyatt? It's been years."

"Miraculously, not in jail. He actually met a nice girl and got his shit together," Wendy says, smiling as she types out a text. "He works for the union, has a dog named Lucy... Heck, I think he's well on his way to becoming fully domesticated." Glancing up at me, she adds, "He sends his congratulations, by the way."

"Really?" My eyebrow lifts.

Wendy snorts, tucking her phone back into her purse. "No, he said to eat a bowl of fuck, but he sent it with a little heart emoji so I think that's basically the same thing."

Mom stiffens behind me and clears her throat as my cheeks stain with blush.

"The food looked great, June. I can't wait to see if Pauly's beef Wellington is as good as Brant's."

My mom changes the subject like a pro.

She is right, though. I can already smell the delicious food that Pauly has been cooking, after he volunteered to be the one-man caterer on our special day. When Pauly moved back to New York this past spring, he ended up purchasing an expansive property with a horse farm, reminiscent of his childhood. He doesn't have any horses yet, but he plans on naming his first horse "Stellina"—the pet name he gave to Wendy, his new fiancée who joined him in New York and is helping him run his restaurants.

Shockingly enough, Wendy and I have become close.

We're friends.

And while Celeste has been swamped with stage shows, earning herself starring roles in critically acclaimed performances, Wendy has stepped in to help me with—

"Oh, Caroline, sweet little love of mine." Dad pushes through the tent opening, his eyes brimming with adoration and his arms full of a tiny, perfect being.

Our daughter.

With tufts of curly brown hair and cheeks fat and pink, she makes little cooing noises that I swear sound like "Aggie." My dad plucks the toy elephant off a folding chair as if hearing what I just heard, and bounces her up and down, still singing his silly rhymes. "Kip and I were putting the finishing touches on the arbor while this little angel serenaded us with baby giggles in her bouncer." He lifts her up high, then brings her back to his chest, holding her head with his big bear paw. "Weren't you, darling girl?"

My father is completely whipped.

He melts into putty every time Caroline gives him a gummy smile or wraps her baby fist around his finger.

I swoon. "Give her here, Dad. I need to smell and squeeze her for good luck."

Caroline just turned four months old. She was born with wayward sprouts of golden hair that have since fallen out, replaced by dark-brown curls. I wonder if her eyes will be blue like mine or hazel like her father's. She has my button nose, Brant's dimples, and a unique birthmark on her hip that Brant says looks like an apple—*the apple of her daddy's eye.*

I think it looks like a peach.

My father hands her over to me, and she smells like lavender, baby powder, and bubble baths; I want to bottle up her sweet scent and savor it for life.

Mom curls a final ribbon of brown hair, letting it flutter between her fingertips. She sighs, and it sounds like something equally melancholy and joyous.

The end of an era.

The beginning of a brand-new journey.

"Goodness…I feel old," Mom reflects, stroking Caroline's little round head. Her eyes lift to me with nostalgia. "It feels like yesterday I was putting pigtails in your hair, pulling pennies from your nose, and washing dirt stains out of your rompers."

I can't help but laugh.

"Now you're getting married," Dad muses.

He shows no sign of resentment or scorn toward the man I'm getting married *to*. We're beyond that now. While our family dynamic isn't conventional, and I realize my parents may never completely approve of the path we've taken, I know there is still acceptance there. And as each day passes, the acceptance grows.

They accept that we are what we are.

They accept that they can't change what we are, and they would rather love us than leave us.

They accept Brant as the boy they raised *and* as the man who fell in love with their daughter.

And above all, they accept this:

Just as we cannot force ourselves to love someone, we cannot force ourselves to unlove them either. Fate can be foolish, and fate can be careless.

But fate is always true.

Placing a glossy kiss on Caroline's head, I smile with fondness, I smile with joy, and I gaze up at my parents with the same sentiment.

"Have a remarkable day, my darling daughter," my father says, his eyes creased with emotion. Canting his head down, he gives my arm a tender squeeze as he whispers in my ear, "Each remarkable day paves the way toward a truly remarkable life."

The expression on our reverend's face concerns me.

My arms start to shake as I clutch the bouquet of flowers to my chest and worry my lip between my teeth. I watch the wrinkles in his forehead furrow as his eyes flare slightly and his lips twitch with a strange combination of professional politeness and…

Amusement? Horror? Confusion?

I simply can't read him. Leaning forward a bit, I whisper, "What is it?"

Glancing at me, the reverend forces a smile, then returns his attention to just over my shoulder.

He winces.

What is happening?

With wobbly knees, I shuffle from foot to foot on the rainbow aisle runner, my eyes flickering across the sky as I tilt my head up to distract myself. I'm jittery with nerves and fighting impatience. What's taking so long? Is Brant having second thoughts? Cold feet?

Is he hurt? Sick? Lost?

Pauly's property is certainly hard to find, tucked away in wooded suburbia, but surely someone would have informed me if Brant was running late to his own wedding before I made it down the aisle.

A family of birds flies overhead, and I smile, inhaling a deep, calming breath.

It's fine, June. Just be patient.

The speakers finally crackle to life with the prelude to our song. My heart races, more nerves coasting through me.

Only…instead of "Over the Rainbow," it's the intro to "Closer" by Nine Inch Nails.

"Shit." I hear Kip curse over the deep bass beats as he frantically adjusts the song. "Sorry, wrong playlist."

Oh my God.

I glance toward the sky again as I fidget in place, assuming that with my luck, the birds will soon be circling back to poop on me.

Sweaty fingers cling to the bouquet stems while everything goes silent, and the reverend clears his throat. He looks dubious. He remains unreadable, but I'm not allowed to look behind me yet.

Brant has a surprise.

I realize it's backwards, having me already at the end of the aisle while Brant walks down to meet me, but I suppose we've always been a little bit backwards. I promised I wouldn't turn around until he told me to, so here I stand—in all of my quivering, sweaty-limbed, heart-palpitating glory.

C'mon, Brant!

Music finally floats through the speakers, and I sigh with relief when it's the beginning of "Over the Rainbow," an acoustic cover performed by Amber Leigh Irish.

Our song.

And I'd be near tears right now if the romantic mood wasn't interrupted by collective gasps, followed by a sound that vaguely resembles a horse.

The reverend's eyebrows lift to his hairline, but he refuses to look at me, crossing his hands at the wrists in front of him.

I blink. "Was that a horse?"

He shakes his head slightly, forcing another taut smile.

Of course I didn't hear a horse.

That would be absurd. It was probably just—

"No! Get back here!" Brant's voice thunders over the melodic song, causing my eyes to pop. "Crap."

What. Is. Going. On?

Voices clamor behind me.

"Should we help him?"

Aunt Kelly.

"He's eating the decorations!"

Mom.

"This was a terrible idea."

Dad.

"Look, he's peeing…for an eternity."

Wendy.

"Will he ever stop peeing?"

Wendy again.

"Ooh, really good dye job."

Celeste.

I can't take it anymore.

I turn around.

And then…

There's a unicorn.

A white horse is decorated like a unicorn, trotting around the small group of folding chairs with a "horn" half falling off its head, a multicolored mane and tail, and letters scrawled across its flank and shoulders in rainbow letters that read "Rupert."

Rupert.

The unicorn in my fever dream when I was twelve.

I told Brant about it, and he'd laughed.

He'd laughed and evidently taken immaculate mental notes.

My hand plants against my chest as my heart beats wildly out of control. "Oh my…" I glance behind me, my eyes landing on a defeated Brant pinching the bridge of his nose in a baby-blue tux and navy bow tie. He shakes his head back and forth with dismay.

Laughter spills out of me as I run to him, lifting up my tulle skirt, hardly able to contain my amusement. "Brant," I choke out. The music goes silent once more, and I fling my arms around his neck. "You remembered my dream."

He makes an *oof* sound when I collide with his chest. Two strong arms wrap around me as he lets out a sigh of disappointment. "That did not go how I expected it to."

I can't help but murmur against his suit vest, "Have we ever gone according to plan?"

"I guess not," he says, laughing.

Pauly is already on his feet, reining in the rebellious horse and walking him toward the back of the aisle as a streamer floats from Rupert's tail that reads "JUST MARRIED." The reverend clears his throat again, still standing beneath our wedding arch, waiting for this circus to mellow out so we can have a proper vow exchange.

Smiling fondly, amusedly, Brant holds his hand out to me. "Ready, Junebug?"

I flash back to my dream.

My eyes case the small group of guests, zoning in on my father holding an elderly Yoshi on a short leash in the front row. The old dachshund is nearly seventeen, having been a loyal friend for almost my whole life.

Something old.

Mom sits beside my father with a pink bundle tucked inside her arms, bouncing the infant up and down in her lap, trying to calm her fussing.

Our baby daughter.

Something new.

Glancing toward the chair that only holds two stuffed elephants and a framed photograph, my eyes start to mist. The pre-prom picture of me standing and laughing between Theo and Brant sits beside Aggie and Bubbles on the seat cushion, serving as a tangible reminder of the brother I miss with my whole heart. The brother who isn't here today because he used his final moments to save someone else.

The brother who will never stop saving *me*, even in death.

My fingers fiddle with the bronze badge pinned to the lacy leotard of my dress.

Theo's badge.

Something borrowed.

A tear slips down my cheek as I stare at the precious photograph, wishing I could hear his speech. Begging to feel his fierce, protective arms around me one last time.

I close my eyes as the breeze picks up, coasting across my face like the hug I crave.

It's warm, it's familiar, and I pretend it's him.

I pretend it's Theo, giving us his blessing and whispering in my ear, *"I'm proud of you, Peach. You know that, right?"*

Yeah, I know.

I readjust the tiara into my curled, glitter-dusted hair, taking Brant by the hand and nodding my head toward Kip to restart the song.

"I'm ready."

"Over the Rainbow" starts to play as we make our way down the aisle together, landing beneath the decorated arch.

It's a rainbow, of course.

It's impossible to predict a rainbow, so we created our very own.

We both glance up at it before our eyes lock with charmed smiles, and the officiant begins the ceremony. It's short and sweet. We didn't want anything drawn-out or extravagant, just as the wedding itself is nothing more than an intimate gathering of close friends and family.

It's a celebration of love on our dear friend's property, with a cake made by the love of my life, an exchange of vows beneath a vibrant sky, and dancing until dusk.

It's perfect.

It's *us*.

As we wrap up our vows and Brant says "I do" with tears in his earth-spun eyes, I can't help myself. I mouth to him, *"You mean it?"*

Grinning, he mouths back, *"Of course I mean it."*

Rupert neighs as the reverend pronounces us man and wife, and then we kiss.

And it's not just any kiss.

It's a kiss of courage, a kiss of comfort, a kiss of two people beating the odds and weaving a love story out of tragedy. It's finding a happily ever after with the one person you least expect yet the only person meant for you.

It's not our first kiss.

It's not our last kiss.

It's a kiss that culminates our past, brings magic to our present, and seals our future forever.

"I love you so much," I murmur, stroking my palm down his stubbled cheek as his dimples wink back at me.

"I love you, Junebug. More than you'll ever know," he replies, planting a kiss on my hairline. He breathes in deeply. "More than you could ever dare to dream."

As Brant pulls back, grinning wide, our guests clap with celebration, and Wendy and Aunt Kelly rise from their seats. They skip over to the tiny birdcage sitting beside us in the grass as another familiar breeze sweeps by.

I take my husband's hand in mine and interlace our fingers, turning toward the women. Emotions run through me like a roaring river.

Wendy picks up the cage, clutching it between her arms as she sends us a beaming smile.

Aunt Kelly lifts her hand and opens the metal door.

And then I start to cry.

I break down in tears, watching as the tiny bluebird spreads its wings and flies free, soaring up to the hazy blue sky and disappearing into a cloud.

Brant pulls me close as he exhales a shuddering breath against my hair, his eyes on the sky, our hands interlocked, and his heart eternally woven with mine.

Something blue.

Epilogue

BRANT, AGE 36

I PULL A PEN OUT OF my back pocket and jot down some notes.

June 1, 2031

It's June's 30th birthday today. THIRTY. We have two children squished on either side of us, but I feel like she wants to celebrate with me already. >:-)

She's biting her lip and giving me the eyes.

You know the eyes.

June stretches out beside me in the little tree house, yawning dramatically, then "accidentally" grazes her fingertips up my thigh as she brings her hand back up.

Yep, she wants me.

Theodore just ran outside, then came back in to tell us that one of the clouds looks like a face with a philtrum. Apparently that's the little groove between the bottom of your nose and your upper lip. Where does he learn this stuff?

Caroline has to pee.

I don't know why I wrote that down.

"I really have to pee, Mommy."

Folding the index card in half, I slip it back into my pocket.

Samantha is way better at this.

All four of us shuffle out of the custom-built tree house, flicking grass blades and dirt stains off our clothes. Andrew helped me build it two years ago—only, it's not *in* the tree; it's built around the tree at ground level.

We learned our lesson.

"Wait! I forgot my sword." Caroline bounces toward the little wooden house and sneaks beneath the curtain, her sable-colored ponytail bouncing against her overalls. She's a tomboy to the max. When she skips back out through the opening, the sword I made for June on Christmas Eve is clutched in her fist. She starts to make swishy noises as the worn wooden blade slices the air, then points right at her brother. "Get back, beast!"

"I'm not a beast, Caroline. I'm a child." He crosses his arms as the setting sun casts a yellowy glow upon his already sandy hair. "You're going to give me splinters if you stab me with that."

"You're no fun at all."

"Want to go inside and crystalize our own rock candy?"

Caroline's face scrunches up with disgust. "That's so boring. I want to fight bad guys with my magic sword and save Aggie and Bubbles from the unpeekable monsters."

"Unspeakable," he corrects. "Hey, don't you have to pee?"

Her eyes widen with remembrance. Squeezing her legs together, she books it through the yard toward the back of the house, Theodore giving chase. When he catches up to her he tugs on her ponytail, and their laughter rings in my ears like the sweetest lullaby.

Two familiar arms encircle me from behind as a warm cheek presses into the center of my back. I grin, placing my hands atop hers. "I saw you eyeing me in the tree house."

"I don't know what you're talking about," she murmurs against my T-shirt, her fingers drifting downward and inching beneath the hem.

"Think we can occupy the kids with a movie while we lock ourselves in the bedroom?"

"You mean, *without* tears or bloodshed?"

"Valid." Taking her by surprise, I bend down, grip her by the thighs, and haul her onto my back. June squeals, wrapping her legs around my waist and burying a fist in my hair for leverage. "I guess I can wait. But the moment you blow out your candles, you better be well on your way to blowing—"

Her hand slaps over my mouth as she laughs out, "Brant!"

"You can't look at me like that and *not* expect me to obsessively think about what that look implies, Junebug."

I start to move toward the open patio door with June bouncing on my back, holding on tight through her giggles.

I'm definitely still owning my title of World's Best Piggyback Giver.

When we step through the back door, Theodore and Caroline are sprawled on the couch with the television on. Theodore has Bubbles clutched in his arms, while Caroline is using Aggie as a pillow. I smile. June and I passed our beloved stuffed elephants down to our children when they were born, and the toys are nearly worn raw from all the love they've received over the years.

"I'm going to check on the cake. It should be cooled down enough to frost," June tells me, sliding down my back.

I give her butt a loving smack as she traipses into the kitchen.

Making my way down the hallway to our master bedroom, I pull the index card out of my pocket and crouch down beside the bed. Underneath hides a slew of shoeboxes. All of them are decorated by the kids with colorful construction paper, markers, paint, glitter, and pipe cleaners.

And inside, they hold our moments.

I pluck a few boxes out and sit down, crossed-legged, a wave of nostalgia coasting through me.

June 15, 2024

It's the last day of our honeymoon in Hawaii. I just realized I didn't write a single card for the past two weeks because all I've done is stare in wonder at my wife.

My. Wife.

I'll never forget the way she looked when a wave tipped her over, and she stood up on shaky legs, soaking wet, shivering, and laughing like she would never again be happier than she was in that moment.

Challenge accepted.

May 16, 2025

Our son was born today. We named him Theodore Andrew, and Samantha Bailey cried when we told her his name. She sobbed into his little blue swaddle blanket, and June cried, too.

It was only the third time I've ever seen Samantha cry.

October 11, 2025

June has decided to retire from dancing to stay home and raise our children. She wants to be a dance teacher, but she said she'll chase that dream when the time comes.

I'm so fucking proud of her.

February 26, 2026

We're moving back home.

Pauly offered me the opportunity of a lifetime, and even though it will be sad to leave him and Wendy behind in New York (and Rupert), it's time to say

goodbye to the big city. Theodore and Caroline deserve to grow up with their grandparents nearby. We'll be flying out to look at properties next week, and we can't wait to lay new roots.
I think I want to build a tree house.

July 18, 2026
Pauly and I opened up a new restaurant in downtown Chicago. I'm the co-owner.
I own a RESTAURANT.
Holy shit...is this real life?
I just got home from work, and Theodore pulled himself up from the couch cushions and took his first steps.
To me.
My son just walked to me.
And I ran down the hallway of our brand-new house, collapsed onto the bed, and cried.

August 5, 2026
We've been stopping by Theo's gravesite every Saturday night since we returned home. June eventually told me that Theo was her mysterious date for all those years, so we decided to keep up the tradition.
Today I stuck around a little longer. I told Theo I was keeping my promise... I'm taking care of June. Our princess is safe. After I said the words, I swore I felt the wind pick up just a little. Almost as if he heard me. Almost as if he was saying, "I know you are, Luigi."
Was that you, Theo?

December 24, 2028

Caroline asked me who the woman was in the photograph ornament on the Christmas tree—the ornament June and Theo gave to me when I was a boy. I told Caroline it was her grandma, the woman we named her after. My sweet mother.

She said she was real pretty. And then she said the stuffed elephant in the picture looked a lot like Bubbles :-)

May 5, 2030

I'm so unbelievably happy.

That's all.

Thirty years ago, I was a terrified six-year-old boy who had just lost his whole world. I was curled up on my bedroom floor, hiding under the bed with a toy elephant as my only comfort.

Now, I'm sitting on the bedroom floor of my forever home while my own six-year-old boy, my precocious daughter, and my Junebug have a tickle fight down the hallway, their giggles and squeals the only comfort I'll ever need again.

I sigh contentedly.

Where has the time gone?

I hope to read through all of those index cards one day, fifty years from now, and know exactly where the time went.

And I'll smile. I'll laugh. I'll cry.

I'll be really damn proud of the life I lived and grateful for all the little moments that created it.

"The pizza just got here." June stands in the doorway to our bedroom, her dress wrinkled and her hair sticking up from the tickle fight with the kids.

God, she's perfect.

I nod, watching as she strolls toward me with that same come-hither look in her eyes. She's holding a paper plate topped with two slices of pizza. "Will you still look at me like that in fifty years when I'm old and wrinkly?" I wonder.

Twirling the skirt of her sundress, she nibbles her bottom lip and crinkles her nose. "Look at you how?"

"That same look you gave me in the treehouse. Like you want to rip off my belt and see what's hiding inside my pants."

She sits down beside me, dropping her forehead to my shoulder. "Of course I'll still look at you like that."

I grin, taking the plate she hands me. "Liar."

"I'm serious. Age doesn't change anything." With her chin propped against my arm, she glances up at me with big, glittering eyes. "You'll still be Brant and I'll still be June."

Her words steal my breath for a moment. Swallowing, I stroke her hair back with my hand, then place a kiss on the top of her head. "Yeah," I murmur. "You're right."

Glancing down at the pizza, I glare at the mushrooms piled onto each piece. Then I hold back a laugh as I return my attention to her. "Mushrooms? We hate mushrooms."

"I know. They messed up the order." She sighs. "The kids love them, so I didn't say anything."

I scrape them off. "Fuck mushrooms."

We share a knowing look, tinged with humor, as June echoes softly, "Fuck mushrooms."

The shoeboxes still lie strewn around us, so she licks her fingers and plucks a random card from a random box. "I love going through these. It's all the beautiful moments that make up our forever," June muses, her eyes scanning over the little white card. "Like this one."

She hands it to me.

I read.

February 2, 2024

June's water broke. I'm going to be a father. My God, I'm going to be a father.

And I'm going to be a good father. Like Andrew.

I'm going to build tree houses and wear funny

slippers and make rhymes and stand at the bus stop every morning before work telling my child to have a remarkable day. I'm going to cook family dinners, host barbecues, sing lullabies by the light of the moon, and look for rainbows after every storm. I'm going to be present. I'm going to be brave.

I'm going to put my family first, like my own father never did.

Always. Forever.

Until my very last breath.

They. Come. First.

I nod, teary-eyed and breathless, wrapping my arm around my wife and placing the card back in the box. I close the lid, pulling June close as we eat terrible mushroom pizza on our bedroom floor on her birthday, making more wishes, more memories, more moments that make up our forever.

That's when our children come barreling into the room with greasy fingers and sauce-covered faces, singing an off-key, high-pitched rendition of "Happy Birthday."

They leap into our laps, and we all collapse with laughter.

With love.

They come first.

And as June squeezes my hand beneath the pile of children and sends me a love-laced smile, her eyes twinkling blue and brilliant, I realize that I no longer fear my lasts.

Because I know—

Every last will be with them.

Want more Jennifer Hartmann?

Read on for an excerpt from ***STILL BEATING***

Available now from Bloom Books.

1

CORA

"YOU'RE INCORRIGIBLE."

I narrow my eyes at the man I've deemed worthy of my most treasured insult.

Incorrigible. It's a damn good word.

The man in question is Dean Asher—my sister's prick of a fiancé.

Dean laughs, seemingly unaffected by the hostility shooting from my eyes like hot lasers. He must be used to it by now. "What the hell does that even mean?"

"Stupid, too," I say, sipping on my watered-down cocktail with one arched eyebrow.

Fifteen years. Fifteen *goddamn* years is the amount of time I've been subjected to Dean's teasing, ridicule, and bad attitude. He's the stereotypical "bad boy"—surly, well muscled, always reeking of cigarettes and leather. Pathetically good-looking.

Asshole.

My sister, Mandy, fell right into his trap. They were high school sweethearts from the start. Mandy was the epitome of popularity with her Prom Queen title, bleached blond hair, and Abercrombie wardrobe. That was the style back in high school.

I, on the other hand, was none of those things—thank *God.* Despite the fact that I'm only ten months younger than Mandy, we could not be more different. She's athletic, bubbly, and vain. I'm a bookworm who would much rather purchase adorable outfits for our family dog than for myself. Mandy is perky, and I'm prickly. I could recite Shakespeare all day, where Mandy likes to quote the gossip headlines off Twitter.

Even though we have our differences, our sisterly bond has strengthened over the years, and now I'm preparing to be the maid of honor in her wedding next month. I'd like to say that Mandy outgrew everything about her high school years, but, alas, Dean Asher somehow made the cut as she enters her thirties. He's clung to Mandy like a disease. She just can't shake him.

I can't shake him.

So, now I have the divine privilege of being Dean's sister-in-law in four short weeks.

Vomit.

"Pretty sure that's not a word."

I swirl the miniature straw around my glass, raising my eyes to the man staring me down with his signature smirk. His gaze is all iron and grit. I shake my head, ashamed I have to call this guy family soon. "Don't make me Google it, Dean. You know I will."

It's Mandy's thirtieth birthday party. We're at the Broken Oar—a laid-back bar in Port Barrington, Illinois, right on the lake. It's a fun place to celebrate, despite the questionable company.

Dean takes a swig of his beer, his pale blue eyes twinkling with mischief. And *not* the fun kind. "You always were the nerdy type, Corabelle."

"Don't call me that."

He winks at me and I shoot him a death glare. Dean is the only person, other than my parents, to call me by my full name—Corabelle. I *hate* the name. Everyone calls me Cora. Dean knows this, of course, but he's always found immense joy in tormenting me.

Our banter is interrupted by the birthday girl, who is currently bringing the phrase "white-girl-wasted" to remarkable levels. Mandy wraps her arms around both me and Dean, squeezing the three of us together in an awkward, smooshed hug.

"I looooove you. You're my bestest friends. I'm marrying my bestest friend," Mandy slurs, having inhaled at least a dozen Sex on the Beach shots at this point. She turns to me, her head falling against my shoulder. "And *you*, Cora. You are going to marry *your* bestest friend really, really soon."

I push myself free of the embrace. The smell of Mandy's overpriced perfume and Dean's whiskey breath is making me want to hurl. "I'm never getting married, Mandy. Divorce just isn't on my bucket list. Maybe in another life."

I begin to turn away, but Mandy stops me. She pokes a French-tipped finger in the middle of my chest, and I flinch back, scratching at the tickle she leaves behind. "Marriage is sacred. Dean and I are never getting a divorce."

Possibly true. Dean seems like the type who would be content staying married, while enjoying his sidechicks along the way. And Mandy is certainly the type to turn a blind eye. "A fairy tale. Color me jealous."

"Can you guys *try* to get along? Please?" Mandy begs, waving her hands around with an air of theatrics. There is an ounce of sincerity mingling with her intoxication.

I sigh, my eyes darting to Dean. He's still smirking. I tap my fingers along the side of my glass as I pretend to consider Mandy's plea. "I mean, I would… maybe, *perhaps*, but…how am I supposed to get over the spider-in-the-shoe incident? How does someone move on from something like that?"

Dean chuckles as he chugs down his beer, clearly amused with his antics. "That was gold. I'll never apologize for it."

"See?" I shove my glass at him, jutting out my pinkie. "He's uncooperative. I tried."

Mandy smacks her fiancé in the chest. "Dean, stop being a dick to my baby sister."

"What? She can hold her own."

I glare at him, and our eyes hold for just a beat. "Well, he's right about something." Then I storm away, swallowing the last few sips of my crummy cocktail as I approach the bar. I slam the empty glass down and perch myself on a stool, eyeing the bartender. "Another one, please. Make it a double."

I should have accepted the ride home.

It's a little after 1:00 a.m., and I managed to find the most boring guy in the bar to get trapped in conversation with. My intoxication is dwindling, so now I'm just tired and crabby as my elbow presses against the bar counter with my head in my hand. I'm staring at the idiot to my left as he blathers on about being a lawyer, his cool car, and something about a reality TV show audition. Honestly, he lost me before he even opened his mouth. He smells like my passion-fruit sugar scrub, and it's *really* unsettling.

I feign a mighty yawn, forcing my head further into my palm. "That's great, Seth. Really great."

"It's Sam."

"That's what I said." I thread my fingers through my long, golden strands of hair as I lift my head and force a smile. "Anyway, I should get going. It's late."

Seth/Sam furrows his bushy eyebrows at me, his thin lips forming a straight line. "It's not that late. I'll buy you one more drink."

Nope. I'll puke. I'll definitely hurl all over his ridiculous sweater vest.

"No thanks," I respond, dismissing him with a quick wave. "I'm gonna go."

"Do you need a ride?"

"No."

Actually, maybe. Mandy and Dean drove me here, and I couldn't stomach another car ride with Satan himself, so I turned down their offer to drive me home.

But that's what Uber is for.

I push myself off the barstool, wobbling on my stupid high heels, and snag my purse off the counter. "See ya."

Seth/Sam grumbles as I fling my purse strap over my shoulder and saunter outside. I've successfully ruined his plans for the evening, and I'm pretty much okay with it. I wouldn't mind a night of drunken shenanigans and questionable decisions—Lord knows my vibrator is sick to death of me—but Seth/Sam lost his appeal faster than the Chicago Bears lost their shot at the Super Bowl this year, which was pretty freakin' fast.

Maybe I'm just too picky.

Mandy says I'm too picky.

Oh well. Looks like my vibrator is stuck with me.

The cool breeze assaults my lungs when I walk along the side of the bar, my heels clacking against the pavement. I tug my cardigan around my navy-blue dress, trying to dilute the chill, then reach into my purse for my cell phone. I've never actually used Uber before—maybe calling a taxi would be less complicated. Do taxis still exist?

I continue to fish through the pockets of my purse and locate my phone, but then my eyebrows crease when I realize my purse is feeling a lot lighter than usual. *Huh.* I shine my cell phone flashlight inside to assess further, and a tight knot of anxiety starts weaving itself in the pit of my stomach.

Well, shit.

My wallet is missing.

Did that son of a bitch inside take it because he knew I wouldn't close the deal?

I storm back into the bar, my heart thumping like a wild stampede beneath my ribs. My credit cards, my driver's license, over one hundred dollars in cash. Photographs, my insurance cards, passwords I'll never remember.

Goddammit.

I smack my hand against Seth/Sam's shoulder with a heaving chest. I don't even wait for him to turn around. "Did you steal my wallet?"

He slowly turns in his chair with a look of disgust. "Excuse me?"

"My wallet is gone. You're the only person I was talking to tonight."

Seth/Sam huffs. "Exactly. You were talking to me all night. When would I have had a chance to steal your wallet?" He shakes his head at me, then turns back around and reaches for his beer. "Sleep it off, bitch."

I ignore the insult, too wrapped up in my current dilemma to slap him. The dude has a point. I was literally facing him the whole time I'd been sitting at the bar—albeit, half-asleep and drooling on my hand—but I would have noticed him messing with my purse. In fact, my purse was perched on the bar counter, slightly behind my right shoulder.

That means someone *behind* me would have stolen my wallet.

Shit, shit, shit.

The bar is almost empty at this point. I question the bartender, who only shrugs at me, then puff my cheeks with air, blowing out a breath of frustration. I wander back outside and mentally prepare myself for begging people for rides since I'm suddenly broke.

I start with Mandy, already knowing she sleeps with her phone on Silent.

Voicemail.

I try my best friend, Lily.

Straight to voicemail.

There's no way in hell I'm calling my parents.

I go through my list of contacts, attempting three more people.

Voicemail, voicemail, voicemail.

My thumb hovers over another name, and I scrunch up my nose and pucker my lips, dreading the mere thought. Walking seven miles home in my high heels sounds more delightful than a ten-minute car ride with Dean Asher.

The wind picks up, forcing my hair to take flight. The cold almost chokes me.

I click on his name and immediately begin muttering profanities into the night.

"Corabelle?"

I don't know if I'm more annoyed or relieved that he picked up. "Don't call me that."

"Why are you drunk dialing me in the middle of the night?" Dean's voice is raspy, laced with sleep. I probably woke him up—*good.* A silver lining.

I'm about to explain, but he interrupts. "Let me guess, you had one too many shots of Fireball and you're calling to confess your undying love. I always knew you had a thing for me."

I grit my teeth, totally regretting my decision. I can feel his smirk from here. "You know what? Forget it. I'll walk home."

I'm about to end the call when Dean cuts in. "Wait, wait—you need a ride? I thought you were calling an Uber."

"Yeah, well, some jerk stole my wallet and now I don't have any money. But it doesn't matter. I'd rather walk." I really want to hang up on him.

"Don't be stupid. Your sister would kill me if I let you walk home."

"Your empathy astounds me."

He chuckles. "Sensitive *and* good-looking. I'm a triple threat."

"You mean a double threat. You only named two things."

"What?"

I pinch the bridge of my nose, searching for some semblance of self-control. *Deep breath.* "Never mind. Just hurry up."

I hit the "end call" button like it's my alarm going off on a Sunday morning. These are the moments I wish I smoked. I debate heading back inside, but I don't have any money for drinks and I really don't want to be sucked into another riveting conversation with Seth/Sam, so I lean back against the brick building instead.

PLAYLIST

"Over the Rainbow"—Amber Leigh Irish
"Everything Under the Sun"—Common Rotation
"Tiny Dancer"—Kurt Hugo Schneider
"Look After You"—The Fray
"Simple Song"—The Shins
"First"—Cold War Kids
"Everything"—Lifehouse
"Crazy for This Girl"—Evan and Jaron
"Sidekick"—Walk the Moon
"Dangerous"—Big Data, Joywave
"Sick Cycle Carousel"—Lifehouse
"It Only Hurts"—Default
"Delivery"—Jimmy Eat World
"Brother"—Kodaline
"Forever Young"—Undressd, Ellie May
"Pain"—The War on Drugs
"Stand by Me"—Joseph Vincent
"Iris"—Ben Hazlewood
"Oceans"—Seafret
"Can't Help Falling in Love"—Boyce Avenue
"When You Come Back Down"—Nickel Creek
"Time after Time"—Boyce Avenue, Megan Davies
"Letters from the Sky"—Civil Twilight
"Until the End"—Quietdrive
"Last Train Home"—Ryan Star
"Born to Die"—JJ Wilde, Billy Raffoul

ACKNOWLEDGMENTS

As always, Jake Hartmann comes first.

Thank you to my incredible husband for accompanying me on another book journey. Every time I finish a story, I say, "I'll never be able to do that again."

And every time he tells me, "Yes, you will."

Thank you for being my biggest fan and supporter, my business partner, and the love of my life. Thank you for being my comfort and my courage.

An overwhelming thanks to Chelley St Clair, the ultimate alpha reader, a huge inspiration to me and the actual reason every book since *Lotus* even exists. *insert burn gifs* Thank you for being my ride-or-die and for convincing me to keep riding every time I doubt myself. (It's fairly often.) Thank you for reading and rereading every chapter I send you, brainstorming with me, and giving me your amazing advice and suggestions.

Even when I throw you under the bus.

Mostly, thank you for all the belly laughter—this journey is hard and draining sometimes. Staying up until midnight, slap-happy and overtired, convinced we're going to write a ghost Theo book one day, helps keep me sane. (And you're totally writing it.)

Thank you to Vanessa Sheets for giving me the heartwarming idea for June's sword. That whole scene where Brant makes June a custom sword on Christmas Eve night stemmed from Vanessa's real-life story. It touched my heart, and I just had to give it life. Thank you for being a constant positive light throughout this journey, Vanessa. I appreciate you.

Big thanks to my wonderful beta readers for helping me through the first draft of this book. And thank you to my friends and readers in my readers' group and promo team for cheering me on with a new story. You guys keep me going creatively. Thank you for the messages, the tags, the comments, and for the sweet encouraging words. Thank you to my early readers for showing your love for this book with shares and reviews. It means the world to me.

Shout-out to my agent, Nicole Resciniti at the Seymour Agency, my invaluable PA, Jennifer Mirabelli, who has been holding my hand throughout the release of this book. I couldn't do any of this without you guys.

Lastly, all the thanks in the world to my amazing children and family for always pushing me, believing in me, and keeping me inspired. You are my greatest gift.

ABOUT THE AUTHOR

Jennifer Hartmann resides in northern Illinois with her devoted husband and three hooligans. When she is not writing angsty love stories, she is likely thinking about writing them. She enjoys sunsets (because mornings are hard), bike riding, traveling, binging *Buffy the Vampire Slayer* reruns, and that time of day when coffee gets replaced by wine. Jennifer is a wedding photographer with her husband. She is also excellent at making puns and finding inappropriate humor in mundane situations. She loves tacos. She also really, really wants to pet your dog.

Follow her at:

Instagram: @author.jenniferhartmann
Facebook: @jenhartmannauthor
Twitter: @authorjhartmann
TikTok: @jenniferhartmannauthor